PRAISE FOR THE NOVELS OF

Surrender to Me

"Full of steam, erotic love, and nonstop, page-turning action, this was one of those books you read in one sitting!" —*Night Owl Reviews*

"Sultry, intoxicating, and super sexy. Do not miss this book!"
—*Bookaholics Romance Book Club*

Delicious

"Shayla Black creates emotional, searingly sexy stories that always leave me wanting more." —Maya Banks, *New York Times* bestselling author

"Too *Delicious* to put down . . . a book to be savored over and over."
—*Romance Junkies*

"Make sure you have something to cool yourself down with, for this one is a scorcher." —*The Romance Readers Connection*

"The characters, the drama, the suspense, the eroticism, and, most important, the heart-stopping romance all combine to make *Delicious* a perfect read . . . Sizzling hot and one for the keeper shelf." —*The Romance Studio*

"Another winner from Black . . . will thrill erotica and mystery fans alike."
—*Romantic Times*

continued . . .

Decadent

"Wickedly seductive from start to finish."

—Jaci Burton, *New York Times* bestselling author

"A lusty page-turner from the get-go, *Decadent* lives up to its title, grabbing readers from the very first chapter and not letting go until the very end with a shuddering climax worthy of any keeper shelf."

—*TwoLips Reviews*

Wicked Ties

"A wicked, sensual thrill from first page to last. I loved it!"

—Lora Leigh, #1 *New York Times* bestselling author

"Not a book to be missed . . . Just be sure that you have something cold to drink while reading it and hopefully someone there afterward to ease away the ache."

—*A Romance Review*

"Absolutely took my breath away . . . *Wicked Ties* wound itself around me and refused to let go. Full of passion and erotic love scenes."

—*Romance Junkies*

Strip Search
(writing as Shelley Bradley)

"Packs a hell of a wallop . . . an exciting, steamy, and magnificent story . . . If I had to rate this book out of ten, it would certainly get a fifteen! Twists, turns, titillating and explosive sexual chemistry, and memorable characters—readers can't ask for more. *Strip Search* is highly recommended!"

—*The Road to Romance*

"An exciting contemporary romance with suspenseful undertones . . . the love scenes are particularly steamy. This book would be perfect for readers who enjoy their romance with a hint of suspense."

—*Curled Up with a Good Book*

Belong to Me

SHAYLA BLACK

HEAT
NEW YORK

THE BERKLEY PUBLISHING GROUP
Published by the Penguin Group
Penguin Group (USA) Inc.
375 Hudson Street, New York, New York 10014, USA
Penguin Group (Canada), 90 Eglinton Avenue East, Suite 700, Toronto, Ontario M4P 2Y3, Canada
(a division of Pearson Penguin Canada Inc.)
Penguin Books Ltd., 80 Strand, London WC2R 0RL, England
Penguin Group Ireland, 25 St. Stephen's Green, Dublin 2, Ireland (a division of Penguin Books Ltd.)
Penguin Group (Australia), 250 Camberwell Road, Camberwell, Victoria 3124, Australia
(a division of Pearson Australia Group Pty. Ltd.)
Penguin Books India Pvt. Ltd., 11 Community Centre, Panchsheel Park, New Delhi—110 017, India
Penguin Group (NZ), 67 Apollo Drive, Rosedale, Auckland 0632, New Zealand
(a division of Pearson New Zealand Ltd.)
Penguin Books (South Africa) (Pty.) Ltd., 24 Sturdee Avenue, Rosebank, Johannesburg 2196,
South Africa

Penguin Books Ltd., Registered Offices: 80 Strand, London WC2R 0RL, England

This book is an original publication of The Berkley Publishing Group.

PRINTING HISTORY
Heat trade paperback edition / October 2011

Library of Congress Cataloging-in-Publication Data

Black, Shayla.
    Belong to me / Shayla Black. — Heat trade pbk. ed.
        p.   cm.
    ISBN 978-0-425-24315-2
    1. Women intelligence officers—Fiction. 2. Undercover operations—Fiction. 3. Sex crimes—Investigation—Fiction. 4. Missing persons—Fiction. 5. Sexual dominance and submission—Fiction. I. Title.
    PS3602.L325245B45 2011
    813'.6—dc23   2011019138

PRINTED IN THE UNITED STATES OF AMERICA

10 9 8 7 6 5 4 3 2 1

For my wonderful husband,
who's taught me so much about giving,
self-sacrifice, and patience.
You balance, temper, and protect me.
This book wouldn't have been possible
without all the good things
you've shown me over the years.
The two decades I've been your wife
have been the best of my life.
I can't wait for many more.

Acknowledgments

As always, a big thanks to the friends, fellow writers, and beta readers who keep me sane:

A huge shout-out to Sophie Oak for being generally awesome, for sharing my love of margaritas, and for telling me that I wasn't insane—at least not totally. And for loving this book as much as I did.

Much appreciation to Sylvia Day for making me look at things a bit differently and pushing me even harder to write a kick-ass heroine with a heart.

A very deep bow to my assistant, Christie Von Ditter, for stepping in and organizing my life and providing research and technical information. Thank you so much for saving me from chaos!

To Kris Cook for being a fabulous cheerleader and rounding up such a great group of Righteous Perverts.

Thanks also to Annee and Natalie for speedy reads and lovely input. Your opinions are truly helpful. Hugs!

And last (but never least), deep gratitude to my agent, Kim Whalen, for getting behind this series, this book, and me.

Chapter One

Club Dominion, Dallas—
Thursday afternoon

THWACK! Logan Edgington smacked the submissive's reddening ass in time with the dark beat of the old-school Depeche Mode tunes pounding through his dungeon at Club Dominion. Clenching his jaw, he curled his palm into a fist, then shook out the sting.

The sub gasped and stuck her butt out for him. Oh yeah, Callie liked pain and punishment, which was why she frequented this BDSM club. But the past two hours had proven that her attitude didn't submit half as well as her body. Given enough time, he'd change that.

Perspiration sheened across her back, and some damp tendrils from her black pixie-cut hair clung to her neck. She bowed her head between her outstretched arms. Logan stood back, watched, while she writhed as much as her bonds allowed. Her pink pussy looked drenched and swollen.

"More!" she demanded.

He leaned down, growled in her ear. "You're not learning. Who's in charge?"

"But I need it," she whined.

"You need discipline, which is why you're here with me now. You say you want to learn to please the Master you hope to have someday, but I'm not seeing the dedication. I think you just like a little pain to make your orgasm better and the rest is bullshit."

"That's not true. Don't be an asshole!"

Smack! "You're disrespectful, sub. What do you call me?"

"Sir," she gasped. "I'm sorry, Sir. I'm so close. You've kept me on edge forever—"

"For thirty minutes," he cut in. "It's your role to stay on edge for as long as I wish and to accept my commands with grace and dignity—and silence."

Callie bowed her head, and Logan pressed his shoulders down, stretching his neck. He waited, swallowing cold water from his bottle. She was going to have to decide whether her long-term goal or her immediate need for orgasm was more important.

Her breath hitched. She sobbed, then caught herself. "Yes, Sir. You're right, Sir. I'm sorry."

Damn, that was the most progress they'd made all afternoon.

"But," she cut in with a mewl, "it would be so much easier to submit if you'd just give me what I want."

And we're back to square one.

Behind her, Logan shook his head in displeasure and walked around the sub in a slow circle. He crouched until she could see the thunder on his face. Callie demanded her orgasm the way a toddler stomped her foot for a doll. She was going to take a lot of taming to reach her submissive potential. Idly, he wondered if he could possibly train her in the less than two weeks left of his leave. He certainly had the time to devote, since the only thing on his calendar until he returned to active duty was his older brother's upcoming vow renewal.

He filtered his fingers into her damp tresses and pulled until she lifted her head. Her blue eyes looked glassy. "That's not how it works. I explained that before we started. I know others have told you, as well. You'd be more likely to get what you want if you showed respect and complied."

"Yes, Sir. It's just . . . I'm so close, I can't think. It's like I'm already talking before my brain has decided what I should say."

So Callie admitted that she had no filter. Since coming to Dominion, she'd been bounced from Dom to Dom. Few wanted to take on a "project." Logan didn't mind; he relished the challenge.

"You're going to have to learn to control yourself."

She bit her lip. "I'm trying, Sir."

"Not hard enough. You know I have to punish you."

Her entire body perked up. "Yes, Sir!"

Logan raced around her and smacked her ass again. "No coming unless I give you permission."

Her head dropped between her shoulders as her hope deflated, but she took his edict in blessed silence.

Turning away, he rummaged through the nearby cabinet until he found what he needed: a pair of unforgiving clamps and a brand-new vibrating egg. Unwrapping both, he cleaned the egg, then inserted the batteries into the remote. After a quick pinch on each nipple, he applied the harsh clamps. This sub didn't need much prepping; her nipples were already stiff red points.

She moaned and tried to claw at the padded mat beneath her. The girl certainly liked pain, and Logan had no problem dishing it out.

Finally, he crouched behind her and slid the egg into her soaking cunt. She tightened around it, bracing. Without a doubt, what he planned was going to be a trial for her.

Logan flipped the egg on.

Callie gasped. Clenching her fists, she wiggled her ass, trying to get enough friction for orgasm, but he'd tied her to a spreader bar, ensuring she couldn't manage to rub anything together between her legs. And when she realized that, she wailed.

"Quiet. Take your punishment. You haven't earned an orgasm. You're not getting one for a long while."

She endured. Not in total silence—that wasn't her style. She cursed below her breath and alternately bit her lip. Logan watched her skin flush even more, her breathing hitch repeatedly, as need filled her. He smoothed his hand over her back, feeling her tremble, feeling her give in.

And finally, he *felt*.

Logan closed his eyes and inhaled, soaking in her uncertainty, her tumult, her quivering need. He savored her ragged breaths, tense mewls, and the pungent scent of her arousal. When he had a woman under his control and he stripped her down to her soul, exposing her most elemental self, *then* he could finally feel more than duty, anger, and nagging emptiness.

His own arousal multiplied. Blood rushed to his cock, hardening him until the sensation was nearly painful. It was perfect.

Well, as perfect as it got anymore.

"Sir!" The sub's keening cry penetrated his haze, jacking him up even more.

He opened his eyes, slid in front of her until he fused their gazes together. Fuck, her wild, fully dilated eyes, red cheeks, and heaving breaths told him that she was close not just to orgasm, but to her breaking point.

"Callie . . ." he warned, dialing back the egg's remote control to let her cool down. "No coming."

This time, she winced, but didn't complain.

"I'm sorry, Sir." Her breathing hitched, and her head bowed completely. "How can I please you?"

He smiled. *Finally . . . some measure of surrender.*

"May I offer you my mouth?" Her voice shook. "My pussy? My ass?"

Technically, it was the right thing to say, but her offer left him cold. "No."

"I want to please you."

One look at the sub's flushed face told Logan that, for once, she actually meant it. He softened. "Watching you, looking so feminine and submissive, so very close to orgasm, is pleasing me. I'm going to ask you to please me like that for a bit longer."

"Yes." Her breath caught. "S-Sir."

Dropping to his knee beside her, Logan wrapped his arm around her waist, pressed his cheek to her back, then put his free hand over her pussy. "I like you on edge, trembling with the bite of pain I've given you, and the swell of need that only grows. Give me more. *That* is how you please me."

Every inch of her skin was flushed rosy. In his head, Logan knew he'd kept her near orgasm for perhaps longer than she could comfortably bear. A part of him whispered that he should throw caution to the wind and enjoy her delicious turmoil for just a few minutes more. God knew she'd earned a little sensual torture for her defiance.

But a sub's responsibility was to please whoever topped her. Still basking in the overspill of her emotion, Logan couldn't deny that he was, in fact, pleased. And she'd even curbed her sass—at least for the moment.

A Dom's role was to give the sub what she needed. Callie needed to come.

Rising to his feet, he made for the door, then pressed the security code. Instantly, the portal clicked open and his pal Xander, whom he'd dubbed his one man cleanup crew, prowled inside. "She ready?"

Logan glanced at the sub. "Just about. Give me thirty seconds."

He turned back and dropped to his knees beside Callie, whispering in her ear, "Are you ready to be fucked? Think carefully about your answer."

When he'd asked this question a few hours ago, she'd replied flippantly, as if she'd been entitled to pleasure. He'd untied her, left her alone in his dungeon while he'd found lunch—let her body cool completely before he'd started arousing her again.

Now, Callie averted her eyes respectfully. "If it pleases you, Sir, I offer myself for your pleasure."

Xander snorted. Logan shot him a quelling glare. Maybe he should take the sub up on that. Maybe it would be all right. Though it would probably be like always. Afterward, he'd only feel crushingly empty and aware of all the fucking mistakes that had led to this shitty, hollow sex life.

"Thank you, little one." He stroked her shoulder as the music throbbed around them. Then he curled a hand under her body, sliding his finger over her clit. "I would be pleased if you came for me. Now."

With a little cry of surprise, she gasped, "Yes, Sir."

Another light circle over her hard little clit, and Callie's whole body shook, convulsed. Her nerve-laden nubbin turned to stone, pulsed under his fingers, as her cries rang in his ears. He opened his pores to her delightful storm of emotion, letting more sink in to him. God, how desperately he needed to feel *something*.

When her orgasm subsided, he removed the plastic egg as he kissed her shoulder. "Very pretty. It would please me now to watch you be fucked."

She stilled. "Watch, Sir? I—I hoped . . . Yes, Sir."

Logan heard the disappointment in her voice. So, she'd gotten the 411 on him, and like most of the other subs here, Callie wanted to be the one he finally fucked. That his celibacy had become a mountain for these women to climb really pissed him off. His reasons for abstaining were his own. He didn't owe anyone an explanation or a stiff dick.

"You knew what would happen when you walked in this dungeon. I stated it clearly, and you agreed. If you've changed your mind, use your safe word and everything ends."

The sub's head snapped up. "No, Sir! If watching pleases you, then I will happily accept another. Please, I ache . . ."

No, it didn't please him exactly, but in the long run, fucking her himself would displease him more. And afterward, he'd inevitably dismiss her harshly and hurt her without meaning to, which would only make him feel worse. It happened every time.

"Very well," he murmured. "Xander?"

When Logan turned, his friend had already shucked his clothes and donned a condom over that big cock that made him a good living, even though he was already filthy rich. On silent footsteps, Xander circled Callie until he crouched in front of her. "I'm going to take care of you from here. Do you understand?"

The sub nodded, keeping her eyes downcast, but her body vibrated with excitement. "Yes, Sir."

"You'll please Master Logan by submitting to me now."

"I understand."

"Good girl." Xander caressed her back, her ass, then helped her to her feet. He guided her to a spanking bench and clipped her in with the rings attached on her wrist and ankle cuffs, tossing the spreader bar aside once he had. With one hand, he plunged two fingers into her pussy. With the other, he smacked her sweetly rosy backside. She gasped.

That quickly, Callie was aroused again. And Xander didn't hesitate. He gripped her hips, aligned his cock, and pushed his way in. She clawed the bench and cried out against the invasion. As Xander slammed her, she came again.

Logan's work here was done. The sub was in the best hands possible. Xander would give her what she needed both during and after sex.

After smoothing a tender hand down Callie's hair, Logan turned and left. Breath sawing in and out of his chest, he pivoted and headed to the end of the hall, pushing his way into the club showers. As he reached for the faucet and waited for the scalding water, his hand shook.

Damn, Callie's lack of filter didn't just apply to her mouth. Her emotions had mounted, one on top of the other, until they'd spilled all over him. Her fear, her thrill, her desire, her trembling greed for more had bled into him—and he'd sucked in every drop. Subs like her were the reason dominance worked for him.

Logan stripped, then stepped into the swirl of spray and hot steam. He wasn't stupid; psychologists would have a field day with him, if he'd ever talk to one. Fuck that. He wasn't opening his head for some shrink. He was simply wired this way, and his emotional disconnect worked professionally. Navy SEALs had to be collected, logic firing on all cylinders. When emotions got involved, people died.

Personally, however, it sucked. Sponging off women like Callie only took him so far. He remembered those high school days when all it had taken was one look, one kiss, and he'd been brimming with so many fantasies and wants that he couldn't process them all. But that had been before . . . *Nope, not thinking about* her.

Still, once she flashed across his brain, he was unable to stop himself from wrapping his hand around the inside of his left thigh and fingering the little tattoo there. Like always, desire roared through him. Just like that, he was desperate to come.

Desperate to have what he knew he never would again.

Blocking out those thoughts, Logan jerked his hand from the tattoo and soaped his palms. He'd better get down to business before his thoughts turned into a total buzz kill.

Drawing in a cleansing breath, he closed his eyes and shut everything out except the vision of how Callie had looked minutes ago under his command. With his back to the spray, he took his cock in hand.

At the first touch, tingles shot through his groin, up his spine. He called forth the memories of the sub's pants and moans. The scent of her arousal still lingered in his nostrils. Her trembling pleas had been hot. Desire simmered in his belly, and another stroke up his dick fanned the fire higher.

The wild need in Callie's eyes pumped Logan with a heavy euphoria. Letting that brew in his brain, he picked up the pace, rubbed his thumb along a sensitive spot on his glans. Fire licked his balls, and the ache tightened, tingled at the base of his spine.

Part of him wished he'd taken her up on her offer and fucked her. It had been more than five years since he'd felt the silken clasp of a woman's pussy. But nothing had changed. He had no reason to hope that being with Callie would provide any different outcome. Crushing emptiness and disappointment would level him the moment the orgasm ended—if he had one at all. The woman always either felt inadequate or irate. Sex had been that way every time he'd tried with anyone after—

No. Damn it, he wasn't having thoughts of *her*. He had to focus on Callie and those swollen lips of hers, begging for the orgasm she'd needed with every nerve in her body, of those pleas filling him with anxious tension, arousal, fueling his own need to come.

Logan stroked faster. She'd been gorgeous. Once he'd curbed her sass a bit, she'd been willing to stay in the raging tumult to please him. And when he'd granted her orgasm, the pure joy in the experience had been completely heady. He'd greedily sucked in that tingling ache. Now, he anticipated that same cataclysm washing over him.

But fucking hell . . . it wasn't happening.

He pumped faster, his arm starting to ache. The orgasm was right there, but all the usual tricks weren't working. And Logan couldn't pretend that he didn't know why.

God damn it, why couldn't he get past *her* after twelve fucking years? Memories of her still plagued him. Her sweet, bee stung lips as she looked up at him, wearing nothing but a shy smile. The vulnerability obvious in her trembling chin, shining from her big brown eyes, when she'd confessed it was her first time. Knowing he'd been the first man to kiss the soft curve of her neck, feel the pink berry nipple against his tongue, lap up the flavor of her sweet cream, and hear the startled cry of her first orgasm . . .

Tension torqued in Logan's gut as the water pounded his back. His palm glided up and down his hungry cock as those well-traveled memories crashed over him again. The trust in her eyes as she'd parted her virgin thighs, the way she'd whispered that she loved him, too, with unblinking honesty as she took him inside her body for the first time.

The only time.

My Cherry.

Now stroking his cock like a wild man, Logan reached down to rub at the tattoo again. He couldn't see it or feel it, but he'd put it there years ago to remind him of her. He pictured her as she'd been that spring afternoon, lying beneath him, eyes wide with startled desire, delicate nails digging into his shoulders. His balls filled with scalding need now, drew up tight. Orgasm sizzled through his blood, then exploded until he released a thick stream of semen onto the shower's black tiles.

In seconds, the sensation fizzled. He panted, propping himself up with a palm against the wall and released his softening cock. His heartbeat slowed.

And once again, he was left to feel exactly how pathetic he was because he could only come by thinking about a girl who'd surely gotten over him long ago. A girl, now a woman, whom he'd never have the chance to touch again.

The self-loathing had barely started to suck the pleasure from his orgasm when a knock sounded. Fuck, that would be Xander. Logan would rather ignore his friend, but he'd put Callie in the other man's hands; ensuring that she was okay now was his responsibility.

Turning off the spray, he yanked a towel off the rack and wrapped it around his waist. "What?"

"You done fingering your cherry yet?"

God damn it, he hated that Xander knew him so well. "Bite my ass."

"I am *not*, nor will I ever be, interested in your ass," Xander called through the door. "You decent? 'Cause I don't want to see your junk."

As if he never had during the course of a scene, which was how Xander knew about his hidden tattoo in the first place.

Logan rolled his eyes. "If you don't like it, don't look."

Xander pushed the door open, his olive cheeks flushed, his dark hair mussed. He looked relieved to see the towel around Logan's waist. "Callie is fine. All sated, praised, and cuddled."

With a nod, Logan turned away, hoping his pal would get the hint.

No such luck. Xander merely crossed his arms over his chest, cocky grin stretched across his face, and looked at him expectantly.

Damn. Logan sighed. "Thanks for taking care of her."

"After working at a BDSM resort where my primary job was to

take care of women like her, it's no sweat. And unlike those women, she didn't act like I was beneath her afterward, which was a nice bonus." Xander shrugged. "It was a good fuck. I should thank you for priming her so thoroughly. I had to pause twice to slow down her slew of orgasms. The girl still doesn't have much self-control."

Another problem for another day. Maybe if he dropped his towel, Xander would leave.

Logan let go of the damp terrycloth. It slithered to the floor as he reached for his leathers.

"Oh, dude." In the mirror, Logan could see Xander turn away with a wince. "Warn a guy next time, huh?"

Shoving on his leathers, he zipped them up and shrugged. "You're the one who insists on barging in on my bathroom time. You get what you deserve."

"You're shooting the messenger. I'm just here to tell you that Thorpe wants to see you."

Mitchell Thorpe. Logan held in a curse, hoping like hell that Dominion's owner wasn't going to chew his ass out for pushing Callie so hard. Thorpe had a soft spot for her. Logan thought it was more like a blind spot. Any other sub who'd been so damn near untrainable would have been out on her ass long ago.

"Why?"

"I'm not exactly sure. He's getting all the Doms together. I'm guessing it has something to do with the FBI being here." Xander slapped him on the back. "Welcome back."

* * *

"YOU dragged my ass out of the shower for—" Logan paused as Mitchell Thorpe glared at him with cold gray eyes, then yanked back the black drape covering the one-way mirror. Logan's jaw dropped at the sight. "Oh, holy shit."

Around him, half a dozen other Doms all whistled and looked their fill.

"I thought she'd get your attention," Thorpe drawled.

Completely. Logan's gaze glued itself hungrily to the graceful line of her spine, cut in half by a gray sports bra. Tight black running shorts barely covered the lush globes of her ass. Though the beauty was way overdressed for her role, she sat back on her knees, legs spread, pose submissive. *Mercy!*

Logan rubbed his jaw. But the ache coursing through him wasn't under his two days' growth of beard; it had quickly settled south, behind his straining zipper, despite his orgasm fifteen minutes ago. Desire sizzled through him, along with shock. For the first time in years, he not only wanted inside a woman, he was desperate for it. Trying to cool down and process this development, he grabbed a bottle of water from the nearby cooler and drained half in two swallows.

Thorpe cleared his throat, clearly expecting a reply. As Logan forced himself to look at the club's owner, a thousand responses ran through his head. Finally, he settled for something factual. "With that curvy ass and fiery hair? Yeah, she's got my attention."

He *really* had a thing for redheads. Always had.

In fact, everything about this woman set off Logan's buttons. Such fair skin. He'd bet it would be damn soft and look so prettily pink after a good spanking. She radiated femininity, from the slender neck just under her pile of vibrant hair atop her head, to the sensual flare of her hips. Already, he wanted her the way he hadn't wanted anyone in years—down, dirty, insatiably. Completely. He wanted to penetrate her, violate her, subjugate her. Every moment he watched her, the desire grew. Logan swallowed.

An unfamiliar thirtysomething man in jeans beside her issued orders. Logan couldn't hear through the glass. Granted, he wasn't the best at reading lips, but he thought the guy told her to bow her head. The stranger's physique looked powerful enough to enforce his will . . . but he lacked any sort of commanding presence.

"Is this poser her Dom?" Logan drained the rest of his water bottle, wondering who the guy on the other side of the glass thought he was kidding.

Thorpe sighed. "Not yet. He needs to be. These two are actually FBI agents, training for an upcoming undercover assignment to break up a sex ring and rescue another agent. They've been in Axel's dungeon for nearly a week. We're not getting anywhere."

"I have to be honest; it's looking hopeless." Axel, the club's resident Dom, sighed.

In that instant, Logan knew that Thorpe had called together all the club's Doms in the hopes that one of them could step in and train the delicious redhead in the next room. Yeah, she was still kneeling at the other man's feet, but she had her hands on her hips. The sway of her body and the bobs of her head told Logan, she was giving her "Dom" an earful. He smiled.

Suddenly, he was damn glad he'd left Tyler, Texas, for Dallas during his leave to blow off some pent-up steam. Logan loved the navy, but constant missions to third world shit holes didn't give him many opportunities to indulge in his kink of choice. But after yesterday, he needed to release tension even more. Over breakfast with his dad, Logan had seen an engagement announcement in the Tyler *Morning Telegraph* that had knocked him flat. *She* was fucking marrying Brad Thompson. Every muscle in Logan's body tensed at the thought of that raving ass-hat touching her, planting his children in her womb.

"You trying to crush that plastic?" Xander whispered, brow raised.

Thorpe, Axel, and the other Doms all stared.

Logan looked down and realized that he'd pulverized his water bottle. Muttering a curse, he threw it in the trash can, then focused on the scene through the glass. "She's not submitting to him and she never will."

"Which is where one of you comes in. Axel has agreed to coach the male agent one-on-one. But that leaves the female, and she needs a *strong* hand. I don't have time for a project."

Before anyone else could say a word, Logan volunteered. "I'll do it."

Thorpe paused, sizing him up. Logan refused to flinch or blink.

"Since you like the defiant ones, I thought this might be up your alley," Thorpe stated. "But will you be too much for our little FBI agent? It's her first field assignment."

"I'll give her whatever she needs," Logan vowed. She was beautiful and seemingly brave. Field assignments with the FBI didn't tend to be cakewalks.

"Except sex," Jason, the bad-boy financial wizard, drawled.

"Fuck off," Logan muttered.

"Sex isn't required," Thorpe advised, tossing a glare Jason's way. "She just needs to learn protocol and obedience."

The normally silent Erik shrugged. "You know I like the putty-in-my-hands type. I can tell by the finger wag, that ain't her."

Logan looked at her again. Watching that finger wag made him hard. Hell, everything about her made him hard. Any time he could spend touching the gorgeous woman in the next room would be time well spent. Maybe even cathartic. He couldn't remember the last time he'd been this stiff so quickly after an orgasm, but looking at the redhead's lush ass, his dick was fully saluting her.

Zeb, the last of the Doms in the room, just grunted. "I'm heading down to Cabo in a few days for vacation. Man, I'd love to—"

"But since you won't be here, and I will . . ." Logan cut him off with a smile.

"Lucky bastard," Zeb groused.

Thorpe stepped between them. "The agents don't have long before their mission begins. They're already working against the clock. The female agent is submissive, in my opinion. But she's not letting go."

Logan already knew the problem. "She doesn't trust that guy."

In fact, the man beside her dropped his shoulders and sighed, clearly trying to reason with her—and showing his frustration. Both were exactly the wrong thing to do to earn obedience.

Axel shook his head. "Dominance isn't Agent York's bag."

"Clearly," Logan drawled, staring at the two through the glass. "Why not find someone else to take his place?"

"Six days ago, one of their fellow agents working undercover was abducted by the leaders of a sex ring they're trying to bust. They sent her in alone as a submissive. The only training she'd received was an hour's briefing."

"Dear God," Erik choked. "What the fuck were they thinking?"

Logan shook his head. Sending an agent in that unprepared was more than stupid; it was downright irresponsible. Submission wasn't something a person learned by reading a piece of paper. Any Dom worth his leathers was able to spot a tourist a mile away. She had been a lamb sent to slaughter. And now the redhead was going in after her, trying to dupe heartless predators for her first undercover assignment? Definitely brave.

"It's worse than you think. Agent York let me read some cursory information on this sex ring so I'd know how to prep the agents," Axel said. "The mastermind of this ring is a ruthless motherfucker. Though he's from somewhere in the U.S., he's apparently got brothels all over the world, from what the FBI can tell. He's made a fortune off the backs of ten-year-old girls in Thailand, along with distributing videos of orgies and gang rapes. Apparently, this sick bastard expanded his business to include high-end slave auctions about six months ago. He's abducting gorgeous, young submissives out of clubs and resorts, then smuggling them out of the country. The minimum bid for the sadistic fucks who want to buy is three million dollars."

"Damn, that's twisted." Zeb frowned. "Who has that kind of cash to drop on pussy?"

"Sheiks, Internet tycoons, obscure European royalty." Thorpe shrugged. "They're out there."

Zeb shook his head as he looked at the woman. "That almost makes me want to change my plans. She's probably scared to have this thrown at her as a first assignment."

"She volunteered," Thorpe clarified, obvious admiration in his voice. "She's never been out from behind a desk, but she's willing to risk her life for this. She deserves the best training we can give her, so these two agents are working to go undercover and hopefully recover the missing agent, who I suspect Agent York cares for as more than merely a peer."

Gorgeous, courageous, submissive. Everything Logan had heard about this woman intrigued him, and Thorpe's last statement perked him up even more. "So he and the redhead aren't an item?"

"Definitely not. They've made their mutual discomfort of this training well known."

Sweet. "And you haven't had any luck handling her?" Logan asked Axel.

"I've spent all my time on York, thinking that if I can train him to lead, she'd follow. Not happening." Axel's long blond hair brushed his shoulders as he shrugged. "We're going to have to divide and conquer. So if you're willing to take on a novice, I'm more than willing to dump her in your lap. Not that it looks like you'll mind."

As he reached for the doorknob, Logan smiled. "I can't wait."

Axel pushed past him. "Slow down. She's a tough cookie. I think she's a natural sub, but this is all new to her, so you can't just barge in there and go all Dom on her ass. Let me do the introductions and hand off. Then you can take the girl down to your dungeon."

"I'll come along, too," Xander cut in with a flashy grin. "Thorpe said sex wasn't required, but you never know what she'll need . . ."

Wherever there was wet pussy, Xander was never far away. But the thought of his friend grinding his dick inside the redhead made Logan seethe. He shot his buddy a scathing glare.

"What? She has a world-class ass," Xander defended. "Sue me."

It was impossible to argue with that. And while he didn't want to think about Xander fucking her, Logan knew that, chances were, his sudden ache for this woman would likely disappear before she'd ever need sex.

Logan gestured to the door, then followed Axel and Xander down the hall to the next opening on the left. York looked up, tensed, clearly not digging the assignment. The female agent just set her shoulders and ignored him. That would change—damn quick. For now, Logan let Axel ease the way.

Quickly, Axel explained the situation. The male agent glanced at his female counterpart as she rose to her feet. Poor bastard actually looked relieved. Logan smiled, fighting back the urge to rub his hands together.

"You want me to introduce you two?" Axel gestured between Logan and the redhead.

He shook his head. "I got it from here. Face me."

The woman gasped, stiffened—then darted to the other side of the room.

So she wanted to play games already? That was no problem for him.

Logan took off after her and grabbed her from behind, grasping a handful of that siren red hair. Damn, it was soft. Her breathing hitched, and he turned harder in an instant.

"On your knees. Stay there until I say otherwise. You're in training with *me* now, and I won't be as lax as Axel. I'd rather complete introductions before I spank you, but that's your choice."

"Let. Go. Of. Me." The woman fought his hold. "Logan."

She knew his name? Her voice resonated in his head, crisp yet feminine. So fucking familiar. Impossible. It couldn't be . . .

He released her hair and grabbed her shoulders, still subduing her struggles. Heart pounding, he spun her to face him. That familiar face, angry dark eyes, and the mulish set of her pert little chin had him mentally flailing with shock. *Holy fuck.*

Logan gasped, stared. "Cherry?"

Chapter Two

"Y*OUR* Cherry?" Xander slanted a questioning glance in his direction.

Logan couldn't take his eyes off her or unscramble his brain enough to answer. He hadn't been this close to her in twelve years, one month, fifteen days, six hours, and a handful of minutes. Now *she* was in a dungeon to train as a submissive. With him.

She jerked from his hold and swatted his hand away, glaring at him with the full force of those furious brown eyes. Logan's belly pulsed with dark thrill and sexual heat. His first urge was to back her against a wall and bury himself deep inside her.

"My name isn't Cherry," she hissed. "It's Tara, not that I expect you remember."

Oh, he remembered. Hell, he couldn't forget. How was it possible that taking her virginity at sixteen had virtually ruined him for every other woman? He wished he could deny it, but if he tried, he'd be lying.

Looking at her now, she was twice the woman she'd been as a young girl. He'd seen more beautiful females, but none who flipped his switch more.

"Tara Jacobs," he murmured, still staring as if she were a mirage that might disappear at any moment. "I wouldn't have passed sophomore lit if you hadn't tutored me." He stared, not really conscious of the words pouring out of his mouth, just the shock fueling them. "Still a tiny thing. Still independent, I gather. Still have that little birthmark on the inside of your left thigh?"

Her jaw dropped, sweet mouth gaping open. God, he'd love to put his cock there. He hadn't had the chance to do that . . . yet.

"That's none of your damn business." She crossed her arms over her chest.

As if that defensive gesture would keep him away. *Pfft.*

"Oh my God," Xander exclaimed. "She *is* your Cherry. It's all over your face."

"Shut the fuck up, Xander," Logan growled. "Get out."

Axel cleared his throat. "It appears that you and Agent Jacobs are acquainted. That's my cue to back off and let you sort this little reunion out. Agent York?" The tattooed Dom turned to the male agent. "Let's go to Thorpe's office and talk."

York speared Tara with a concerned glance that rubbed Logan the wrong way. Just as he was about to offer to rearrange the agent's face, Tara sent the man a decisive nod.

"Xander, you, too," Axel said. "Something tells me Logan won't need your help with this one."

His one-man cleanup crew shrugged and followed Axel to the door. "We'll see."

Beating back his annoyance, Logan watched the trio file out. The door closed behind them with a soft click.

Now could he push Cherry up against the wall and bury himself inside her? One look at her face told him that she was less than amenable to that idea. But now that he was training her, he'd have time alone with her. Get to simply touch her. God, he couldn't have planned this better if he'd tried.

Tara stormed across the room, her fiery hair loosening from its clip after his manhandling. She removed it. The fiery tresses fell halfway down her back as she grabbed a robe out of the armoire against the far wall and thrust it on. "What are you doing here?"

He hadn't given her permission to put that little silken robe on, but they'd get to that. He had questions, and was sure that she did, as well.

Logan shrugged. "I spend a lot of time here, actually. At least when I'm on leave."

She frowned. "I'd heard you joined the service. Army?"

"Navy," he corrected. "SEAL."

That had her raising her delicate ginger brows. "From jock to frogman. That's a stretch. Still a team player, I guess."

Oddly, her razor-sharp sarcasm, even in high school, was one of the things he'd missed most about her after their split. The other thing had been her compassion.

A dozen years ago, he'd hurt her badly—and it had nearly killed him to rip her heart out. That she could still spare him even a shred of anger after all these years he took as a good sign. If he was irrelevant to her now, she'd have no emotion beyond mild surprise. She certainly wouldn't bother to bristle and clutch that robe like a shield.

"From budding author to FBI Agent. That *is* a stretch."

Then it dawned on him; he would be training *his* Cherry to go into the field, to submit to some unscrupulous asshole who sold females for a living, a man who would touch her, maybe hurt her. One agent had already disappeared, might even be dead. She'd volunteered for immense danger. And he wouldn't be there to guide her. But York would.

Damn it.

He crossed his arms over his chest. Maybe that way she wouldn't see how hard his heart was pounding at the idea of her volunteering to walk into a snake pit. "Since you're FBI, I presume you're proficient with a gun and hand-to-hand, but if you don't have the time or guts to fully prepare for a potentially dangerous BDSM environment, then I won't train you for this mission."

"Oh, I have the time and the guts, but you're right; you won't train me. I'll find someone else. But I *am* going to do my job. Darcy

Miles, the missing agent, is my friend. And what I do is none of your business."

Because he'd thrown away the right to say anything when they'd been sixteen, near the end of their sophomore year. She didn't spit out that she was no longer his, but the unspoken words hung brittle in the air, taking him back to that terrible day . . .

Tyler High School—Twelve years ago

Logan pulled out his cell phone and tried Tara's number again. Once more, he heard her cheerful little voice telling him to leave a message—just like the last hundred times he'd called. He snapped his phone shut and raked a hand through his hair. God, this couldn't be happening. Where was she? Why hadn't she been in British Lit this morning? Clenching his fingers around his open locker, he tried not to hyperventilate or think about the menacing letter.

"Bro." Hunter, his older brother, stopped beside his locker, wearing a scowl. His blue eyes softened with concern.

"So they just let seniors roam the halls now?" he tried to joke.

Hunter's mouth curled up, but it wasn't a smile. "I got a hall pass to check on you after I heard that you'd ditched out of Brit Lit earlier. How are you doing?"

"Well, Mom was murdered yesterday, and I found her body. How am I supposed to feel?"

Logan couldn't seem to stop the flashes of his mother's lifeless body, his horror at the spray of red running down the wall as she lay in a sludgy pool of her own blood.

At Hunter's sigh, Logan raked a hand through his hair. "Sorry. I know it hasn't been easy on you, either."

"But it's harder on you. You'd maintained a tight relationship with Mom after the divorce. I hadn't spoken to her since she left Dad last year. And I'll have to live with that." Hunter's eyes narrowed.

"But just now, you seemed more concerned than grief-stricken. The worst has already happened. So what's up? It have anything to do with Tara being absent?"

Logan opened his mouth, but nothing came out. He wanted to confide . . . but did he dare? Grappling with possibilities, he froze. Though he trusted Hunter with his life, the note had been very clear on the terrible consequences for failing to keep this to himself.

Hunter grabbed his shoulder. "Look, I heard that you freaked out when she didn't show up for class. You wanna tell me something?"

Maybe. Logan truly hoped his brother had decided to pull a sick prank last night. If Hunter was behind this, Logan would totally rearrange his face—then breathe a sigh of relief.

"Did you jack with me yesterday by leaving a note on my pillow?"

Hunter scowled at him as if he thought Logan had a few screws loose. "No. When would I have done it? While we were at the police station? While I rocked Kimber to sleep?"

Right. At eight, their little sister had been terrified last night. After hours at the police station, she'd come away wise enough to understand that she'd never see her mom again, but too young to cope alone. Hunter had stepped in and stayed all night. And he wasn't known for his levity, so hoping he'd pulled the prank had been a stretch.

Which meant the threat was real. Logan swore under his breath. What the hell should he do?

Scanning the hall to make sure he and Hunter were alone, Logan gulped down nerves about to make his stomach revolt. "Last night, not long after we got home from the police station, I found a note on my pillow. I—it was from Mom's killer, threatening to kill Tara if I don't stay away from her."

His blue eyes widened with shock. "*What?* Did you tell Dad or call the police?"

"I can't," he choked out. "The note said that if I told anyone, she'd 'suffer.' Last night, I hoped it was just a sick prank. And I . . . needed to talk to Tara."

"You called her?" Hunter's grim tone said he disapproved of that impulse.

After all the police interviews, after they'd removed his mom's body, Logan had *needed* to talk to the one person who understood what it was like to lose a mother. He'd also wanted to check on her, make sure no one had harmed her. And after he'd taken her virginity yesterday, she'd surely ached for some reassurance. Yet his Cherry had brushed aside her own needs to help him. She'd been so sympathetic on the phone, so understanding of his disbelief, anger, and confusion. Her voice alone had soothed him.

But after giving in to his need to hear her voice, he couldn't find her.

Dread pounded his stomach as he nodded. "She agreed to meet me at the park at nine. I waited an hour, but she never showed. On my way to her house, Dad found me and dragged me home and . . ." He let out a sick sigh of worry. "I tried to call Tara all night. She didn't answer or show up for class this morning." Logan crushed the heels of his hands into his eyes. "I'm so fucking afraid that I got her killed."

The bell ending third period sounded. He looked frantically for Tara in the crowding halls, but saw no sign of her. Panic nearly choked him.

Damn it, why hadn't he heeded the threat?

Hunter frowned. "Given Mom's brutal murder, if some asshole is threatening Tara, I'd take it seriously and walk away."

Do without Cherry? Tears stung Logan's eyes. Until yesterday, he hadn't cried about anything or anyone since he was nine. But he'd shed tears for Mom—and now for Tara.

Maybe dealing with all the shock and death of the last twenty-four hours had changed him, but Logan feared that he couldn't live without Tara Jacobs. And he couldn't take another loss now, especially not hers.

"But I love her."

Hunter's face turned grim. "If that's the case, then you'd rather see her alive, right?"

God, what kind of question was that? Of course. But . . . Jesus. He hated this feeling of helplessness, of his entire life being ripped apart all at once and him being unable to stop it.

With a clap on the back, Hunter said, "I get that this is hurting you, man. But better you hurt than her."

He's right. Swallowing the feeling of sick dread roiling through him, Logan turned away, opened his locker. Relief poured over him to find a neatly folded piece of paper. Maybe Tara had been running late this morning to school and left a note. She'd done that once after a dentist appointment. God, let her be all right. With shaking hands, he tore into the white paper.

You didn't listen. Tara paid.

Air left his body with a *whoosh* as if he'd been punched by a battering ram. *Oh shit!* He couldn't breathe, couldn't blink. People moved in the halls around Logan, but for him, time stood still, while inside, he screamed a silent *no!!!!*

Over his shoulder, Hunter read the note and cursed. "Whoever's behind this isn't fucking around. They know who you are, where you live, and how you feel."

Every word of truth Hunter spoke stabbed him. What the fuck was he going to do? "Why her? What if she's been killed?"

"I don't know. But if, by some chance, Tara is still alive, you need to stay away from that girl."

Crumpling the note in his fist, Logan tried not to cry again as he shoved it in his pocket and reached for his phone and dialed once more. He just needed to know that she was all right. Tara's voicemail picked up. He closed the phone and shoved it in his pocket.

Please be okay. Please . . . She had to be safe. If she wasn't, it would be his fault for calling her, for doing exactly what he'd been warned against. And he'd lose another loved one to terrible, sudden violence.

"I have to take a Government test," Hunter murmured. "I'll see you at lunch. We'll talk more."

Absently, Logan nodded, his head still spinning as his brother walked away.

Fourth period was about to begin. And still, Tara hadn't come to her locker, only three down from his own. If she didn't, it would all be his fault. Logan raked a hand through his hair. Tara was so smart and responsible. She would never have missed school unless something was wrong.

On autopilot, he grabbed his books and closed his locker, fear eating at his composure. To say that the day before had been both the best and the worst of his life would be a gross understatement. His thrill that he'd finally made Cherry his had totally amplified the horror of discovering his mom's body. The worry that he'd spelled Tara's doom only made it all worse.

"Logan?" a shy voice whispered.

Cherry!

He whirled to find her standing beside her locker, pretty brown eyes bouncing up to his face, her expression concerned. Relief poured thorough him, and he ached to grab her, kiss her, get inside her again. They'd get busted in the hallways if he did more than hold her hand. He didn't care about getting caught himself, but her overprotective stepfather already disapproved of him, an experienced jock sniffing around his pristine daughter. If Logan lured Adam Sterling's valedictorian-in-training into trouble, the man would only try harder to pull them apart.

"I've been trying to call you." It came out like an accusation, but Logan was too strung out on worry to take it back.

"Sorry. I dropped my phone last night. It broke."

Logan released the last of his breath he'd been holding. That was it? Thank God it hadn't been anything more serious. Thank God no one had harmed her.

At least not yet.

He stared, not sure how to how to explain his behavior. Not sure how much longer he could stop himself from touching her.

Then he realized that he shouldn't do either. He shouldn't even be talking to her now.

Under his intent gaze, a flush crawled up her skin, from the pale flesh above her little white cardigan, all the way to her lightly freckled nose. She nervously fingered a heart-shaped pendant around her neck, eyes cast down demurely. Was she remembering yesterday after school, when they'd gone all the way? Logan ached to return to that blissful moment, when he'd been able to truly experience first love—without knowing any of the horrors that awaited.

A vision of Tara brutalized like his mother flashed through his head. If he didn't want that to become reality, he had to end this now.

Damn it, she stood two feet from him, and he could barely keep himself from reaching out to touch her. How agonizing would it be to see her every day but know that she might as well be a million miles away?

Logan swallowed all that down. "I have to go."

She grabbed his arm. With that one touch, she soothed him. He closed his eyes and savored her for one selfish second, wishing it could last forever.

Then he jerked away.

"I'm sorry I couldn't make it last night," she apologized, her sweet face all but pleading with him to understand. "You needed me, and I—"

"It's fine." He was sure there was a good reason she hadn't made it. His Cherry was nothing if not caring and conscientious. Maybe her stepdad had found out they'd made love. Maybe she'd gotten grounded. Logan frowned.

"It's not fine. Logan, you found your mother murdered yesterday. Why are you even here today?"

"My dad insisted on normalcy. You know the Colonel. Why

deal with anything as paltry as emotion?" And Logan knew that he shouldn't be seen talking to her now. Anyone—a killer—could be watching them. "I've gotta go."

"Logan, you look . . . devastated. I'm sorry I couldn't be there when you needed me." Her eyes filled with tears. For him. "I'm here now. I know how the death of a mom feels. I'll help you through it. We'll talk, or whatever you need."

He swallowed. That was his Cherry—giving, willing to do anything to soothe and please him. But he wanted her to live more.

"I don't need anything from you." He turned away.

"Wait!" She grabbed his shoulder, pulled him back. "Let me explain last night. I snuck out and got on my bike to come to the park and see you. I didn't get two blocks before a car nearly ran me over."

Logan's heart seized up. "Oh my— Are you hurt?"

She angled her arm around from under her sweater. It was covered in a big white cast. The entire arm was in a sling. "The car came out of an alley. I guess whoever was driving didn't see my reflectors. I jerked away so they didn't mow me down, and they drove off. I hit the fence and fell. Dropped my phone. The jerk drove off. My shoulder was dislocated and my arm broken. My stepdad and I were in the ER until after midnight."

You didn't listen. Tara paid. The warning burned through Logan's head.

He swallowed down fear. "The driver didn't stop to help you?"

"No." She looked down and shook her head. "He screeched off, like he was in a hurry."

Or like he didn't want any witnesses. Tara's "accident" had been Logan's last warning; he felt it all the way to his bones. Even now, standing in the hall with her, he could be signing her death warrant. Whoever had written this note had also killed his mother—brutally. Bled her out and enjoyed her slow, torturous death. Logan knew that if he stayed near Tara . . .

Fuck, he couldn't even finish the sentence. The images pummel-
ing his brain filled him with fresh panic. He forced himself to shake
off her touch and back away.

"It doesn't matter," Logan choked out and turned away to shut
his locker.

For a moment, he squeezed his eyes closed. He didn't want to do
this. Being without Cherry was going to hurt so fucking bad. He
needed her, loved her. But this wasn't about him.

He drew in a deep breath. Once he turned and spoke to her,
she'd never look at him the same way again. In fact, she was so caring
and certain to be worried about his grief that he'd have to make sure
she never wanted to speak to him again.

God, she was going to hate him for this. Hurting her was going
to kill him.

Logan hesitated, pressed his lips together. No matter how excru-
ciating, he needed to grow a set—now. Better his heartache than her
death.

Shoving down the anguish ripping him to pieces, Logan turned.
"I'm sorry you got hurt, but you not showing doesn't matter. Tara,
we can't be together anymore."

Her expression became guarded. "Did you finally decide that
jocks like you can't be with brains like me?"

Tara looked ready to tear into him for that, filling him with a
bittersweet pride. He'd love to take her to the prom, shock all his
friends. Yeah, he was dating a smart girl. And he loved her. If they
didn't like it, they could kiss his ass.

But the opportunity to show her off as his would never come
now.

She shook her finger at him. "I won't believe it. You've spent
three months convincing me that was my hang up, not yours. You
haven't suddenly had a change of heart."

"It's just not working for me. I'm used to dating a certain kind of
girl." Vapid, sleazy, and utterly dull. God, he'd miss Cherry.

Tears filled her big brown eyes. "You're going to fail the *Romeo and Juliet* test without me."

Yeah, he was, but he'd scrape by for the semester. His grade was now the least of his worries.

The fourth-period bell rang. Tara looked up, realized the halls were empty. "I'm late to class. Can we talk about this after school?"

He forced himself to spear her with a cold glare. "Why bother?"

She trembled as she tried to draw in a breath. "But after yesterday . . ."

Yesterday. When he'd shoved their books to the floor, laid her across his bed, and kissed Cherry out of her sweater and T-shirt, her shoes and pants, then finally her bra and panties. He'd touched her all over. When he'd finished, other than her red hair, he had no reason to call her Cherry anymore.

"Hi, Logan." Brittany Fuller, his ex-girlfriend, sauntered by with a wink.

"Brit." He nodded, hoping like hell that she'd keep walking.

She was pretty, had big tits, and loved every variety of sex, the wilder the better. But Tara had taught Logan that he required a brain and a heart in a woman. Brittany lacked both.

Thankfully, she kept walking to her next class.

Cherry's face screwed up with jealousy. She couldn't stand the cheerleader on principle. Brit was lazy and slid by on her looks. Tara was a hard worker, blisteringly smart. She'd made her contempt for Brittany's type well known. Once he'd thought about it, Logan had realized that Tara was right. Which made what he was about to do all the more heinous.

He clenched his fists. "It's over. The tutoring, the sex. Don't call me anymore."

She sucked in a breath, her creamy pale skin going ghostly white. Tears gathered in her pained dark eyes. "You—you're upset. Your mom just died. Last night, you needed me a-and I didn't show up."

"You've said for weeks that we had nothing in common." He

shrugged. "I'm just admitting now that you're right. I'm getting back together with Brittany."

She was the last girl Logan wanted, but a couple of weeks with her would surely convince Tara to keep her distance.

"B-But yesterday. We . . ."

"Fucked. Yeah?"

She gaped, shock blanching her face. "You said that you loved me."

He had, and he'd meant it. But Logan loved her enough to cut his own heart out to keep her alive. "Let that be a lesson not to believe everything you hear."

Tara lurched back as if he'd stabbed her. "You bastard! My step-dad swore you'd only hurt me. He gave me this necklace last night and told me to guard my heart. Too bad he was a few hours too late!" She bit her lip, furiously fighting more tears. "I hope someone breaks your heart someday, you son of a bitch."

Gripping her books in one hand, Tara turned away, then ran down the hall before she shoved into the girls' bathroom.

Logan watched, breaking apart into a million pieces inside. "Someone just did. I'm so damn sorry, Cherry."

Dominion—Present day

Pressing her lips together, Tara grabbed her purse and clothes from the armoire, shoving the latter into a ball. It was either that or stare at Logan Edgington. If she did, she'd have to acknowledge that he was more gorgeous than ever and still made her weak-kneed—and that would only piss her off more. No way would she give the prick that satisfaction.

Twelve years ago, he'd been a pretty, if somewhat gawky boy. Tall and thin with a hint of the broad chest to come and a mischievous smile. Today, he'd grown into that body. Wide, bronzed shoulders bulged out beneath a white tank. Muscled pectorals that no T-shirt could conceal. The angles of his face, stark cheekbones, razor-sharp jaw, and dimpled chin, had once made him interesting. Now, they gave him the look of a predator, topped off by that dangerous blue stare.

God, why was he *here*? Didn't matter. She was leaving, right this minute.

Tara tucked the clothes under her arm. She would have loved to don them. Wearing little more than a bra and panties around the jerk who'd conned her out of her virginity wasn't exactly comfortable, but no way would she give him the slightest hint that burning stare of his unnerved her. And no way in hell was she staying in this BDSM palace with him for even two more seconds.

God, it figures he'd wind up spending "a lot of time" in a place where men played mind games and used women for pleasure. Logan had excelled at that, even in high school. And she refused to let him use her again.

Not sparing him a glance, she stormed toward the door.

"Tara."

Her first instinct was to turn and look at him. Because his voice snapped with command and made her pussy ache for some mysterious reason? Because she'd deluded herself into thinking that she heard pain?

Tara kept walking.

She was so angry she could spit nails. It was irrational, she knew. Logan hadn't done anything to her today but surprise her. Too much frustration piled onto too little sleep, mixed with too much fear that her friend and fellow agent, Darcy Miles, could die any minute she spent in this tie-'em-down-whip-'em-up dungeon learning her role.

But her new boss, Jon Bocelli, had been perfectly clear when finally granting her this assignment. She'd been given this opportunity because she solved mysteries well, kept her cool, was hell with a gun, and fit the victims' general background. Of course, he could find all that among existing agents. She'd also been told she was the perfect bait because she had the physical attributes these men seemed to want. She was voluptuous and had a soft look about her. It didn't hurt that word had it they were looking for redheads. Beyond all that, though, what she possessed that others lacked, according to her psychological profile, was a submissive streak. Tara shuddered. Even the suggestion made her bristle. She *hated* being told what to do, but if the misconception worked in her favor, Bocelli could believe whatever he wanted. If she patently denied her "nature," Bocelli would shuttle her behind a desk again, filtering intel.

She'd volunteered for a field assignment to see if she was cut out to be an agent . . . and to see if following in Adam's footsteps would make her stepfather proud. She'd only been given this assignment now because Bocelli didn't have a better option. No one would work harder to rescue Darcy.

And Tara knew that, unless she did something, Logan would be squarely in her way.

If she wanted him gone, she'd have to talk to the club's owner. Mr. Thorpe seemed like a calm, rational man. Then, hopefully, she'd never see her high school flame again.

But Logan was faster than her and took hold of her elbow.

He didn't exert pressure; he didn't need to. His touch alone sizzled through her like the shock of a live wire. To her horror, Tara felt her entire body heat up.

"Stop."

His snapped command detonated through her system, his voice so hypnotic, so deep, it compelled her to obey. The need was almost more than she could resist. Her nipples peaked. An ache took up residence between her legs.

She hesitated, though her entire body stayed tensed for flight.

"Look at me," he demanded.

Damn it, she didn't want to. But that tone alone nearly seduced her compliance. Refusing would only make her look ridiculously stubborn. Or scared. The last thing Tara wanted to do was give Logan a reason to think he mattered, to presume for an instant that she'd measured all lovers against him and found each lacking.

Drawing in a bracing breath, she met his gaze.

"Good," he murmured. "Let's sit and talk. You can tell me more about this mission, and we'll talk about our best next steps."

No way was she going to risk Darcy's safety any more by wasting time with Logan. Yes, Tara was a professional, but she'd have to be dead not to be distracted by the perceptive, gorgeous man staring at her now. Toss in their crappy history, and this had train wreck written all over it.

"Or you could fuck off." Tara jerked from his grasp and marched out the door, giving it a satisfying slam behind her.

She didn't delude herself; if Logan wanted to make something of their unlikely meeting, he would. God knew, he'd once pursued her with a single-minded intensity that had made her sixteen-year-old heart flutter. But unlike her teenage self, she knew better than to give him a second more of her time or mental energy.

And no, she wouldn't think about him at all when she lay in her bed late at night and put her hand on her clit, seeking satisfaction. Damn it.

After sneaking into a restroom in the hall, Tara wriggled into her gray suit and tucked her hair back into her professional chignon. She stepped into her heels and repaired her makeup. Feeling a thousand percent more confident, she wrenched open the door, half expecting to find Logan blocking her way. The hall was empty.

Hoping he'd taken the hint, she made her way to Mr. Thorpe's office, the echo of her heels against the concrete floors too loud. At the office door, she knocked and waited.

"You may come in, Agent Jacobs."

Tara smothered her surprise as she opened the door. He'd either known her identity because he had cameras installed in the hall or Logan had told him to expect her. Either way, she didn't care. "Hello."

The tight smile playing at his full mouth pricked her with unease. "Sit."

It was an order; not an invitation. If she wanted his cooperation, she shouldn't risk pissing him off.

Quickly, she settled into the stylish leather chair in front of the gigantic walnut desk and crossed her legs. Brushed nickel accented the rest of the office, along with glass shelves peppered with books, silk plants, and heinously expensive pottery. A Picasso hung on his wall. She was pretty sure it was real.

"Mr. Thorpe, I know you're busy, so I'll get to the point."

"You want someone else to train you." He peered at her with a penetrating stare, steepling his long fingers in front of his strong jaw. "Tell me why."

So Logan had filled him in. "Mr. Edgington and I knew each other in high school. To be blunt, I don't trust him. I never will."

From her research, she knew that trust was big in the Dom/sub relationship. She'd start there. Tara sat back in the chair and waited.

As soon as she got settled, Thorpe stood, using his height advantage. He looked urbane enough, but under that expensive white dress shirt and impeccable chocolate slacks, she saw lots of muscle. He pinned her with a piercing stare, as if trying to read her mind. To hell with that.

"Because?"

"He's a liar." A ruthless one who didn't blink as he tore out a young girl's heart.

Thorpe stroked his close-cropped beard. "Have you changed at all since high school, Agent Jacobs?"

She knew where he was going, and she'd have to cut short that line of thinking. "One hopes we've all matured since high school, but fundamentally, some things about a person remain the same, no matter how 'grown up' they are."

"Hmm." He paced the room. "Distant past aside, do you have any current objections to Logan?"

What about the trust issue? "Are you listening? There's no way I can put myself completely in his hands while I learn to say 'Sir' and 'please' every half second. I know Agent York needs quite a bit of training before he can assume the role, and I'm fully aware that time is of the essence. I'll be happy to have anyone train me. Except Mr. Edgington."

His mouth twitched, and he looked like he was suppressing a smile. She didn't need this asshole to be amused at her expense.

"Answer my question." His quiet demand snapped in the air like a whip. "Do you have any current objections against Logan? He's a highly decorated Navy SEAL with eight solid years in this club. I trained him myself, so I know very well who he is and what he's like. Do you?"

God, Logan had gotten into this stuff a couple years after high school? Why? What need of his did it feed? Tara shook her head. It didn't matter. He wasn't her problem.

"His military service, while admirable, is of no comfort to me. His training, while I'm sure thorough, can't make up for the fact that I distrust him. And I can't change how I feel. Mr. Thorpe, you're the best in the region, and the Bureau hired you to prepare me for this field mission—"

"They did," he cut in. "And I am trying to live up to my end of the contract. It's been frustrating to Axel that you've been resistant and bratty all week. Uncooperative."

Determined to remain professional, Tara refused to betray her anger. "I disagree. I've been here, half dressed and on my knees, for ten hours a day, every day. I've spent my nights and weekends researching the lifestyle—reading, interviewing, whatever necessary to increase my knowledge."

He acknowledged her with a nod. "Physically, you've done as asked. Intellectually, you've got the fundamentals. Mentally and emotionally, you've erected walls against participating in the power exchange. A shame, really, denying your submissive nature."

There was that ridiculous assertion again. Just like Bocelli, Thorpe didn't know her at all.

"Mr. Thorpe, my nature isn't up for discussion. I'm here to learn whatever I need to fake it and rescue Agent Miles."

"'Faking it' probably got Agent Miles captured. A Dom worth his salt can dig out a sub's true desires quickly. If she's not genuine about embracing her need to please her Master, he'll know. If you truly want to help your fellow agent, focus on finding the true sub within you."

His words wrapped around her neck like a vise grip and choked. Her stepfather had always called her a pleaser, which was why she'd allowed Logan to take advantage of her. Of course she liked the idea of a man who knew her, body and soul, and fulfilled every dark fantasy. Nor could she deny having a bondage fantasy or two. But that hardly made her submissive. The thought of giving up her free will entirely to another . . . Tara shuddered inwardly. Hell no.

Still, being here at Dominion was about the friend she'd gone to college with, first gotten drunk with, shared holidays, beauty tips, illness, and breakups with. It had nothing to do with Logan.

"I will do my best to embrace the role. I will work harder to internalize whatever I must before going undercover. But please, I'm asking you to find anyone else but Mr. Edgington."

Thorpe sat on the edge of the desk, hovering. No doubt, he knew that the way he towered over her discomfited her. "A pretty plea . . . but no. First, I won't let you top from the bottom."

"I am *not* manipulating a Dom to get my way."

At that, he sent her a sly, white grin. "You are—and if you were mine, I'd paddle you for that lie. In fact, your stubbornness is one reason Agent York isn't progressing. He's placating you instead of getting his act together. Second, Logan is the best at training subs who need, shall we say, an attitude adjustment. He's patient, logical, and unyielding. You, Agent Jacobs, need a firm hand. He'll give it to you, make no mistake."

Bastard! "You're dragging out this training unnecessarily. Instead of simply getting comfortable with the lifestyle, you're forcing me to deal with a Dom I will never trust. How is that helpful?"

"Your employer paid me handsomely to prepare you for an urgent mission. Everything I have done is to prepare you, including taking away your choices. You have to get used to that since a submissive may only say yes or quit. That's what you haven't gotten through your head yet. The contract states that I'm able, within legal bounds, to use my discretion and do whatever necessary to ensure your readiness. That's what I'm going to do. Or do you wish to quit before truly trying?"

Low blow. Tara refused to give up on Darcy, and Thorpe knew it. She fought to hold down an angry flush. "No."

He raised a dark brow. He wanted a "Sir" out of her, damn him. But giving it would prove to him that she understood protocol—and could embrace it.

And if she wanted another Dom, she needed to play his game.

"No, Sir," she murmured. "But—"

"That was slow and insincere. Your manners need work, Agent Jacobs. Logan may make you uncomfortable, but I believe he will be effective. I've watched you with Axel this week. I saw from the observation room when you first realized that Logan had come for you. Your reaction was . . .very enlightening." He prowled around to the edge of his desk again. "For the first time since you stepped in this door, you snapped to attention and listened. I'll bet he made you wet. There's a reason a sweet sub like you denies her nature, and Logan will get to the bottom of that. Besides, if you truly are unable to trust him ever again, this will be good training for your mission. You'll never trust an international slave dealer who wants you to kneel at his feet so he can sell you to the highest bidder. Pretending obedience will do you good."

"But wouldn't it take less time to prepare me if—"

"You are not without recourse," Thorpe broke in. "You will be monitored, for safety's sake. If Logan genuinely pushes you past what's bearable or forces any act on you, you always have your safe word. Should you truly need to use it, we'll discuss your options then." He rose from the desk and opened his door. "Good-bye."

Tara rose to her feet stiffly. The bastard thought he had this all figured out. Fine. If he wasn't going to believe her, there was no sense wasting more time arguing. Giving one hundred percent to her mission and rescuing Darcy was the priority. Thorpe had all but told her the way out of this nonsense. Now all she needed was an opportunity.

Whirling to face the club's owner, she opened her mouth—and closed it when she saw they were no longer alone. Logan leaned against the doorjamb, staring at her with a dissecting blue gaze that promised punishment. Against her will, her womb clenched.

"C'mon, Cherry. Apparently, I need to start with that spanking, after all. Let's go."

Chapter Three

TARA swallowed. Her heart fell to her knees as Logan stepped aside just enough for her to exit Thorpe's office. She didn't look his way as she turned down the hall. Even without seeing the harsh angles of Logan's face, she felt his heat and leashed anger simmering behind her. He was furious that she'd tried to have him replaced. Why the hell did he care? He'd cast her aside twelve years ago. Yes, he'd been reeling after his mother's murder, and she would have excused anger or aloofness. But not his cruelty. What the hell did he want now? The sick thrill of hurting her again? She'd be damned if she let him, because she—and more important, Darcy—didn't need Logan's head games.

But she couldn't deny that rankling his Edgington pride had given her a thrill.

Logan steered her with a light touch at the small of her back, his fingertips like a brand as he guided her down the long hallway that led to more shadowy rooms with equipment that shocked her—and jolted her with a shameful hot spark. Tara hated that, almost as much as she wanted to hate his touch.

"We're going to be spending a lot of time in my dungeon, Cherry."

"Don't call me that," she hissed.

"While you're training, you have no control over what I call you, what you do, or what you wear. Your only choices are to obey or quit."

Immediately, Tara got his game. "And you're going to push in every way possible to induce me to throw in the towel, aren't you?"

He raised an intimidating brow, but said nothing.

Bastard. Clearly he didn't know how much spine she'd grown since high school. Yet.

"You think I can't handle it."

"I'd prefer you out of harm's way."

"It's my job to do everything possible to save Agent Miles. I don't give a shit what you want."

Logan clenched his jaw. "Going undercover when you have no experience in either covert operations or submissive behavior is incredibly brave. But it's also very dangerous. You should have more field experience first. Since you don't, it's *my* job to thoroughly prepare you."

"Why not let someone else do the job?" She thrust her hand on her hip. "You made it crystal clear years ago that you don't care."

"Think of this as my atonement for our past. Now let's go."

With a nudge, he urged her forward. Anger shimmered off of him. His presence filled the air around her, forbidding. *Atonement, my ass.*

Repressing a quiver of apprehension, Tara moved forward, heels clicking on the hard floors as he stalked behind her. He might be in charge . . . for now. But she had one power that Logan absolutely must respect. The minute he tried to exert his will? She'd blurt her safe word faster than he could spit. Thorpe, watching their exchange, would be forced to replace Logan with another Dom. Then she could get down to serious training. But whatever her first lover's game, she wasn't playing.

Logan guided her to a room she'd never seen and flicked on the overhead lights. The space was utilitarian, with gray concrete floors and black walls. A padded table, a spanking bench that looked like a sawhorse, a large wooden X, and a bed outfitted with nothing but a fitted, black silk sheet. Was this his dungeon?

"Inside."

She stepped in and whirled on him as he slammed the door. And locked it.

Tara shot him a cold glare. "Don't try to scare me by playing the heavy."

He pierced her with a stare as he crossed the floor to stand beside the giant wooden X. Manacles dangled from heavy-duty bolts both at top and bottom. "I'm not playing. Come here and present yourself."

She looked at the apparatus, shoving down a shiver of apprehension. "If we're a team, I need to know what's going on. We should discuss how to proceed with this training."

His stare grew icy. "We may be a team, but I'm in charge. I didn't give you permission to speak. First warning. Come here and do as you're told or we'll start our time together with a hell of a spanking."

Spanking, as in his hand on my ass? The thought rippled through her with an involuntary blast of heat. Tara didn't waste her breath to challenge Logan and say that he wouldn't dare. He would.

Damn it. Why did that make her panties damp?

She approached him, stopping a few safe feet away.

He raised a brow. "You can't follow my simple instructions, but you're going to breeze through some slave-peddling asshole trying to mold you into the perfect submissive while you search for your missing agent?"

Tara paused. As much as she wanted to hate him now . . . he was right. Until Thorpe assigned her a new Dom, she was stuck with Logan. And whatever the situation, she had to control her anger—and her anxiety that Logan would touch her.

Drawing in a deep breath, Tara dropped down into the pose Axel had taught her, sitting back on her heels, legs spread as much as her skirt allowed, palms up on her thighs, shoulders back, head down.

Logan walked a slow circle around her, his stare touching her everywhere. Though she kept in good shape, Tara had a generous booty no matter how much she exercised. But she didn't care if Logan loathed her figure. Brad, her fiancé, liked it just fine.

Logan crouched in front of her. "Look at me."

Tara met his stare with cool challenge.

That blue gaze penetrated her defenses, and despite wearing a skirt, blouse, and heels, she felt stark naked. Her skin grew hot and tight as he scrutinized her.

"There's nothing wrong with the form of the pose itself, as I'm sure you know. You always studied every subject thoroughly. That won't be enough to slide by with submission. What matters is not merely that you obey, but that there's obedience in your heart.

"You dropped into position quickly when I reminded you about your fellow agent's well-being," he went on. "But you didn't come to me with any desire to please me. You spoke after I told you to remain silent. I see anger all over your face."

She blanked her expression and stared through him. "I'll try harder next time."

"You may not have a next time. Agent Miles doesn't."

He was right. Shit, this arrangement was never going to work. Yes, she needed to keep her head in the game, but there was too much past between them that she couldn't seem to forget. If she was going to stop wasting time and get rid of Logan, she needed to do it now.

Tara slanted him an innocent stare. "Did you wish to spank me?"

"Yep, like the bratty sub you're being, until you think twice about letting your temper get the best of you. That will be fatal in the field. Unless, of course, you'd like to quit the mission and send a more experienced agent in your place."

"Hell no. Unlike you, I don't turn my back on others."

A muscle ticked in Logan's cheek. "I still didn't give you permission to speak. That's something that won't be tolerated when you're undercover. For that, I'll punish you with two swats, in addition to

the five I'd already decided to give you for running to Thorpe instead
of working your differences out with me. For cursing, I'm adding
another two. For failing to address me as 'Logan,' I'll add three more."

Neither Axel nor Robert had touched her all week. Nor had she
wanted them to. But against her will, Tara flashed hot at the dizzying
number of blows Logan promised to inflict on her ass. Her womb
cramped. Damn it, she shouldn't react like this with him. "Don't
most of you control freaks want to be called Sir or Master?"

He laughed. It wasn't a nice sound. "Usually. For you, I'm making
an exception. I want to hear *my* name on your lips so I know you're
aware of exactly who's making you come."

Tara bit her tongue. She'd love to toss his self-assurance back in
his face and vow there was no way in hell he'd arouse her enough to
climax. But if he'd managed to make a virgin gasp and claw and melt
in his arms at sixteen, what could a grown man do to a woman hungry for another orgasm like that? It was a nonissue. They wouldn't
be together that long.

"You don't get to make me come. That's my *fiancé's* role."

"I'd read that you were engaged to Brad Thompson. I figured
you'd fall in love with someone who had at least a shred of honor."

"Since he didn't lie to me to steal my innocence, then dump me
flat the next day, I'd say he's a huge step up from you."

Logan tensed, fists clenching, muscles bunching, veins bulging.
"When you're with me, the man is irrelevant. His name does not
cross your lips. That ring comes off your finger. Are we clear?"

It bothered him to see her wearing a symbol of Brad's possession. She smiled and slowly peeled it off before placing it in her skirt
pocket. "As long as you understand that you're not to touch me sexually. I choose to give him my orgasms."

And she would . . . if Brad could arouse her enough to have one.

His smug smile made her heart stutter. "You agreed to be trained.
That means I'll push you far beyond your comfort level so that you'll
become accustomed to acts that, right now, may be uncomfortable.

We'll see what your body says when I've got your legs spread and my tongue all over your clit. Again."

Tara bit her lip to keep from sucking in an inflamed breath. His words flared heat between her legs as memories bombarded her. More moisture coated her panties. Damn it, why did her body react to him with anything other than disgust?

"No commentary?" he asked with an arched brow. "Good. Now where was I? Oh, for your disrespect in calling me a control freak, I'll add another three smacks. How many is that so far?"

God, she wanted to spit in his face. "Fifteen."

Logan smiled. "You're going to have the most gorgeous rosy ass when I'm through with you, Cherry."

Tara wished she had the luxury of telling him there was no way she was letting him touch her ass, but she needed to rid herself of Logan and get another Dom. Until then, she'd stick it out, no matter how difficult or distasteful.

"Your temper is brewing again. We'll work on that. But first, I told you to present yourself, not merely pose."

She froze as his meaning sank in. "You want me naked?"

"Yes. And watch your tone, or I'll add more punishment."

"Axel allowed me to train in my bra and panties so I'd be relaxed and comfortable for our lessons."

Logan snorted. "In BUDs training for SEALs, the instructors deprive the trainees of all relaxation and comfort for hours on end to more closely simulate the stress and difficulty of real combat and covert situations. I subscribe to their theory that immersion training is most effective. What's this called?" He pointed to the wooden X with dangling manacles. A something-or-other cross. Her terrible curiosity about what it would feel like to be bare as he secured her to one scared the hell out of her.

She willed herself to find the term, but with apprehension and unwanted lust clouding her brain, it didn't happen in the long, silent minute.

"A St. Andrew's Cross," he said into her silence. "What kind of ring is this?" He pointed to the thick metal implement from which the manacles at the top and bottom of the cross dangled.

Tara went blank. "A metal ring?"

"It's an O ring," he supplied. "And you 'learned' this while in your bra and panties?"

Crap.

"We agreed to train in bathing suits or lingerie. Besides my being engaged, Robert—Agent York—is a coworker. We'll have to work together after this is over, and we both wanted to avoid as much of the awkwardness as possible."

"You and York are now undergoing separate training, so problem solved. And I've already seen it all, Cherry."

"Thorpe is watching."

"He's likely not the only man who will see you naked before this mission is over. You're going to last longer if you focus only on pleasing the Dom in front of you. When you're ready to work, remove everything, fold it neatly at my feet, then resume your position. Hesitating will cost you another ten swats."

Fury broiled her composure. God, what had she ever seen in him besides those shiver-worthy blue eyes?

Once upon a time, he'd seemed really, really genuine with her. In high school, they'd studied British literature classics, and she'd learned a lot about his heart. He'd debated Shakespeare's star-crossed teen lovers, worried about Tiny Tim. He'd even wrung his hands waiting for Elizabeth Bennett to have her happily ever after with Mr. Darcy. And she'd delighted at his capacity to feel.

That boy was long gone, if he'd ever really existed.

Now, the bastard was doing everything possible to make her job hell. Tara pressed her lips together and wiped the mulish expression off her face. *Think proving yourself on this mission, think Darcy.*

"Now," he barked. "That position you're in is not only for you to show your obedience, but your willingness to accept your Dom in whatever way he wishes to have you. It's also to tempt him by showing off your body. I can't see what you've covered, Cherry. Strip."

Her breath caught. Being naked again for Logan . . . The cold ball of dread settling in her gut warred with the hot ache brewing between her legs. Baring herself to him would make her frighteningly vulnerable, but submitting to his demand so they could get on with this farce was necessary. She swallowed down her nerves.

After a few swats of his hand on her ass, Tara vowed that Logan would be out of her life again—this time for good.

She stood and stepped out of her heels, sliding them aside, then removed her bracelet, earrings, and chunky silver necklace. She shrugged out of her suit coat and unbuttoned her rumpled eggshell blouse, closing her eyes to block out his presence.

"Look at me."

His voice compelled her. Almost against her will, Tara complied. Logan stood mere inches away, watching intently as she stripped the blouse from her pale shoulders, revealing her nude lace bra. His eyes heated. His nostrils flared. Her heart pounded. The sheer fabric did nothing to hide her peaked nipples as she folded the silky shirt. A shuddering inhalation later, she unhooked her bra and let it drop to the floor. His fists tightened at his side.

He wanted her. A quick glance down the front of his leather pants proved that she was turning him on. Tara didn't want to care that she got to him, but dangerous feminine thrill zipped through her.

Still, this was the first weakness he'd displayed. Maybe she could use it to her advantage.

Tara retrieved her bra, folded it, then set it on top of her blouse and coat. When she stood again, she infused her stare with a bit of challenge and come-hither. His whole body went taut.

"The rest," he growled.

Heart racing, she shimmied out of her knee-length gray skirt, putting a bit of extra sway in her hips. She used it as camouflage, folding it very slowly to avoid losing her engagement ring—and to tease him by delaying the moment he'd see her tiny lace thong. Tara held her breath as she made the final fold, then set it on top of her bra.

She looked up at Logan. His heated gaze devoured her flushing face, swelling breasts, dampening sex. His severely short hair emphasized his high cheekbones, his hard jaw. He looked ready to eat her alive. A fresh jolt of desire pounded through her, as subtle as a sledgehammer.

When had Brad ever looked at her like that?

Shoving the thought aside, she hooked her thumbs on the sides of her ruffled panties. All she had to do was inflame Logan and let him spank her a little—after she revealed her body and let him touch her one last time.

She pulled the thong down.

* * *

HOLY shit.

As Cherry peeled those little panties down her feminine thighs, Logan nearly swallowed his tongue. She'd definitely grown from a girl to a woman. She'd put on twenty pounds since sixteen, all in her hips, ass, and breasts. Tara's tiny waist and dainty shoulders offset all that lush, rounded perfection. And the best part? Fiery red hair dusted her puffy pink mound. She was so damn pretty everywhere. And he wanted his mouth on her so badly, he'd fucking beg.

Setting his jaw into a grim line, Logan tried to wrangle in this feeling. She hated him—and had every right to. Besides, she was all but married. The thought that an ass like Brad Thompson had her heart damn near brought him to his knees. Logan had known for a long time that he hadn't gotten over Tara sexually, but had hoped the fixation stopped at his dick.

Now he knew he hadn't been that lucky.

All the emotion he'd been trying to manufacture with Callie and countless other subs just so he could jack off? A pale comparison. Tara had barely gotten naked, and already he felt like sinking his cock into her and staying until, oh . . . next month. But he also wanted the right to cover her plump bow of a mouth with his own, put his arms around her, and tuck her beside him and . . . just be.

Impossible. Tara was on a dangerous mission. If he didn't train her well, she was going to give herself away and die—unless he could talk her out of this suicide operation. Maybe, if she got a firsthand taste of how men capable of spending millions of dollars on "disposable pussy" would treat her, she'd bail. The Cherry he'd known had been fanciful, hadn't possessed a violent thought, and had no capacity for subterfuge. Though she'd clearly improved her poker face since high school, he didn't want her on this mission. She wasn't stupid or incapable at all, but she couldn't possibly have the frame of reference to understand the kind of scum she was up against.

The last thing Logan wanted to do was hurt her again, but he had to give her a clue.

As he stepped toward her, she looked braced for battle. Challenge sparkled in her pretty dark eyes. He stared. She was up to something. Whatever it was, he couldn't let her win. He'd been a prick to her once to save her life. History was destined to fucking repeat itself.

His gaze brushed over her rosy, hard nipples as she folded her tiny little thong and set it on top of her clothes. Obediently, she dropped into position, on her knees, head down, palms up.

God damn, what he wouldn't give for her submission to be real.

"Better, Cherry."

He glanced across the room at the mat Callie had occupied earlier. The thought of putting Tara in that same spot curdled his gut. Ditto for the spanking bench. Logan didn't want to do the usual with her. His eyes lit on the bed he'd never used. Xander had insisted on something cozier, and Logan hadn't cared enough to refuse.

Perfect.

"On your feet."

Tara hesitated, a moment's surprise flashing across her delicate face, before she stood gracefully, eyes still downcast. She'd been doing her homework, and he applauded that. It also meant that it might take more than he'd planned to rattle her.

"Walk to the bed. Stand beside it and wait for me."

Shoulders set with determination, she made her way across the room. Logan watched the sway of her hips, the roll of her prime ass. When she reached the foot of the bed, she turned to face him, her skin was flushed, her expression sultry. She was enjoying the knowledge that he wanted her. The thought of keeping her naked and aroused, her sweet cunt ready for him . . .

No, he had to prepare her for a mission or goad her into quitting.

Logan prowled toward her, then sat on the silk sheet. "Come closer."

"Don't I get a safe word first?"

Cherry was more interested in a safe word than beginning her training? She was definitely up to something. "How about . . . *Romeo.* If that word clears your lips, we're done."

She shot him a startled glance, then cleared her features. "*Romeo.* Okay."

"Good. Lay yourself across my lap and present your ass for punishment. No coming."

"What the—" Tara stopped herself and bit back her irritation.

"And no talking. If I was capable of selling you to a Colombian drug lord willing to pay five million dollars for the privilege of raping you, do you think I'd be letting you speak? Follow directions or suffer more punishment."

Her body tensed as she lowered herself awkwardly over his thighs. Immediately, he knew Cherry had never done this. She wasn't sure how to balance her weight, where to perch. That fact pleased him more than it should.

With a guiding hand on soft skin that only made him want to fuck her more, he helped her settle. "Count for me, Cherry. Lose track, and we start over."

He needed to get on with scaring her half to death, but the sight of that pale, curvy ass spread across his thighs had Logan swallowing down a fireball of lust. Nothing was going to help his cock. It poked Tara, desperately seeking her heat. She kept trying to shift away, and instead rubbed herself all over it.

Logan stopped her with a hand at the small of her back. She'd stilled, but he could hear her heavy breathing as he caressed down until he palmed her sweet ass. He nearly groaned. God, he could sink his fingers, his teeth, his cock into that flesh and be one happy bastard.

Focus.

Raising his hand, Logan hesitated. He didn't want to hurt her, but damn, he couldn't afford to back off. If he had any hope of getting her to quit, he had to unleash some bad shit.

Steeling himself, he bypassed the warm up and struck her harder than he'd ever hit a sub. His swat landed on her right check with a deafening *smack*. She yelped, jerked. Logan winced. His palm stung like a bitch, so he could only imagine how poor Cherry felt.

"Count," he choked out.

"One." Her voice wobbled.

Ruthlessly, he squelched his guilt. "Ready for more?"

Under him, she tensed, clearly bracing for more pain. "Yes."

She wasn't, but she'd never admit it. As much as he admired tenacity, not curbing her stubbornness could get her killed on this mission.

As he lifted his hand again, he saw the clear red print of his hand on her ass. His cock jerked. He'd love to put his stamp all over her. No doubt, she would think that made him a sick fuck, but Logan knew that ship had sailed long ago.

He gave her another harsh slap on her left cheek. Tara cried out, her body jolting, as she took the blow. Her nails dug into his calf as she tried to process the pain.

"Get your nails out of my skin and count," he demanded.

Tara's back stiffened, and she shuddered, panted. "Two."

She'd silently punctuated the statement with *you asshole*. He could hear it hanging in the air. When he saw her struggling to accept his blows, he *felt* like an asshole.

Logan drew his arm up to deliver another swift blow to her upper thigh. She tensed, every line in her body screeching with anger. He hesitated. This wasn't scaring her, just reinforcing her low opinion. She expected pain from him. In fact, she was holding her breath expectantly, like she was waiting . . .

What the hell was she up to? What would a novice sub trying to control a scene do?

Immediately, Logan knew he was playing right into Tara's hand. *Shit.* He lowered his arm.

"On your feet," he ordered.

Tara froze. "Wh-what about the rest of the spankings?"

Fully capable of math—she'd kicked his ass in algebra, too—she knew they hadn't completed fifteen swats. Nor had she been looking forward to the rest of such a brutal spanking. She'd merely been looking for an excuse to scream her safe word.

Logan gave her credit; she'd always been clever.

"The rest of your punishment will wait. When we're together, I want you to look at me. Always at me."

That chocolate gaze zipped up to his—hard, resolved. No fucking way was she backing down. And cutting her off before she could credibly use her safe word had pissed her off. If she'd succeeded, how quickly would Thorpe hustle her out the door? PDQ, no doubt. Likely, Logan would never see her again.

He needed another tactic. How would Tara respond to his genuine desire for her? She might hate what he'd done to her in high school. But as he admired her body, Logan saw that didn't stop her from wanting him. Hard pink nipples stood up and beckoned. The plump lips of her pussy glistened. Something about this—about him—was getting to her. Mentally, she'd write off his spanking as abuse and cast him in the villain role. But what if he gave her what he ached to? What he'd bet that her body, deep down, wanted as well? How long would those walls she'd erected between them last? Maybe then they could get to something honest so they could sort this mission out—and he could heal himself.

Logan gripped his thighs through his leathers. "Take my shirt off, Cherry."

Her gaze went saucer wide, locking with his. That look sizzled him, settling down in his throbbing cock. He vowed to drink in the arousal burning through him. For as long as he had her, he was going to gorge on her every reaction—and anything else she gave him.

Tara pressed her lips together, clearly reluctant. He watched her steel herself, then lift her hands to the hem of his T-shirt. She trembled as she did her best to lift up the cotton knit with an impersonal thumb and forefinger, and he thanked God for the tight garment. It forced her to lay her palms against his abdomen and shove the shirt up his torso, dragging across his skin, over muscle, so near his nipples. She brushed fire everywhere she touched. He repressed a shiver. When the shirt bunched under his arms, she stopped.

"What's the problem, Cherry? Keep going."

He knew full well it would force her up on her tiptoes, putting her face breathlessly close to his.

Raising up, Tara grabbed a handful of shirt and yanked.

Logan grabbed her wrist. "Slowly."

Bastard! Her expression screamed it. Her fists clenched.

He did nothing to help her as she raised the white cotton, dragging it up one arm, then the other, her mouth a bare inch under his own. He could smell mint on her breath. And that cherry-vanilla scent he'd always known as hers wafted between them. His mouth watered.

Her gaze fell on the bold black tattoo she'd revealed, etched permanently on his ribs from armpit to hip.

Logan tensed. "You read Japanese?"

She shook her head. "What does it say?"

"Never quit," he lied. The truth would freak her out.

Finally, she jerked the shirt over his face, then stepped back the instant the cotton cleared his head. That wouldn't do.

With one hand, he grabbed the garment and tossed it to a far corner of the room. With the other, he latched his hand around her neck. "You never back away from me without permission."

"You going to spank me again?" she challenged.

No way would he give Tara the perfect means to ditch him. "Lie down on the bed, back flat against the mattress, legs spread."

Though she didn't gasp or betray herself, her shock rippled across the tense silence. He could almost read her thoughts whirling as she wondered, worried, what the hell he was going to do.

"Cherry, is there a problem?" He repressed a smile and crossed his arms over his chest.

Slowly, Tara dropped one knee to the bed, then caught her weight on her outstretched hands. After a pause, she turned over, until her back hit the cool sheet. She hissed at the unexpected chill, arched, then settled.

Fuck, all that red hair spread out across black silk, along with the sweet purity of her pale skin. Incredibly, he got harder. His dick would have a permanent zipper imprint if he didn't get his leathers off soon.

Tara was, no doubt, the fantasy he'd harbored all these years—only better. As a teen, she'd been a little shy. He'd never understood why she lacked self-confidence; from his perspective she'd had it all. Tara now knew who she was, wasn't afraid to exert her independence. She was still clever and a bit of a mystery . . . but Logan still knew her, *felt* her.

Right now, her trembling apprehension and anticipation damn near stole his breath and strangled his cock. Shit, he'd better get himself under control and seduce her into quitting or obeying, or he'd forget his purpose and do whatever it took to steal her for himself.

As before, saving her life was more important than saving his heart.

"I don't remember you ever having trouble following directions, Cherry. There's one more part of the instruction."

She had to be mad enough to spit nails. But she hid any anger or apprehension fairly well as she complied, slowly drawing her slender thighs apart, revealing the inside of her knees, the creamy expanse of skin up the inside of her leg. More . . . more, until the little birthmark appeared on the inside of her left thigh, exactly as he remembered.

Satisfaction roared through him. Rightness. No matter what happened, a part of him would always belong to Cherry—and she to him.

Finally, she eased her legs far enough apart to show every bit of the pink, swollen heaven he was dying to sink into. Sheer fucking orgasmic heaven awaited. He belonged there. Connected to her—skin, breaths, hearts.

Logan edged closer and lowered himself to the bed. With his heart racing, he rolled beside her and propped his head on his hand. Cherry's guarded brown gaze met his. Oh yeah, she was dying to know what he had planned.

He could ease her into his touch, and if he was playing for keeps, that's exactly what he'd do, give her a slow, sweet ramp up to an undeniable arousal that would have her gasping and clinging and begging to follow his every demand to the ultimate pleasure again and again.

But he had to make her not just want to escape him, but the whole assignment. Regret stabbed him, and he had the most insane urge to do nothing more than wrap his arms around her, bring her body flush against his and simply hold her until she lost all that starch.

He couldn't afford it.

Wrapping his hand under her neck, he tilted her head up until he was fully in control, then covered her mouth in a greedy kiss. He didn't ease inside or wait for her acceptance; he prowled in.

Instantly, hunger roared through his belly, mowing down his good intentions, screaming at him to get deeper and consume her. She stiffened against him at first, struggled for a moment, only to realize that he'd positioned her so that she couldn't move. When she gasped, he plunged in again, so ravenous for her his entire body was taut, aching. Tara anchored her hands on his shoulders. Logan braced for her to push him away. Instead, after a moment's pause, she curled her hands around his neck, urged him closer, and twined her tongue around his hungrily.

Shock vibrated down his spine. Searing arousal followed.

His Cherry tasted like . . . everything. All he'd wanted for years. The essence that had haunted him. This is what he'd been missing. What he needed. Her.

Deeper he pressed into her mouth, laving, tasting, possessing. She met him, frenzied stroke for stroke as he wrapped an arm around her waist and crushed her bare torso against his own in a sizzle of skin. He slid a leg between hers. She cried out as he rubbed his thigh against her folds. The wetness of her pussy coated his leather-clad thigh so he slid against her more easily than melted butter. He fucking ached with the knowledge that she wanted him, too.

For the first time in a decade, Logan felt complete.

How the fuck was he going to goad her into ending this mission, knowing he'd likely never see her again? He knew he should, but now that he'd touched her, he needed at least a few precious moments more to savor her before she was gone forever.

"Cherry, baby . . ." he murmured against her soft lips, so sweet with a flavor so uniquely her. "Open to me."

Without hesitation, she did, plunging her tongue in his mouth again and clinging like he mattered, like she'd starve without him.

The feeling was mutual. There'd be time later to make her flee this mission and hate him for it.

Easing over Tara, their lips and breaths still entwined, he savored every touch. His palms caressed her nape, glided over the dainty slope of her collarbone, before his fingers splayed across the slight incline of her breast. Then he swept down, cupped the firm little mound. Her nipple burned his fingertips.

Damn, he wanted that against his tongue. Cherry mewled, shifting restlessly beneath him.

With a last deep kiss and a nibble at her sweet lips, he kissed his way down her feverish skin, lapping at the soft expanse of pale silk that he ached to explore for hours, days.

Her fingers wound their way into his hair, dragging him closer to that delectable pink nipple.

No way was he going to refuse her silent plea. Yes, he was supposed to be in command, and Logan knew this was reckless as hell. He'd reassert himself, after another taste or two . . .

Cradling her breast in his hand, he plumped it up for his descending lips. He soaked the reddening bud in his mouth, dragging his tongue over the hard tip.

"Yes," she panted. "Logan, yes."

Hearing her moan his name, desire whipped through him, torquing the ache in his cock. She arched closer, like she'd die if he released her now.

Sucking her breast deep into his mouth until his tongue flattened her nipple against the roof, he delved down her body with his hand, sliding between the sweet folds of her pussy.

Fuck, she was more than wet. Soaked. And so damn responsive. He prayed she wanted him at least a tenth as much as he was dying for her.

He plunged two fingers inside her, sinking in as far as he could. She jerked her hips up to him.

"You're so wet, baby. You're making my mouth water. And you're tight."

"It's been a while," she panted.

A while? Wasn't she engaged?

"Get all wet for me, Cherry. That's it." He lifted his wet fingertips from her slick folds and brushed them over her nipple, then sucked it into his mouth, starved for her taste. Her sweetness hit his tongue, sending him spiraling further out of control.

God, he needed more of her. All of her. Endless days and nights beside her, inside her. If she were his, Logan would keep her constantly wet, aroused, just for the pleasure of satisfying her.

Need driving him, Logan settled his fingers over her clit, thrilled to feel the bud so hard and swollen. For him. He settled in to touch her, do whatever necessary, until she surrendered her will to him.

* * *

DROWNING in sensation, tingles razing her, Tara could hardly breathe.

She tried to suck in a breath, but it wasn't enough. Dizziness swam through her head, along with his masculine scent, like spice and earth. Logan oozed testosterone, drugging her senses. High on him, she soared, breath sawing, blood churning, flesh on fire.

God, this needed to stop, and yet . . . his very touch made her feel not only powerfully female, but desired in a way she hadn't experienced since the last time he'd held her.

As his fingers glided through her slick folds again, Tara held her breath, waiting. Euphoria and need balled between her thighs. When he brushed over her clit, she rushed closer to the edge.

Normally, she was professional and able to hide her emotions. Logan completely stripped that from her. Why him? Why did he always get to her in a way no man ever had?

Too far gone to puzzle it out, she lifted to him. "Logan, please."

He growled against her throbbing nipple. "I'm going to ramp you up without mercy, Cherry, then take you over the edge, again and again. When you're boneless and wrung out, I'll just keep petting this pussy with my fingers, my tongue, taking you up, up, up until you shatter. When you think you can't take it anymore, I'll fill you with every inch of my cock, until I'm all you can see and feel. We'll take a hard, wild ride—the first time."

He inhaled against the damp skin of her neck as if he could breathe her in, all the while rubbing her clit in slow, tender circles that only made her entire body clench with arousal. She flattened her feet on the bed, legs spread, and shifted, lifted, silently urging him on.

"After that, I'll slide inside you again and pull every gasping, keening little breath out of you while this sweet cunt clamps down on me. Over and over. Even then, I won't stop."

Every word made Tara gasp harder for her next breath. How badly she wanted to forget their painful past, her fiancé, the dangerous mission to come, and sink into the pleasure she knew Logan could deliver, this connection that she'd only ever felt with him. Desire roared like a runaway train, making a blur of her resistance and good intentions. Being with him like this was wrong in so many ways, but it felt so damn right.

When Logan's mouth crashed over hers, he opened her wide for his kiss. He didn't just enter; he conquered and ravaged. He possessed.

Tara met him, hungry, greedy, opening herself deep to him, then demanding more. His clever fingers grazed her clit, toying, brushing, sensitizing. Arousal wound fist-tight in her belly.

"You feel so good." He scraped the dark shadow of his whiskers covering his jaw over her sensitive nipple.

A million new tingles cascaded over her. She gasped his name, clutching him tighter, lost in the feel of him.

"That's it," he murmured. "You're almost ready to come for me, Cherry. Wait for my command. I'm going to make it the best you've ever felt, baby."

It would be. Oh God, she wanted it so bad. Every nerve in her body trembled in anticipation, quivered, as she held her breath, willing to give him anything—everything—if he'd satisfy this ache.

But if she let him, how betrayed would Brad feel? How much more would Logan tighten his twelve-year grip on her body? How much more of her soul would he steal? Tara had teased Logan in high school that if someone gave him a yard, he'd take the whole football field. Nothing had changed—except that he'd grown more ruthless.

After a mere hour in Logan's presence, she was too entangled. As much as her body wanted Logan, what she needed was a new trainer so she could keep her head on straight, tackle her first undercover mission, and save her friend.

Closing her eyes, she drew in a shaky breath, then uttered the one word she hoped she wouldn't regret. *"Romeo."*

Chapter Four

LOGAN froze. "What did you say?"

Every muscle in Tara's body protested the loss of his touch. If she didn't get distance between them now, she wasn't sure she'd find the strength to push him away again.

She glanced toward the two-way mirror from which Thorpe must be watching and shouted, *"Romeo!"*

Logan's stricken face said that if she'd pulled his heart from his chest with her bare hands, he couldn't have been more shocked. He jerked back, staggered to his feet.

An instant later, Thorpe barged in with a blanket and enveloped her in it protectively. "Come with me."

Logan launched himself toward them. "Don't take her! She's topping us both from the bottom, trying to force you to replace me."

Thorpe held up a hand to stop him. "It doesn't matter. You know how this works. You're done. I'll get Agent Jacobs someone else. Stay the fuck away from her."

Logan's condo—Thursday evening

Logan paced his living room two hours later, gripping the back of his neck in one hand. He jammed the phone to his ear with the other.

His older brother, Hunter, hadn't even greeted him before Logan
started in. "Question."

"Shoot."

Sighing in agitation, Logan paced across the floor again, from
the St. Andrew's Cross against the wall, past the spanking bench, to
the padded table in the corner. God damn it, Tara should be here,
strapped down, taking him in every way he needed. That she needed.
She was a fever, boiling him up from the inside, and he'd be damned
before he gave her up. No Dom was better equipped to train her for
this mission—for her life. No man could love her the way he did.

And after this afternoon, Logan had no doubt whatsoever that
he still loved her every bit as much as he had at sixteen. Maybe more.
She felt something for him, too. In order to exploit that, keep her
safe and make her his, he had to overcome a few obstacles.

"I don't have time for the long explanation now, so I'll give you
the CliffsNotes. I saw Tara today." Logan struggled to get his breathing back under control as memories bombarded him.

"You said her name. That's progress. Congratulations!"

"Save it. She wants nothing to do with me. For her, the past isn't
dead and buried."

"The way you broke up with her was ugly. You knew it was
permanent."

"I hated every fucking second that I hurt her. Because of me, she
transferred to that prissy private girls' academy the very next day. I
rarely saw her after that." Other than the Christmas he'd gone to see
her, and she'd slammed the door in his face. "But I dealt because it
kept her safe."

"With Mom's murder unsolved and the sick bastard having Tara
on his radar, you didn't have a choice."

"I still don't understand the killer's motives. Why come between
me and Tara?" Logan shook his head. "That isn't the issue right now.
It's her safety. Since the case has never been solved, we have to assume Mom's killer is still on the loose. He hasn't threatened me since

I broke up with Tara. It's been a dozen years. You think it's safe for me to pursue her now?"

"One chance meeting, and you're ready to chase this girl again?"

Since their breakup, Logan had hoped that Cherry was happy. She'd gone to college, gotten a great job, and as much as it bugged the shit out of him, she'd gotten engaged. As long as he'd believed all was right for her, he'd been able to cope with the gaping hole in his heart. After all, she wouldn't be able to handle his needs—or so he'd believed. When he'd kissed her today, touched and restrained her, he'd figured out real quick that Tara's nature ran sweetly submissive.

And the way she'd responded to him . . . That kiss hadn't come from a woman happily in love with her fiancé, but a hungry female craving the satisfaction she needed and wasn't getting. Logan would move heaven and earth to give it to her.

"Yes." Logan didn't hesitate. "I want to make her mine. Forever."

"Hell, I shouldn't be surprised. You never got over her. Maybe she's what you need."

"I'm working on a plan, but I can't execute it if I'd be putting her in danger."

"What do *you* think?"

Logan sighed. "Right now, I'm not doing a good job of thinking past my dick."

Hunter's deep laugh resounded in his ear. "If you're ready to fuck her and end this crazy five year abstinence, I'm definitely in favor."

He only said that because he could barely stand to leave the bed he shared with his wife.

"But what about Tara?" Logan prodded. "I won't put her in danger."

"It's been a dozen years. I don't think you can answer that question without going for it and seeing what happens. If you don't, you'll be one miserable bastard, always wondering 'what if.'"

Shit, Hunter was right. Agitation stabbed Logan. He didn't like unnecessary risk of any kind, but like his missions as a SEAL, he couldn't predict the exact outcome before putting forth the effort. Planning, keeping calm, paying attention to detail—those things gave him an edge. When he did them right, he succeeded.

He paced back to the St. Andrew's Cross, imagining Tara there. She would look amazing, bound and bare, wet and begging for him. That fantasy wasn't helping him think clearly.

He let out a pent-up breath. At sixteen, Logan hadn't had the first clue how to protect Tara. Today, he was an adult, a highly trained operator. He could—and had—killed enemy combatants in seconds with his bare hands. He'd do anything to keep her from harm's way.

"You're right. If anyone threatens her, I'll tear out their mother-fucking throat and spit in the empty hole."

"That's the Logan I know and love. I'll help you, by the way. Go after her."

Just one small problem . . . "She said her safe word. Thorpe won't let me near her now."

"Oh, this *is* good. She submitted? Willingly? Knowing *you* were topping her?"

Logan wished Hunter wasn't enjoying the speculation quite so much. "We were getting there, but I lost my head. Came at her too hard and fast. I need to downshift and regroup before I approach her again."

"Yeah, you'll have to hurdle Thorpe. Once you do, then you absolutely have to tell Tara why you left her years ago, if you're going to earn her trust."

Again, Hunter was right, but even that wasn't simple. First, Logan could count on Thorpe to be a real hard-ass about enforcing the club's rules.

Even if Logan found a way around that, then came the hard part: explaining the reason for their painful breakup to Tara. He refused to do it at Dominion. No way was he sharing something so personal with Thorpe. Training? Fine. Actual feelings? No.

And Logan had no doubt that revealing the truth about their

past to Tara was going to get sticky. She was no longer a pliant young girl who would listen to his explanation because he asked her to. She'd definitely grown more spine. Now, he might be able to top her into giving him a blow job, but not forgiveness. As much as he'd love the first, it was the latter he'd do anything to have. If he pushed her, she might hate him more.

Logan grimaced. "I've been thinking about that. I doubt she cares now why I left her. Even if I could make her listen, would she believe me? If I hadn't been through it, a killer threatening her would sound far-fetched. Tara might want me, but she doesn't trust me for an instant. I'm not sure how to work past that. Unlike you, I'm not devious enough to marry a drunk girl."

"Hey, it was Kata's idea."

"And you didn't encourage that at all, huh?"

Hunter laughed. "Maybe a little, but it worked out. Speaking of which, my wife is on her way home, so if there's anything else, make it quick."

"What? Are you going to be waiting naked?"

"Good idea, bro."

"Sick fuck. You'll scare the poor girl."

"Nah. Kata is made of stern stuff."

"She has to be if she's going to stay married to you."

"Funny." Hunter sighed. "Seriously, I know you can't force it down her throat, but you've got to find some way to tell Tara why you broke it off with her in high school."

Yeah. It would go over better once he'd reconnected his bond with her, established some trust. Even then, would she believe him? Damn it. If he was in her shoes, he probably wouldn't. A mysterious stranger threatening a high school girl? It made way more sense that he'd just wanted to screw other girls. But maybe if he could earn Tara's trust, he could find some way to make her believe him. Right now, she was too angry to hear any postmortem of their high school drama. And damn it, Logan wanted Tara to *want* to hear the truth.

"When the time is right, I will," Logan murmured.

"Good luck."

"Thanks." He hung up and prowled into the bedroom, tossing his phone on the bed. He rifled through his paperwork. Dominion's rules would be among them.

Forty-six minutes later Logan found exactly the loophole he needed. Tucking the papers in his back pocket, he sprinted out his door, locking it behind him. Rush hour traffic would be thick now, and he had to reach Dominion before Thorpe left for the day because he intended to fucking settle this now.

Club Dominion—Thursday evening

In less than eight minutes, Logan climbed off his motorcycle in Dominion's parking lot and slammed through the front door, past Thorpe's usual bouncers and the crew setting up for the night. Axel was preparing for a demonstration with a single tail whip. Jason was checking the club's public playroom. Logan was supposed to be helping, but first, he and Thorpe were going to have it out.

Logan stalked down the hall, his boots striking the concrete floors, the pendant lights above providing one soft pool of light after another on the otherwise unrelenting gray. When he reached Thorpe's door, he entered without knocking.

The club's owner looked up, then glared. "Whatever you have to say, I don't want to hear it. Agent Jacobs warned me that she couldn't work with you. You got her naked and lost all control. There was no training happening there. I don't know what the fuck your problem is, but it's not mine or hers. Get out."

Logan slapped his copy of the club's rules on Thorpe's desk. "Rule twenty-one dot three dot five. I'm invoking it."

"Prior claim?" Thorpe wouldn't have been more surprised if he'd said he was the freaking Easter Bunny. "Because you fucked this girl in the past."

"Yes."

Thorpe slanted him a long, considering look. "If I hadn't heard her say so during your session, I'd think you were full of shit, given how many women you've refused to share your sheets with."

Logan forced down his impatience and leaned over the desk. "If you heard everything she said, then you heard that I have the ultimate prior claim: her virginity."

"So?" He braced his elbows on the desk. "This clause doesn't exist for you to protect your old stomping grounds. It's to keep two Doms from fighting over a sub. No one else is threatening violence, so . . ."

"I am. If anyone touches *my* Tara, I will bust them wide open."

"This territorial crap is unlike you."

Thorpe sent him a Dom-like stare and waited for him to break. Logan glared back.

"You still haven't met all the clause's stipulations," the club owner pointed out. "Prior Claim can only be invoked if the Dom doing so intends to either collar or marry the sub in question."

If he could earn her trust again and make her happier than Brad Thompson? And see her through this mission? She'd given up a much desired orgasm when she said her safe word. There was a reason Tara had used such grit to maintain her self-control. Hell, Logan knew he hadn't. He doubted she'd kept a clear head and manipulated the situation because she was afraid or wanted to quit the mission. She'd never quit anything before. He knew Cherry. She was going to dig in and do the job no matter what he said. She'd simply wanted to shed him as her trainer so she could continue on without him.

"Both."

"You intend to tie yourself to Agent Jacobs permanently, even though she loathes you?"

"She doesn't, and yes. I plan on making her mine in every way."

"You're actually going to have sex with her yourself, and not send in Xander?"

Logan smiled wide. "In every conceivable way. As soon as possible."

Thorpe considered him for a very long moment. "You've cited a viable club rule and you sound very serious. The clause gives you a week to win her without obstruction or interference. But the FBI is paying me to ensure their agent is trained. Your love life isn't important to them. Another woman's life hangs in the balance."

"I've considered that. No Dom will be more invested in Tara than me. No one will have a greater stake in making sure she comes out of this mission alive. I understand that I only have a week. If I'm forced to choose between winning her or preparing her for the mission . . . keeping her safe is my first priority."

Thorpe kept staring. "The thought of putting the enforcement of her safe word entirely in your hands for the next seven days doesn't set well with me."

"If she knows saying it means she'll get her way, she'll be a broken record. I *will* take care of her, but it has to be on my terms or she'll never truly submit. You can't throw away your own rulebook for a paycheck. She's going into our world, or a twisted version of it anyway. She's going to have to conform to rules or everyone is going to see straight through her."

Logan stood firm and waited. Doms were sometimes victims of their own rules, like now. Tara couldn't learn—or succeed—if she didn't get a dose of true club life. Nor would Thorpe's selective enforcement of the rules be well received by other club members—and he would know that.

"You're a shrewd son of a bitch." Thorpe rose, agitated. "All right. You have seven days, but I'm not letting you off the leash entirely. If I think you've crossed the line with Agent Jacobs, or that you're not adequately preparing her, I'll revoke both your claim and your membership. Of course, the same holds true if you fail to win her in a week. Do you understand?"

The bastard drove a hard bargain, but Logan smiled. "Perfectly."

Club Dominion—Friday morning

The following morning, Tara slammed into Logan's dungeon, fire charring her veins.

She'd arrived expecting to train with another Dom, one she hadn't stupidly rubbed up against like a cat. But no. Thorpe had explained that she was completely in Logan's hands for the next week. She'd have to look at the man and remember how utterly she'd responded.

Worse, last night she and Brad had argued; he'd seen the whisker burns on her chin, neck . . . and breasts. If he'd known who'd given them to her, he would have completely lost his mind, especially after he'd asked her to drop the case, and she'd refused.

Damn it, her life would be much easier if Logan would just get the hell out of it.

As Tara set her purse down and tugged at her black pencil skirt, she struggled to get control of her temper; anger wouldn't help her focus. But the sight of Logan, brow raised, like he knew she was pissed and didn't care, nearly derailed her good intentions. Not to mention the hungry blue stare that said he couldn't wait to unleash his raw sexuality on her again. Tara resented like hell that he got under her skin.

"Good morning." He glanced at his watch. "You're three minutes late. Strip and we'll get started."

As if nothing important had happened yesterday? Tara hadn't slept a wink, rehashing where she had gone wrong, unable to forget Logan's mouth and hands on her, making her feel alive again. Damn it, she had a job to perform, and he was doing his level best to screw that up.

She tugged the lapels of her suit jacket together. "No. I've just talked to Thorpe. What kind of game are you playing?"

He cocked his head. "I'm not. We'll talk, but now isn't the time, and here isn't the place."

"Since this is the only place I see you, I disagree. What happened yesterday—"

"Isn't the issue. The elephant in the room, our breakup in high school, is."

His words couldn't have shocked Tara more, especially when something somber and pensive crossed his face. Why would he want to discuss that?

"I was a naïve girl, and you were a hormonal teenage prick. After your mom's death, you were hurting and lashed out at me. End of story."

Logan shook his head. "There was *far* more involved. I'd like to explain."

Was he out of his mind? Give a player like him more opportunities to spin his lies and woo her back into bed so he could hurt her again? "No."

He looked disappointed, but resigned. "This isn't a part of your training. This is personal between us. If you change your mind, ask me outside this place, when we don't have an audience. I genuinely believe it will change the way you feel."

Tara opened her mouth, then snapped it closed. That crushed, angry girl still inside of her wanted to hear his explanation, but only if it ended with some confession of Logan's undying love. She gave a cynical snort. *Stupid.* Far more likely that he'd been confused and grieving, and received a great deal of comfort in Brittany Fuller's legendary blow jobs. Besides, what good would rehashing the past do? She needed to keep him at arm's length and focus on her job.

"I doubt that, so I'll skip it."

"That offer is always on the table. But we'll get back to training for now. I gave you an order to strip. And while it wasn't first on my agenda, we can finish yesterday's punishment now. If you're disobedient, I'll add to it."

"I said my safe word. You should respect that, as should Thorpe. Why the hell is he violating his own club's rules by giving me back to you?"

Logan stalked closer, and she didn't want to notice the way his black T-shirt hugged each rippling muscle of his torso or that his leather pants clung to every inch of his erection. Nothing to the imagination there. No denying, he looked good. Okay, great. Mouthwatering. But he was definitely up to no good.

"Thorpe and I had a . . . heart-to-heart yesterday. We understand each other, and for the next seven days, you are completely in my hands. End of story. Any questions, Cherry?"

"What's your angle? Are you hoping to nail me so you can cut me cold and see if I bleed again. You get off on my humiliation?"

"I've never wanted to hurt you. I didn't then, and I don't now. Besides, do you really think humiliating you crossed my mind yesterday when I had my tongue in your mouth and my fingers in your pussy?"

Tara wanted to cringe—but refused. "Thank God my taste in men has improved since I was sixteen."

"Brad sold exam keys and crystal meth to anyone with cash back in high school, so I'm gonna disagree." Logan smiled tightly. "Understand that invoking the safe word only ends the current scene, it doesn't sever the contact between us. So you can stop me if you're very uncomfortable with whatever is happening. But screaming 'Romeo' won't make me disappear. Do you understand?"

That unless she wanted to let Darcy die and give up on following in her stepfather's footsteps to make him proud, she was stuck with Logan with virtually no recourse for a week? Fine, she'd suck it up. She was the perfect bait and she wasn't going to let her colleagues down. "Yes."

Besides, no way in hell would she let him get the best of her ever again.

"Yes, *Logan*," he corrected. "I want to hear my name on your lips."

She gave him a long-suffering sigh. "Yes, Logan."

"That attitude is going to get your ass spanked a lot. I'd think carefully, if I were you."

"But you're not me, *Logan*."

He gritted his teeth. "True, and we'll get back to your attitude. Right now, I'd like to apologize for losing control of the situation yesterday and pushing you so hard and so quickly."

That set her back. Was he trying to get under her guard to seduce her again? Did that explain why he suddenly wanted to discuss their past? Logan looked sincere . . . but he'd only apologized for pushing her, not for kissing her in the first place.

"Assuming you actually mean that and given that we're going to be working together, I have a condition: Don't kiss me again. You're supposed to be mentally preparing me to submit for a mission, not seducing me."

A faint smile curled up the edges of his mouth, but he wasn't amused. "Mental preparation is at the top of my agenda, but that's going to involve touching you in about every way possible. You don't get to give me any parameters. So if you'd like to stop arguing and get down to work so you can save Agent Miles, I suggest you strip."

God, she hated that command. It made her vulnerable to him, which was precisely why he was so fond of it. But it turned him on, too. She'd use that to her advantage if he pressed her again.

"If I have to repeat the command again, it won't be pretty." Logan crossed his arms over his chest, waiting.

Tara tried not to grit her teeth. Once undercover, she might be given to a Dom who would insist on her nudity twenty-four/seven. She had to ditch her inhibitions and the discomfort of having her less-than-perfect body scrutinized. And she had to stop interacting with Logan on a personal level. He was her trainer. He wanted her naked. She needed to comply.

"Should I fold my garments and lay them at your feet?" Even saying the words burned through her anger and began a dangerous pulse of hunger in her belly.

His blue eyes darkened. "Yes."

Without another word, she stepped out of her clothes, one garment at a time, then neatly folded each into a little pile, which she set before him. Once done, she stood, waiting, cool air brushing over her nipples, making them tight. They throbbed. Logan sent her a hot stare that nearly made her toes curl.

Damn it, why did he still get to her? She had to overcome this arousal. Her body and feelings weren't important, just the mission.

Easy to think, but hard to remember when Logan stepped so close she felt heat pouring off his hard, substantial body. He lifted a finger to her, its tip settling between her breasts, and brushed a soft, tantalizing line directly down her abdomen slowly, pausing just above the mound of her sex. He waited there, unmoving. Incredibly, his light touch made her pussy clench with emptiness. Blood rushed between her thighs, moisture pooled, coating her folds, though he'd barely touched her.

Finally, his finger descended again. He smiled as it drifted through her damp red curls to nestle against her hard clit, which swelled under his touch.

His smile only widened. "Good, Cherry. Today, we're going to start with a demonstration. It will provide you instruction, as well as help me understand how best to proceed. Let's go."

He tugged her toward the door, and she pulled from his grasp. "I can't go out there naked."

The second her words were out, Tara knew she'd made a mistake.

"Your nudity isn't your concern." Logan's face was a thunderclap of displeasure. "While you train with me, you and your body belong to me. As always, you can say your safe word. In that case, we will discuss and resolve the issue, then resume training. Or you may quit the mission altogether, in which case I'm sure that Thorpe and the FBI will happily sever all contact between us."

His cold speech set her teeth on edge. She was a grown, capable woman. Putting herself in someone else's hands so utterly felt foreign. She worked every day in an environment where she was expected to suppress her own emotions and use her logic, so suddenly having to do the opposite wasn't easy. Training with Logan scared her to death. But if she was going to solve this case and possibly be a successful agent, she had to suck up her courage and swallow her pride.

"Understood, Logan."

She expected amusement to flash across his features. Instead, searing desire glowed in his dark blue eyes, flushed the slashes of his cheekbones. A glance down told her that his erection still bulged in his leather pants.

Her breathing grew unstable when he turned her away, took her arm in one hand and slung the other low on her opposite hip, and led her out of the dungeon. A frightening sense of exposure washed over her as they walked down the hall. Though the club wasn't quite open for public play yet, Thorpe and some of the other resident Doms were already roaming. She'd run into a few as she rushed to confront Logan. But then, she'd been clothed. Now, he was parading her though the halls without a stitch, his touch all but branding her.

It terrified her, and yet . . . Tara felt Logan's desire spilling hotly in the air between them, along with his pride and pleasure that she overcame her own fears to follow his command. As much as she hated to admit it, it turned her on.

She turned to him with a puzzled glance over her shoulder. "I don't understand what's happening."

He glanced at her hot cheeks. "You want to know why you're responding to this. Because deep inside, you feel sensual in your own skin. And you know that you're pleasing your Dom by trusting me, which for a submissive, is a pleasure all its own."

"I shouldn't give a god damn whether you're happy. You don't care whether I am."

Logan leveled her with a direct blue stare. "You're dead wrong. There are things you don't know, and I want to tell you . . ." He shook his head. "When you're ready. Just know that your happiness matters more than anything. If you let me, I'll fulfill your fantasies. Your submission, if you truly give it, will allow me the privilege of doing so."

His words sent a fission of heat through her, which she ruthlessly pressed down. *Focus on the academic.* "None of this makes a damn bit of sense."

"It will. Come with me."

As they rounded a corner, they came face-to-face with another Dom. She didn't know his name, but he had that sharp, shrewd way about him. He'd be dangerous across a negotiating table. Under that pristine dress shirt and tailored slacks beat the heart of a predator. He and Logan had that in common.

"Jason," Logan greeted.

"Edgington." His gray eyes flickered over to her.

Tara squirmed as she felt the man's gaze touch her face, her breasts, the flat of her belly, then settle for a brief moment on the red curls guarding her sex. Tara crossed one leg in front of the other, settled her arms over her chest.

"Hands at your sides and feet apart," Logan demanded.

He *wanted* Jason to look at her? Knowing she had to get past this hurdle for her mission, Tara forced herself to comply. Logan rewarded her with a smile of approval that lit her up inside.

Damn it, why? Normally, she'd be running for cover, refusing to let a stranger see her and wondering if he found her lacking. She'd be fuming that Logan demanded she show herself. She damn sure wouldn't care what he thought of her behavior. But all of those mores and insecurities paled when she saw the flash of his smile. Why?

"Get out of your head," Logan instructed. "Don't look for logic. Just feel."

Right. Her discomfort wasn't the point. Learning to give herself over to the mission—to him—was.

Jason grinned, then glanced back at Logan. "How's your slave in training?"

"In need of a lot of instruction. I was actually coming to ask if you're seeing the policewoman today."

"Greta should be here in ten minutes. It was the only time she had today, so I took an early lunch." He grinned. "Gotta love nooners."

"Do you mind if we use your observation room? This sub needs to see what submission truly means."

"Sure. I think you'll find Greta has been both an apt and eager pupil."

Tara tried to leash her curiosity as they entered the observation room. The tiny space was dark, dominated by one huge window that overlooked an unfamiliar play room. A futon, the only thing in the room, stood in the shadowed corner, allowing occupants some comfort while they watched. It could also be pulled into a bed at a moment's notice.

"What was that about, Logan?"

He shut the door behind them, enclosing them in the small space. The wall trapped her on one side, Logan on the other as he turned to her in the shadowed room. "You want to know why I allowed Jason to see you naked."

"Encouraged it, even."

"It's not about him, and normally, I wouldn't share you. But you're going to have to be comfortable with your own nudity on this mission, regardless of who's around. I'll be testing you until you overcome your discomfort. It's a telltale sign of an untrained sub."

And that's probably what had gotten Darcy made and abducted. Tara's past, both distant and recent, with Logan didn't matter. Training to succeed at this mission did.

"Will you genuinely prepare me to go undercover? No mind games?"

"I'll make sure you're prepared for any situation you encounter." He sent her a serious stare. "But mind games come with the territory. Domination and submission is one giant mind fuck."

"As long as I'm prepared to hold my own, I can live with that."

"You're good with firearms and hand-to-hand?"

"Yeah, but I'm sparring every night to keep myself sharp. That's one thing Robert is damn good at."

"York is never going to be a convincing Dom."

Exactly as she'd feared. "Maybe Axel can keep working with—"

"Never," Logan underscored. "And that's something I'm going to talk to Thorpe about. Starting tomorrow, Axel and I will both be checking in with your boss, Bocelli, daily. If York can't pull this off, we're going to be brutally honest."

"You can't have Robert yanked off this case. It will take too long to bring someone else in. We've already invested dozens of hours in—"

"Let us worry about that. You have enough on your plate, learning to be a convincing sub in seven days."

"But—"

"For the next week, who is your Dom?" Even in the dark, she discerned his raised brow, his more aggressive stance.

"You are." When he threw her a pointed glare, she sighed. "Logan."

"What does any Dom desire above all else?"

"Obedience."

He shook his head. "Trust. With that, obedience naturally follows. And underneath all that tough-girl FBI training, that's who you are. I realize trust is going to be more difficult with our history, but I need you to understand that I would never do anything to put you in jeopardy. *Ever*. I'd make myself bleed first."

Wow. The gravity of his emphatic tone confused Tara, like he had some hidden message beyond his actual words. She frowned. But she wasn't here to get personal with Logan, so she wasn't touching that statement with a ten-foot pole.

"Tell me about Agent Miles' disappearance," he said into her silence, switching topics.

It was a command—one Tara found easy to comply with. "Darcy was sent near Key West to attend a singles' weekend at a resort that caters to dominance and submission. That's where Darcy and two other women have gone missing. Darcy reported in during her first two days at the resort to say that she'd attended lectures and demonstrations. They paired her up with a few Doms, but nothing out of the ordinary happened. Then she said she'd been invited to a special demonstration by the resort's director, Lincoln Kantor. Three hours later, we received eight seconds of distress signal from her before the transmission ended abruptly. We haven't heard from her since. That was seven days ago."

"And now you're against a ticking clock."

Tara nodded, worry twisting her stomach in knots. "I know I'm supposed to train with you for a week. I'm not sure Darcy has that long."

Logan took her hand in his, lacing their fingers together. She found the gesture ridiculously comforting. "But I won't send you in unprepared. The FBI will only lose another agent."

"I know."

With a squeeze of her hand, he acknowledged her difficulty in dealing with this reality. "If there's a way to save Darcy, we will. Let's focus on getting you ready."

She nodded, and a few moments later, Jason and his police-woman entered the room. The instant the door shut, Jason's shoulders squared. He appeared bigger, adopted a mantle of authority.

He didn't say a word to the woman, just sent her an expectant stare. Immediately, she removed her uniform, one garment at a time, until she stood completely bare, the ends of her long, dark hair brushing her mid-back. Then she kneeled at his feet, knees spread, palms up, head down. Even from here, Tara felt her desperation to please.

Jason ruffled her hair. "Very good, pet. Have you done as I asked during our last session?"

"Yes, Master."

"Show me."

Greta didn't hesitate before she uncurled her legs from beneath her, rocked back on her ass, legs spread wide for Jason's view.

He dropped to one knee and his hand disappeared between her legs. "Very nice. Shaved or waxed?"

"Waxed," she panted. "Brazilian."

"And I see you've complied with regard to the anal plug. Is this the largest?"

"Yes, Master. I put it in this morning. It was challenging, but I'm ready for you now."

In Greta's voice, Tara heard the need for Jason's acceptance and pleasure. Her own knowledge about the shadowy world of BDSM was almost exclusively academic and yet . . . Tara already understood exactly how the other woman felt. It struck a chord in her, all the times she'd done her best to please Brad or another lover by cutting her hair a certain way or buying a sexy pair of shoes. Most of her efforts had gone unnoticed.

For a crazy moment, Tara wanted a man who would truly notice her, down to the last detail. A man like—

She didn't dare finish that thought.

But memories filtered in as her gaze skittered Logan's way. In high school, he'd usually noticed when she'd even changed her sweater. The afternoon he'd taken her innocence, he remarked on everything, all the way down to her birthmarks and the way she flushed before she came.

Jason smiled, stroking between her legs again. Greta's thigh blocked her view, but whatever was going on, the woman moaned.

"I'm very proud of you, pet," Jason crooned. "You deserve a reward, which you'll get as soon as we deal with your punishment for Tuesday."

Despite being nearly flat on her back, Greta managed to cast her gaze down. She was the picture of contrition. "I'm sorry, Master. I won't fail you again. I was . . . apprehensive."

"You uphold the law, and I would never want you to be arrested for public indecency. The exercise was intended to test your trust in me, and you failed. Did you think I would let you be reproached professionally?"

Greta bit her plump lip. "I didn't think. I panicked."

"And you didn't trust me."

The woman bowed her dark head. "I wish to please you, Master. I'll take any punishment you see fit."

He nodded. "First, I will give you another opportunity to do what you refused on Tuesday and please me. We are, even now, being watched. I won't say by whom or why. Stroke your clit."

She cast a quick glance toward the mirror. The stunning beauty's sultry eyes looked both wide and dilated. She was afraid . . . but aroused.

Jason snapped his fingers. "They are not your concern. I am."

With a shaky nod, Greta reclined on her elbows and drew her hand shyly between her spread legs.

"Turn your body to face the mirror," he demanded.

Greta froze.

"Why is he pushing her when she's so obviously apprehensive?" Tara whispered.

"She wants it, and Jason knows it. The sub is trying so hard to control the scene that she's not letting go and putting her well-being in his hands. Logically, she knows she has nothing to fear in this situation. Jason's job is to push her past her inhibitions until she's able to submit and experience her fantasy."

Tara understood, but she related to Greta's discomfort. The thought of masturbating in front of a lover and unknown witnesses made her squirm with both apprehension and a disturbing thread of arousal.

Finally, Greta gathered her courage and turned her body to face the window. Tara saw every goose bump on the woman's flesh, every jagged breath, the peaked nipples topping her plump breasts, the slick lips of her bare sex, along with the pink base of the plug tucked into her anus.

Greta's hand slid between her legs. She closed her eyes and began to rub slow fingers over the little bundle of nerves.

"He wanted her to do this in public?" Tara couldn't fathom that, but the idea of having that sort of faith in a partner made something inside her curl with unwanted warmth.

"Tuesday, after her shift ended, he met her at a park. It was dark and empty. He didn't tell her, but he'd actually swept it and had a couple of buddies guarding the entrances. Jason has a real hard-on for outdoor sex, and Greta gets off on the thought that she might be watched."

"But I can see her uneasiness." Tara frowned. Every muscle in the woman's body tensed, shook.

"She's also flushed. She keeps spreading her legs wider. Her nipples are diamond hard."

Tara's gaze skated over the other woman. He was right. Now that she saw the sub's reactions through a Dom's eyes, she also noticed something else. "She's beginning to stroke herself faster."

"Exactly. Does she truly look uncomfortable? Perturbed? Inhibited?"

After another glance, Tara had to shake her head. "Not anymore."

"He's helping her bring out her true nature and fulfilling her fantasies. That's his role."

"Is that why you do this?" The question slipped out before she could stop it.

Logan turned her way, hesitated. "That's what every Dom aspires to. Some make it, some don't."

Tara was sure Logan was right . . . but he hadn't really answered her question.

"Stop," Jason demanded of the woman.

Greta sobbed as she lifted her fingers to hover over her clit. Her back arched, teeth grinding together. She'd been just on the verge. Tara's body clenched in empathy. Sitting next to Logan in this small, dark space made Tara fidget, hyperaware of the ache that started in the pit of her stomach and grew between her thighs.

"Sit still," Logan demanded, as if he knew exactly the uncomfortable desire brewing inside her.

"Stand," Jason demanded of Greta.

Slowly, the policewoman rose to her feet. She cast a pleading glance at her Dom. He looked unmoved as he sat on a plush ottoman squatting nearby.

He patted his thigh. "Over my knees, pet."

"Master . . ." Greta looked ready to cry.

"You've been doing so well. Don't spoil it now."

Greta closed her eyes, her face tense as she searched for the courage to carry on. Finally, she draped herself over Jason's impeccable charcoal slacks. "Count each spanking. No coming."

The Dom began peppering a stinging volley of slaps across the woman's pert ass. Greta counted each, becoming breathier with every number. Tara squirmed.

"If you're wondering," Logan murmured, "you weren't aroused when I spanked you earlier because I meant to punish, not pleasure you. Next time I spank you, you'll feel the difference. And if all that fidgeting you can't seem to stop is any indication, you'll like it."

If anyone had asked her ten minutes ago if she'd be aroused by an erotic spanking, she would have laughed, but now Tara couldn't deny that she'd become more than curious. There was a rhythm to their bodies, a push-pull, almost like a well-choreographed dance. As he struck, she gasped and counted breathlessly. Then he groaned. He rubbed his worshipping palm across her reddening cheeks, and she lifted her butt into his hand—again and again.

Suddenly, Greta's body tightened. Jason lifted her until she straddled his thighs, then fused his mouth to hers. In seconds, he'd shoved his pants down and rolled a condom on.

Grabbing her hips, Jason bared his teeth. "Take me inside you."

With a cry of relief, she impaled herself on his thick cock, shoving it deep in her sex in one brutal thrust.

Jason tossed his head back with a groan. On the next down stroke, he swept his thumb over her clit. "Come, Greta."

He didn't have to ask her twice. Her lithe body tensed up, fingers digging into his shoulders as she met his gaze with a helplessly erotic stare, then closed her eyes in pleasure, releasing everything to him.

It didn't take long for Jason to fuck her through the first orgasm, then a second. When Greta ramped up for her third, her face rosy, her breath stuttering, the Dom finally let go, one hand splayed behind her back, the other tangled in her hair. Not a bit of air passed between them as he kissed her all through their shuddering joint climax.

Tara let out the breath she didn't realize she'd been holding. Her entire body shook, pulsed. Desire pooled in her pussy. Jason and Greta had been visually arousing . . . but far more. Deeper. He'd given; she'd taken—and given everything back in return. The act looked like one of such togetherness. That sort of connection of bodies, of minds and souls, that made poets and songwriters dash madly for their pens. Tara had never seen or felt anything like it.

And, in that moment, she wanted it—desperately.

She risked a glance at Logan. He met her stare with silent confidence that said, *yes, I can give you that.*

"Do you understand now?"

She couldn't find the words to tell him how deeply she was moved and how completely she understood. "Yes, Logan."

He held out his hand. "Let's get started."

Chapter Five

LOGAN'S heart beat faster and more forcefully than a sledgehammer. He tried not to crush Tara's hand in his as he forced down his impatience. No matter how badly he itched to touch her, get inside her and stay, he had to focus first on teaching her.

At the door to his dungeon, he pushed it open, let her walk through. Her clothes still lay on the floor, her engagement ring peeking out from her skirt pocket, winking in the light from overhead. With his blood already pumping, knowing that she still planned to tie herself to Brad Thompson made him damn near violent.

Calm. Breathe. Focus. He had to be smart, pay attention to detail. The reality was, right now, Cherry was flushed, aroused. She'd seen the power exchange and found beauty in it. She wanted it for herself. She needed it for her mission. Their biggest impediment now was his own impatience . . . and her unwillingness to hear his reason for their breakup. But that was another issue for another time. Now, he'd begin to bind her to him sexually, as a way to reach her emotions, because he wasn't going to make Hunter's mistake and try to force them. Logan had seven days; no need for panic. He had to believe that her heart would be roused before their time ran out.

"Kneel," he ordered softly. "Get into position."

Without hesitation, she slid to her knees and parted them, then met his gaze. Her nipples stood up, begged for his mouth. Her pussy had swollen to a deep, rosy red.

"Beautiful," he praised. "Tell me what equipment Axel walked you through."

"You mean, what did he use on me? He didn't actually do anything to me, Logan."

Hearing his name slide off her tongue with that reverent tone any other sub would use to say "Master," revved him up. He'd been hard nearly every moment he'd been with Tara, but when she said his name like that . . . Damn, he had to keep his head in the game.

"On your feet. Over to the St. Andrew's Cross."

Tara stood and stared at the giant wooden X, stained a rich walnut, padded manacles affixed at top and bottom. With a hesitant gait, she made her way across the floor.

Logan stopped her by taking her hips and pulling her back against his chest. The vanilla-fruity sweet scent of her skin grabbed him by the balls. "What are you afraid of, Cherry?"

"Being helpless." Even her voice quivered.

"You will be. Trust me with your safety and training," he murmured in her ear. "Will I let anything bad happen to you?"

She swallowed. "Define bad."

He repressed a smile. Tara had always looked at every angle. "Will I make you bleed?"

"No."

She hadn't hesitated with that answer, which filled Logan with relief and pride. She was scared, but her logic was shining through. "Will I mark your skin in any permanent way?"

"I know you won't."

"Will I give you more pain than you can bear?"

A small pause. "No. But what will you make me feel?"

She looked over her shoulder and met his gaze. Since they'd begun working together, Tara had been desperately trying to hide her apprehension and desire, but in that moment, she dropped her mask. Her face glowed with arousal—and tightened with worry. Both were so honest that triumph rushed through him. Some small part of her was beginning to trust him with her feelings.

"You'll feel whatever needed so that you're willingly in my control. While our interaction may be different than Jason and Greta's, I will do whatever necessary to make you give yourself over to me. Step up, Cherry." He waved her against the cross. "Normally, I'd have you face away from me, but I want to see your every reaction. Back against the cross."

She smoothed out a shuddering breath, then turned, easing against the smooth, dark wood. Every muscle in her soft body went tight. Under that pretty, pale skin, Logan was sure she fought the urge to fidget and shiver. That instinct would serve her well.

"Place yourself in the manacles and lock them."

Her brown eyes flew up to him with a startled glance. Wisely, she held her tongue. After a moment's hesitation, she secured her left ankle, then her right. The second she straightened up and glanced at the wrist shackles, Logan knew she was questioning her own wisdom.

He gave her a moment to work it out in her head. As their training went on, her response times would have to become instant and fluid. Behaving like an untrained sub would only make her stand out. Like a soldier unable to complete an evolution of any special forces training, negative attention wasn't the kind anyone sought.

"What is your hesitation, Cherry?"

"I've never been restrained."

That fact thrilled Logan. He'd be the first—and last—man to show her the true joy of the power exchange she secretly ached for. She might experience a dark version of it during her mission, but she'd only truly submit to him.

He lowered his voice, peppering it with disapproval. "We've been over this. I won't hurt you. What is the real issue?"

"It's a logical fear to put yourself at someone else's mercy."

Especially someone who has hurt you. Tara didn't say it, but Logan heard the subtext.

"It is, but I'll reward your trust. And you'll be one step closer to saving Agent Miles."

With that, she nodded, then drew in a bracing breath as she stretched one hand up to a manacle and closed it with other. Then she looked to him for approval, and that expression, her need to please, went straight to his cock.

He drew off his T-shirt, gratified as her eyes widened, then he stepped close, lifting her chin with his finger. "Very good, Cherry. You're being very brave."

Then he laid his lips over hers, a small, reassuring peck. Her breath caught. It was almost indiscernible—but he felt it, felt her begin to give herself over. His chest tightening, Logan took her free hand, leaned in, and slowly pressed it to his torso. She took over, moving across his skin. God, those soft little fingers were like brands sizzling across his abdomen, brushing over his nipple. Her delicate palm settling over his heartbeat all but seared him.

With every moment that passed between them, Logan was more certain that he'd made the right decision to risk everything to win Cherry back. Smiling, he lifted her hand to his mouth, pressed a kiss to her palm, then eased it into the last manacle.

As it snapped shut, the little red light in the corner flashed, indicating that someone had tripped the motion detector in his observation room. Someone had entered without his knowledge or permission. It wasn't Thorpe; he'd scheduled a tour of the facility to a new member. Had he sent someone to watch in his stead? Possibly, but Jason had to get back to work. Xander rarely showed up before noon. Most of the other Doms weren't here, and Thorpe would never allow any of the casual club members this deep into the club. He didn't think Axel would waste his needed time with Agent York to watch Tara's progress. So who the hell was spying on them?

"Wait here."

"But—"

"Cherry," he cut her off. "I promise I'll be back. Nothing will happen to you. I'm watching from the next room."

It pained Logan to leave her naked and hanging on the cross, looking so beautiful and uncertain that she hurt his eyes. But whoever observed them without obtaining permission was breaching protocol. And it pissed Logan off.

He shoved out of the dungeon, stalked a few steps to the observation room, and pushed the door open, ready to see just about anyone—except Tara's fiancé, Brad Thompson.

"What the fuck are you doing here?" Logan demanded.

Brad stood under the harsh glare of the industrial light with his face red and his fists clenched. "What the fuck are *you* doing here, Edgington? I pounded on that damn door, and you ignored me."

"It's soundproof for a reason."

"You underhanded bastard. I don't know how you talked Tara into participating in this degrading tie-'em-up crap with you, of all people, but I demand that you to unchain her and return her clothes now." The man looked him up and down with disdain. "My God, what kind of animal are you?"

The kind of animal who made Cherry flushed and wet. The kind who looked forward to getting her off until she screamed her throat raw. But Logan didn't mention that.

Instead, he crossed his arms over his chest and looked at Brad like he was an insect. "What do you want?"

"Tara is not your damn toy anymore. She's my fiancée, and I won't let you hurt her. Let her go this second."

Like hell. "How did you get down to the dungeon level? This area is security restricted."

"Flashing the credentials of an Assistant District Attorney at stupid receptionists usually works. She nearly fell all over herself to help me find you down in this labyrinth."

Misty, or Sweet Pea, as everyone called her, was an efficient receptionist and a sweet little sub, but skittish around anyone with a badge. She'd nearly fainted when meeting York.

"Get the fuck out before I call security." Logan turned his back to leave.

Thompson grabbed his shoulder and spun him around, throwing a left hook. Logan had known it was coming from the way the man's body tensed. He ducked, then recovered, shoving his right fist into Brad's stomach. Thompson grunted and turned an even darker shade of red.

"Listen up, because I'll only say this once. On a professional level, stalking your fiancée while she's working won't go over well with her superiors or help her learn the skills necessary to survive her mission."

Brad jerked away. "I saw your whisker burn on her body last night. You're not teaching her a damn thing, just setting her up to hurt her again."

Logan shook his head. "You're wrong. And on a personal level, do you think spying on Tara is going to win you any brownie points?"

"I care about her well-being. It's my responsibility to keep her safe." Brad glared.

"While we're working, she's *my* responsibility. I'll take excellent care of her—always."

"Is that some kind of innuendo? A veiled threat that you're going to try to seduce her?"

"No innuendo at all. I'll lay it flat out for you right now." Logan got in Brad's face. "Tara is made for what I can give her, and whatever vanilla sex you're having with her isn't getting the job done. Her heart was mine first. If she wants me, I won't rest until it's mine again."

"Tara will be my wife, the mother of my children. You're not getting in my way."

Thompson swung at him again, and Logan plowed his fist into the man's jaw. Brad staggered back, nearly tripping over some folding chairs. Logan helped out by backing him into the concrete wall, then shoving a forearm to his throat. "I don't know how you duped her into marrying you, but I know the kind of scab you are."

"And you're a real gentleman, chaining women up," he croaked.

"Do you honestly think she'll fall for that?" With narrowed eyes and ruthless pleasure, Thompson smiled. "But go ahead and hit me some more. She'll hate you even more, not that it matters. Regardless of what you do, she'll never love you again."

That possibility worried Logan. He could train her to be submissive. She had both the urge and the aptitude. He could even make her want him; already she responded. But was it possible to make her fall for him again in a week? Logan was tempted to blurt the truth about their breakup to Cherry, whether or not she wanted to hear it. But he'd taken so many other choices from her when pressing Thorpe to honor his prior claim. Trying to wrestle absolution from her was counterproductive. He had to tamp down his impatience and let things play out.

"Get the fuck out and don't ever darken my dungeon door again."

Logan slammed his way out of the observation room. In the hallway, he let out a calming breath, rolled his shoulders to clear the tension. It wasn't working. Motherfucker. He'd always hated Brad Thompson in high school, the slimy, two-faced bastard.

But now he had to focus on Cherry.

Letting himself in his dungeon, Logan locked the door behind him once more. If Thompson was smart he'd leave. And yeah, he could call security and have the asshole tossed out. But Logan was betting that Tara's fiancé wasn't smart. He'd stay and watch out of some misguided sense of duty. Or maybe because he wasn't as sure of Tara's love as he pretended. Logan didn't really give a shit. But if Thompson was fool enough to hang around . . . well, Logan would be happy to put on a show and do whatever necessary to prove that he pleased Tara sexually in a way Brad couldn't because her feelings for him lingered. It ought to be a big wake-up call for the ass wipe.

Logan sighed. Tara's reaction worried him. Guilt niggled. In the short term, she'd be pissed. But he wouldn't do this if he didn't genuinely believe that they belonged together.

Pushing his concerns aside, he approached Cherry, sweeping her hair away from her face with a soft palm. "You okay, baby?"

A shiver ran through her. "A little cold."

And a little scared. Not that she'd say it. Tara was stubborn, but he admired her moxie.

"I'm sorry. I had to deal with someone unpleasant. You have my undivided attention now. I'll make it up to you."

"Then let's get to work." She sent him a brave smile.

Logan slanted her a grin. "I'll do my best to not make it too tedious."

Her expression turned wary, and she opened her mouth. Before she could say a word, he laid a finger over his lips and shook his head. "Who are you going to obey?"

Tara licked her lips, her eyes dilating a bit. "You, Logan."

Hearing those words made not just his cock jerk, but his heart sing. "Good girl."

He pressed kisses across the soft slope of her shoulder, up her neck, then whispered for her ears alone, "You look beautiful restrained for me."

She wrinkled her nose. "At least you can't see my ass."

Normally, he'd discipline her for thinking anything negative about her body. In fact, he should already be disciplining her for yesterday's offenses. But after seeing Jason and Greta, she now knew the beauty of this kind of relationship. Before giving her more of the unpleasant so that she could cope with this mission, he wanted to give her a bit more of the wonderful—for them. And if that pissed their peeping Thompson off, so much the better.

"I already have, and I love it. Hmm . . ." He nipped on her earlobe. "I can't wait to fondle and kiss it." *And fuck it.*

"Logan . . ." she warned. "This is business."

"And pleasure." He cradled her face in his hands and compelled her wary stare up to him. "Breathe with me."

Tara did. As he inhaled, she did the same. Ditto with the exhalations. Soon they were in sync, but he didn't look away. Her gaze clung to him, fell down into him, and Logan edged closer. Their toes touched. Her icy feet sent a shiver through him.

"You said you were cold, not frozen. Why didn't you tell me you were uncomfortable?" he demanded, kneeling to envelop her cold feet in his hot grip.

Relief relaxed her face, and she moaned. "I didn't think it would matter to you."

"Your discomfort always matters. Some pain is intentional and is meant to arouse you physically and emotionally. Neglect never falls in that category."

Logan crossed the room and rummaged through the little closet. He found a clean pair of his tube socks, left over from his stop here last winter. He unfolded them, approached Tara, then slipped one on each foot, bunching them under the restraints. "Better?"

He wouldn't relent until he'd taken care of her. Granted, giving her socks was a small gesture, one not likely to win her heart. But her expression softened.

"Thank you, Logan."

Every word was breathy. His touch and simple care were getting to her, it seemed. Deep down, was she looking for signs that she mattered to him?

The thought made him smile. If she wanted some measure of his caring, he'd be more than happy to give her all she could handle.

* * *

TARA looked at Logan. Uh-oh, there was a dangerous gleam in his eye, the one that said he was up to something.

"No more cold feet. Now we can get back to work," she reminded him.

"You don't have cold feet at all?"

Did he mean physically or metaphorically? If the latter, oh hell yeah, her feet were freezing. But no way was she going to show her weakness or give up on this mission. No way was she going to give up on experiencing the sort of power exchange Jason and Greta shared. She needed it for herself, just once.

"Bring it."

The second she issued the challenge, Tara knew it was the wrong thing to say. If she'd simply agreed with him and used that deferential tone when speaking his name . . . he liked that. It soothed him. When she tossed out something like this? She was just asking for the beast.

His hands caressed their way up her calves, behind her sensitive knees, inching up her thighs until he gripped her hips, his fingers sinking into her ass. He looked straight forward—right at her pussy. He licked his lips, staring like he couldn't wait to devour her. Her heart started tripping over itself, beating triple time. In this position, she was desperately aware that her legs were spread, her body bare. She could do nothing to stop him.

Her entire body jolted with the thought of his mouth on her most secret flesh again.

"Wait, Log— Oh my God." She swallowed as his tongue pressed torturously slow over her clit, the tip toying with the protective hood. Then he slipped two fingers inside her, lazily fondling her slick walls. She struggled for her next breath.

No man made her feel like Logan. Through college and her mid-twenties, she'd taken a few guys for a "test drive." Some had performed better than others. A few had even made her motor rev a little. But no one had given her the same high-octane thrill as Logan. He was the Ferrari of lovers.

"You're wet, Cherry."

"You just put your saliva on me." She dished out the excuse with a voice that trembled more than she liked.

Logan raised a brow in displeasure. "Were you wet before?"

He knew the answer, but was making her say it. Damn him. Why? To professionally push her past her comfort level? Or to personally bring about her submission? Could she ever experience the kind of connection she'd witnessed today if she wasn't honest? No. The woman had faced her desire for Jason's demands head-on, determined to please him and find the pleasure she fantasized about.

"Yes, Logan." She closed her eyes. "I was wet before you touched me with your mouth."

"Open your eyes. Always look at me."

She did, her lashes fluttering wide until she had nowhere to look but his intent blue stare.

"Good." He breathed against her mound, and every nerve below her waist tensed, pooled hot with need. "Your kiss yesterday told me how hungry you are for satisfaction. I know you want it even now. Will you be brave enough to accept it?"

Oh, God. He'd read her like an open book. Tara drew in a deep breath. She had to do this. For Darcy and her own success as a field agent, she'd need to be able to perform any act asked of her. For herself, she needed to see if this time with Logan would patch up the empty, gaping hole of unfulfilled desire inside her.

"Yes, Logan."

"Excellent."

He didn't hesitate for an instant before settling his mouth over her pussy again and swiping his tongue underneath her clit, then over it, laving the little bud with almost more friction than she could take. But somehow, he knew exactly how far he could push her before the pleasure became too much. Logan backed away, blowing cool air over her slick, overheated folds, and rubbed his thumb over the needy bundle of nerves. Her entire body jerked and heat brewed between her trembling legs.

"Hmm, Cherry. You're as sweet as I remember." He brushed his tongue over her birthmark, the one inside her thigh that he'd been seemingly fascinated with at sixteen. "I'd love to spend a day with my mouth on your pussy, lapping at you while you shiver and swell. And give me all that sweet cream. I want you to come. I want to stay at you until you shake and cry and beg, not sure if you want me to stop or taste that pretty cunt all over again."

A big boom of desire dropped right between her legs, adding to the already torturous ache. How did he do that to her, so quickly and easily? Mere seconds, and she was panting. Arousal overtook her senses. No way she could pretend that she didn't want every tingling bit of sin his deep voice promised.

"Logan . . ."

"I'm here, baby."

Not a moment passed before he pried her open with his thumbs and stroked his tongue all the way from her seeping hole up, up, over the hard knot of her clit. Dizziness swept over Tara in waves, euphoric, surreal. God, at sixteen, he'd made her feel so good. Given her first orgasm ever with that patient, talented tongue. Then, it had taken time, and his endless little licks had built, finally escalating into something spectacular.

This orgasm was going to burst over her in a flash like a fireball of sensation. It would make every self-induced climax for the last dozen years feel like a lame joke. She clenched her fists. Climbing desire tightened her body until every muscle clenched. As wrong as Logan was for her, she needed this orgasm, and only he seemed able to give it to her.

Instead of pushing her over the edge, Logan sat back on his heels and looked up expectantly. What did he want from her? Tara clenched her fists above the unyielding manacles, dying a small death inside as she panted and writhed. "Logan . . ."

"Tell me you need it."

Below the ridge of his dark brow, he stared at her with eyes like blue fire. His nostrils flared. His taut mouth twitched, as if lifting into a snarl, before he forced it back in line.

That expression said that he wanted her—badly. Worse, he looked willing to do anything to make her want him that badly in return.

But he didn't have to try at all.

Tara's shaky breath couldn't quite fill her lungs. He was breaking her down, and somehow, being on this cross, at his mercy, stripped her bravado and revealed the woman beneath. Even if her mind shied away, her body craved it. Worse, no matter how badly he'd burned her before, some part of her trusted his strength, his tenacity, that searing desire all over his face.

"I—I need it," she admitted.

From her knee, he smoothed his hand upward. Tara couldn't take her eyes off the contrast of those strong, dark fingers against the pale flesh of her thigh. Her breathing hitched as his touch inched closer and closer to the burning ache in her pussy.

He planted a soft kiss on her hip and teasing her clit with his thumb again. "Thank you for your honesty. Your body is so sweetly ripe. Flushed, wet, trembling. I can barely wait to get my mouth on you again."

Tara cried out at his words. She couldn't move much, but wriggled her hips, urging her pussy closer to his waiting lips just a few inches away.

Logan inched back, then lifted his thumb off her aching clit.

"Please . . ." She was begging and she knew it. He knew it. Yet she'd never needed pleasure this desperately. Her body felt as if she'd been waiting for twelve cold years for him.

Slowly, he swiped his thumb, all but dripping with her cream, over his tongue. Then he closed his lips around the digit and sucked with closed eyes and a moan. "Fuck, yeah."

The ecstasy prowling across his face aroused her even more.

Before she could take a breath, that thumb was back on her exposed, engorged nubbin, rubbing in slow circles. "You really need it, Cherry?"

"Yes!" she gasped, willing to say anything. She'd worry about repairing the damage to her pride and her engagement later.

"All you have to do is say that you need *me* to give it to you."

Shock ricocheted through her. It was true, but admitting that to him gave him so much power over her. "I already said that I need to come."

He shook his head. "That's only half of the admission. Give me the rest."

Logan was going to make her surrender both body and mind—
to him. She wanted to despise him for it, but she needed him too
damn badly. His Cheshire cat smile said that he knew it.

"Fine. I—I need you to give it to me."

"Not good enough. Be specific. Address me properly."

Having him this near was an aphrodisiac, not to mention the
hypnotic rhythm of his thumb over her responsive flesh. With every
pass, every bit of friction he bestowed on the little bud, it swelled
more, poked out from its hood, exposing the delicate, sensitive organ
beneath. Tara gasped as he unraveled her. She ached to reach out
and touch him. Since she couldn't, she dug her nails into her palms.
Her thighs clenched.

He started to back away again.

"Don't!" she protested. "I need to come. I need *you* to make me
come, Logan. Please."

"You still owe me another thirteen spankings on that pretty bare
ass for yesterday's transgressions, but for your sweet request just now,
I'll grant your wish—with one condition: No holding back your
screams."

She gave him a feverish nod, willing to say or do almost anything for Logan.

If she wanted to know if he could ease the constant ache of her
body, then she had to be woman enough to accept everything he
gave her. Overcoming her apprehension and learning to give over
control would be imperative to succeed on this the case, too.

His blue eyes darkened to something like midnight. Then he
smiled—and leaned in.

The moment his mouth opened over her pussy and his tongue
slid through her juices, her breath caught. God, it was like he hadn't
paused at all. Her desire was still pooled right on the edge, just waiting for that last shove over.

Logan moaned, and the vibrations made her clit tighten, tremble. If she'd had her hands free, Tara would have loved to plunge her

fingers into that short hair and push his face deeper into her. But as he nibbled gently, then sucked her clit into his mouth, she moaned in return. Somehow, being manacled so that she couldn't direct what Logan did was the most freeing thing of all. She had no responsibility. And she had no choice but to stay and take the pleasure he gave her.

"You're so sweet, Cherry," he whispered against her pussy, then shoved his fingers into the hot well of her sex.

It took him less than two seconds to find a spot that made her gasp with a sharp pleasure, so unlike anything she'd ever felt before.

"Y-Yes," Tara sputtered. "Oh my God . . ."

"Never had your G-spot stimulated?"

Never. "Not like that," she hedged.

"Hmm. I love being your first at so many things."

Before she could process his words, he brushed his fingertips over that nerve-laden spot again and circled his tongue over her clit. Friction sparked fire all through her body.

"You're ready now. Come for me, Cherry."

With those magic words, Tara came apart in an instant, every nerve in her body escalating to a shattering crescendo unlike anything she'd ever felt. As promised, she screamed. And screamed. He didn't relent until he'd wrung every spasm, shiver, and moan out of her.

The violent sensations raged through her body in a seemingly endless blast until the tension finally left her. As she sagged against the manacles, anger seeped out. Bravado buckled under the strain. He'd stripped away her ability to put on a front, leaving behind a terrible sense of naked vulnerability.

Logan pulled away from her pussy, licking his lips. He placed a reverent kiss on her lower abdomen, still twitching with aftershocks. With soft fingers, he petted her mound, kissing his way up her body. "Gorgeous. You did well, Cherry."

When he stood, she didn't know where to look. The floor? The bed across the room? Not at him. She feared begging for more. So she closed her eyes, but a terrible sense of exposure hit her. Tears leaked out. Her chest bucked with a sob. God, the release he'd given her had scrubbed her psyche cleaner than steel wool. She felt new and raw.

Tara sucked in a ragged breath, tried to bottle up her haywire emotions.

Logan wasn't having any of that. Quickly, he released her manacles. Her rubbery legs wouldn't support her weight, and she crashed into his arms. He caught her and carried her to the bed. Once he laid them down, he rolled to his back, draping her on top, soothing her with his body and a rhythmic caress up and down her spine.

"Let it out," he encouraged.

She shook her head with a sniff, trying again to hold in all the emotions. "I'm sorry. I need to stop. This isn't professional."

"It's necessary." He cupped her face in the steely heat of his hands. "Doms will expect an honest response. Don't lie and don't front—or there will be punishment. Whatever you need to feel, feel it."

His gentle voice encouraged, but Tara still wanted to crawl into a hole. She had to stop bawling and clinging to him. Instead, she buried her face in Logan's neck and availed herself of the earthy musk and leather scents. She cuddled closer. How could he comfort her when he was the source of her distress?

"B-But I'm a damn FBI agent. I need t-to act like one."

Quite simply, Logan brought out every emotion in her. She was usually good at keeping all that in; she had to be. But with him, she couldn't seem to turn it off.

Logan wiped her fresh tears away with the pad of his thumb. "You have. This is part of training. You're learning to give into your submissive nature. That's what this mission requires."

Perhaps, but she hadn't been thinking about her mission with Logan's mouth on her pussy. She'd been focused on pleasure, on her need for more. That reality filled her with shame.

"This feels so personal." She scrambled off of his body to sit beside him, curling her knees into her chest.

"You feel off balance, and you're not used to that." He tucked a strand of fiery hair behind her ear. "That's okay. Since you're independent, you're going to feel that way in a D/s relationship until you learn to flow with it and trust me. I'll help you through it. Lie back." With a gentle, but insistent hand, he pushed her to her back. "Right now, just breathe with me. In . . ."

He demonstrated, lying beside her, inhaling through his nose until his chest rose. Tara followed suit.

"Now let it out." Logan exhaled until the air was gone, his shoulders slightly slumped.

Again, she did the same. Amazingly, her tears began to dry up. A sense of calm settled over her. It wouldn't last. She had mountains to climb with this case—and Logan. But right now, she felt more settled than she had in months, maybe years.

But she also felt more connected to him than she ever had to any lover.

Before the alarm bells could go off in her head, Logan rolled over, his body half covering hers, and he possessed her mouth with his in a slow kiss of reverence. Endless, deep. It wasn't meant to arouse. Instead, Tara had to fight the urge to burrow deeper into his embrace and cling. To connect with him again in every way.

Feelings like that could lead nowhere good. Logan would train her and disappear from her life. She had to be ready to feign an appropriate response to York or any other Dom presented to her.

She broke the kiss and eased to her feet, praying her legs would support her.

"I need a minute. Please. Then we'll get back to work." Tara reached for her clothes on the concrete floor.

Logan scooped them up before she could grab the first garment. He tucked the stack against his chest. "When you're in my dungeon— in most Dom's dungeons—you won't be dressed beyond what they

allow. If you need to go down the hall to the ladies' room, I'll give
you your robe." He placed her clothes in the wardrobe, then handed
her the silky cream-colored garment. It wasn't sheer, but it clung to
every bump on her body, especially her stiff, aching nipples. She
crossed her arms over her chest.

*Tsk*ing, Logan pushed them down to her sides. "No hiding."

He cradled her breast in his hand, thumbing her engorged nipple
through the silk. Fresh pleasure arced through her body. Her head
told her that she should be pulling away. She was engaged. None of
the soft touches Logan lavished on her forwarded her training. But
her body didn't care. It wanted him.

"Yes, Logan."

"Excellent, Cherry." In reward, he eased the silky lapels of the robe
apart, anchoring them on the sides of her exposed breasts. He leaned
in and kissed one nipple, suckled and nipped it gently. More blood
rushed to the tip in a flash of sensitivity. Logan did the same to the
other hard tip. More desire gathered hotly between her thighs.

As she arched toward him in silent offering, he covered her
breasts up and spun her toward the door.

"Still want a few minutes alone?" he murmured in her ear.

Distance between them would be good, but she no longer wanted
it. But was it really wise to experience all that passion again when she
was marrying someone else? Someone like Brad, whom her stepfather
approved of. Brad shared her desire for marriage and children. He did
absolutely nothing for her in bed and could never use sex to control
her. Logan could do that twenty-four/seven. Tara sighed. Maybe she
should ease her own ache in the bathroom and come back with re-
newed focus, a clearer head.

"Yes, Logan."

"Ten minutes. No masturbating. Or that will cost you twenty-
five swats and a whole lot of orgasm deprivation. That would be a
damn shame . . ." He smiled as if he knew that he'd thwarted her
plans.

Damn him. He wanted her totally at his mercy. For the case—or for himself? Was he really trying so hard to train her simply for the mission? Did he want to talk about their past merely to clear the air so their rapport would be easier and facilitate the training? Or was this personal for him? His every touch seemed to say so. Tara had to ask herself why. And what was she going to do about the fact that both the scared girl and aching woman inside her wanted to cling to Logan and ask the answers to all her questions?

Tara drew in a bracing breath and opened the dungeon's door. To her utter horror, Brad stood directly in her path.

Chapter Six

"B-BRAD?" Tara's heart dropped to her knees. She had trouble drawing in a breath. "What are you doing here?"

He crossed his arms over his chest, anger radiating from his nearly black eyes, glittering with betrayal. "After the marks I saw on your body last night and our argument, I came to find out what's going on."

Tara swallowed. How much of this morning's session with Logan had he seen? "You shouldn't be here."

"Neither should you." Brad stepped into the room on heavy footsteps. "Why didn't you tell me that your first lover was working you over—excuse me, working with you on this case? Did that fact slip your mind, dear?"

Crap. She'd stepped deep in it now, and had no one to blame but herself. "No. I was reassigned to Logan yesterday. I didn't tell you because I didn't want you to overreact."

"Or you didn't want me wondering if you were having feelings for him again."

Okay, that, too. Brad's sarcasm made his fury painfully obvious. Maybe she should have handled things differently, but it was too late now. Clearly, Logan was always going to elicit some response in her. It was like her body was hardwired to his, and she'd been naïve to hope otherwise.

"I'm sorry," she murmured.

"You're damn right, you should be sorry! You took off every stitch of clothing and let him put his fucking tongue all over you. And you came for him like a bitch in heat. You *begged* for him. I have always treated you like a lady, been gentle and deferential. And this is how you screw me over?"

Tara felt two inches tall—and wished she could disappear altogether. "It—I didn't arrange to have Logan as my trainer. That decision rests with my superior and the club owner. You know Darcy is in imminent danger. What kind of friend, what kind of FBI agent, would I be if I held up this case for my personal—"

"Our wedding is in eight weeks. Our invitations arrived yesterday afternoon. Now, I'm standing here wondering if I know you at all. I've always thought you were honest and forthright. That you'd never cheat because this bastard"—he pointed to Logan angrily—"taught you how much it hurts."

Brad was right. The fact that he was a lawyer, capable of tossing together great arguments on the fly, didn't help, either. Worse, she couldn't say that she hadn't cheated. She may not have had sex with Logan, but if he'd dropped his leather pants and crawled between her thighs ten minutes ago, would she have found the strength to stop him?

Tara feared she knew the answer.

"You're right." She shook her head, not knowing what else to say. "About everything."

"Call Bocelli and tell him you need to be reassigned."

"I did. Yesterday afternoon."

"Damn it, Cherry," Logan cursed softly.

Tara glanced his way. Hurt flashed across his face. And somehow, his pain hurt her.

Why? She didn't owe him anything, except hard work on this case. But engaging in a bit of the power exchange today had reforged the connection she'd once felt with Logan. It was back—but stronger.

Damn. The last thing she wanted to do was hurt Brad. If she'd seen him having oral sex with another woman, even for the sake of his job, she'd feel betrayed, too.

Pressing her lips together, she turned back to her fiancé. "Bocelli refused me. The club's owner insists that Logan will get the job done, and my boss is sticking by that. Logan has a lot of valuable experience in this environment. I know what you're thinking, but this is my *job*. I have to see this through. And quite frankly, I understand where they're coming from. Look, Brad, I know this seems weird to you, but I'm about to go into a different world. These people are criminals and don't play by the rules. If I'm going to do this job right, I have to fit into their world and that includes accepting certain things I might not like."

Brad paced. "So I'm supposed to watch you walk out the door every morning, knowing that you're strutting around naked for him, letting him touch you so he can dig his way back into your heart? He's been a ghost between us since day one, Tara."

She wished she could refute Brad.

He lifted her chin and forced her stare to lock with his. "What else don't I know? Have you fucked him again?"

"No. Brad, don't do this . . ."

"What, seek the truth? I shouldn't point out that, in the three years we've been together, I've never heard you scream during sex. Hell, I'd wondered if you even liked it, but that was okay because I love you and wanted to be with you, regardless. I guess I should be wondering now about your feelings for me."

Tara was questioning them herself. But aside from her stepfather, Adam, Brad had been the most stable force in her life. "I would never have agreed to marry you if I didn't care."

"Are you going to try to tell me that nothing has changed for you?" he challenged.

Tara hesitated. No. Everything had changed. She closed her eyes. How had that happened? When? Did she even want to know why?

It sucked caring about two men who were so damn different.

They were like comparing a sunny morning to a midnight storm. Brad usually brought his kindness, his well-developed sense of justice to everything he did. Logan charged in with a bang—all testosterone and demand with a little mischief thrown in—then wrought difficulty and destruction before disappearing like a wraith.

But she couldn't stop wanting him. Maybe she'd never stopped.

God, her life was falling apart. She hoped that when this case was over, her fever for Logan would be, too. But she feared that was wishful thinking.

"Brad, this isn't the place to discuss us. Let me get dressed. We'll talk in the car for a bit."

"Our relationship is a mess, and you want to give me ten minutes in the Audi?"

His sarcasm made her wince. "It's all I can spare now. Tonight, we'll talk—"

"No. Right here, right now, I want to know what's most important to you. Either you—"

"Don't do this." Tara had a terrible felling that she knew what his next words would be and she wasn't ready to face this so soon after Logan had opened up everything vulnerable inside her.

"Quit this case—"

"Stop. Brad . . ." Distress stabbed her chest.

"Or give me back my ring. Because I'll be god damned if I'm going to do nothing while you come here every day to play kinky personal trainer with your ex-boyfriend for your 'job.'"

Dread made her stomach plummet to her knees. Since yesterday, Tara had feared that if Brad learned Logan was prepping her for this mission that he'd blow a gasket, but this wasn't the reaction she'd imagined. Anger, yes. Betrayal, absolutely. But this?

"You're reading this wrong, Brad. Logan is a highly skilled non-Bureau contractor assigned to teach me everything I need to succeed and save Darcy. You know how important this is to me, to make Adam proud, see if the field is where I belong."

"You talked about interviews, maybe a demonstration or a walk-through of all this BDSM shit. Not hands-on experience with your ex."

Logan got in his face. "Are you really such a prick that you'd want her to go into a potentially dangerous situation without the proper training?"

"Someone else can teach her what she needs to know."

"I told you," Tara insisted. "The brass put my training in Dominion's hands because no one at the Bureau is equipped to teach me properly. The head of this club thinks Logan can prepare me to survive in this world. At this point, I think the smartest thing is for me to listen to the people who know what the hell they're doing. What's the brass going to say if I walk in as a junior agent on her first assignment and tell them how it's going to go down? They would laugh at me. Nor can I walk off this case without losing credibility."

"Maybe so, but they can't force you stay with this job."

Tara's jaw dropped. "You're asking me to quit the FBI for you?"

That took his jealousy too far. It was a betrayal of everything she wanted and believed in. Brad worked to all hours of the night. He'd asked her to sacrifice for his career, claiming that it was for the good of both of them. But her job didn't mean anything?

"For *us*," he stressed. "I'm asking you to think about our future. Take a job that doesn't put you in the hands of ruthless bastards and criminals for a paycheck. A job you won't have to prostitute your integrity for."

"You're asking me to choose between my aspirations and my fiancé? I *need* to know if I'm meant to spend my life in the field. And I can't leave my maid of honor in some sick bastard's dungeon. What about Darcy and the other victims? Am I supposed to just let them die?"

"C'mon, Tara. As much as I hate to say it, they're probably either already dead or sold. Let's say what this really is about. Do you want a man who wants to love you for the rest of your life, or the douche bag who's going to treat you like a piece of ass—again."

Brad wanted her to choose between Logan and himself, between the past and the future. He was forcing her to lay her cards on the table now.

"You don't know a damn thing about me or how I feel about Tara," Logan growled, suddenly standing protectively by her side. "You've said a lot of really ugly things about the woman you supposedly love. Have to guilt her into staying with you?"

"You really want to go there?" Brad glared at Logan, despite being four inches shorter and having thirty fewer pounds of pure muscle. "From here, it looks like you have to tie them down to keep them from running away, screaming."

"Stop it, both of you!" Tara glared from one to the other. "Brad, this isn't about Logan."

Fists clenched, Brad looked like a kettle ready to blow, all red and worked up. Logan appeared calm on the surface, but she wasn't fooled. Under that façade was a deadly force he could unleash at will.

"Don't kid yourself, Tara." Brad shook his head. "Either get your clothes on and come with me or give me back my ring."

"Who's the douche bag now?" Logan said, staring at Brad with disdain.

"Yeah, if the shoe was on the other foot?"

Logan laughed. The sound wasn't nice. "I'd spend every night satisfying her to make sure she knew how much I loved her, so that the last thing on her mind during the day was another man. But I'm guessing you didn't try that."

"I've been working late. I have a big case," Brad defended.

"She does, too."

"I don't have to prance around naked for mine."

"This attitude only shows that you know squat about working undercover. Solving crime and stopping bad shit is more important than modesty or your tight-ass idea of morality."

Tara jumped into the fray before Logan and Brad started dismantling one another. "Please, Brad . . . You're asking me to give up the opportunity to nail a guy who kidnaps ten-year-old girls, then sells them to perverts in brothels. So what if someone sees my boobs? I'm an adult; I can handle it. What about these poor girls? Who is going to fight for them? Should I apologize to them because my fiancé is squeamish?"

"You're being obtuse. I'm not objecting to the case; I'm objecting to him." Brad pointed.

Logan smiled. "From the FBI's perspective, we're a package deal."

"He could be anyone else, and you still wouldn't want another man touching me this way," Tara pointed out.

One look at Brad's face told her that rationale wasn't going to cut it for him. Anxiety clawed through her, along with a fear of letting go of her status quo. What would she do without his anchoring influence? And what about her stepfather? He'd be so disappointed, then disapproving if he found out Logan was back in her life. No, she wasn't a teenager anymore, could choose who she wanted to be with, but Adam was all the family she had left. She hated letting him down after he'd all but raised her.

Even so, the big question loomed: What did she want? In the end, she was going to have to battle her natural inclination to please everyone and decide what *she* wanted.

"Maybe not," Brad conceded. "But he makes it worse. It took years to exorcise his ghost from between us. Last year, when I finally thought you'd overcome him, I proposed. Now he's back, and this time it'll be worse. Just to inflate his ego, he'll make sure you won't forget him, even as he's ripping your heart to shreds."

"Brad—"

"Choose, Tara. Come with me or give me the ring."

She didn't dare look at Logan. She didn't want to look at Brad. A million thoughts swirled in her head. The need to help Darcy. The crusading spirit in her chest to stop the abduction of these poor young girls sold into sex. The fire in her belly to be a good agent. The ache Logan stirred in her warred with the fear of losing Brad's stability. If Logan knew she was no longer engaged, he'd ruthlessly go after her body. And her heart would follow.

If she was that worried about Logan stealing her heart, how in love with Brad could she be? The too-honest question made her flinch. But there was no taking it back. The risk in losing Brad wasn't in losing the love of her life, but the man who made her feel like she'd finally have the family she wanted. After losing her mother young and being bounced around between her grandparents and an aunt until Adam stepped in and adopted her, she craved having one roof and one man to come home to. She wanted to know that her children would never wonder where they'd live tomorrow. Brad could give that to her.

But was it fair to hang on to someone who'd been nothing but patient and kind to her when that family was off in the future and she wasn't sure that she loved him now?

Without looking at either man, she made her way to Logan's little cabinet on the far side of the room. She doffed the socks and the robe, feeling both men's eyes searing her bare backside. Then she donned her suit, buttoned her blouse, adjusted the lapels of her coat, stepped into her heels.

She grabbed the ring in her hand, then crossed the room again, focusing on Brad. "Shall we go?"

Astonishment flashed across Brad's face, then an exultant smile that had Tara wincing.

"Tara." Logan grabbed her hand, his dark brows bunched over his stunned gaze.

God, every time he touched her, her body flared hot. She didn't want to leave him.

"Get your hand off her," Brad growled, placing his arm around her waist.

It was one of the few times he'd ever been possessive.

"I can't do this, Logan. Not now." Tara squelched her guilt, then eased away from them both before addressing Brad. "Let's go."

"Gladly," Brad said as he shot Logan a triumphant glare.

Then he slammed the dungeon door behind them, and the last thing Tara saw was shock and agony ripping across Logan's face. Her heart squeezed painfully in her chest.

With a kiss at her temple, Brad threw his arm around her again and drew her close as they walked down the hall. "Thank you. I was so afraid I was going to lose you."

In a few minutes, he'd hate her so much that he wouldn't care. But for everything he'd done for her, been for her, for the past three years, he deserved the respect of privacy for this conversation. "Where can we talk?"

Ten minutes later, they were back at the house they shared. It had been investment property for Brad, but when the previous tenants had moved out and she'd accepted Brad's proposal, he'd given up his studio apartment and asked her to move in here with him. As he opened the front door, into the living room, Tara was struck by the fact that this place had never felt like home.

"Do you want to eat first, then talk?" he asked gently.

"I'm not—" Tara shook her head. "No." She drew in a long breath and held the engagement ring out to Brad. "I'm sorry but I can't marry you."

Shock blanched his face as he stared, frozen. When she pressed the ring into his hand, his fingers curled slowly around it. "You're picking him over me?"

"This isn't about Logan. It's about making the right choices for me."

Brad's anger took over. "Tell yourself that all you want. I know the truth. He will, too."

"It's about my case and my friend and the duty I swore to uphold when I joined the FBI. It's about what I want to accomplish. I won't quit." *And I won't continue pretending that I love you as much as you want me to.*

Brad shook his head as he pocketed the ring. "I wonder if he knew when he staged that demonstration for me earlier that he'd break us apart."

Demonstration? "What d-do you mean?"

"He must have known that my watching you with him would tear me apart inside."

Shock turned the blood in her veins to ice. Logan had known that Brad was watching him go down on her? Horror washed over Tara. And certainty. Of course Logan had known. Brad had been the "someone unpleasant" he'd had to deal with.

That son of a bitch. Betrayal scalded her. And fury. She'd trusted him enough to submit, so she could feel for herself the connection that Jason and Greta shared. He'd used the scene as a way to rub her desire in Brad's face.

"He's a fucking bastard, Tara," Brad spat. "Enjoy the hell out of your life, especially after he makes you miserable again. Screaming orgasms aside, you know that day is coming. And I won't be around to pick up the pieces. Leave your key on the kitchen counter."

Brad stormed through the front door—and out of her life.

Just like that, her perfect picket-fence future was gone. How the hell had that happened so quickly?

Tara braced herself on the back of the sofa with shaking hands. She needed a few minutes to process the fact that she was no longer engaged to an up-and-coming ADA who'd sworn he'd love her forever—and that her first lover had done his level best to break them up. And why? Just to see if she'd be gullible enough to fall for him twice? All the bullshit earlier about him caring for her and wanting to protect her . . . She suspected all he'd really wanted was to strip Brad from her life so he could have her back at his mercy. No way was she going to give him the satisfaction.

Club Dominion—Friday afternoon

Two hours later, Tara walked back into the dungeon. Logan felt his entire body go rubbery with relief. He'd feared that when she'd left with Brad, she'd never return, that she'd marry the schmuck and leave Logan alone and fucking miserable for the rest of his crappy life.

"You're back?" God, even his voice wobbled nervously.

When she stepped closer, he looked under that furious glare to see that she'd been crying. Something in his chest seized up. Her expression told him that she hadn't shed all her tears yet. Was she that miserable being here with him?

Logan raked a hand through his hair. If she stayed, he'd train her. But damn it, he wanted to do everything possible to make her happy. He couldn't stand that anguished face. He hoped like hell that he could make her fall in love with him again, not only because he'd told Thorpe he was going to collar and marry her, but because he didn't think his god damn sanity would last without her.

But if, after her training, he only made her miserable, he'd let her go.

"I'm back." She raised her chin proudly. "Don't gloat. If it weren't for my job, I swear to God, I'd never come within ten feet of you again."

Without another word, she took off her clothes, folded them at his feet, then assumed the slave position. Despite being posed in a way meant to communicate her desire to serve, her body shook with fury, complete with a "fuck off" vibe.

Shit. She looked so lovely, and it was all he could do to keep his hands off. But he had to figure out what was in her heart first. So the bad news he'd received while she'd been gone would have to wait.

"Cherry, tell me what happened."

Tara glared at him with the fire of a thousand suns. "I ended my engagement to Brad."

Hope and triumph spiked inside him. She'd left the asshole? Thank God. Not only was Brad a distraction Tara didn't need right now, he was completely wrong for her. He'd been standing squarely in Logan's way. It was a relief to have that obstacle removed.

"But then, I suppose you manipulated the situation—and me—

as always." She tossed him a bitter glare. "Why else would you go down on me and force me to beg for orgasm, unless you knew he was watching."

Shit. She'd totally mistaken his utter need to fight for her as a betrayal. "I'd be happy to do that every day. Brad watching was merely a bonus. I told him to leave, but I suspected he'd be stupid enough to stay and watch. Did I want to piss him off? I didn't really care how he felt. Did I hope to come between the two of you? He and I had already covered that. He knew the score. But I didn't do it for him; I did it because I couldn't stay away from you for another god damned minute. I *needed* to touch you."

She hesitated. "What did you cover with Brad?"

Tara didn't want to listen to him. Frustration gnawed at his stomach. He'd been right to put the decision to hear him out in her hands. He wasn't going to be able to force her to believe him, especially a few minutes after breaking up with her fiancé. Unlike her behavior in the dungeon, this had to be her choice. She'd been through a lot already today, and it was barely after noon.

"Tell you what, Cherry. We'll talk about it when we're both in a better place."

Tara was silent for such a long moment, her face so angry and full of hurt. Dread wound its way through Logan's system. "You manipulated my future. I started to trust you and . . . you hurt me."

He winced. Every word was true. He was used to being ruthless; fighting terrorist thugs required it, and sometimes, he forgot to turn that off.

"Baby, I didn't mean . . ." To come between Tara and Brad? Yeah, he had. Or at least he'd hoped to make her think about where her heart truly lay. "I'm sorry if I hurt you."

Logan couldn't say that he was sorry for the result—but he was sorry for her pain.

She wouldn't even look at him. "What you did was despicable, but I shouldn't have expected any different. It doesn't matter.

I won't let you matter. Physically, you'll teach me and keep me safe, and that's all I need. So let's get back to business. *Strictly* business. The sooner I learn what I need to know, the sooner I'll be away from you."

Ouch. He probably deserved that. He still had plenty to say on this topic, but he'd play it her way for now. Forcing her to talk before she was ready wasn't going to make her feel any better or get him what he wanted.

"All right, work it is," he conceded. "But we *will* revisit the subject later."

"You've just stabbed me in the back and exploded my personal life all to hell. From now on, it's off-limits to you."

"You really think that your breakup with Brad had *nothing* to do with me?" Logan knew he should shut up, but if Tara imagined that to be true for a second, then she'd lied to her former fiancé—and herself. "The way I see it, you responded to my hands on your body, my mouth on your clit so completely that there's no way you don't have feelings for me. You've never been the kind of girl to get off with a guy she doesn't care for. I'm guessing that was your problem with Brad."

She flushed, but still managed to scowl. "You're delusional. Go fuck yourself."

Not gonna happen. He had six days to convince Tara that he'd always loved her and that she was his. He refused to waste another second.

"You want to get down to business, fine. Lose the chip on your shoulder, get your ass over to the bed, then wait for my command."

"You're such a prick," she muttered as she made her way across the room.

Logan caught up to her in a heartbeat. "That's Master Prick to you."

Tara rolled her eyes. With that attitude, she wouldn't learn anything about how to behave with a suspect trying to dominate her.

She was also testing his authority. Yes, she was angry, but she'd broken her engagement to roll the dice with him again. Deep down, she knew it, even if she wasn't ready to admit it.

But if she wanted to work, the first thing he was going to do was put a stop to her shitty attitude—quickly.

He grabbed her wrist and turned her around, thrusting his hand into the silky length of that fiery red hair. Fuck, he wanted to slide his tongue along her skin, his cock deeper into her body than any man ever had, and stay there until she acknowledged who she belonged to.

Taking a calming breath, Logan released her and sat on the bed, then pulled her naked backside across his lap.

Tara stiffened. "You're not abusing my ass again, you bastard! *Romeo!*"

He smoothed a hand across her firm, pale cheeks as he held her struggling form. Tara was topping from the bottom. But in case she was actually scared, he paused.

"Am I going to hurt you past what you can bear? Make you bleed? Permanently mark you?"

"No, but I—"

"Do you fear for your physical safety?"

She sighed. "No."

"No what? Rephrase your answer."

A long pause later, she grumbled, "No, I don't fear for my physical safety, Logan."

"I've barely touched you, but I've pushed you beyond what you can endure?"

Tara didn't answer, just wriggled, trying to displace his hold on her.

Logan held her steady across his lap. "Stay still and answer the question."

With a huff, she stilled. "I don't like being spanked."

"Had a lot of experience with it, have you?"

"What you did yesterday was—"

"Not meant to pleasure you. It was meant to punish. I told you that. Now I'll show you the difference."

"If I said no, you'd do it anyway. If I told you to fuck off, you'd only add more. At least the safe word stops you."

"It does, but if you can't take a spanking or a little mind fuck, how will you save Darcy or succeed on this mission? If a training exercise scares you this much, then I can't let you proceed any further."

Her back went ramrod straight. "I'm *not* scared. You just . . . annoy me."

Annoy wasn't the right word; he got under her skin. This emotional block was one they had to get past. She could probably learn to submit for this assignment, but these walls she thrust between them wouldn't fly if they were going to progress as a couple. "So you're giving me a red light because you're annoyed with me. Is that what a safe word is for? How do you think that's going to work undercover?"

Her fists clenched, and Logan heard her curse under her breath. Time to pull out his ace in the hole. "I'm scheduled to chat with Thorpe and Bocelli later this afternoon. Cherry, if you can't do this, then you're in over your head. You have a submissive nature, but mentally, you're not allowing yourself to give up control so that you can learn—and get—what you need. I'll ask Bocelli if he can think of another agent who could pull off the case. I'm in town for another ten days, so I can train—"

"Don't you dare," she snarled.

The situation was serious, but Logan had to work to suppress his smile. He knew Cherry. Yeah, she didn't want to give up this assignment, but she really didn't like the idea of him training another woman. Whether she knew it or not, by giving up her fiancé and refusing to let another woman take her place in his dungeon, Tara was telling him that he mattered to her.

"I'll dare if I think you're not ready. So either admit that you can't handle this case or take the punishment you've earned."

Tara didn't say anything for a long moment. Finally, she drew in an angry breath. "The thirteen swats I had left over from yesterday? Should I count them, Logan?"

He smiled and refrained from a rousing fist pump. "Yes. And I'm adding another seven for your generally bad attitude and leaving without permission. Get ready."

"Fine." Her entire body tensed, as if bracing for a mortal blow.

Logan caressed her ass again. She'd find this spanking much different than yesterday's. This one would push her to the brink until she begged for more.

* * *

A strange curl of anticipation writhed in Tara's belly as Logan braced one palm on the back of her thigh—a gentle reminder of who was in charge—and lifted the other hand to deliver a light smack to the middle of her right cheek. A little sting spread over her flesh with a sizzle.

That was it? No terrible blow? No awful pain? She wanted to ask, but didn't. Quickly, the sting dissipated. She found herself almost . . . disappointed.

"One." Tara spoke the number more like a question, feeling decidedly off guard.

Then she waited. So did Logan. As long seconds ticked by, she wondered what the hell he was up to. Tara fought off the urge to look over her shoulder. Instead, she bit her lip and forced herself to remain still.

Finally, he raised his hand, this time smacking her left cheek lower, with a bit more force.

"Two," she counted with more confidence as the slight tingle flitted across her ass again, then slowly faded. Tara squirmed, trying to extend the sensation, but it didn't work.

The good news was, she'd easily make it through twenty of these.

"Is there a problem?"

She wriggled again, but the sweet ache was gone. Instead, a more insistent one had taken up residence between her thighs. And she was getting wet. Damn it.

"No problem."

"Then hold still and take the rest of your punishment."

Bastard. Tara scowled and held her breath.

Lifting his hand again, Logan rained a series of swats across her ass—on her right thigh, high on her left cheek, over the line that bisected her cheeks.

The sizzle heated up again, a little faster and harder. A little hotter. She closed her eyes to enjoy the burn seeping through her.

"Cherry?"

"Three, four, five."

"Good." He stroked her ass, the heat of his palms intensifying the crackling warmth.

Her breathing was a bit heavier now, her voice shakier. No doubt, he heard it, too. She wanted to hang on to her fury, but she was finding it more difficult to concentrate on anything except her anticipation of Logan's next slap. His movements had a rhythm Tara couldn't escape. Lured by the cadence, she sank into sensation.

"Feeling warm back here, Cherry?" He rubbed his palm over the fading sting of her right thigh, and the friction of his skin sliding against hers did something to Tara that she didn't understand. The sensations felt almost dreamlike. The peace of it lulled her.

"Yes."

"You finding a little place in your head to sink into?"

How had he known?

"It's called subspace," he offered. "All submissives go there when they're getting what they want and need. It's their happy place. Get cozy, baby. You'll be spending a lot of time there."

Before she could ask what he meant, he rained down another series of blows on her tender ass, each a bit more forceful than the last. A slow fire began to burn. Everything between her hips and her knees throbbed, especially her pussy. With the slaps ringing in her ears and the prickling heat quivering across her skin, she lost count of his blows.

"Cherry, where are we? How many?"

She blinked and realized that she'd zoned out looking at the concrete floor and feeling the erotic rhythm of his hand striking her, skin on skin.

"Six, seven, eight, nine."

He smacked the side of her thigh. "Focus. That was six through ten. Do I need to start over?"

"No, Logan." But she swallowed at the thought of staying here, pinned helplessly across his lap while he heaped one slap after another across her tender buttocks. She should hate his guts, but imagining that he might continue to spank her to his satisfaction made her impossibly hot and wet.

Suddenly, he thrust a hand between her legs, his fingers sliding through her copious juices to brush across her clit. She gasped and tried to twist away. No luck. He circled the sensitive nub once, twice. Tara couldn't hold in her moan.

"You going to tell me now that you don't like to be spanked?"

She bit her lip. How could she be aroused so completely by someone who'd broken her heart in the past and done his part to ruin her future? Then again, she had no way to lie. Given her very fair skin, she was going to bruise. And yet knowing he'd leave his mark on her somehow turned her on more.

"Cherry, I asked you a question."

"No," she choked. "I'm not going to tell you that I don't like it."

Beneath her, Tara felt Logan's whole body relax. Did her feelings really matter to him?

Gently, he glided his palm down her spine, over her warmed ass, as he pressed a soft kiss between her shoulder blades. She had to remind herself that his tenderness was a lie.

"Thank you for your honesty," he said softly. "I know that was difficult for you."

Very. And she didn't want to give him anymore ammunition, so she said nothing.

Logan stroked a hand down her hair, then cradled her head in his palm with one hand. With the other, he started raining down a series of blows again.

"Keep counting, baby," he crooned.

"Eleven, twelve, thirteen . . ." The numbers poured out automatically, but the rest of her body was anything but machinelike. The fire spreading over her skin became a blaze burning through her blood. As her body revved up, her brain shut down. And the pain dazzled. It stripped her bravado, her barriers, until it poured into her very soul—then back out again. The hurts that had bruised her heart, both now and then, welled up and swirled together with the inferno of her backside to break her apart. Tears pooled, overflowed, slid down her cheeks.

She should be pissed, fighting and screaming being treated like a naughty child. Instead, she murmured "twenty" and prayed like hell that he wouldn't leave her like this, alone, aching for release, and spread wide open emotionally. He'd driven her to a place so frighteningly personal.

"Good." Logan lifted her to face him. He searched her watery eyes and teary face, then yanked her against his chest. "Cherry . . ."

Tara knew that she shouldn't do it, but the concern and warmth on his face drew her in. She *needed* comfort—from him. The why of that didn't compute. He was the one who had helped to ruin her future, then spanked her into this hot mess. But for some reason, she knew only he could put her back together.

"Shh." He cuddled her close, soothing her with a soft touch to her hair, down her back. "You did really well, baby."

"No," she sobbed. "I—I have to get control. This is un-p-professional."

And it was humiliating to admit that, despite everything, Logan could still make her want him more than any other man.

Somewhere in that alpha male head of his, she feared that he'd labeled her not just a challenge, but the ultimate one. The one who got away. Other than the one time he'd knocked on her door a few years back and she'd slammed it in his face, he'd never contacted her after their breakup. Now, he sought to seduce the little lovesick twit back to his bed. She'd become his personal Mount Everest. Clinging to him made her feel stupid.

"Cherry, we've covered this. Your response is honest, and that's what I need from you. You want to come?"

Yes. Desperately. And what kind of girl got off on having her ass smacked, especially by a guy trying to fuck her over for a second time?

Tara resisted answering, wanting so badly to keep clinging to his neck, drawing in his musky earth scent . . . and avoiding that question. Instead, she pulled away, letting her arms fall to her sides.

Logan shot her a stern glance. "Be honest. Did you want to come?"

"I . . ." She squeezed her eyes shut, then forced herself to face the truth. "Yes, Logan."

He kissed her softly in reward. "Really good, baby. Soon. What else did you feel?"

How could she explain it? She shook her head. "Like a bunch of feelings welled up inside me. With every swat, there was physical pain, but somehow that released more of it inside me."

"Pain you've been holding on to?"

"I guess." She shrugged, playing it off. "I'm more emotional today since I lost a fiancé."

He clasped her head in his hands and drew her gaze squarely to his. "Cherry, if he'd been really important to you, you'd still be with him now, trying to patch up your engagement, not here falling into subspace for me. Think about that tonight for me. Please."

Tara blinked at him. God, was he right? She tried to wipe the emotion off her face, but feared that she was failing.

"And now I have something else to tell you." He caressed her back, his face full of regret. "When you left, you forgot your phone. Bocelli couldn't reach you, so he called Thorpe."

Her stomach clenched with fear. She grabbed Logan. "Please tell me that Darcy isn't . . ."

"Not that we know." He soothed her shoulder with a light touch. "But the first submissive to disappear, Laken Fox? A fisherman off the coast of Key West found her body, bound, tortured, and strangled, early this morning."

Chapter Seven

Tara felt the bottom fall out of her stomach. God, she was going to be sick.

"Th-They killed her? I thought their plans were to sell submissives and . . ."

Logan nodded, looking pensive. "Based on the fact that they found her in the U.S., I don't think the victim had been sold yet. And given the description of her corpse, I'd say someone lost patience during the training or likes to play way outside the boundaries of the safe, sane, and consensual. These people are beyond hard core, Cherry. If you're going to pursue this case—and I wish to hell you wouldn't—then you have to set aside everything. You can't hold back with me."

Fear tasted brackish in her mouth, but Tara had no doubt about the resolution beating inside her. No way was she leaving Darcy or any other woman to suffer. No way was she giving up on this case. This had gone way beyond pleasing Adam or serving some uncertain ambition of being a field agent, and into crusading. She *needed* to save these victims.

Logan was right; she had to step up to the plate. Kidnapping and sex trafficking was terrible enough, but adding torture and murder upped the stakes. No matter how she felt about Logan personally or his motives, the last twenty-four hours had taught her that she'd be hard-pressed to hide her true responses from a well-trained Dom. Learning to submit was necessary for her mission. And if she was brutally honest, being submissive was filling some void inside her that she hadn't wanted to acknowledge. It scared the crap out of her, and she'd been fighting Logan from the second she'd hit his dungeon door. Now, she didn't have that luxury.

"Point taken," she agreed. "I'll focus completely on learning."

Both relief and pride crossed his face as he brushed a hand over her cheek. "Excellent, Cherry. You're so damn brave."

Tara swallowed. She didn't want to think about how good his approval made her feel. As Brad had pointed out, Logan had wreaked a lot of misery on her life. If she was going to truly submit to him, then she had to put that out of her head. But she had to protect herself somehow. Otherwise, she wouldn't make it through this training with her heart intact.

"You have to promise me something."

He cocked his head. "Tell me, and I'll consider it."

"I'll give you everything I've got. No more fighting or holding back. No pretending that submitting to you doesn't arouse me. I'll give you total honesty sexually. In exchange, once this mission is over, you'll walk away and never seek me out again. If those terms aren't acceptable, I believe my stepfather is still in contact with Admiral Pierce, who can revoke your leave immediately," she bluffed. "What's it going to be?"

* * *

LOGAN stared at his clever little Cherry. Getting angry would be easy—and pointless. If he didn't agree to her deal, he'd likely be back in some third world shithole by tomorrow, fighting tangos, which would pave the way for another Dom to train her.

Fuck, no.

Logan set her aside on the silken sheets and rose, scrubbing a harsh hand down his face. Talk about topping from the bottom. Either he refused her deal and gave her up now, or he took his chances and hoped that in their remaining time together, he could both teach her what she needed to know and recapture her heart. No contest.

"All right." He grabbed her chin, forcing her gaze up to his. "But I need your complete cooperation to get this done, so I have terms of my own: if you push back even once, if you lie or fail to trust me, the deal is off."

"Fine." She bristled.

"Make no mistake, Cherry. If that happens, once this mission is over, I *will* come after you hard, with everything I've got."

Tara jerked her chin from his grasp and glared, clearly trying to understand his motivation. If he hadn't known her well, he would have missed the curiosity and confusion she tried like hell to bury. He wished she'd just ask; he'd be more than happy to tell her why he'd cut her loose years ago. He'd gladly admit that he still loved her so much that it hurt. But she didn't trust him yet. That stunt he'd pulled with Brad earlier today hadn't helped his cause. Logan knew that if he blurted his feelings now, she likely wouldn't believe him. And why should she? It wasn't like he'd been at her door every day, trying to win her back. No, he'd been trying, in his way, to move on, just as she had.

She glared, then nodded once. "All right. But I need to speak with Bocelli before it gets any later on the East Coast. I have a sparring appointment with Agent York at six, then dinner with my stepfather at seven thirty. Somewhere between all of that, I need to find a place to stay, since I moved my things out of Brad's house."

She'd been living with the asshole? It probably shouldn't have shocked Logan, but her words were a blow to his gut.

"You can stay with me."

Tara just shook her head. "That's not a good idea. Misty said she knew of some decent nearby motels. I'll start there. It won't interfere with work."

"If that's the way you want it. But you're not leaving this dungeon before five today. I have something planned for you this afternoon. In fact, we've got a lot to cover before you're ready, so we'll be putting in long hours. For the rest of the week, we'll start at oh six hundred."

"Fine," she bit out.

Logan let out a breath, tried to stay focused. All he could think about was picking Cherry up and throwing her in his truck, taking her to his condo, to his bed—where he'd never taken any woman— then strapping her down and getting deep inside her. So fucking deep, she'd never forget the way he filled her up.

God damn it, what irony. He'd refused a string of subs who'd assumed that giving him sex would please him. He finally found one he was dying for, and he couldn't have her.

At least not yet.

While she spent tonight dealing with all the crap in her life, he'd get his head screwed on straight. And plan. His time with Cherry was limited, so he had to pull out all the stops to show her how he felt. He'd do his fucking best to ensure that by the end of the week there was no way she could fail on this mission—and no way she'd ever again deny that he was in her heart.

* * *

"STAND for me," Logan commanded.

Without a word or a moment's hesitation, Tara rose to her feet before him, hands behind her back, breasts outthrust, defiant stare glued to his.

"Careful with your attitude," he warned, voice silky. "Ever heard of edge play?"

"I have." She struggled to retrieve the information from her brain with Logan's unnerving gaze on every naked inch of her. "It can mean activities on the 'edge' of the safe, sane, consensual, like breathplay or cutting."

"Right. That's a hard limit for many, including me, so we won't go there. I'm talking about a different sort of edge."

Moments later, Logan punched in his security code to the dungeon door. Tara looked up to see another man saunter inside.

He was tall, with dark hair, and eyes somewhere between green and gold. Hispanic? Italian? His bronzed complexion bespoke some exotic race. When he entered, he'd looked bored. The second his eyes latched on to her, they lit up like he'd found a fascinating new toy and couldn't wait to play.

Tara raised her arms, intent on crossing them over her chest.

"Stop," Logan demanded, his voice low.

Body taut, she forced herself to drop her hands to her sides.

Logan nodded his praise. "This is my friend and fellow Dom, Xander."

"What's he doing here?"

"Normally, I wouldn't answer that question for a sub, but since we're training for a mission, I'll explain. In the BDSM world, it's considered polite to share your subs with other Doms. Agent York may be called upon while you're undercover to let others touch you. You have to get used to the idea that it will both happen and that you'll have absolutely no control. Now, present yourself to us."

A thousand thoughts swirled through her head. Anger and shock that Logan wanted another man to look at her. To touch her? He'd just done everything possible to remove Brad from her life.

But he also had to prepare her for whatever might happen undercover.

Tara refused to reveal her anxiety or renege on their deal, so she merely nodded and did as Logan demanded, sliding onto the cold concrete on her knees in front of them both. Xander looked at every inch of her bare skin, just as Logan had ordered her to let him.

"She's gorgeous." Xander's deep voice slid over her skin, and she tingled with the sincerity in those words.

"Cherry always has been."

Warmth sang in Logan's tone. The whole situation was twisted, but for some reason, hearing his desire and pride made her hopelessly wet.

"She's also smart and prickly sweet," Logan added. "And submissive."

"Lucky bastard," Xander murmured. "May I?"

"Go. I'll direct."

Before Tara could wonder what their exchange meant, Xander held out a hand. What did they expect? She cast Logan a questioning glance.

"She already looks to you," Xander said, clearly impressed. "You've made a lot of progress in barely twenty-four hours."

"We have a lot more to go," Logan replied, then turned to her. "Put your hand in his, Cherry. Do whatever he asks unless I say otherwise. Do you understand?"

"O-Okay, Logan." She laid her fingertips across Xander's rough palm. His skin was burning hot. He smelled like cut wood and rain and something very male. Without a word, he helped her to her feet and guided her toward the bed.

Logan crossed his arms over his chest, watching. Knowing that he wasn't too far away was somehow comforting, even if his next words weren't. "Strap her down, wrists and ankles."

Tara's immediate response was to protest, but she bit it back and forced herself to examine her reaction. The command caused a pulse of sensation behind her clit and it scared her. She hated to admit that. But she'd promised honesty and couldn't squirm away from it. If she allowed Xander to do as Logan had ordered, it would make her utterly vulnerable to them. It would also arouse her more. Somehow, Logan knew that.

"What's going on, Logan?"

"You don't get to ask that, Cherry. Unless you're pushing back?"

"I'm not."

Tara took a breath, willed herself to remain calm. Then Xander's large hand all but swallowed hers as he led her to the black silk sheets, melting her composure. With her heart racing, she clenched her fist. Gently, Xander squeezed back in reassurance.

"I won't hurt you," he whispered.

No, but he'd push her way beyond her comfort zone. And Logan would tell him exactly how to do it. And as much as it discomfited her to admit it, that thought made her flushed and faint.

All too quickly, they reached the bed. Xander helped her onto the mattress, then secured her ankles with Velcro straps at each corner. She squeezed her eyes shut for a moment, achingly aware of her naked sex.

Sitting back on his heels, Xander spread her thighs wider with searing palms and stared directly at her pussy. Lust narrowed his dark-lashed hazel eyes. He reached out, rubbed a thumb directly over her slick clit.

The shock of arousal stung her. Her body bucked.

"Hmm," Xander murmured. "I love bare pussy, but I can see why you haven't shaved hers. With this deep red fringe and pink flesh, she's like a jewel."

Logan edged closer, brushed a hand over her aching nipple, her cheek. "I could spend a whole day playing with her, touching, toying, tasting, watching her come over and over."

Tara gasped. Logan's words turned her inside out. Being held down helplessly as he teased her with his fingers and lips, teeth, and tongue, all for the purpose of giving her unending pleasure . . . Need tightened her body.

Unable to keep her reaction in, she moaned.

"Nice," Logan praised. "That's an honest response."

She bit her lip. *Too honest.*

Xander ran a finger through her very wet pussy. "She definitely likes that idea."

"Remember, Cherry, no coming unless I say so." He turned to Xander. "Blindfold her."

Xander grinned as he went to the cabinet in the corner and came back toward her with something that looked like a black, lacy sleep mask.

She struggled, shaking her head. "I need to see what's happening."

"Remember your promise. You get no say in this scene, so you don't need to know anything. I'm calling the shots."

"If I can't see, how will I understand the point of this exercise," she improvised.

The truth was, being blindfolded and touched by both of them excited her and scared her spitless at once.

A sexy smile lifted Logan's lips. "Trust me, you'll get the point quickly. Xander, go."

All too quickly, the mask settled over her eyes, and Tara was plunged into darkness. Immediately, she worked to tamp down her panic and focused in on her other senses. The cold air grazing her hard nipples and the wet folds of her heated flesh. Xander's breath on her face as he hovered. The tangy taste of apprehension in her mouth. The rustling of clothing as Xander moved away, then returned. He brushed a thumb over her clit once, twice. The need in her belly twisted tighter. Again, he pulled away. A few moments later, a mechanical humming buzzed—just before he settled something that vibrated directly over her clit. It gave her a jolt of pleasure.

"Oh God," she cried out.

"Is he hurting you?" Logan asked.

Xander moved the little device to one side of her clit, then another, awakening more nerves. Just when his stimulation of that spot made her desire spiral, he eased back over the hood and started the cycle all over again. He moved the toy around until the fire engulfed not just her greedy nerve-filled nub, but her very skin and blood. Tara's sex clenched with aching emptiness. Every time Xander eased that little rubbery device over her, he made her arch, gasp, burn just a little bit more.

"Is he?" Logan demanded.

What was the question? Damn, she couldn't recall, could only drown in desire.

"Is he hurting you?" Logan snapped. "I'm not going to ask again."

"N-No." She was panting now. There was no denying that orgasm was mere seconds away—all the more potent because Logan had demanded that a stranger, his friend, make her body want it.

Even so, some part of her didn't want to climax for Xander. Instead, she wanted to beg Logan to touch her and drive her to ecstasy in his arms. It made no sense to want the conniving bastard, but the thought pushed her even closer to the edge. God, just another second . . .

"Stop," Logan demanded.

Instantly, Xander lifted the device from her clit, then settled two stationary fingers over her plush, sensitive flesh. She shuddered, mewled.

"It's hard and shuddering," Xander said as if that excited the hell out of him.

Then his warm touch left her. The slide of leather told her that he'd stepped back.

"Excellent." Logan sounded vastly pleased.

Later, she'd want to die of shame and clobber him, but now she ached too much. What sort of game was he playing? Trying to prove that he controlled her orgasm, and therefore, controlled her? The whole thing was so caveman . . . but knowing that she was helpless for him, that he would only give her pleasure when he deemed it, made her dangerously excited.

"No more." She shook her head from side to side.

"We're just getting started," Logan vowed.

Xander—funny how she could already tell them apart—laughed in amusement.

The pair of them stepped away from the bed, their low voices unintelligible. Her body protested, clamoring for another touch, a bit more friction. Instead, a squeak, a whoosh, from her left. They'd opened the door to the cabinet in the corner again. What the hell else did Logan keep in there?

Tara feared that she was about to find out.

Moments later, Xander stepped close again. She could tell from his scent. He leaned in, brushed his lips against the skin between her shoulder and the swell of her breast. She gasped. It didn't feel either good or bad, but rather shocked her with sensation.

Suddenly, there was a rustle of cloth, a *thump*, then Xander let loose a long-suffering sigh. Tara had no idea what to make of that. But she felt Xander approach again and braced herself. She could almost feel Logan watching intently.

This time, something cool and rubbery traced the wet, swollen lips of her pussy, coating it with her cream. Then Xander slipped it inside her. Plastic also touched her clit. Tara held her breath, not sure what to expect.

Her friends all talked about sex toys being a single girl's best friend. Tara had never invested in any. Now she was paying the price because she had no idea what this thing was or what Xander planned to do.

She held her breath.

There was a little click, a nudge of the slippery gadget deeper into her. Then the torturous pleasure began. The little bit of plastic nestled against her clit began to vibrate, working the already stimulated bundle. Worse, this toy feathered across a sensitive spot inside the clasp of her pussy, and the second she felt that startling pleasure, she clamped down and cried out.

"That's it," Xander encouraged. "Oh, she likes having her G-spot stimulated. This is going to be fun."

His voice rang with a naughty glee that made Tara both want more and fear more.

"Stick to the plan." Logan sounded like he was gritting his teeth.
What plan?

"All right." Xander sounded glum.

He began to rock the toy against all her most sensitive spots, a gentle back and forth that hyperfocused her pleasure until she gasped and arched and cried out. Helplessly, Tara clenched her fists, her body bowing as the need for orgasm stacked up into unrelieved torture. She bit her lip, trying desperately to keep herself together. Logan had forced Xander to stop last time her mewl had given her imminent orgasm away. Maybe if she stayed mute, he wouldn't notice until it was too late.

The sensations crept up, wrenching, tightening, pounding through her. Her heart raced. She couldn't keep the muscles of her shoulders, thighs, and butt from tensing. Almost there . . .

"Stop," Logan demanded.

Xander snapped off the device.

"No!"

"You won't be sneaking in an orgasm, Cherry. I ought to spank you for trying."

"Don't do this." The plea was out of her mouth before she could stop it.

"What do you think I'm doing, exactly?" Logan asked.

Xander pulled the toy from the clinging depths of her body. In its place, his fingers slid through the slippery flesh between her legs, hovering near her clit, rubbing all around it, but never over it, never giving her enough stimulation to do anything but make her aware that they held her body—and her pleasure—in their hands.

"You're keeping me on edge."

"Yep. It's a facet of edge play. I could do this all day, baby. How about you?"

Oh God, he was going to leave her like this, a pleading mass of nerves and need until she begged. "Bastard! You're punishing me."

"For walking out on me without permission or a single god damn word, maybe."

And maybe she ought to be asking herself why she responded to this. Yes, Xander was exciting her body through the clever use of toys, but that wasn't what aroused her half as much as knowing that Logan controlled her pleasure. Tara sensed that, as her desire grew frantic, his also rose to a fever pitch. *That* flipped her switch. What the hell did it mean?

After setting the toy down with a soft tap on the bedside table,

Xander again walked away. This time, Logan stayed rooted in place. Tara felt his stare burn all over her. Her skin flared with heat, her breasts tightened, her clit tingled. God, with him looking at her, desiring her, she wasn't coming off this arousal high.

"I get it," she insisted. "Someone else is going to touch me. I've proven that I'm not a shrinking violet since Xander put his hand between my legs and I didn't flinch."

"That's not the only purpose. A well-trained sub holds her orgasm until she's given permission to release it, when it will please her Master most. Yesterday, you screamed and pleaded and came almost the moment I put my mouth on your pussy."

She flushed. "Thanks for sharing that with Xander."

"Privacy and modesty don't belong in a BDSM club. Some Doms won't tolerate you coming without permission. If you want to save Agent Miles and do this job properly, start focusing and stop worrying about what you can't control. Are we clear?"

Again, Logan reminded her to closet the anger she felt toward him and focused her on her purpose. She'd promised to let go and she needed to live up to her end of the bargain.

"Yes, Logan."

"Good girl. Xander?"

Instantly, Tara tensed. Round three; here it came. With her blindfold on, she had no idea what to expect. She shivered in both fear and anticipation, focusing on getting out of her body and head, and just letting whatever was going to happen, happen.

A wet tongue rolled over her taut nipple. Xander's. The little point tightened even more. Tara breathed through the sensation, then again when he took the whole nipple in the heat of his mouth and sucked until she gasped, fists clenched.

Slowly, Xander released the hard point, only to repeat the process with the other nipple while twisting the other between a firm thumb and forefinger.

Against her will, her back arched in a silent plea for more.

A second later, he lifted away. Before she could process her disappointment and thrill that Logan was still watching intently, she felt twin shots of pain, one wrenching each of her nipples.

Tara gasped. "Oh God. I don't . . . I can't . . ."

"Breathe through the pain," Logan demanded. "You can take it."

Was he insane? "No."

"Are you saying your safe word?"

She couldn't take the easy way out. "No."

"Then take the pain. For me."

God, for some twisted reason, those words melted her. She felt helpless in a way she never had. She could do nothing but accept what he chose to give her. And for some damn reason, she didn't want to let him down.

Since she couldn't change it, she let in the pain. Slowly, the bite rolled through her system, settling into a smooth throb. The hurt lashed her pussy with a direct jolt of fire. She cried out.

"Do you want to come?" Logan asked.

"Yes!"

"Rephrase."

"Yes, Logan! Please . . ."

A hand drifted over her stomach, fingers prowling lower until sure fingers slipped through her drenched folds and circled her clit. She knew by the touch and scent that it was Logan.

"Xander," Logan prompted him, but no other explanation was forthcoming.

He caressed her breasts, tugging gently on the clamps. Tara bucked, begged. They both petted her, keeping her just shy of climax.

Tears leaked from her eyes as her body felt like a building storm. So many sensations piled on top of emotions. She couldn't block them, couldn't process them, couldn't do anything but let them pour in.

Suddenly, Xander removed the clamps. Blood rushed back to her nipples in an uproar of tingles. And Logan's fingers toyed with her clit again. Tara thrust and wriggled, trying to manipulate more pressure where she needed it.

Logan stopped instantly, then spanked her pussy lightly with the pads of his fingers. "Stop moving. No coming."

Tara bit back a curse, nearly out of her mind with need. "What do you want from me?"

"Breathe, Cherry," he whispered in her ear. "I'll start with your submission. We'll talk about the rest later. Focus on holding back your orgasm."

She clenched everything inside her to stop the pending climax. The sensation was so intense, it was like physical pain. She tried to gulp in deep breaths, calm herself. Slowly, it worked.

Tara unclenched her fists and dug her nails out of her palms. She eased her butt and thighs back to the bed, then forced her shoulders against the silk sheets. Another long exhalation later she hoped—prayed—that she had it under control.

The rip of Velcro and the easing of her restraints told her that she was free. Xander removed her mask. Together, they rubbed her wrists and ankles.

After a long minute, Logan edged his way in front of her and took her face in his hands. "You okay now, Cherry? Breathing and calm?"

"That's it? You're not going to let me come?"

With a shake of his head, Logan retrieved the silk robe and tossed at her. As she scrambled into it, he glanced at his watch. She couldn't miss his tense shoulders and the sizeable erection behind his zipper.

"Training isn't always going to feel good. It's seventeen hundred. Go home. No masturbating or I'll know, and your ass will be redder than . . . well, a cherry. I'll see you bright and early tomorrow." He shifted his gaze to Xander. "Don't piss me off."

His exotic friend held up a hand. "Wouldn't dream of it. We'll talk when you're out of the shower."

"Fucker," Logan muttered, then hurried toward the door.

No way was she letting him leave her like this.

Fuming and aching all over, Tara charged after him and grabbed his granite arm. "What the hell kind of power trip is this?"

He raised an ominous brow at her. "I explained."

"I heard a lot of blah, blah, blah. Haven't you taken enough from me today? I lost my fiancé. God knows, you quickly stripped me of dignity. Because of you, I have no privacy. You don't allow me modesty. You shove everything on me. This is just about you having your sick pleasure, bending me—"

"Ohhh." Xander shook his head at her. "I'd run if I were you."

Tara stood her ground, tightening her grip on Logan's biceps. "I'm not going anywhere until he explains what the fuck he's trying to pull."

"I *explained.*" Logan enunciated each syllable with quiet bite. "You heard me. But that's not what you're pissed about. You're angry because I'm withholding this."

Before Tara could even blink, Logan scooped her up in his arms and stalked toward the bed, jaw clenched. Every muscle in his body felt tense. She had a feeling that she'd awakened the sleeping beast.

Her heart seized up in her chest. "Put me down!"

"You don't give the orders, Cherry." With that reminder, Logan plopped down on the bed, then turned her to face him, shoving her legs on either side of her hips. "I do. If you want this, scoot in."

She had no idea what he was up to, but the opportunity to be closer to him was a lure she knew she should resist, but couldn't. Bracing her hands on his shoulders, she moved her hips closer until her wet folds were nestled against the hard ridge of his cock.

"Wrap your arms around my neck."

Breath coming in pants, she slid her palms over his hard shoulders, then curled her arms around his nape. Their faces were inches apart, and the heat blaring from his eyes blasted her with something that made her stomach tighten, her pussy clench.

"What's you're safe word?" he barked.

"*R-Romeo.*"

"Yes. Either use it or rub that pretty pussy over my cock until you come."

Oh God, his actions became crystal clear in a second. He was forcing her to either deny that she wanted him or to use him to pleasure herself. No matter what she did, she was going to lose.

God damn it, wasn't that a metaphor for her whole relationship with Logan?

"Bastard," she hissed.

"Choose, Cherry. You've got three seconds."

Fury and desire had whipped her into a froth. She wanted him so badly that she hated him. But he'd always been like gravity for her; the pull to him was undeniable and inevitable.

Tara slanted her mouth over his and took his lips in a fierce kiss, rocking her aching clit directly over the thick stalk of his cock. She gasped into his mouth as need streamed through her body, lacing her veins. Logan met her tongue with his, fisting one hand in her hair.

She writhed like a wild thing, panting, straining, needing everything he could give her. And it wasn't enough yet. Mewling, she clawed at his back, desperate for the orgasm beckoning with frightening intensity just out of reach.

Suddenly, he ripped away from her kiss. "You want to come?"

God, she could barely focus through her haze of need. But those blue eyes were an inescapable lure; she couldn't look away from the hot demand slowly burning her alive.

"Yes," she gasped. "Please, give it to me."

"No. Take it." His eyes burned into her. "Take it now."

As if his words had been precisely what she needed, the wall of sensation flattened her. She screamed, then she couldn't breathe at all, just feel herself open wide to the pleasure pouring in.

And her soul pouring out.

As the deep pulses of her womb subsided, Tara stilled, sucked in a deep breath. Then she looked at Logan, as still as a statue, his face like a time bomb with a short fuse.

"Logan?"

"Did I take anything from you? Force anything on you?"

His questions made her feel small—and forced her to acknowledge the truth. Tears pricked her eyes, but she blinked them back. "No."

"Then I'll see you at oh six hundred." Logan pressed a hard, fast kiss to her lips, then set her down on the silk sheet beside him. She barely had time to notice the wet spot she'd left on the front of his leather pants before he stormed across the room, slamming the door behind him.

Tara watched Logan go, feeling as if she was watching a part of her walk away. He was angry; it felt painful. The tears returned. What the hell had happened? One minute she'd been furious with him. Then he'd forced her to admit her need, take what she craved— and torn her wide open again.

Xander laughed, a bemused expression lighting his face.

Tara belted the robe more tightly around her waist. "What's so funny, damn it?"

"I've never seen him so off balance. That orgasm was for you, you know. The normal Logan would have made a sub suffer to teach her a valuable lesson." He turned to her, cocking his head. "But he let you come because he couldn't stand to leave you hurting. God, you're . . . perfect for him. I'm laughing because he's going to the shower to think about you while he masturbates, as usual. But I don't think that ritual is going to stand much longer."

So much of Xander's speech startled Tara that she almost didn't know where to start. "You think that Logan thinks about me when he masturbates?"

"I *know* he does. Every day I've ever spent with him for the last five years."

"For the last—" *Impossible.*

She opened her mouth to sputter . . . she wasn't exactly sure what. Then she closed it. But the myriad of questions kept coming at her. "How would you know that he thinks about me?"

"He admitted it after a few too many shots of tequila. We've talked about it. I've even had the misfortune to walk into the bathroom and see it." Xander sent her a quizzical expression. "Have you seen his tattoos?"

"I—I saw the Japanese on his ribs."

"And you can't read it," Xander stated, quirking a dark brow.

"He told me it says 'never quit.'"

"And he's a fucking liar. Have you gotten a close look at him without his leathers?"

What was Xander trying to tell her? "No. He hasn't taken them off."

"Make him. I'll tell you something straight up: Logan hasn't had sex with a woman as long as I've known him."

Tara's jaw dropped. "No way. He spends a lot of time here and—"

"When he's on leave, yeah. He spanks the subs, works them up, makes them come. He never kisses them. And he definitely never fucks them. When he wants that done, he calls me."

Shock pinged through Tara's system. "Bullshit."

"Ask anyone here at Dominion." Xander sidled closer, dropped his voice. "Look, he's my friend, and I've been worried as hell about him for a long time. His behavior isn't normal. For a Dom, he's an awful lot like a monk."

It still wasn't adding up for her. She understood Xander's implication that Logan was hung up on her, but how was that possible? Logan had broken it off with her. Why would he be hung up on a relationship he'd ended so brutally? "I don't understand. Why tell me this?"

He shook his head. "I've pushed the door open a bit. Now you have to choose to walk through it. Or not."

After everything that had happened today, she couldn't take more mind games. "Logan left *me*. He crushed me and walked away without a backward glance when we were sophomores in high school. I make him feel guilty, but he doesn't actually care."

Xander shook his head. "For him, the sun rises and sets on you. If you decide to seek the truth, once you see and understand *all* of his tattoos, maybe you'll believe me."

Chapter Eight

Nearby motel—Friday night

HAIR wet from her recent shower, Tara combed her tresses with one hand and rifled through her suitcase absently with the other. She grabbed a cotton floral nightie from inside, stared at the duffel bag by her feet, then frowned. In the year she'd been living with Brad, this was all she had come away with? She'd walked in with the clothes on her back and walked out with the same. Everything in the house had been his when they'd moved in together. She'd never bought a stick of furniture with him. Hell, not even a toaster.

What did that say about their relationship? Had she unconsciously known that it wouldn't last?

Tara swallowed as she flipped the lid of the suitcase closed and shoved on her pajamas. She poured more wine into one of the hotel's cheap plastic cups and grimaced. By far, she preferred tequila for a good, rousing drunk, but being in a part of town that only allowed beer and wine sales, she'd had to make do. After half the bottle, however, she couldn't say that she felt any better.

Not that she felt bad exactly, just somewhat numb. And that was the problem. On a day she'd come twice for a man she had refused to miss in years and the case she worked on being complicated by a dead body, not to mention the fact that she'd lost her fiancé, she should feel *something*. But Tara wondered now if she'd been truly feeling for years.

Everything came back to Logan. Somehow, over the miles and years, he'd continued his hold on her without a single touch. Now suddenly, he was back in her life. In fact, he was the center of her world this week. Could she make it to the next without losing her heart again?

She wanted to talk to Logan, ached to ask him questions. But that wasn't smart. What if the truth made her want him more? If she embraced him now, how broken would she be if he walked away again? After everything he'd taken from her today, and, damn him, given her, she wasn't ready for any sort of soul baring. Tears lurked under the surface of her haze; she could feel them. Just like her adolescent self, she couldn't seem to hold anything back from him. Logan was her downfall, probably always would be.

Tara downed the rest of the wine in her cup. Damn, she wished this stuff would work faster.

A boom blasted through her room, startling her. Someone was pounding on her door.

No one knew she was here, not even Adam. Her stepfather would not be pleased with today's developments. He thought Brad was perfect, and Logan was Satan's spawn, so she'd bailed on dinner with her stepfather tonight, not having the energy to explain herself and defend her actions. So who the hell wanted in her room at nearly ten p.m.?

She tiptoed to the door and peeked out the hole. Logan, wearing all black and carrying a grocery sack packed full. For a moment, she debated not opening the door, but he already knew she was inside. He wasn't going to go away.

With a sigh, Tara pulled the door open, then leaned against it. "Why are you here?"

"I'm a Dom; it's my job to take care of you."

That was the last damn thing she wanted to hear. "Only when we're working. Otherwise, I can take care of myself. You've already been up in my face for most of the day. I don't need you here tonight, too, ordering me around and—"

"I'm not here to tell you what to do, Cherry." He gripped the bag tighter. "I just came to bring you a few things, see what else you needed."

Without another word, he held out the bag to her. Curiosity got the better of her, and she grabbed it. A peek inside revealed some bottled water, toothbrush and toothpaste, dental floss, shampoo, and a comb.

She looked at him with a questioning gaze, and he shrugged. "I wasn't sure if you'd been able to get anything from Brad's house, and I didn't like the thought of you shopping at night by yourself, especially around here."

Against her better judgment she was touched. "I managed to get all my things from his house, but thank you. Come in."

As she stepped back, he edged inside, looking around at the run-down dump. He scowled. "This is . . . No, Cherry, come stay with me. I promise, I won't touch you if you don't want me to, but you—"

"Will be fine." Tara marveled that he seemed genuinely concerned as she set the grocery bag on a nearby Formica table. "I know it's not the Ritz, but Misty said the place was reputable enough. I've got lots of locks on the doors and bolts on the windows. No one is getting in here to hurt me."

Logan blew out a deep breath, clearly pensive. "This is another reason I wish I was your Dom. I could just tell you to come with me so I could sleep beside your warm body peacefully, knowing that you're safe."

Another reason? "I *am* an FBI agent, you know."

"But you're also a beautiful woman in a world with a lot of predators."

She softened again. "I'm fine. Really."

"Yeah. And smart and capable. This visit was for my peace of mind. Thanks for humoring me."

"You're really different away from the club."

Logan shrugged, his smile self-deprecating. "I'm not a twenty-four/seven kind of Dom. In the club, subs better not fuck with me or there's going to be punishment. Outside the club? I'm just a guy, with other concerns and thoughts . . . and regrets."

He was going to get personal, and a part of her didn't want to stop him.

Her hand shook as she poured herself another glass of wine, then held up the bottle. "Drink?"

"No, thanks. I won't overstay my welcome." Logan turned for the door.

Tara didn't examine the feeling, but she knew that she wasn't ready to see him go. "Logan?"

He turned. "You need something, baby?"

Before she could talk herself out of it, she nodded. "Answers."

She settled herself on the edge of the bed, then watched as he folded his big form into an ugly green plastic chair with sleek economy of movement.

"I'm wide open."

God, where the hell should she begin? It had been an eventful day by any standards, but the information Xander had dumped on her late this evening gnawed at her brain. How much of what he'd said was true?

"What does the tattoo on your ribs *really* say? I know what you told me but . . ."

"That's not important." He dipped his head, looked away. "What happened in high school is. Don't you want to know about that?"

In the past twelve years, she'd sworn that she had gotten over Logan. Now she knew she'd been fooling herself. Brad had accused her of giving him up for Logan. He'd been right. Logan had reminded her what it was like to truly feel and want and hurt again. The avalanche of emotion had smacked her hard. Had she, maybe, not built much of a life with Brad because she'd been subconsciously waiting for her withered relationship with Logan to blossom to life again?

It sounded absurd on the surface—but Tara couldn't deny that his pull still lured her in like no man ever had.

Eventually, she'd have to listen to his explanation, but she wanted this conversation on her terms. "Do you have other tattoos?"

He pinned her with a cautious look. "Yeah. I'm in the navy, and I've been drunk overseas more than once."

"You regret them?"

His somber stare wiped away any levity. "No. Cherry, ask me about our breakup."

He'd promised that he wouldn't explain until she asked him, and he was trying to live up to his word. Tara bit her lip. What if there was some explanation for everything? What if it was something that made her want to forgive him? After the magnitude of his betrayal years ago, did she want to? She was damn sure that it would be easier—and safer to her heart—to go on being angry with him.

But maybe, a voice whispered in her head, it was no longer realistic.

"Is it true that you haven't had sex in the last five years?"

"God damn Xander," Logan cursed, closing his eyes. "What didn't he tell you?"

"If what he said is true, he didn't hold much back."

He rose, paced, stared out the window into the shabby parking lot. A moment later, he seemed to come to some decision and turned back to her. "Yeah, it's true. Even before then, sex had become . . . infrequent."

When Xander had spilled this secret, Tara had been sure the guy was insane. To hear Logan fess up to this absolutely blew her mind. "Why? In high school, you loved sex. If those rumors were true, you had a lot of it."

"I don't know exactly what you heard back then, but yeah. I took advantage of the fact that I was the J.V. quarterback and the tallest guy in my class. I figured out quick that if you could make a girl feel special for a moment, then it wasn't too hard to get her horizontal."

Tara grimaced. "God, you sound like a pig."

Logan shrugged, the black T-shirt lovingly hugging his wide shoulders and muscled chest. "I was sixteen. I'm sure I was a pig. Then came you."

She rolled her eyes. "It was a long time ago, and I don't think for one minute that I had any lasting effect on you. You fell right back into bed with Brittany Fuller a few hours after we broke up."

"I was drunk, and I was angry." He swallowed. "Afterward, I felt really empty. When she left . . . I cried."

She reared back, looking up into his taut face. She'd expected to see him laugh, but Logan was dead serious. Shock pinged through her body.

"The pattern sort of repeated itself a lot for the next few years. I'd meet a random girl, pick her up hoping she could bring me out of my funk. At first, I'd realize how lousy I felt *after* the sex. Then the feeling began to hit me in the middle. I got a lot of girls off, then sent them on their way, leaving them to wonder why I hadn't finished fucking them." He shrugged. "Masturbating was easier, less emotional.

"Then I found BDSM and met Mitchell Thorpe. A whole new avenue opened to me. I suddenly controlled everything. The females didn't expect sex. And I realized that I could absorb a sub's sexual energy and use it to propel me to my next self-induced orgasm. It worked."

"Logan . . ." God, such a damaged life broke her heart. Because of her? Really? Tara didn't know what to say.

He stepped closer and wrapped a hand around her nape, his hot touch searing her skin. "It worked until I saw you again. I never got over you. A week ago, I couldn't find a woman on the planet who could tempt me to want to have sex with her. One look at you—even before I knew it was you—and my first thought was of getting deep inside you and never leaving." He trailed his thumb down her cheek. "That's what I think every time I look at you, Cherry."

A whole new wave of shock reverberated through her body. The girl who had once loved him wanted to leap up, wrap her arms around him, and offer him whatever he needed to feel whole. The woman she'd become after he'd burned her wasn't sure how to believe him. He'd said that he loved her the day he took her virginity. Barely twenty-four hours later, he'd broken her heart and taken another girl to bed.

"We weren't together long enough for you to get that hung up on me, and I—"

"Yeah, we were." He closed his eyes. "And I think I left scars on you, too. Cherry, please, ask me why I broke up with you."

Tara trembled. The million-dollar question. If she asked it, she feared that everything would change, that the answer could throw her into a tailspin all over again. Being able to open up physically and emotionally to Brad had been a real step up for her. In college, she'd only managed drunk sex. Sober, she couldn't bring herself to let anyone touch her. But she'd broken through with Brad.

And now he was gone.

If she didn't get the answer to this question, would she remain in limbo, hung up on Logan forever? Maybe they both needed this to cleanse themselves of the past and move on.

That didn't mean that she wasn't scared as hell to hear the answer.

"A- All right, Logan. Tell me." Her voice broke up as tears welled. She was fucking terrified. "Why?"

"Thank you." He leaped on the bed, pushing her flat on her back and covering her body with his own. He pressed their foreheads together and drew in a deep breath.

"Logan . . ." He was so close, felt so good, that she couldn't breathe.

"Tara, I had to protect you. The sick fuck who'd killed my mother sent me more than one note threatening to kill you if I didn't walk away. Then when you showed up at school late that day with a broken arm . . ." Logan told the entire story, the words halting at first, as though recounting all this hurt him, but Tara could feel his will and his anguish as he explained.

When he was done, she blinked and tears filled her eyes. If he'd told her this story earlier, she would have tossed it back in his face angrily and called him a liar. She would have assumed it was some sob tale he'd spent years inventing, designed to dupe her into dropping her panties so he could get her into bed again. Now, looking at the torment tightening his face, she couldn't doubt that this was the truth as he knew it.

"Why didn't you tell the police? Or tell *me*?"

"There was no way I was going to risk you any further. You were beyond precious to me." He cupped her cheek. "I would have done anything to keep you safe, and at sixteen, I couldn't think of another way. Please understand."

Oddly, given the circumstances and their age, she did. And she was both touched and crushed by his words. All the time they'd never had together, all the things they'd never had the opportunity to do . . . The relationship may not have been one to last happily ever after. But how much pain would they have never experienced if it hadn't been for that note on his pillow and the relationship had come to its natural conclusion?

"Your mom was such a nice lady. I'm sorry. And the police never caught her killer?"

Logan shook his head with deep regret. "It's in cold-case status now. A new detective tried to tackle it about four years ago. He called my dad and me, checked with some of Mom's old neighbors, asked questions of the people she once worked for. Nothing. One of her neighbors said she thought she saw a man entering her apartment that afternoon, but she was elderly and a bit senile. My mother never mentioned a boyfriend, not to me, to her neighbors, or her coworkers. There were no prints at the scene, no DNA left behind. This psycho randomly chose my mother. The police have no record of any similar case, either." He squeezed his eyes shut and pain crawled all over his face. "I am never going to forget what it was like to drive to her house, so excited to tell her about us, then find her so still. Dead."

Her heart went out to Logan. It was a lot to deal with at sixteen. He'd been reeling, grief-stricken. A note like the one he'd received from the killer warning him away from her would have both scared and confused him. Tara couldn't blame him for the decisions he'd made then.

"Cherry, if I'd had my way, we would have stayed together, gone to prom as a couple, graduated hand-in-hand." He shrugged. "Built a life together."

A part of her really wanted to believe that, but after everything that had happened, she couldn't imagine that alternate universe. "Why didn't you ever try to tell me all this after your mom's case cooled down?"

"After you changed your cell, I only had your stepfather's home number."

And she'd always made Adam answer the phone and tell him off. "You could have come to see me."

"I tried. Remember a couple of Christmases ago? You slammed the door in my face."

She had. And now she regretted it like hell. "We'll never know the paths our lives would have taken if things had been different. I may be training to be a submissive. I may even have submissive tendencies. I don't know that I could live this life."

"You could, baby, under the right circumstances. It doesn't have to be in a club, if you don't like that setting. I just want to be with you. I'd vow to be the most loving Dom ever."

"Isn't that kind of an oxymoron? What, you'd boss me around in a tender way?" She raised a disbelieving brow.

"Yeah. Say the word, Cherry, and I'll show you exactly what I mean."

His words, along with his body heat settling under her skin, made her tremble. "I just lost a fiancé today, and there's been too much water under the bridge. Maybe . . . your hang-up isn't about me in particular. Is there another incident—"

"I know what happened. I know what's in my heart," he growled each word fiercely, fisting the cheap bedspread beneath her. "It was you. It's always been you."

Those words sounded so romantic, and the female in her really, really wanted to believe them. But they almost didn't compute. Yes, she'd pined for Logan, but him for her?

Oh, God. Her next confession was going to open her up wide, but he'd been so painfully honest, how could she be anything less? "I saw a therapist shortly after college. I went to him for a good two years. He suggested that my hang-up about you stemmed from the fact that our break was really sudden. He suggested that I simply needed to talk it all out and know the score—"

"No. I know what I need, what I've always needed." Logan wriggled his hips between the slight spread of her thighs, forcing them wider, until his cock settled right against her pussy. "Cherry, I need you."

Then he rocked against her, igniting her body with sensation to match all the emotions swirling inside her. Tara closed her eyes. God, it would be so easy to give in. He wanted her. Between her tears and her loathing, she'd fantasized more than once about what it would be like for Logan to make love to her again. Never in her wildest fantasies had she imagined that she'd actually have this opportunity again.

She licked her lips. "Logan, really, maybe you're mistaking some old emotion or the need for closure for actual love. Someday, you will fall in love with the right person and—"

"You think I've never been in love? Baby, I never fell out of love with you."

Tara's heart lurched in her chest. And something that felt way too much like joy raced through her veins like a heady drug. She had to take a deep breath and stop herself. Everything on his face underscored his honesty—at least as he believed it. But how could he know for certain? If what he said was true, he'd never really been in another relationship, so it was possible he'd fixated on her because she was the last girl he'd tried to love. There was too much behind them, and even if she put the BDSM thing aside, their lives were going in opposite directions. She might have a mountain of feelings for Logan, but being with him so soon after getting out of a relationship with Brad . . . Frying pan, meet fire.

But she wasn't immune to his pain. If he was stuck here, then perhaps she could help him out. Maybe it would be good for both of them to get the closure they'd never had.

"Kiss me, Logan." When his entire body tensed, she added, "Please."

"If I start, Cherry, I won't be able to stop." He caressed a gentle hand down her hair, over her shoulder, brushing the side of her breast to settle at her waist.

"You sure? It's been five years . . ." Would he still be able to? Would he feel empty afterward, as he did with the others?

"Oh, I'm dying to prove that, with you, everything will work just fine."

"Then kiss me," Tara repeated.

She'd worry about tomorrow when tomorrow came. Tonight, she'd be with him, try to heal his pain, scar over her own. He'd done an incredibly selfless thing to protect her all those years ago. She might wish that he'd told her what was going on. But at the end of the day, he'd been young and he'd done what he thought would be best for her, shattering his own heart in the process.

Clearly, he cared about her. But unending love?

They were going to be together until she went undercover. Maybe it would be best, for both of them, to spend the rest of the week together, training hard by day, working through their issues by night. Maybe by the end of the week, both of them would be ready to move on with their lives, sane, happy, and whole.

"Cherry, baby . . ." he breathed out, then settled his mouth over hers.

The kiss was soft as a rose petal. He clearly leashed himself, sinking into her mouth slowly, as if worried that he would scare her.

When his tongue brushed her bottom lip, then curled into her mouth, Tara opened to him. There was no place she'd rather be than here tonight with Logan. Maybe they weren't meant to be together forever, but every time he touched her she felt some inexorable bond with him, an invisible line that ran between them over the years, unchanged, unbroken.

Logan moaned, then nudged the little spaghetti strap of her nightie down her shoulder, then shoved the garment under her breast. The cool air hit her nipple, and it puckered. He covered the little bud with his hand, pinched it with his fingers. Then he looked down at her with burning blue eyes, already panting.

"Take it off for me."

That was his Dom voice. She couldn't fail to recognize the lower, silkier tone. Her pussy clenched. She nodded.

He eased off of her, still hovering above her. He gave her just enough room to pull the garment up her body and over her head. She used it to shield herself.

Logan's stare raked her body. Around the edges of the little nightie, he could surely see that she hadn't been wearing any panties. "Fuck, Cherry. I can't wait to get inside you, baby. Hand the nightgown to me."

Those hushed words, his low command, made her insides flip, then melt. Of the lovers she ever had, none had ever made her feel as beautiful and desired as Logan.

Tara was shocked to feel a blush creeping up her skin as she handed the little cotton garment to him. "Can we kill the lights?"

Logan shook his head. "I'm going to enjoy seeing your every expression while I'm deep inside you."

As her belly dipped in reaction, he flung her nightgown to the other side of the room. Despite the anticipation charging through her system, she laughed.

"Hey," he defended, "if I had my way, I'd burn it. As it is, I'll make sure you don't need that for the rest of the night."

Her belly quivered. "Kiss me, Logan. Don't stop."

"Yes, ma'am," he promised, before dropping his hand to her hair, tucking his fingers beneath her head, and bringing her close.

This time, his mouth settled over hers firmly. He didn't merely seduce her with his kiss; he took charge, nudging her lips apart with his own, tasting her deep inside, an endless tangle of lips and tongues that had her breathless and clinging. She wrapped her arms around his sizeable shoulders, fingers grasping into the hard flesh of his back as he moved between her thighs and began working his way down her body.

His lips caressed her everywhere. She shivered as they drifted down her neck, to the sensitive little spot where it joined with her shoulder. Those same sure lips pressed tender kisses across her collarbone as his palm cradled her breast in his hand. Languid honey rolled through her blood, and yet, every sense felt attuned to him. Even her skin seemed to strain closer to him.

"I fantasized about this a lot," he whispered against her skin. "From the day I met you, I used to think about getting you alone and naked for uninterrupted hours, exploring every part of your body over and over."

His words alone made her shiver, but when he closed his lips over the hard bud of her nipple, she cried out and arched toward him. Instantly, he wrapped an arm under her back to support her—and keep her there.

"When I've been drunk or just really damn lonely, I'd let myself think of you. You don't know how fucking often I'd roll over in bed and wish you were there."

The sincerity pouring off of Logan made her want to cry. "I thought of you, too. When I realized I was doing it, I'd try to force myself to stop. But sometimes, I couldn't. I'd remember the way you made me feel, like a woman, like . . . someone special. No one else has ever made me feel that way."

"Cherry, you *are* special. I'm never going to let you forget it."

Tears stung her eyes, and she slammed them shut. If he kept talking like that, they wouldn't get closure; she wouldn't want it. She'd want nothing more than to cling to Logan and pretend the last twelve years had never happened. She'd want to pretend they could have a fairy-tale ending.

That would most likely lead to another broken heart.

Tara forced out a saucy grin. "Shut up and take your clothes off."

He paused, then smiled down at her. "You're awfully demanding tonight, baby. If you're not careful, that's going to cost you tomorrow."

She shrugged, but excitement raced through her veins, pulsed between her legs. She would never have considered herself a glutton for punishment, but the way Logan dished out pain, it felt awfully sweet going down.

But he did as she asked, and shrugged off his tight black T-shirt. Every time she saw him exposed, she wanted to swallow her tongue.

"Are you going to tell me what this really means?" She traced the Japanese lettering along his bronzed, muscled torso.

"How much of yourself are you going to share with me?"

He'd dangled the answer to her question like a carrot, wiggling it in front of her face as bait, hoping she'd expose all her secrets to him.

Tara couldn't lie and say that she wasn't disappointed—or terrified.

He sighed. "If you can't share everything with me tonight, Cherry, I understand. It's been a long time for us, and Brad . . . I know it just ended. All I'm asking is that you share as much of yourself with me tonight as you can."

He acted as if this was meaningful, almost momentous, not merely closure. Tara swallowed. Eventually he'd see that, while there was something wonderful between them, it wasn't a forever kind of thing.

Was it?

She gnawed on her lip. "Is there anything else you won't share with me?"

"No. I'm going to give you everything you'll let me."

That made her swallow against a new tide of desire. According to Xander, Logan had shared next to nothing of himself with anyone in years. The fact that he felt differently about her warmed something dangerous in her chest. She shouldn't be more to him than the means to heal a wound. But she couldn't deny that part of her wanted more.

Without another word, he stood and unfastened his jeans, then slid them down his hips, taking his boxer briefs with them. Slim hips, jutting hipbones and a dark cluster of pubic hair revealed themselves before his cock sprung free. She blinked.

Tara hadn't looked at him when he'd taken her virginity. At sixteen, she'd been too embarrassed. The moment between them then had been tender, but now she knew why it had hurt so damn bad initially. He was long and incredibly thick and very hard. His stalk stood straight up, its head flaring bluish and wide and fascinating. He had, by far, the biggest cock she'd ever seen.

Unconsciously, she licked her lips nervously.

He groaned. "Baby, don't tease me like that. You're killing me."

Instantly, she understood—and wanted the opportunity to drive him mad. Since she'd walked into his dungeon, he'd had more than one chance to dish out the sensual torture. This could be hers, and she wanted it.

"I'm not teasing," she whispered.

"Shit, Cherry." He drew in a shuddering breath and stepped closer, wrapping his hands around her head. "This has been one of the most potent fantasies I've had for years. Suck me."

When he drew her down to his turgid cock, she opened her mouth, conscious that he watched her every move with unblinking eyes. She could feel his rapt attention all through her body. Excitement settled right beneath her clit.

She licked the head once experimentally. Salty, musky, earthy. All man. She shivered as his flavor flared through her, addictive on her tongue. So she lapped at him again.

His hands tightened on her head and he hissed in a breath. "You're trying to kill me."

No, but she couldn't lift her mouth from his thick stalk to tell him so. Instead, she closed her lips over the bulbous tip and shook her head, humming a little denial. His hips jerked, his body bucked.

"Deeper, Cherry."

She sank lower on his cock, her lips skimming as much of the velvety flesh as she could. There was no way she could take him in completely, so she settled for lapping her tongue around him on her way back up, tasting the head again in a series of little licks, then cradling him as she worked back down. He jerked once more, his body tightening as she braced her hands on his hard thighs. God, he was like a rock everywhere, and while that was sexy, what got to her more was how much she aroused him. The fisting of his hands in her hair and the little curses he couldn't hold in spurred her on to take him deeper again and again, until he pushed at the back of her throat.

Tara's mouth felt overfull. Suddenly, she felt as if she couldn't breathe. She panicked and tried to shove him back. Logan held firm.

"Calm down, baby. You're not choking. I'll stay as still as I can. Breathe through your nose. It's okay." She heard his words, but they didn't compute until he added, "I won't let anything happen to you."

He wouldn't; she knew that without hesitation. With that thought foremost in her mind, Tara focused on breathing through her nostrils. Relief hit her. She swallowed, and the back of her throat pushed against the swollen head of his dick.

Logan cursed again. "Jesus. I'm trying really hard to go easy on you, but damn . . ."

Her inexperience was showing. She'd given a few drunken blow jobs in college and been criticized for her technique once. Brad had never seemed that enthusiastic when she'd gone down on him. Maybe she sucked, and not in the good way.

Tara backed away, and his wet cock slipped from her mouth. "Sorry if it's not working for you. I don't do this a lot."

That made him grin from ear to ear. "Cherry, you were doing

wonderful, but it does my heart good to know I'm one of the few who've been in your mouth." He tapped her cheek. "Open up, tongue out."

Automatically, she complied, and something inside her heated at his gentle command. Logan took himself in hand and eased his hard flesh back onto her tongue.

"Don't move yet," he advised. "I want to watch this."

Slowly, he slid his cock against her tongue, from the large, salty head leaking fluid, past the ridge, down the entire silky length, until he was pressing back against her throat again.

"Now close your lips around me."

Tara didn't hesitate, and the heat of his flesh in her mouth fit perfectly. She moaned.

"Good girl. I want to fuck your mouth. If it's too much, snap your fingers, okay?"

She'd barely finished nodding before he set a blistering pace as he thrust past her lips. His fingers tangled themselves in her hair again as he groaned and slid over her tongue, to the back of her throat again and again.

The taste of him suffused her. His scent sank into her pores.

"That's it, Cherry. Dear fucking God, you're going to kill me. Yes, baby! Oh, yeah. Damn . . . I'm not going to last. Now swallow me, every drop."

Tara tensed. She'd never actually swallowed. The few times she'd managed to finish the job, she'd always discreetly spit into a nearby cup or sink. But the thought of this intimate act with Logan, pleasing him, she was nervous, but not scared.

She sucked harder, pulling against his thrusts to create more friction, running her tongue all up and down his length, nipping at the head with her teeth.

"That's it. I'm . . . there. Damn." His fingers tightened in her hair. He pulsed on her tongue. "Fuck!"

Warm jets of salty fluid sprayed to the back of her throat, coating her tongue. Feeling the way his body shuddered, hearing his whispered "Cherry, baby, yes . . ." filled her with something she couldn't quite explain. Happiness was too simple, as was pride. It was a deepening connection, a gladness that she'd given him something he desired.

She softened her suction, lapping at him, bringing him down slowly. He cradled her head at the crown, then caressed her hair, filtering the strands through his hair for a long moment until he pulled free.

When she looked up to meet his gaze, he wore this dazed, happy expression. Every muscle in his body was relaxed. He was so blindingly handsome when he smiled that the sight of him almost hurt.

He sighed, then leaned down to kiss the tip of her nose just before he stumbled to the bed and fell flat on his back with a wobbly smile. "That was . . . awesome. No, incredible." Logan shifted his body to his side, then propped his head on his hand to look at her. "I needed that."

Warmth suffused her. As broken as he'd been, she was happy to offer him some form of release that hadn't come from his own hand.

"You don't let the subs at the club do that to you?"

Logan shook his head. "The last one who tried spent twenty minutes at it. It wasn't going to happen, so I let her off the hook. My fault, not hers."

Conflicting emotions clashed inside her: pride that she'd succeeded where others had failed, but jealousy that other women had taken him in their mouth. It wasn't rational or fair. If anything, he had more reason to be jealous. She'd been engaged, had sex in the last five years. Feeling proprietary wasn't smart. She was supposed to be getting over him, helping him let go. But she supposed it was only natural to feel close to him when his scent and taste still lingered and he laid beside her, watching intently. The right time to say good-bye would hit them both, and they'd be done, whole people ready to face their lives.

"You're staring off into space. Did I lose you already?"

She shook her head. "It's just been a momentous day."

He winced. "Two orgasms, a spanking, being fondled by a stranger, and a breakup. If you're too tired for more, I'd be perfectly happy to get you off with my tongue, then let you go to sleep. Is that what you want, Cherry?"

Chapter Nine

WAS Logan suggesting they not make love? Or rather, not have sex. They weren't *in* love anymore. Freudian slip. As much as she loved his tongue on her—she coiled tight with desire as she remembered the feel of his mouth pushing her up and over—that wasn't what Tara wanted. Besides, she didn't think they'd ever be able to move on again until they'd truly connected.

"I'd rather have you inside me."

His blue eyes darkened. "Come here, baby."

Tara eased back on the bed, closer to him.

"Let me see those pretty nipples."

Blushing, she did as he asked, then sucked in a breath when he drew one into his mouth, then pinched the other between this thumb and fingers. Tara gasped as the sensation shot directly to her clit. When his teeth nipped at the sensitive bud, her body jolted with sensation.

"Spread your legs," he whispered against her breast.

There was no way she couldn't obey that. Slowly, intentionally teasing him, she parted her thighs. Logan grunted, growled a warning, then shoved his body between her knees and pried her thighs open wide.

"I ought to spank you for that."

Tara grimaced at the thought.

He grinned. "You sore, baby?"

"A little."

"Let me see."

She hesitated. God, she hated to show anyone her less-than-perfect backside, but especially perfectly yummy Logan. But he'd only push her until she complied. With a sigh, Tara rolled over.

He hissed out a curse. "I'm so sorry I bruised you, Cherry. I won't do it again."

"Yes, you will. I bruise really easily. It didn't hurt. Well, not too much."

Logan caressed her ass with gentle fingers, then rolled her back to face him, his expression full of concern that melted her more than it should. "If I ever truly hurt you, I expect you to use your safe word. Understood?"

"I got it. I'm a big girl; I can take care of myself."

He nodded. "You've done well, adapted faster than many would, despite the other issues going on in your life now. I'm proud of you."

His words shouldn't mean anything to her. They were just finding a way to get past each other and moving on. But his praise warmed her. "Thanks."

"In the meantime, I think I can make up for these bruises." He dragged one finger through her soaking folds. She'd been aware that she was wet, but this was almost embarrassing. "Someone's aroused."

As she watched his cock rise up hard and tall again, Tara gave him a pointed glance down, then slanted him a saucy smile. "Clearly."

"Bratty girl. I'll definitely spank you again." He lowered himself over her, covering her thighs, belly, and chest, before buying his face in her neck. "Later."

At the feel of him on top of her, heat raced through her veins like a drug. She clutched him, held him tight. Probably not smart, but Logan's tenderness was getting to her. Like this, he made everything feel so intimate.

He inhaled her, drawing in her fragrance. "Hmm. Sweet and

spicy, like cherry-vanilla. I used to promise myself that I'd lick your skin again if I ever got the chance."

And he did, drawing his tongue over her neck, her shoulder, breathing fire all over her. Tara shuddered.

Then he eased down her body and sucked her nipples into his mouth, one at a time. The little points ached from everything they'd endured today. Brad had always been an ass man, so he'd paid little attention to her breasts. The one time she and Logan had had sex, he'd taken a ravenous interest in her wide pink areolas and hard nipples.

Every flick of his tongue, every nip of his teeth now only enthralled her more. She writhed under his body, unconsciously spreading her legs wider.

"Do you want me, Cherry?" He nibbled on the underswell of her breast, then dragged his tongue to the tip before sucking it deep inside, then giving it a dizzying little bite.

Even if she hadn't already decided this would be the best way for them both to move on, Tara wouldn't have been able to resist him. "Please."

"A sweet little plea. You, I'd never even try to resist. I'd fail miserably."

She barely managed to smile at his sweet words before his hips slid between her thighs and he settled the head of his cock to her entrance. Tara tensed. It had been over a month since she'd had sex, and Logan was much bigger than Brad. This was going to stretch and burn—in a good way.

He cradled her cheek, caressing with his thumb. "Take me, Cherry. All of me."

Then he pushed into her slowly, inexorably, one torturous inch at a time, no pausing, no waiting, just a slow, relentless entry.

She wriggled against the slight sting of discomfort, but kept taking him. She wanted to feel him deep and know that, for that moment, he was totally hers. Thrill and pride filled her because he chose to be with her after he'd denied all others for years.

With that thought, Tara lifted her hips to him, impaling herself on the last of his hard length. She gasped as she stretched wide to accommodate him. God, he seared her. Everywhere inside her, so big, filling her so perfectly.

"That's a snug fit, baby." He threw back his head and groaned. "So fucking good."

Tara felt the sound resonate through her body, seep all the way down to her bones. She hadn't been this close to Logan Edgington in a dozen years, and in some ways being with him felt so extraordinary. In others, it felt so natural.

She eased her legs up higher on his hips. He sank down into her until his balls rested against her. The dizzying feelings of his hard cock filling her rivaled her amazement that he was inside her, joined with her, once again. "You're really here."

"Yeah, Cherry. And I'm going to stay here as long as you'll let me."

His low, sensual words made her shiver as he eased back, almost to the point of withdrawal. The friction made her gasp. With anyone other than Logan, the pleasure gleaned during sex had been fleeting, because she'd been making someone else happy more than feeling real ecstasy herself. Now, every nerve in her body pinged with life, every cell attuned to him. Her whole body was strung up, the rest of the world fading away, until only Logan existed as he filled her again, nudging all the way up at the end of her channel.

"Cherry, give me your hands."

Her hands? Tara frowned, then realized that she'd dug her nails into his shoulders already. She lifted them away and set her hands on the bed, next to his. "Sorry if I hurt you."

"No." Those burning blue eyes of his stared down at her, into her soul, and his body began working in deep, rhythmic strokes in and out of her. Tingles drifted like snow flurries through her veins. "I want to touch you everywhere. I need more control."

She barely nodded before he took both her wrists and gathered them together in one firm hand, stringing them over her head. He ran his free hand down her body, then under her ass, angling her to take him even deeper. She gasped at the sensation, the burning full-ness. He plunged in again, every rhythmic thrust stimulating her swollen clit.

Under him, she writhed, moaned. "Faster."

He didn't change pace. "Soon."

With Logan's entire torso covering her, the crisp hair on his chest rasped against her taut nipples. His so-blue eyes kept her gaze pris-oner as he moved inside her again and again, sinking deeper with every thrust, not just into her body, but with his gaze, with his will. *Take all of me,* it said.

Tara hoped that being with him would heal him, make him a whole, happy man again—and allow her to move on finally, too. But it wasn't her concern for him that had her mewling, helpless to the charge and flash of sensations bursting all through her body as she thrashed under him. It was simply Logan and the way he made her feel special. Possessed.

So she took all of him, every grunted thrust, every wild kiss, every whispered word.

"You're so incredible, Cherry." He closed his eyes. "Nothing has ever felt better. I could stay inside you all night, all day, all eternity, and still want you more."

Everything within her responded to him. Together, they strained for more pleasure, two halves of a whole both aching for something desperately that they could only get from the other.

With her hands pinned immobile by his grip, Tara had no way to exorcise her need to touch him except to lift her head and press her lips to his. Immediately, he took complete possession of her mouth. She melted, opening herself, unfurling, almost as if she could feel her mind, her heart, her very soul welcoming him.

Oh, God. This was dangerous. And there was no way she could stop.

"Yeah, Cherry." He swallowed, panted, fused their gazes together. "I." *Thrust.* "Can't." *Thrust.* "Take." *Thrust.* "Another." *Thrust.* "Min-ute." *Thrust.* "Without." *Thrust.* "You."

Tara cried out as his words sizzled clear through her. Pleasure spiraled, a hot drizzle of sensation that burned her all the way to her core until she clenched down on him tight, hanging on the edge of the precipice. She writhed, cried out.

"Say you need this," he demanded as he slammed into her again.

"Yes!" Tara arched beneath him, willing him deeper still.

"Say you need *me*."

"God, yes!" Never, ever had she experienced this incredible rush to pleasure or felt closer to the man giving it to her. "I need you, please, Logan . . ."

Incredibly, he hardened even more, his thrusts became piston-fast. He stared down into her eyes as he slid his hand between their bodies and settled his thumb right in her clit. "Come with me."

There was no stopping her orgasm. It was a brilliant surge of sensation charging through her system, swelling into something enormous, transcendent. She held her breath as every molecule in her body converged in the center, spreading not just from her pussy, but seizing up her chest until it radiated down every nerve. Even her fingers and toes tingled. The pleasure burst, splintering her into a million pieces as she felt Logan jolt, grip her hands tightly, then shout out his own release, hot and liquid inside her.

For a long moment, her body pulsed, unable to stop the reactive shaking. Logan released her hands and wrapped his steely arms around her, dragging her against his slowing heartbeat. She threw her arms around his neck and clung. She'd never required someone for her next breath the way she did Logan in that moment. God, she'd been hoping to bring them both closure, but now he felt like a part of her . . . so necessary to her existence.

No, it was a mirage, her delusion left over from the pleasure. It would fade. It had to.

"Cherry?" he breathed heavily, his gaze fixed on her as he pushed stray tresses from her face. "You okay, baby?"

"Fine."

But she wasn't. Tears lurked under the surface. He'd broken her wide open again, persuaded her to give to him again some deep part of her she scarcely understood. Tara swallowed back the tears.

"No, you're not." Concern spread across his face. "Be honest with me. Let it out."

She shook her head. "I just feel . . . raw, Logan. I don't know what I expected, but . . ."

It wasn't to feel as if she'd been turned inside out and ripped in two.

"It was everything to me, baby. Whatever you think, know that. Please believe me when I say I want to hold you all night and assure you that I'm going to be here for you as long as you'll let me."

Tara's sigh trembled, and Logan frowned. She tried to send him a reassuring smile. The truth was, she was utterly overwrought. It had been naïve of her to think that either of them would get over a dozen years of pining in one night. Maybe their sex had been explosive because it had been so long and they'd needed each other so desperately. Maybe if she just . . . gave herself over to whatever it was they had for the next week, this thing would burn itself out and they could go on with their lives.

Maybe.

"It was important to me, too." Whatever she said to him, she wasn't going to lie. "Being with you again is better than anything I imagined."

"So you'll let me hold you tonight?"

How could she say no? The truth was, she craved feeling close to him as much as he seemed to need to hold her.

She nodded, tears welling up. "Yeah. That would be perfect."

Nearby motel—Saturday morning

"Would you care to explain why you left me a voicemail canceling dinner last night at the last minute and why I couldn't reach you all night long?" Tara's stepfather, Adam Sterling, asked in her ear, his voice unnervingly calm, at five thirty the next morning.

Tara sighed. When Logan had popped in the shower a few minutes ago, she'd taken her phone off vibrate, only to realize her stepfather had left her nine messages since seven last night, each one more concerned than the last. His question weighed on her mind, along with her broken engagement, the terrible turn in her case, and everything she'd done between the sheets last night.

Logan had awakened her twice more during the night to make love to her, once rolling her to her stomach, cupping her sensitive breasts and pinching her stiff nipples until her pussy flowed wet for him. He'd pushed inside and rode her with a desperation that had her clawing the sheets and gasping his name. Then, just an hour ago, he'd slid into her again and awakened her with molasses strokes and a devastating smile.

"Tara?" Her stepfather's voice rang with concern. "Where have you been? Are you all right, princess? Tell me what's going on so I can help."

She was going to have to tell Adam something about why she'd broken things off with Brad and moved out or else he'd keep badgering her. She stuck to the factual. "Brad and I called it quits yesterday. It's better for both of us. I'm fine, just tired."

"He called me to tell me that you'd ended the engagement. I want to hear your side of this."

Oh, crap. What exactly had Brad told Adam? Her stepfather had loathed Logan when she'd merely been his tutor. After he'd broken her heart, protective Adam had hated him with a vengeance. She didn't want to imagine his reaction if Brad had told him that Logan was back in her life. She had to hope that since Adam hadn't mentioned it, neither had Brad.

As a grown woman, she should be able to tell the man who had raised her through her teenage years that she was working with Logan. But Tara didn't want to rehash the ancient argument with Adam, especially if he thought that Logan had had a hand in ending her engagement. Besides, whatever Logan said, he'd likely be out of her life in less than a week. Telling her stepfather the truth served no purpose except to worry—and rile—him needlessly.

"Tara, please. You've been missing all night, and I've been frantic. What's going on? Why did you suddenly break up with Brad? Are you all right?"

Maybe. No. Tara wasn't really sure. "I didn't mean to worry you. I'm sorry. I wasn't ready to talk about it yet. Our breakup was sudden, but I'll be fine."

"Really? I'm concerned about you."

Adam had always been concerned. True, he'd always been busy. Lately, more so. Adam simply wasn't the sort of man to show much outward affection, but he'd always been there when she needed him.

"Everything will be all right."

Her stepfather sighed. "Where are you? Do you have a place to stay until you can find a new one? You're always welcome to move back home."

"Thanks, but I'm good. I found a decent motel for a few days near my latest assignment. I'll find a new apartment afterward."

"If you're sure. Tell me what happened with Brad."

"It's this case," she finally said, choosing her words carefully. "The mission is to retrieve my friend Darcy. You remember her, right?"

"Of course. She's spent a few Christmases with us. Sad that her parents died so horrifically."

"Yes. She went undercover inside a sex ring based in Florida. I'd like to snuff the ring and nail the bastard who runs it. So I'm getting some training to go undercover myself to this 'adult' resort. You've always said missions are taxing, and that sometimes you have to give yourself over to them. Brad couldn't handle it."

"You're taking a field position?" He didn't sound pleased, but she could do this.

"This is more like an audition. I volunteered, and my boss agreed because I fit the right age and . . . characteristics. And he knows how badly I'd like to make a difference in this case beyond analyzing the papers shuffling across my desk." She shrugged. "We'll see how it turns out. It's demanding; I'm managing."

"What are you training for?"

This was where the explanation was going to get hairy. "To be a sexual submissive. Before you say anything, don't worry. I can handle it."

"*What?!* This is the big leagues." The worry in her stepfather's voice deepened. "Princess, I don't want to see you get hurt. Drop the case, go back to Brad, and work out your issues, please. He loves you and he's good for you. He'll give you everything you need."

No, Brad wouldn't. Last night with Logan had proven that. Sex wasn't everything, but the needs he was unlocking inside her weren't just those of her body. The intimacy that she and Logan shared resulted from some deep, organic bond—a connection she'd never felt with her ex-fiancé.

And she'd discovered over the last two days a certain . . . pride that she was learning to submit. Tara knew she wasn't perfect, but was doing pretty well at living up to Logan's demands. Even more, she'd done it on pure grit. Somehow, obeying him made her feel stronger. As powerless as she'd felt as a child without a home, as a teenager with a broken heart, as an agent wondering if she was ready for field assignments, *this* made her feel damn capable.

"No, he won't. He wants me to quit my job."

Adam sighed. "Would that be so bad? Field work will consume your life. Take it from someone who's been there."

Of course Adam knew. The fact that he'd rarely come home during some of those years and often been absent mentally had caused Adam's separation from her mother. He'd only changed after her mother had died suddenly in a single-car accident.

"I thought you'd be proud of me, following in your footsteps." Tara was somewhat hurt that he wasn't and pushed back. "Now that I don't have anyone to come home to, the job taking over my life is a nonissue. Really, it's for the best."

"It's dangerous." He sounded almost frantic to get that point across.

"And I love you for caring. I need to catch these people, for them—and for me. They've got Darcy, and I want her back."

"If you won't listen to me as a father, listen to me as a retired agent. What you're heading into is going to be ugly."

"I know. And I know you don't want to think about me in danger. But I'd appreciate your support. I need it."

"Damn it, I was never good at saying no to you." He sighed. "You want to talk about what've you got so far?"

Tara gnawed on her lip. This was against protocol, but Adam had been a damn good agent with a stellar track record in the field. That track record was one of the factors that allowed Adam to retire early and open his own security consulting firm. He traveled the world now, helping clients learn to stay as safe as possible. He made oodles of money doing it. She could benefit from his experience. And if using him brought Darcy home safely, Tara had no problem bending rules.

She filled Adam in on the case. "We have almost nothing on the ringleader, not even a name. This guy's greedy, and he doesn't care who he has to step on. He's got connections in hellholes all over the world."

"Makes sense," Adam agreed. "I'll tell you what else I'll bet is true: he's got a kink no one knows about, maybe it's BDSM or a serious hard-on for little girls. Whatever it is, he's figured out how to monetize it. My guess is that we're looking for an educated white male between the ages of thirty-five and fifty-five. Someone affluent, who travels easily. Maybe someone who speaks multiple languages."

"I thought as much. We're definitely dealing with someone who has no conscience and no heart. I need to catch this dirtbag."

"When do you leave?"

"Agent York and I are scheduled to travel to one of his resorts on Wednesday. It's on a private island off of Key West. I'll check in with you if I can. I don't want you to worry."

Adam smiled wryly. "You know me too well. Who's training you, anyone I know?"

"Non-Bureau contractor."

Not for a million dollars would she tell Adam the truth. He'd only start on a pointless diatribe, ticking off all the reasons he hated Logan. And Tara wasn't sure what she'd say. After his revelations and the toe-curling way he'd made love to her, she wasn't sure how she felt.

On the way to Club Dominion—Saturday morning

Logan glanced across the cab of his truck at Tara. As close as they'd been last night, as responsive and tuned to him as she'd been, his Cherry was now someplace else mentally. And he didn't like it one bit. Did she think that he'd be pacified with one night of sex? Was she feeling guilty that she'd spent the night with him hours after breaking up with her fiancé?

"What's running through that pretty head?"

She smiled wanly, looking tired. "The need for coffee."

He accepted her deflection for now. Maybe she was just processing and needed space. But she'd kissed him so wholly when he'd awakened her—then seemed like a completely different person once he'd emerged from the shower.

"I'll fix you up before we start working. Anything else bothering you?"

Tara slanted a glance his way. The shrug she gave him was one of the fakest gestures he'd ever seen. "No."

"I thought I heard you talking when I was in the shower. On the phone?"

She gave a long-suffering sigh. "Can't you just leave it alone?"

"Not if it's bothering you. Did Brad call you? Do I need to have a chat with him?"

"You're kidding, right?" She scoffed. "I can just imagine how that would go. I doubt there'd be much talking."

"Not if I had my way."

"Leave it be. Brad didn't call. My stepfather did."

"I'm guessing you didn't tell him that you were with me," he said.

"Um . . . no. Not in the mood to start World War Three. He was already unhappy that I'd ended things with Brad." She stared pensively out the windshield. "Then he begged me to walk away from this case."

"Probably the only thing we've ever agreed on."

Tara turned to him, looking stunned. "After all the progress I've made, you *still* want me to quit? You think I can't handle it, but you're dead wrong. I'll have you know that—"

"Down, tigress." Logan stopped at a red light that seemed pointless in the sparse Saturday predawn streets. "I agree that you've been doing well. I've always known that you're absolutely capable of doing whatever you set your mind to, and I respect the hell out of that. As the man who loves you, though, I'd rather have you out of danger."

There it was again, his seemingly casual declaration of love, spoken as he pulled into a fast food drive thru. *Nice weather. Pass the creamer. I love you.* Tara shook her head.

After last night, they'd been as close as two people could get. It was only natural, she supposed, that he'd feel *something* for her. As he got closure and started to move on, he'd likely see that it wasn't really love, not anymore. Even so, his words softened her.

As soon as they got their food and steaming caffeine, she turned to Logan. "I can't back out. Darcy was my roommate in college. She lost her parents on 9/11. They were on the plane that crashed into the South Tower. She'd been an admin of justice major anyway, but after that day . . . I held her hands a lot, cried with her. I even talked her into joining the FBI as a way to honor their memories and protect others from suffering the same loss. I feel partially responsible and—"

"Cherry, shh. You may have given her the idea, but she followed through because she wanted to. Would she want you going undercover to save her before you're ready?"

Darcy probably wouldn't want her to go at all. "I have to. She's tough and smart, and I know if anyone could stay alive in a hostile situation, she'd be the one."

"You didn't answer the question. Would Darcy want you to do this before you're ready?"

God, he just didn't give up. "No. According to her, I have a lot of fortitude but the heart of a marshmallow."

Logan had never met Darcy, but he liked her already. "That sounds about right. Really, I want you to think carefully about this."

"I'm committed." She crossed her arms over her petite chest, looking as determined as he'd ever seen her. "I owe it to her. And I owe it to me. I'm not unhappy behind a desk, but I need to know if the field is where I belong. My life has been missing something, and I keep thinking that it's—I don't know—having an actual life."

Boy, Brad had bored the shit out of her, and Tara had taken the blame upon herself. In Logan's mind, she thrived behind a desk, solving riddles that most people would never fathom. She'd always loved puzzles and brainteasers, but this was one she was going to have to figure out for herself.

And it was his job to make sure she stayed alive long enough to do it.

"Then let's focus on getting you ready. We've got four days. We're going to need every minute."

He parked the truck, and they both climbed out. Despite spending half the night inside her, Logan was hard as nails just thinking about the preparation she needed next.

As they entered the building, he grabbed her hand. She tried to pull away discreetly. Fuck that.

He leveled her a stare heavy with disapproval. "You're kidding? After last night, you won't touch me?"

"That was separate from this. I don't think we should bring our personal stuff into our training sessions."

Logan held her hand tighter. "You're not putting distance between us when what we need most is trust and connection."

Cherry gnawed on her bottom lip as she walked down Dominion's long corridor, clearly thinking. He knew why she was backing away; she wasn't ready to admit yet that last night was the birth of something new, rather than the burial of old feelings. He'd make sure she understood the difference soon.

"Fine."

Logan ran his key card through the mechanism beside his dungeon door. It popped open, and he pushed it wide, easing her in. He left the door cracked behind him.

"We're in the dungeon now. Rephrase."

Tara didn't look pleased. "Yes, Logan."

But she was so damn adorable that he wanted to kiss her senseless.

"Good. What else should you be doing now that we're here?"

She rolled her eyes and started to pull off her clothes. "What is your fascination with me being naked?"

He nuzzled her neck, running his tongue over one of the love bites he'd left there. "If you have to ask that after last night, I'd be happy to demonstrate again."

With a frown, she landed a mock punch on his shoulder. "I meant Doms in general. Does the sub having clothes put them on too level a playing field?"

"Not exactly. It's that subs are often feeling their most vulnerable and open when they're naked. It's a natural state, but for most of our lives, we're told that it's not. The Dom's job, in part, is to strip off the artifice to get to the real person underneath. So in that way, clothes are symbolic. And subs are less likely to put on a front with nothing to hide behind."

"I don't like it," she said, folding the last of her clothes and handing them to him.

"Because it makes you feel vulnerable. I see it in the flush that pinks up your skin, in the slouching of your shoulders, the way you try to look anywhere but at me."

Tara glared. "Now I just don't like you."

She was teasing . . . and yet not. She really didn't like feeling vulnerable with him when she was so off balance. Time and trust would heal that. He just hoped he could convince her of his abiding love, that it was safe to give him her trust, before his time with her ran out.

"Undercover, that won't be tolerated. Shoulders back, breasts out. Eyes on me, Cherry. Now."

Dragging in a deep breath, she did as she was told. Her posture improved a hundred percent. His respect for her determination went up a thousand.

"Did you kids start without me?" Xander called from the doorway, then sauntered across the room.

Tara stiffened. She didn't cover up, but he could tell she fought the urge. Pride at her progress surged, even as he wanted to clobber Xander for his mischief. This wasn't how he'd wanted to explain today's lesson to Tara.

"Damn, she looks pretty," Xander commented. "Edible, even. I need a taste."

Logan glared at his friend as he circled Tara to wrap a naked hand on her hip and drop a kiss on her bare shoulder. When he saw Xander's tongue hit her soft skin, Logan nearly lost it.

"Get your fucking hands off her."

Xander smiled as he pulled back.

"What is going on here?" Tara demanded.

Both he and Xander turned disapproving stares on her.

"Watch your attitude, Cherry," he warned. "I won't spank your ass again until the bruises fade, but I know plenty of other ways to make you suffer. You won't come for hours until you remember how you do and don't address me on this assignment."

Instantly, she pressed her lips together. "Yes, Logan."

"Good." He rubbed a soothing hand across her shoulder. "Xander is here to help us with the next phase of your training. I'm not going to tell you too much about it yet, because you need to learn to be ready for anything. Understood?"

Tara wanted to argue, but didn't. "Yes, Logan."

"Good girl. Stay here." Then he scowled at Xander as he moved to the cabinet in the corner. "Keep your hands off. Take a seat."

Xander strolled to the bed and sat. "This ought to be a great show. Wish I'd brought popcorn."

Out of the corner of his eye, Logan saw Tara shoot Xander a quelling glare and pretended not to notice. The bastard deserved that and more. Logan would have to make sure that she knew better than to disrespect any other Doms . . . but he was getting ahead of himself.

"Cherry, lean over the spanking bench."

She glanced at the apparatus, hesitated, then looked at him. He raised a brow, but waited wordlessly. Logan saw her brace herself, then comply, draping her figure over the leather top with grace.

After gathering the things he needed, he crossed the room and set everything on a table out of Tara's sight. Quickly, he clipped her in, then took a breath.

For the purposes of this mission, this preparation may save her pain. For their relationship, it was equally important. If she didn't enjoy this, Logan wouldn't love her less—but he'd always want to possess her more completely. After years of barriers between them, he didn't like the idea of enduring more.

In fact, last night, he'd been aware that he hadn't used a condom. They hadn't discussed birth control at all. Children were something they should talk about, but he wanted them with Tara, and everything about her made him want to embrace life full throttle. For the first time in years, he felt truly alive and he wanted to share it, spread it, breed it.

He glanced at Tara, and the thought she could already be pregnant made him harder than steel. *One thing at a time, buddy. Get her out of this mission alive. Then get a collar around her neck and a ring on her finger.*

Logan unscrewed the tube of lube, then squeezed it on the pink plastic plug. *Moment of truth . . .*

He sidled up behind her. "You ever been taken anally?"

His guess was that she hadn't, but he needed to hear her say it. Tara stiffened. "No."

"That's okay. We'll get you ready."

"F-For anal sex?

"Yes." He bent over her, draping her gorgeous ivory skin with his body. He whispered, "And before you ask, yes, with me. I want to be the first one to take you here."

The only one.

She shivered, and he placed a palm on her bare back. "Don't tense. We'll go slow."

But she wasn't relaxing. Logan rubbed his palms across her stiff shoulders, dragged his thumbs down the outline of her spine, easing tight muscles. He traced the curve of her waist, kissed her shoulder blade. Gradually, the tension left her body.

"Good girl. I'm starting simple. This shouldn't hurt. You have a few days to take something more substantial. For now, the plug should simply feel foreign. If it hurts, say so. If it really hurts, say your safe word. Do you understand?"

"Yes, Logan." Her reply sounded breathy.

God, that sound went straight to his dick, too. He'd imagined that fucking her repeatedly last night would give him more self-control. Today, he was fighting for it harder than ever.

He curled one palm around her hip, sliding back across the lush globe of one cheek, frowning at the fading purplish bruise there. On her other cheek, he saw another that looked fainter, a greenish-yellow. And he chastised himself. He was going to have to be damn careful with her.

Squeezing some lube on his fingers, Logan rubbed it with his thumb to warm it a bit, then inserted his fingers between her delectable cheeks until he found her untried opening. As he touched her there, she clenched tight.

Slowly, patiently, he pressed in with the tip of his finger. "Relax, Cherry. Breathe."

She did as he asked. Her muscles let go, and he slipped inside her, up to the first knuckle.

Shit. Hot, tight, she felt like heaven. Once he got his dick inside her here, no way he would last long. He was damn well going to have to temper himself until she got acclimated to anal penetration.

Provided she even liked it.

Tara drew in a shuddering breath. Her head lifted and she turned to glance at him over her shoulder. Her cheeks were rosy with color, her brown eyes slowly dilating. He couldn't stand not feeling her reaction for another second, so he wedged his free hand between the bench and her body, then lowered his fingers to her pussy—and he smiled.

"You like this, Cherry?"

"I don't know."

"You're wet."

"I like the idea of it."

That was honest—and half the battle. Maybe she just needed a bit more to figure it out.

"But it scares me a little," she admitted.

"I'm glad you shared that." He kissed her back again, then whispered for her ears alone. "I'm going to make this so good for you, baby. I want you to imagine what it would be like to take me here, my chest covering your back as I pump you full and we breathe together. Can you feel the pleasure climbing?"

"Yes." The sound was a breathy whimper.

"Me, too, baby. To get there, first you're going to have to be ready. Can you push out on me? Yeah, like that. Bear down."

In seconds, his finger slid completely inside, suddenly surrounded by hot satin fire. Logan began to sweat. God, something had changed between them last night, something fundamental. She'd tried to hide behind her professional façade and keep her distance, but now that he was stripping her of all those artificial barriers, he could see how she really felt. And her trust was so damn beautiful. He couldn't wait to fuck her ass, to completely own her. It would require her to have a bit more faith in him, but if he was patient and gave her what she needed, it would happen.

The minute she let him slide completely into that pretty backside, he'd know that she truly trusted him. He'd ask her to stay with him, wear his collar. And no matter what he'd promised her earlier, as soon as this fucking assignment was over, he was going ask her to be his wife.

"Logan . . ."

"Yeah, Cherry? You okay?"

Her whole body tensed. "Do something."

He dragged his fingers up her swollen labia, over the hard, needy knot of her clit. God, how responsive Tara was. She was more than ready to come. He was more than ready to let her, too.

But he had to finish his task first.

Slowly, he withdrew his fingers from her backside, quickly washed them, then rushed back to grab the plug he'd prepared. "I'm going to slide this in. It's a little bigger than my fingers, but you can handle it. Just stay relaxed."

Tara gave him a jerky nod. "Okay."

His heart drummed in his ears as he pulled her cheeks apart with a thumb and finger, then settled the edge of the plug against her rosette. Slowly, he sank it into her depths, watching her closely for cues.

Her back stiffened. When he paused, she forced a breath out. As he resumed, her fists clenched. But when he paused again, she shook her head frantically.

"Don't stop."

Caressing his way down her ass again, Logan pushed the plug in a bit more. As he eased the thicker end into her virgin backside, Tara gasped.

"Too much, Cherry?"

Her breath shuddered, and he could almost hear her trying to collect her thoughts. "M-More intense than I expected."

Intense in a good way? Logan eased his fingers between her

thighs again. Wetter than before. Wetter than ever. He petted her clit, then settled a pair of fingers at her entrance. They slipped inside as if eased by melted butter. Slick. Smooth. Perfect.

"You want to come." It wasn't a question; he knew.

"I don't understand."

"You don't have to, baby. It's all about feeling. Just hold back a few minutes for me. I want to share this orgasm with you."

Tara whimpered, but sent him a shaky nod.

"Answer me," he demanded.

"Yes, Logan."

Her breathy submission went straight to his cock, as usual. God, she had another inch of the plug to take, and watching it slide into her body, seeing her incredible arousal soar, was getting to him. He'd been inside her less than two hours ago, and already he was dying for her again.

"Good girl. This is going to feel so good. You're going to take the rest of this plug, baby. Then you're going to take me. I'm going to fill this pretty wet pussy with my cock," he whispered in her ear. "And I'm going to rub your hard little clit while I fuck you smooth and deep. You're going to scream for me."

She didn't say anything, just panted.

"Do you want that?" Logan knew she did, but he wanted to hear her admit it. Being with her this way, her body so in tune with his, was drawing forth his every primal instinct.

Take. Possess. Own.

"Yes, Logan."

Jesus, somehow when she said those two simple words, his dick pulsed in response, more than ready to give her everything he could.

With a deep breath, he withdrew his fingers from her pussy. She whined in protest, but a second later, he seated the plug deep in her ass, and that whine became a mewl.

"Fuck, she looks pretty," Xander murmured from the bed.

As if Tara suddenly remembered they had an audience, she stiffened. "Is he staying?"

"Yes, you always have to be ready to perform for an audience. Now stop asking questions, Cherry. You take what I give or say your safe word. Everything I'm doing is designed to prepare you for what's ahead. If you can't handle it, say so."

That would get her back up.

Sure enough, her spine stiffened. Logan distracted her by rubbing a pair of fingers across her clit again, settling his touch into little circles.

She didn't say another word.

With a quick flick of his wrist and a lowering of his zipper, he freed his cock and settled himself against her wet portal. With his other hand, he grabbed the base of the plug. Then he eased into her hot, so-tight silken pussy, the feel of his bare cock against her flesh the most mind-blowing sensation ever. Yes, he was playing with fire without protection, and his brain knew they should discuss this, but he needed her this way so badly. The image of her round with his child almost made him come then and there.

Instead, he gritted his teeth, sucked it up, then withdrew the plug a fraction. Before she could even finish gasping, he shoved the little pink device into her ass as he eased back from her pussy, then repeated the process. Tara started to scratch at the spanking bench, her nails digging into the dark leather. Her body clamped down on him until his eyes nearly fucking crossed. Her response was hot in itself, but it was her trust driving him to the edge. The connection. He could literally feel her body overheating, overloading, going exactly where he led her. With every sigh and groan, every tensing of her muscles and shake of her head, she sent a message to him, telling him exactly how to finish unraveling her.

Fuck, he'd better do it quick. He wasn't going to last.

He settled his left hand over her clit again, swiped her fingers across the little bud. Tara was hard, primed. Her orgasm was going to drag him with her, and he couldn't wait.

Logan circled her clit again, then drove deep into her pussy. "Come!"

The word was barely out before her body began jolting with the force of her pleasure. She clamped down on his cock and she screamed, her body bucking, pulsing with release. A moment later, the climax that had been brewing at the base of his spine shot through his balls and sped up his cock like white-hot lightning. As he plunged with feral strokes into her pussy, the fire erupted and he convulsed, emptying himself inside her with a soul-deep groan.

And as he laid his sweat-slick chest over the heated skin of her back and wrapped his arm around her, he knew that he would do whatever necessary to keep her safe and make her his forever.

Chapter Ten

Club Dominion—
Saturday afternoon

LOGAN entered the dungeon again, balancing a white paper bag in each hand and gripping a plastic bag with his teeth. Seeing him, Tara tossed her phone into the cabinet, then rushed to help him, relieving him of the bulk he held with his mouth first.

He sighed with relief. "Who knew sodas were so heavy?"

"That's bad for your teeth," she scolded.

"They're all still here." He grinned.

"Yeah, but if you want to continue chewing food in the future, you probably ought not to use them as tools, you know."

With a wink, he maneuvered across the room and set the bags on the table. It struck her that this was a bit like high school. Then, she'd been forever trying to point out the smart thing, the logical thing. He'd always pushed back with a bit of mischief that inevitably made something inside her melt. By nature, she tended to be serious. She had a sense of humor, but too often let it get buried under duty and responsibility. Logan's wit was relaxed, closer to the surface, and during their time together in high school, she'd always felt more . . . balanced around him. Happy.

She felt happier and lighter today than someone who'd just lost a fiancé, than a woman trying to rescue her best friend from sex slavers, than the female who'd been glutting on sex with the jerk who'd broken her heart once upon a time. That made her pause.

"Uh-oh," Logan said, tearing into the first bag and withdrawing a tin round with a cardboard lid.

The food smelled heavenly, but her stomach was so tight, she wondered if she could eat. "What?"

"I know that look. You're getting serious on me."

And not for anything would she tell him that being with him now felt right. He already had these crazy ideas of love that she feared would fade once he realized that he was just getting her out of his system. She didn't want to be crushed by this incredible hunk of man again. Yes, he'd left her last time for extenuating circumstances; she didn't blame him. But the fact that he'd walked away with such seeming ease scared her.

"Thinking about the case," she lied. "I leave in four days."

"You'll be ready, I promise. Have you heard any news from Bocelli?"

Tara shook her head. "I checked in while you were gone. The call was brief, but he said there was nothing new yet."

"No more dead bodies is a good development, Cherry."

Logan was right, but that didn't make the worry any easier. She'd pushed her apprehension for Darcy's safety and the mission's success to the back of her mind by telling herself that panic would only slow down her training. But the second she closed her eyes, Darcy was there, sometimes screaming for help, sometimes already dead.

"Baby, now you're just worrying me." He set the food aside and crossed the room. "You've gone pale."

"Sorry. I really am concerned about Darcy."

"You're doing your best."

"What if it isn't good enough?" The thought brought a rush of tears.

He cupped her shoulders, his blue eyes delving deep into hers. "It's all you can do. Be comforted by the fact that the abductor's goal isn't to kill the women. It gives you more time."

"I just wonder what she's enduring now."

"I don't know Darcy, but if she's a field agent for the Bureau, then she's a tough woman."

"She is," Tara agreed, a bit of the anxiety in her stomach easing. "But . . . do you think they've figured out that she's not really submissive?" And if so, would she end up like Laken Fox?

Logan hesitated. "Hard to say. If they were convinced of that, I think they'd have killed her already. They may think she's just really bratty and needs a seriously firm hand."

Tara swallowed. "In the wrong hands, that sounds terrible."

"It could be. But you've got to worry about you now. You have to focus on being ready to rescue her or you'll both wind up in serious trouble."

"I know." And she did. It just didn't make the situation any easier. "What about Robert? Any updates from Axel?"

This time, Logan sighed. The hesitation on his face worried her.

"He's not cut out for this, Cherry. I told you that. Axel says York has the self-control, but not the drive to earn submission. He brought in one of the club subs yesterday. Apparently, she topped from the bottom the entire time. York said he was sick of head games and walked out. Are he and Darcy an item?"

"No one is supposed to know, but yeah. I think he meant to propose soon. At least Darcy suspected so."

"York is not only wrong for this assignment, he's not focusing on what he needs to learn. He's too anxious. I've told Bocelli that. So has Axel. Baby, you need a plan B."

She chewed on her bottom lip. "I know it's smart to have one. I just don't think I could go to this resort and hand over my body to someone I don't know, not the way I give myself over to you."

He cupped her cheek, and his face softened. "And you do it because you trust me."

That expression scared the hell out of her, like he was expecting her to love him back. "With my body, yes."

Logan narrowed his eyes, clearly not liking the way she qualified that statement. "We're going to broaden that trust, Cherry. I'm going to earn it all, every last drop of forgiveness and lo—"

"Stop."

Her heart pounded. She knew what he was going to say, and she wasn't strong enough to resist it right now. Last night, he'd scaled so many of her defenses. If he'd been demanding or bossy, she could have easily told him to go fuck himself. But he'd been patient, tender, seductive. Even today . . . Who would have thought that taking the anal plug he'd inserted could seem like a bonding experience? Yet no denying that she felt even closer to him.

Tara couldn't afford any of this, especially right now.

"I'm starving, and that smells good." She nodded at the tin rounds of food. Definitely Italian.

He heaved a disappointed sigh at her, then removed the lids. "Lasagna. Salad is in plastic containers in the other bag."

"Thanks." And she felt like a heel for hurting him. That she had was written all over his face. "I really do appreciate it."

"If you'd let me, I'd take care of you always."

God, it was getting hard to say no. She couldn't imagine what another three days with him would do. "Can we just focus on the case right now?"

"Yeah."

But he didn't look happy about it.

"What's on tap for the rest of the day?"

"Not telling. It's the first real test I've prepared, which will encompass a lot of what you've learned into one scene. You'll need to remember to stay in protocol and submit to the best of your ability."

A bit of foreboding filled her. "Will Thorpe be there?"

"You can bet on it."

She grimaced, but couldn't stand to tackle this fear alone. She took Logan by the hand. "I'm afraid of failing."

He slid a hand behind her neck. "Don't be. I won't let you. Focus on me, on being with me and pleasing me. The rest will come."

Club Dominion—Saturday night

With a reassuring hand at the small of her back, Logan led her out of his dungeon and down the club's hall. It would be a simple act . . . except she was wearing nothing but the short buttery, pale silk robe he kept in his armoire.

Tara didn't think for a second that she'd be wearing it for long.

She knew better than to ask again where they were going and what was going to happen. He'd refused to answer the question twice and vowed that if she asked again, she wouldn't come for the rest of the night.

This was a trial run for her work at Fantasy Key, the resort where she'd go undercover. Eventually, Robert would lead, and she'd follow. Since he wasn't proving to be a strong Dom, she'd have to fill in the gaps by being especially submissive to him. Somehow.

"You're shaking," Logan whispered. "Nothing to be afraid of. I won't let anything happen to you."

He wouldn't; she knew that. "It doesn't make the unknown easier to take."

"Deep breath. I know you like to plan everything and run all the contingencies in your head, but don't. Submission works for you, in part, because it's the one place in your life where you let go. Relax into it and know that I'll take care of you."

It all came down to trust. She was shocked to realize how totally she trusted him to keep her safe. He'd push her, but not beyond what she could endure.

The nervous flutters didn't go away, but the fear gripping her eased. "Thanks."

As they approached another door, he opened it. Immediately a wall of grinding, sexy music filled the cavernous space. The slap of leather resounded, followed by cries of passion. A man to her right groaned, and she was shocked to see a naked woman kneeling before him, taking the hard stalk of cock in her mouth as he fucked her lips rapidly. About twenty feet away, a woman in full leather had bound a man to a St. Andrew's Cross and was whacking his ass with a cane. His abundant muscles rippled with every blow.

"She's marking him!" Tara's first instinct was to race across the room and rescue him.

Logan's hand at her elbow silently reminded her that the submissive man had signed up for this and had a safe word if he really wanted out. "He likes it. And those are your last words until I ask you to speak. Are we clear?"

Protocol. People were watching. Around her, she saw stares, some lustful, some curious. One sub with short pixie dark hair served another Dom a drink, stabbing Tara with a dark glare. A former sub of Logan's? In her head, she knew it didn't matter; he hadn't had sex with the girl, whoever she was. But it wasn't just about sex. Logan showed genuine caring when he topped, and the thought that this woman had experienced that for herself . . .

"You've gone tense." Logan caressed her hip.

When she looked back, he'd already followed the line of her vision and his gaze fell on the sub, who quickly wiped the expression off her face. He clenched his jaw.

"Hey, Logan." Xander approached from their right. "Tara."

"Watch Cherry for a minute," Logan said to his friend. "I need to have a word with Callie."

"Good call. Since she found out you've been holed up in your dungeon with Tara, she's been in a foul mood."

"I'll nip it now."

With that, Logan stalked off. He'd said no talking, but . . .

Xander raised a brow at her. "Ask quickly, sweet thing."

"What's her problem?"

"She wanted your boy something fierce. She's tried really hard to get him to fuck her." Xander shook his head. "Callie's not dumb. She can already see that he's different with you."

Logan might believe that he loved her—and an insidious part of her wished that were true since she still cared for him. But wishful thinking would get her nowhere. He didn't truly know the woman she'd become; just the girl he'd crushed on in high school. Their unresolved feelings and the case were drawing them together temporarily. Once this was over, and he no longer had to train her, he'd get some clarity and likely be ready to move on. He'd probably do so with a sense of relief.

Whatever conversation Logan had with this Callie woman was short. He scolded her, his expression firm, then motioned to a dungeon monitor, who escorted her away. Then Logan headed back toward her.

"What will they do to her?" she whispered to Xander.

"Punish her, Cherry. Which is what I'm going to do if you open your mouth one more time," Logan warned.

And he would. She pressed her lips together.

"Let's go." He leaned over to Xander. "You get everything in place?"

"It's exactly like you requested."

The not knowing was making Tara's imagination work overtime. Her belly twisted in knots, and she took a deep breath, willing herself to calm as Logan guided her deeper into the club's public area. Still, she couldn't decide if Xander having a hand in whatever it was made her less apprehensive or more.

Finally, they reached a fork in the main hallway and turned left. Xander took point, and suddenly the crowd parted, letting them through, closer and closer to— *Oh shit, no.*

A stage.

Suddenly, Tara felt all the eyes in the room on her. She wasn't just going to do a scene; she was going to publicly submit to Logan for this swelling audience. Panic tore through her, along with the edges of a humiliating sting. People wanted to watch her bow and scrape and beg . . .

Tara turned to Logan, giving him a look that both resisted and pleaded.

"Speak," he demanded.

"I'm going to be sick. It's one thing to submit to you in private, but in front of all these people—"

"Stop." He took her hand. "You did brilliantly in front of Xander. We've got a few more days to perfect this, and I'll make sure you're absolutely ready before the mission. But don't forget, you have a safe word if the scene becomes too much. Other than that, focus on me. Trust me to make this not about you bending for me, but about us connecting by giving one another what we need. That's the beauty of what happens here, Cherry. Haven't you felt that?"

Yes, she had, earlier today especially. He'd expanded her horizons because she'd trusted him, and she'd given him a way to experience the sex he hadn't had in five years—all because they were connected by this mysterious power exchange and emotions she didn't completely understand.

Tara nodded.

He squeezed her hand. "Come with me."

Biting her lip nervously, she did, following Xander.

As they grew closer to the stage, a golden glow flickered all around the perimeter. Dozens of tea light candles burned softly. It was almost romantic, and the fact that Logan had asked Xander to do this for her touched Tara. Then she realized the candles illuminated a small padded ottoman and a pair of leather-lined shackles hanging from the ceiling.

Her belly did a flip, and her first instinct was to turn around and run. But she felt dozens of eyes on her, including Thorpe, who now stood at the edge of the crowd, near the front, watching her with a critical eye. Beside him stood a man in a pristine suit with dark hair and piercing black eyes like she'd never seen. He put off an intense vibe like nobody's business—and looked straight at her, assessing her almost clinically.

Instinctively, she dropped her gaze to the floor, figuring the gesture would help her submissive image. But inside, her stomach was rolling with apprehension. How the hell could she go through with this?

No idea, but if she left now, all these people would think she was a coward. Thorpe would undoubtedly report the development to Bocelli. Since she'd only been working with her new boss for two weeks, he'd assume she didn't have to right stuff for this mission and maybe choose someone else. If she bailed, she wouldn't be helping to rescue Darcy. And she'd let Logan down. To her surprise, the thought of disappointing him hurt more than she could stand.

Tara took a deep breath and stepped toward the stage. Other people survived this. If there was a way to make this good for her, Logan would find it. She knew that as well as she knew her own name.

With a tender hand at her elbow, he helped her up the stairs to the stage. She saw a table in the shadows, its top dotted with a coiled whip, a long rectangular paddle, and a flogger with soft leather strips.

She gulped.

"Eyes on me, slave." Logan's voice sounded deep and downright commanding, making her shiver. She couldn't do anything but obey. "What is your safe word? Say it loud enough for everyone to hear."

"*R-Romeo.*"

"Very good. Strip and hand your robe to Master Xander."

She'd known this command was coming, yet it startled her. Still, hesitation wasn't going to accomplish anything, so she forced herself past her nerves and unbelted the little silk garment, shrugging it off her shoulders, down her arms. When Xander held out a hand, she gave it to him, not surprised to find that she was trembling.

Logan nodded, his expression full of approval. "Face the wall and kneel here." He pointed to the ottoman.

Tara fought the urge to glare at Logan and instead looked at the padded cube like it was a snake. Once she complied, everyone would see her abundant ass. But her insecurities weren't the issue. Submission was. She could do this for Darcy, for her own sense of success. And she would make Logan proud.

Facing the wall, she settled one knee down on the black vinyl, then another . . . The surface was cool, but soon warmed under her skin. But those shackles dangled just above eye level, and Xander turned a crank to raise them, they clinked against the wall, stirring up a whole new batch of fears.

Logan reached one and pried it open. "Give me your wrist."

Oh God, oh God, oh God. She forced down nausea, forced herself to forget that people were watching. She couldn't see them, and they'd gone silent. She knew from her research, from being restrained earlier while Xander watched, that the best coping mechanism she had was to focus on Logan.

Finally, she drew in a rattling breath, then held out her wrist to him. He snapped it into the cuff just above her head, and she was startled to find that the snug way it hugged her skin was almost comforting.

"Another hesitation will cost you, slave."

A few feet away, Xander picked up the paddle from the nearby table and smacked it lustily against his hand with a grin. A part of her feared something that solid against her rear, having everyone watch her punishment. But some other part of her must like it because moisture gushed from her slit. Shocked, she gasped.

Logan sent her a secretive little smile. "Your other wrist."

This time, she didn't dither. Logan's touch calmed her even more as he settled her into the next shackle, then he squeezed her fingers before releasing her and walking over to the little table in the shadows.

Her belly clenched and turned again.

He took a long moment, then selected something. Tara couldn't see what, since his body blocked her view. But once he had an instrument in hand, he walked behind her and caressed his way down her back, over her ass, lingering on one cheek.

"Bend at the waist."

Tara sucked in a deep breath. Okay, he was going to spank her.

She'd managed this before, but tonight he was adding something new into the mix. The thought of that whip scared the hell out of her. She tensed, but complied as much she could, until her arms dangled from the shackles, pulling at her shoulders. The sensation felt foreign, but so submissive that it aroused something in her. Then she realized that, as she'd bent, she'd given the audience a perfect view of her pussy.

More embarrassment swirled with arousal through her body. A fresh flush crawled up her skin. Additional moisture coated her folds.

Circling her again, Logan fused his gaze to hers and cupped her breast. Though her back faced the audience, no one would have any doubt that he was fondling her in public. It should bother her . . . but any time Logan touched her, it felt so damn good. When he pinched her nipple, rubbing it between his thumb and forefinger, nothing but sensation and his touch mattered.

Unable to stop the sound, she moaned.

Logan scraped a thumbnail gently across her erect nipple. "Nice."

Then he withdrew a pair of clamps from his pocket, attached to one another by a chain. Each end had two plastic balls attached that looked like . . . cherries? She glanced back up at him.

"There are weights at each end. And yes, I bought these just for you."

It seemed silly to think that she welcomed nipple clamps because he'd been thinking of her when he purchased them, but she did. Of course, when he secured the first, it pinched and burned—for a moment. Just as it settled into a mellow numb haze, he repeated the process with the other nipple.

Heat rolled through her, and the ache behind her clit began to pulse in demand. No denying how wet she was now. Her labia felt slick, unbearably swollen. No doubt, everyone in the audience could see, but somehow that only aroused her more. She whimpered.

"Quiet," he demanded.

Not a second later, she heard a *whoosh*, then felt the tails of the flogger, almost like soft leather fringe, striking her ass. The sensation wasn't pain exactly; it was too diffused for that. Instead, it felt more like a dozen fingers firmly caressing her, heating her skin. No way could she bruise from this, only catch fire.

Tara found herself arching, sticking her ass back for more. Logan splayed his palm in the middle of her spine and pressed gently, raising her backside another inch. Then he struck her with the flogger again, a bit harder than before. Still, it was pleasant, and she felt her mind begin to float away.

Smacks three and four each hit one of her cheeks. With her skin already sensitive, the burn kindled into a blaze. That heat spread outward, seeping into her bones. Her pussy clenched in protest against the emptiness that ratcheted up her hunger. And as he dragged the soft leather strips across her ass, fire burned under her skin, topped by a sweet sting that soon eased into a gentle tingle.

Closing her eyes, she gave more of herself to Logan, letting the shackles assume more of her weight. Her blood hummed as she awaited another smack with the flogger.

It never came.

Instead, he circled in front of her once more. "Look at me."

She did, and the electric need in his eyes created an answering ping in her body. Whatever he wanted, yes. Tara knew she would give it to him, no questions asked.

"Good girl. Straighten up and spread your knees as wide as the pedestal allows."

Pleasure and the sharp pang of want made her brain sluggish. It took her a second to process his command, but she complied finally. He nodded in approval, then tugged on the little weights one at a time. Fresh heat jolted down to her pussy. Her entire body tensed in need, and she whimpered.

"You look beautiful," he murmured, his low, velvety tone warming her.

Then, with a flick of his wrist, he unleashed the flogger's supple leather. The ends landed with a gentle slap right on her mound. The ache expanded, rocketing upward, outward until she swore that every nerve in her body was wired straight to her swollen clit. But it wasn't quite enough to push her over the edge.

Tara tossed her head back and cried out, forcing herself to hold back a plea. She *needed* him inside her. She'd wanted him last night and this morning, but this ache was a living, breathing entity taking over her whole being, suppressing all but the desperate craving to feel Logan filling up every empty bit of her with every hard inch of him.

His burning blue eyes told her he knew that.

"Are you wet, slave?" he asked loudly. He wanted the audience to hear.

"Yes, Logan."

"You've been very good. I'll reward you soon."

He dropped the flogger and stepped forward, wrapping one hand around her waist, anchoring the other in her hair. His mouth covered hers, his tongue demanding entrance, seducing her submission.

Feminine gasps erupted around the room. They confused Tara until she remembered Xander saying that not only did Logan never have sex with the subs, he never kissed them. And suddenly, she understood: Logan wasn't just having her publicly submit. He was explicitly staking his claim.

Something warm erupted inside her. Though she couldn't touch him with her hands because of the shackles, she met every nuance of the kiss with her own delight and need, showing him—and everyone—how totally she accepted him in this moment as the master of her body. He pulled her against every hard inch of his frame, her clamped nipples rasping against his bare chest. And she melted.

When Logan pulled back and searched her eyes with curiosity and wonder, he was panting. Tara wanted nothing more than to sink back down into that endless kiss and join with him forever, but he caressed her face, then stepped away. Every part of her ached for him, so focused on his actions, on pleasing him.

Then Xander stepped forward.

Tara sucked in a breath. He was going to touch her? In public?

"Accept his touch because I demand it of you, slave," Logan's voice rang harsh in the air, but his blue eyes scanned her, concerned and checking her response.

"Yes, Logan." The words slipped out automatically.

With a wicked grin, Xander approached, trailing a finger in the valley between her breasts, caressing the underswell of one. Then he disappeared behind her and breathed kisses along her shoulders. Her skin tingled; she shuddered. Her belly knotted.

"If Logan gave me the chance, I'd fuck you here," he whispered, caressing her ass. "I'd sink my cock so deep inside you while Logan plundered your sweet pussy. It is sweet, right?"

She whimpered. Her body craved Logan's, answered to him, but this man skewed her system in some odd way. Maybe it was because Logan watched with a hot gaze. Had he overheard? Did he want to possess her pussy while Xander plunged his cock into her backside?

His sizzling words played in her head while he glided gentle fingertips over her body. A surge of passion from the audience swelled around her, nearly overcoming her. She could almost feel them holding their collective breath. But nothing affected her more than the need in Logan's eyes. She swayed closer to him.

With his signature musky heat surrounding her, he approached, all business—and all man. He uncrossed his arms from his chest and settled his fingers over her clit, fondling her without hurry, for no other purpose than to jack up her need and watch her twist. Pleasure jackknifed through her body, a spike of need she found impossible to ignore.

"Is Xander whispering naughty suggestions to you?" He gripped her chin and forced her to meet his gaze.

"Yes, Logan."

"Every time you say that, Cherry, it goes straight to my cock. You like his suggestions?"

"I'm not sure." Her breath hitched.

"Let's experiment," Xander murmured for her ears only. "I'd love to lick your creamy little pussy while I watch you suck his cock. Would you like that?"

"Whatever you said," Logan directed at Xander, "she just got a whole bunch wetter."

"You've got a dirty girl."

Logan nodded and released her with a wicked smile, and Tara caught her breath. "Let's see how dirty."

A moment later, she felt Xander's fingers on her pussy, searching, sinking deep, before circling her clit in lip-biting little circles.

"Do you want to come for us, baby?" Logan murmured, spreading kisses across her face, down her neck, then bending to trace his tongue around her clamped nipples.

Her breath caught, froze, at the exquisite sensations racing between her breasts and wet sex. "Yes, Logan. Please . . ."

"Aww," Xander crooned as he speared her pussy with two fingers. "She even said please. How sweet." Then, with a mischievous smile, he withdrew his fingers from her slit and licked them with a groan. "Very, very sweet."

She flushed all over, tension coiling up under the tight knot of her clit until she thought she'd explode.

"Xander," Logan growled in warning.

"Just checking."

"Never," Logan vowed. "*Ever.*"

Tara understood his message loud and clear, but he shot her a warning, just in case—an emphatic declaration that, while he'd let Xander touch her for training purposes, there was no fucking way that Logan would ever let it go beyond this right now.

As hot as this scene was, that fact relieved her. Knowing he had no further expectations of what she'd do with or for Xander allowed her to simply relax and enjoy whatever came next.

"I know, I know . . ." Xander groused. "Just enjoying it while I can."

And he did, gliding his fingers back inside her. Instantly, he found her G-spot and rubbed, his thumb still circling her clit.

As Logan caressed her sensitive breasts, her body caught fire again. It swept through her like a conflagration that she couldn't control.

"Don't come before I give you permission," he reminded. "I don't want to have to spank you again tonight."

She drew in a deep breath, closed her eyes to focus inward.

"No. Look at me," Logan barked. "Always at me."

Tara opened her eyes, lashes fluttering. Logan grasped her chin and lifted her face to him for another deep, mad kiss—a tangle of tongues and passion, breaths and desperation. And, God, the need that seized her every muscle as he removed the first of her weighted clamps and blood roared back into her nipple.

Suddenly, he tore his mouth away and fastened it over the throbbing little bud. A second later, he removed the other clamp, and suddenly Xander's mouth was there to breathe more fire into the aching tips of her breasts. Both men sucked gently on her nipples as Xander plucked at her aching clit with lazy fingers and teased her mercilessly.

She groaned, clenched tight, trying to fight the lure of the pleasure roaring inside her as her heartbeat boomed like a cannon in her ear. With her gaze riveted to Logan's and his thick-fringed blue eyes silently shouting of untold pleasure, Tara nearly lost her restraint.

"Cherry, come now!" he demanded.

Instantly, ecstasy bloomed inside her, expanding outward, alighting every nerve ending in her body. Like a leaf in the wind, she swayed, arched, but the pleasure kept bowling her over as the men suckled her nipples. She jolted, and her clit pulsed again and again under Xander's deft fingers.

Slowly, Tara came down, her body releasing the gripping tension by degrees until she fell lax. Logan was there to support her weight as her legs went boneless beneath her. Suddenly, she became aware of people clapping—and suddenly remembered the audience. She stiffened.

"Relax," Logan murmured, caressing her cheek. "That was so sweet, Cherry. You did great."

Lacking the energy to reply, she merely nodded as Xander opened her shackles.

The instant her arms were free, Logan was there to catch her. He picked her up, cradling her against his chest, then rushed off the stage, past the crowd stumbling to get out of his way. With ground-eating strides, he darted toward the secured door that led to the restricted areas of the club, fusing his mouth over hers. His demanding lips, every caress of his tongue, shouted his need for her with eloquent silence.

When he reached the door, he tore his mouth away reluctantly, those blue eyes burning for her.

"Cherry, I've got to have you now."

Fresh heat flared through her at his words. The orgasm he and Xander had given her on stage should have sated her, but knowing that he intended to be deep inside her in mere seconds awakened all her nerve endings and hot fantasies again.

He fished a key card out of his pocket and handed it to her. "Unlock the door."

With shaking hands, Tara grabbed the card and swiped it through the apparatus. A quiet click resounded over the din of the crowd noise in the background. Then Logan yanked the door open and charged through it like a bull.

On the other side, he grabbed the handle and slammed it shut, then shoved her against the adjacent wall. Tara felt her heart beating triple time as he covered her naked body with his overwhelming heat. His stare singed her with intent, telling her silently that he intended to get inside deep, drive her to screaming pleasure, and leave her no doubt who she belonged to.

"You want to say your safe word now?" His voice was gravelly, strained.

Her stomach tightened. Her pussy clenched. "No, Logan."

Triumph mixed with his predatory stare. That hot lust on his face turned the ache brewing in her clit to a burn. He'd show her no mercy, and she didn't want any.

Logan unfastened his leather pants, watching her with that unflinching gaze. With one hand, he lifted her against his body and braced her back against the wall. "Spread your legs. Put them around my waist."

Tara didn't hesitate, pulsing with an impatient thrill. Within an instant, he held the stalk of his cock in his free hand and lined it up to her weeping entrance.

"Cherry, baby . . ." His hands clinched around her waist, then shoved her down on his cock, one hot, uncompromising inch at a time.

He sank into her, stretching her with the perfect tingle of pleasure and just the right bite of pain. He shuddered as he filled her. Tara focused entirely on him, flowered around his cock. She cried out, digging her nails into his back as fire seared its way through her blood.

"Fuck, yes, Cherry." The low groan sounded as if it had been ripped from his chest.

Except for his panting and pounding heart, he remained totally still, as if he could absorb her into his body. But Tara needed him now. With a whimper, she wriggled on him, pleading for more.

"Give me a second, baby. I'm trying to find some restraint so I don't fuck you raw."

His words, the uncontrolled passion in his growl, made her sheath flutter around him in hunger, her blood sear with scalding desire. "Don't hold back for me."

His entire body taut, Logan fisted his hand in her hair and forced her gaze to his. His expression was a silent warning that she shouldn't have given him such free license. But that didn't stop him from gripping her hips, lifting her up, then slamming her body down helplessly on his steely length.

The friction of his cock plowed through her sensitive sex. Her body flared with white-hot life. But he didn't go slowly, linger. Logan shoved her up again, then savagely pushed her down as he arched into her cunt, working even deeper than before.

"There's nothing like being inside you, Cherry."

And no one fueled her need like Logan when he filled every empty space inside her.

"I fantasize about fucking you all the time, about waking you up to the feel of my cock deep in your sweet little pussy. I get hard all over thinking about laying you across my table and taking my dessert between your legs. I come wishing I could take you back to my bed and shackle you to it, then spend all night, every night, inside you, pounding away until you want me half as much as I crave you."

"I do," Tara groaned.

His words burned through her until she swore she was on the edge of combusting. Her every sense felt attuned to him, the hard rhythm of his hot breaths as he lifted her and thrust deep, the chugging of his heart. The smell of earth, manly sweat, and musky spice filled her head, mingling with the bite of his fingers on her hips, controlling her every move.

"Ah, your pussy clamped down on me, Cherry. You like that? You like the thought that I want to possess you constantly, in every way possible? Because I do. I'm fucking obsessed with it." He pulled on her hair, arching her neck for him. Raking his teeth across the sensitive skin, he kissed his way up to her ear. "I want to suck your nipples hard every chance I get. I fantasize about that, and about binding you so that I can open up that pretty lush ass for me—and me alone."

More heat clawed through her body. Every one of his words drove up higher. Her body tightened desperately on his cock, and he had to work twice as hard to maintain those rhythmic strokes that were unraveling her one at a time. But Logan wasn't faltering. He just kept filling her one deep thrust after another as her sheath clung and rippled.

Sweat beaded at his temples, ran down his neck. "You ready to come, baby? I need you."

Nothing could have set her off faster than hearing the raspy demand in his voice. Suddenly, the ache between her legs gathered, heated, then boiled over until it became a fire that consumed her whole body. She tossed back her head and screamed, feeling Logan's straining shoulders beneath her fingertips.

His pace quickened, a brutal shuttling of his hard stalk inside her clenching pussy. He grunted every time he plunged deep, nudging her cervix, rolling a new orgasm over her before the last one had even finished.

Fingers digging into her ass, he stilled inside her, cock pulsing as he released deep inside her, shouting, "Cherry!"

Tara clung to Logan tighter. God, she couldn't catch her breath, and tears stung her eyes. In every word and deed this week, he'd told her that he still had feelings for her—strong ones. Real ones. She was supposed to be helping him get over their past while he taught her everything she needed for this mission. But nothing between them felt that way. She was losing herself in him. The connection between them kept growing, like vines curling through her chest until they nearly wrapped around her heart.

God, she couldn't afford to fall in love with Logan again, not now. Probably not ever.

Gingerly, he lifted her off his still-hard penis and set her on her feet. Semen dripped down her thighs, triggering a realization. She froze.

"Did I hurt you, baby?" he sounded half panicked by the prospect as he took her face in his hands, gaze delving deep.

"We didn't use a condom." A wave of memory swept through her. "We haven't used one at all."

Logan closed his eyes, winced. "I should say I'm sorry, but I . . .

haven't been able to bring myself to put barriers between us. I'm clean and—"

"I've been on the pill for a while, but with everything that's been happening I've forgotten to take it the last two days."

His face softened and he actually looked thrilled. "I'm ready for whatever happens."

Tara blinked in shock. They might be playing Russian roulette with her womb, and he was okay with that? The steadiness of his deep, direct gaze told her that he was completely serious.

"I'd love our baby every bit as much as I love you."

When he said things like that, she melted all over. It was hard to remember that his affection was most likely past emotions lingering before a soft death, rather than the resurgence of secret devotion roaring to life again.

Unless she was totally underestimating his feelings for her.

Before she could reply, a *whoosh* and a *click* from the other side of the door had Logan scrambling to tuck himself back in his pants and zip them up so he could stand protectively in front of her naked body.

Thorpe and the black-haired stranger made their way through the door, stopping short at the sight of them, perspiring and disheveled.

The club owner gave them the once-over, then handed Tara's little silk robe to Logan. "Dress your . . . trainee and come to my office. We have problems."

When Thorpe would have turned away, Logan gripped the man's arm, staying him. "Tara did a damn fine job tonight. A few hesitations, yes, but—"

"The problem is way beyond whatever is going on with the two of you, Edgington."

Thorpe's gray stare wasn't angry, but ice cold. That, along with the presence of the stranger beside her, told Tara that something was very wrong.

Terror gripped her throat until she nearly couldn't speak. "Is this about Darcy, Sir?"

He hesitated, glanced at the stranger, then nodded.

Terrible images pelted her, one after the other, as Logan draped her in the robe, then wrapped his arms around her, providing shelter, comfort. He sent Thorpe a grave gaze. "Give us a minute, and we'll be there."

Chapter Eleven

Logan didn't have a good feeling about this. After cleaning Cherry with a warm, wet washcloth, he pushed aside her trembling fingers and helped her dress quickly. Once done, they left the room, and she settled into a grim silence.

He took her hand, wrapping her cold fingers in his. "You don't know that Darcy is dead."

"No," she admitted, her face taut and pale. "But something is very wrong."

Unable to refute that, Logan guided her toward Thorpe's office. Xander entered the secure area, glanced their way, and frowned. "What's wrong, dude? And don't say 'nothing' because one look at Tara and I know that's a lie."

His friend meant well, but now wasn't the time. "We don't know. Might have something to do with Cherry's case."

Xander nodded. "If I can do anything to help, let me know."

"Thanks, man."

Guiding her down the hall, he and Tara entered Thorpe's office and shut the door behind them. Thorpe sat, resting his chin on his steepled fingers, his mouth a thin white line. A snowy envelope lay on the desk in front of him. The dark stranger in the suit paced the side of the room like a caged animal.

Both gazes rested on Tara, and Logan instinctively wrapped his arm around her.

"Relax, Edgington," Thorpe snapped. "We're not going to tear into her."

"Has he behaved this way since he began training her?" the stranger asked.

"If you have something to say," Logan growled, "you say it to *me*."

"Sit," Thorpe demanded of both of them.

Cherry did so quickly—a submissive's internal urge to respond to a Dominant's command. Logan had no such urge, but the look on the club owner's face warned that arguing now would only be counterproductive to solving the problems at hand.

Glaring at the stranger in the corner, Logan sat beside Cherry, gripping her hand again.

"Good," Thorpe said, tapping his toe against the concrete floor.

He was edgy, wired-up. Since Thorpe was usually one of the fucking calmest customers Logan had ever met, that worried the shit out of him.

"You want to tell us what's going on?" he asked.

Thorpe shook his head. "I'm trying to decide where to start. The night has turned into one giant clusterfuck."

The stranger stepped toward Tara, his dark eyes dissecting her. "I think introductions are in order first."

When he stuck out his hand toward her, Logan tensed.

"I'm Jon Bocelli."

Her new boss. Cherry rose to her feet and shook his hand, chin raised confidently. But Logan knew she had to be cringing at the thought that her boss had both seen her in an act of public submission and in the aftermath of passion. Yes, she'd been training for a dangerous assignment, but responses like hers couldn't be feigned. Logan vowed to pull Bocelli aside if necessary and explain that the sex against the wall, which her boss would likely see as misconduct, had been his own fault.

"It's nice to finally meet you, Agent Jacobs."

"You, too, sir."

"Edgington," Bocelli greeted, hand outstretched.

Logan shook it as Tara said, "I didn't expect you in from D.C. Do you have news about Darcy?"

"Yes. We'll come back to that. I flew into Dallas to check your progress and ask you a few questions."

Tara swallowed, and Logan could sense her nerves. He longed to grab her hand again and squeeze it, just to let her know that he was here for her. But it could be construed as a lack of faith on his part or seem unprofessional in front of her boss, and the last thing he wanted to do now was undermine her when she must feel as if she already had a strike against her.

"Fire away, sir."

Bocelli gestured at her to sit, and she complied once more, her gaze pinging around her room. The tension was thick, and Tara was too smart to miss the fact that they were tight-lipped about something.

"Have you seen Agent York today?"

She hesitated, cocked her head. "No."

"He hasn't contacted you at all?"

"No." She turned to Thorpe. "Isn't he training with Axel?"

"He hasn't seen Agent York since last night."

Bocelli cut in. "A quick search of his apartment revealed a very orderly place, but some of his clothes are gone. His suitcase and toiletries are missing. His dog is nowhere to be found. Nothing looks disturbed. The door was locked right and tight."

"He left voluntarily?" Tara frowned.

"That's how it appears."

"Robert took the death of the first victim, Laken Fox, pretty hard. I'm not suggesting he cracked. Maybe he needed a day or two . . ." She trailed off with a shrug.

"I hear that Agents York and Miles were romantically involved. Any reason you didn't share that with me when I assigned him to this case?"

"You didn't ask. Darcy asked me to keep it on the down low, but I didn't think it would take you long to figure it out. Besides, no one, other than me, would fight harder to get Darcy back."

"But now York has disappeared." Bocelli raised a dark brow, pinning her with a stare that stopped just short of accusing. "Anything else you're holding back?"

"No. But I don't think for one second that he's given up on finding Darcy alive."

"Is it possible he knows something we don't?"

She shrugged. "We're not close. But he knows I'd do anything to help him save Darcy, so I believe he'd tell me about any new developments."

"I hope he'd tell us all, but that doesn't change the fact that he's missing, probably of his own accord." Bocelli's dark gaze shifted from Tara to Logan. "Agent Jacobs did well in public, far better, I gather, than she would have before you took her under your wing. Is she ready?"

Tara shot him a glance filled with quiet plea. Logan understood her need to impress her new boss, but he wasn't going to compromise her safety. "Not quite. I haven't had the chance to put her through all the exercises she'll likely need. There's still some hesitation and fear."

Back ramrod straight, Tara settled into the far side of her chair, away from him. Oh yeah, she wasn't happy with that response.

Nodding, Bocelli appeared to mull his reply. "Couldn't she pass as a slightly bratty sub in need of a firm hand?"

"Maybe, but even if you could find York, like I've been saying for two days, he couldn't handle her. Tara isn't ready to face unknown Doms. Her trust is . . . fragile."

"Your demonstration tonight proves aptly that she trusts you."

The fact that even an outsider could sense that thrilled Logan, but he knew there were chinks in their armor. "We're getting there."

"Why the twenty questions?" Tara demanded. "Clearly, you're not thinking of aborting the mission, given this verbal fishing expedition about my readiness. But if Robert is gone, we have to devise another plan. I understand our options are limited. I'll do whatever needs to be done."

"Axel, Logan, and I have had a few conference calls since Logan assumed your training," Thorpe admitted. "We've suspected for some time that Agent York wasn't going to be successful in the role of your Dom, so we've been devising a plan B."

Tara blinked. Something in her manner made Logan think that she couldn't decide whether she was happy that the mission to rescue her friend would move forward despite York's absence or furious that no one had kept her apprised. Probably a bit of both.

She licked her lips. "And that would be?"

"Me," Logan confessed.

"At least that was the idea," Thorpe said.

"*Was?*" Logan glared at the club owner. With York's disappearance, didn't that make their backup plan more the most viable option.

"You don't work for the FBI," she pointed out.

To Logan's relief, she didn't seem pissed about the idea, just hung up on procedure.

"It's taken some jumping through hoops, but I've got the brass to approve using Edgington as a military contractor to assist with this mission," Bocelli assured. "He's got the unique skill set necessary, and I think that bond brewing between you two will allow you to submit as needed and create a more convincing cover."

Tara flushed, but looked a bit relieved; Logan relaxed.

"I understand, sir," she said. "And I agree."

"Just don't let your feelings interfere with this case. If you want to fuck him in your spare time, that's on you. But once you hit that resort, you keep your eye on the mission."

Logan could see Tara both flushing and restraining her temper. In truth, he wanted to rip Bocelli a new one, too, but that wouldn't do Tara a damn bit of good.

Instead, he leaned forward and met her boss's stare straight on. "We'll get the job done, but whatever happens between us will contribute to our 'convincing cover,' so don't knock it."

Tara thanked him with a silent stare, and Logan nodded, happy to defend her in whatever way he could.

"Your role on this mission has become more complicated. I have something you need to see." Thorpe reached for the envelope on his desk. He toyed with it between his long fingers, as if considering, then held it out to Logan. "A man wearing shades and a dark hoodie paid Misty to give this to you just after Tara's public submission. When she couldn't find you because you were . . . busy, she found Xander, who found me. She said this dude gave her the creeps. By the time I got it, too many people had touched it to bother dusting it for prints, so you can touch it. None of the security cameras got a good look at the guy's face. We already checked. Do you know what the hell this is about?"

With a frown, Logan took the envelope and ripped it open. Clearly, Thorpe had already been into it himself. For the moment, Logan shoved down his irritation and withdrew the piece of paper inside.

Have you forgotten my warning? Stay away from Tara. Or she dies.

Horror froze Logan's entire body. His mother's killer was still keeping tabs on him a dozen years later?

He sucked in a breath, then turned to look at his Cherry, who watched him expectantly. This was a complication they fucking didn't need. Thorpe's and Bocelli's silent gazes settled on him. They were leaving the next move to him, allowing him to bow out if he wanted.

No way was he making the same mistake he'd made a dozen years ago. At sixteen, he couldn't begin to protect Tara. At twenty-eight? Bring it on. This time, he'd handle everything differently. Whoever this motherfucker was, Logan couldn't wait to take him apart.

He handed the note to Tara. Quickly, her eyes scanned the page, then she gasped.

"Your mother's killer is back?"

Logan nodded, feeling his back teeth grind. "This reads like his work, yeah."

"What do you mean, 'back'? You've received notes like this one before?" Bocelli asked.

"Not since high school." Logan grabbed Tara's hand because he needed to feel her, then met her boss's gaze and told him about his mother's murder and the subsequent fallout. "It's a complication, but not a problem. I'll handle it."

"We may have to rethink this, Edgington. This is someone determined, who's followed you for years and watched your scene with Tara tonight. He may follow you to Florida."

"From everything you've told me, Fantasy Key isn't easy to get into," Logan argued. No way was his involvement in this mission going to unravel now. He couldn't send Tara in without an experienced Dom to protect her—and he refused to let this asshole come between him and the woman he loved a second time.

"It's not," Bocelli conceded. "We had to pull a lot of strings to bypass the six month waiting list."

"We may have another alternative." Thorpe rose and crossed the room, opening the door, only to stop short. "Eavesdropping?"

"Sorry. I couldn't make myself stop."

Xander. Thorpe was going to suggest that his best friend replace him? *Oh, hell no.*

Thorpe led him in, and Xander leaned against the wall, brow raised.

"You assisted Edgington during the scene," Bocelli said.

"Yes."

The Fed extended a hand and introduced himself. After the pleasantries, Bocelli briefed Xander on the base facts of their mission to Fantasy Key. Xander listened without expression or comment.

"I could definitely help. I worked there off and on for three years."

No shit? Logan stared at his pal. He didn't talk much about his past. He'd grown up in L.A. and left home young—and refused to say why. Logan knew a few things about Xander's past, like the fact that he'd worked at a BDSM resort, but details had been nonexistent.

"The private resort you topped at . . . that was Fantasy Key?"

"Yeah." Xander turned to Bocelli. "I still have friends there. They're good people. If there's something bad going down, I'd like to help."

Thorpe turned to Bocelli. "That's a plus. And your agent needs a strong, experienced Dom she can trust to lead her through the resort's activities and hopefully attract the notice of the scumbags behind the illegal activity. Xander can do that. And he doesn't bring an extra threat to the table, like Edgington."

Logan's first response was towering rage. After angling for nearly two days solid to accompany Tara on this mission, no way was he backing down in favor of his buddy.

But nothing Thorpe said was incorrect. In his shoes, Logan figured he'd be making the same suggestion. It still pissed him off, but he had to think about Cherry. Did he want what was most advantageous for his future with her or what was best for her safety?

"Since Xander has already touched her," Thorpe added, "she's familiar with him on some level. You saw she responded well to him during her public submission. In fact, he got her off. So they could make their way convincingly enough through sex, if necessary."

Xander and Cherry? Oh, fuck no! Logan wanted to rip the club owner in two. Beside him, Tara tried to school her expression, but a flush crept up her face.

Xander cleared his throat. "My first thought was simply to ask some of my friends to help you. But you might be right, Thorpe. I know most everyone there, not to mention each nook and cranny of the place. I know how to manipulate the security." He turned to Tara. "But . . . I think I could be pretty good with you, and we don't have any history to overcome."

Logan couldn't refute any of Xander's words, having topped others at Fantasy Key and knowing the people inside would lend credibility to their cover. No one would think it odd that Xander showed up with a sub. Hell, he might even get a discount.

"Any military or law enforcement in your background?" Bocelli barked.

"No, but I'm a black belt and I'm good with a gun. I wouldn't let anything happen to her." Xander sent a reassuring glance at Cherry, who bit her lip, clearly thinking things through.

This situation was killing Logan, but he had to put Tara first. "My role is to support Agent Jacobs. She doesn't need my military background to do her job, but if Xander will prove more useful and bring less complication—"

"I'll do whatever necessary, but I'm more likely to maintain my cover at this resort if I feel really comfortable. If Xander can help us with information or inside connections, great. But I've trained with Logan. Despite everything else, going with him makes more sense."

Logan's heart melted. Underneath all the complexities of their past and this case, she truly trusted him to keep her safe, even in the face of a threat. That thrilled him to death and gave him a foundation to build on, but none of that mattered if she didn't come home alive.

"Cherry, the guy who killed my mother is a smart psychopath. I see Thorpe's point about not borrowing more trouble now."

"Maybe so, but he probably lacks the clout necessary to get into the resort at the last minute," Tara argued. "And since Fantasy Key has such tight security, this killer won't be sneaking on the grounds while we're undercover. Being on this mission will probably be the safest place for me."

Thorpe shrugged, glancing at Bocelli. "SEALs aren't exactly pussies, and Edgington is a tough bastard. He's capable of doing whatever necessary to keep your agent safe. But you knew that or you wouldn't have run him up the FBI's internal flagpole."

Still, Bocelli remained wordless, his face giving nothing away.

"My life for Tara's." Logan stood and braced his hands on Thorpe's desk, leveling a grave stare at the Fed. "I swear it. I'll come home in a pine box before I let anything happen to her."

Behind him, Tara gasped. He couldn't turn his attention to her now, not when he had a point to make.

"This is my job, Logan. Not yours. If there's danger, I'll face it."

"Like hell. If you're in it, I'm in it, too, Cherry. I'll protect you with my dying breath."

Her gaze skittered away, and he couldn't tell if she was touched or horrified. Probably both.

Bocelli didn't like the situation, Logan could tell. He paced Thorpe's office in silence, clearly running scenarios in his head. Finally, he turned back. "Getting my superiors to approve Xander as her partner would be a harder sell, since he's neither law enforcement nor military. And a change now would delay the mission."

Tara's face reflected the relief that Logan felt.

"All right, Edgington, you stay. But there are parameters. First, I'm going to put a few agents nearby, as close as I can get them. They'll be invisible to you, but will serve as backup and be armed to the teeth."

Logan cast a glance at Tara, who nodded. "We're okay with that."

Bocelli turned. "Xander, can you help us decide where the agents are best placed and how to get management to insert them there without tipping anyone off?"

"Absolutely."

"Great. I'll be in touch. You're excused."

It wasn't a subtle dismissal, but Xander let himself out.

Bocelli looked back at Logan. "Now, we discuss your behavior."

Swallowing back what he really wanted to say, Logan merely raised a brow.

"It's obvious you have feelings for my agent that run deep. I don't give a shit about the details. And if you're mentally prepping a denial, don't. I'm not stupid. But you're going to have to shelve those feelings during this mission. Agent Jacobs can't be a target for these people unless they believe she's going to be easy to pluck away from you. You'll pose as a new couple, and you'll seem less than committed to her. Have a roving eye, wander off to chase other subs—whatever. The kidnappers have to believe that you won't move heaven and earth to find her if she disappears."

As much as Logan hated to admit it, Bocelli was right. "I'll do my best."

"You damn well better succeed. Treat her as if she's disposable. Be dismissive, detached. You have to leave her vulnerable so the kidnappers think she's an easy mark."

Logan didn't like it one damn bit . . . but that was reality. "I'll manage."

The Fed turned to Tara. "You have to seem adoring with a hint of rebellion. As we've done more research, we've learned that the two victims so far, besides Darcy, both had Doms but neither had been in a long-term relationship. By all accounts, none had family who would miss them. Only one was employed outside her home, and she'd been gone for days before anyone reported her missing. You'll need to be self-employed for your cover. Any ideas?"

"I spent some time as a freelance copyeditor in college. I can speak intelligently about it if the subject comes up."

"Perfect. Realistically, you would have had deadlines, but cleared them before coming to Fantasy Key."

"Yes."

Tara's boss paced more, his whole Brooks Brothers vibe just adding to the image of a stressed-out Fed. He turned to Logan. "You're absolutely sure you want to go, despite this threat?"

He planned to fight for Tara, and she wanted him by her side. "Yes."

Bocelli glanced Tara's way. "If his mother's killer follows and somehow finds his way onto the resort, you understand this makes you his target, in addition to being set up to be abducted by these slavers?"

"I do. I'm willing to assume the risk. Logan will be the best Dom for me on this case."

"And you know that if the killer can't sneak into Fantasy Key, he probably isn't going to call it a day and leave you alone once you've returned home?" her boss asked.

"It should be a nonissue once we've finished this mission. Mr. Edgington and I . . . We'll be going our separate ways."

What the fuck? Logan turned to stare at her as if she'd lost her ever-loving mind, because clearly she had. Tara would spend the rest of her life without him over his dead body. But he'd correct her gross misconception later; now wasn't the time.

"You're willing to assume the extra risk?"

"Sir, with all due respect, it's not as if we have better options. Robert is gone, Darcy's abduction has proven that it's not good to go undercover alone, and Logan is well trained to handle all phases of this mission. Can we end this conversation now so that we can prepare for our departure Wednesday? I'm sure Logan has a lot of training he'd like to cram in before then."

Bocelli raised a brow. "Fine. You're both in. If you've duly noted all the risks, I have nothing left to say on that score. Now to the evening's biggest problem."

"Darcy?" That note of alarm crept back in Tara's voice.

"Yes. One of your fellow analysts found this online advertisement about noon today. We were running a new program that checks the web for certain key words and images that tap into our open cases. We found this." Bocelli turned to Thorpe.

The club's owner grabbed his laptop from the corner of the desk and pressed a few buttons before turning the screen toward him and Tara. Logan watched with horror as a bound woman wearing too much makeup around her glassy eyes—and nothing else—was fondled by four hooded, leather-clad men.

"Darcy . . ." Tara's broken whisper rang with fear and pain. "Oh my God."

Logan hurt for her. How terrible it must be to see a loved one at the mercy of strangers willing to degrade her for a sick thrill—and profit.

Then it got worse as the ad's words began to scroll across the screen.

Tara gasped, slapping a hand over her mouth as she read.

Another rung of horror gripped Logan. "They're going to force her to star in a snuff film?"

"A gang rape snuff film, yes."

Her face turned ashen. "They're going to strangle her while they . . ."

"Yeah," Bocelli confirmed grimly. "Friday night. It's a pay-per-view event, then they'll distribute through all their usual illegal channels. I don't think they'll kill her on U.S. soil since it would likely be too easy to trace their location via IP addresses and whatnot, so we have to find her before they smuggle her out of the country. So you're leaving tomorrow morning."

Beside Logan, Tara stiffened but nodded. "I'll be ready."

"*We'll* be ready," he corrected.

"Excellent. I'll provide you some last-minute instruction. Your flight leaves just after nine in the morning. I want to see you back here by six."

"Done," Logan assured as he stood, then held out his hand for Tara.

She glanced up at him, and though she did her best to hide it, he read the trepidation in her body language, the bleak line of her lips. Now that she was committed, the reality of this mission was setting in. It would only be natural for her to be afraid, especially since she had both white slavers and a killer after her. Still, she refused to back down. His brave little Cherry just kept on impressing the hell out of him.

Finally, she placed her hand in his, but the second she had her feet underneath her, she let go.

Frowning, Logan watched her approach Bocelli. "I won't let you down."

"Be smart. Stay safe."

She nodded, and as Thorpe approached her, she turned to him warily. Logan was taken aback when the notoriously chilly club owner pressed a kiss to her forehead. "Listen to your Dom and submit with honesty."

As Tara stepped back, she frowned. Logan wondered if she could even follow Thorpe's advice. Yesterday, she'd been engaged to another man. Since then, she'd fallen back into her first lover's bed, submitted to him again and again, and was about to place her safety in his hands as she put herself in the path of really dangerous men. She was confused and, no doubt, afraid.

Above all, she was burying her feelings, protecting herself after the hurt he'd dealt her years ago.

The case was going to take time to unravel. He might have to act distant in public, but by damned, when they were alone, Logan was going to make her face exactly what was in her heart.

* * *

THE second they cleared Thorpe's office, Logan draped his arm around her and led her to his dungeon.

Tara shivered in the shadowy chill of the room as Logan raced around, collecting various items and yanking on his T-shirt. She made her way to the armoire, withdrew her bag, and turned to leave.

"I didn't give you permission to go," he pointed out sharply, suddenly by her side.

She glanced at her cell phone. "It's after midnight, and I've been here since six this morning. I'm tired, hungry, I want a shower, and I have a lot of thinking to do. We have to be here early tomorrow, and I haven't yet packed. You can resume your Dom thing tomorrow. Good night."

He extracted her duffle from her hands, disapproval all over his face. "Here's how it's going to go, Cherry: Your boss basically gave you to me until the end of this mission. We're not slipping in and out of roles when it's convenient for you. I'm the Dom, you're the sub, period. First, you wear what I say."

Logan studied her with a critical eye. "Give me your undergarments and suit coat."

"What the hell? I can't walk out of here without a bra. Everyone will know I'm not wearing one. It's not like I won't jiggle under silk."

He raised a brow. "You'll be walking past everyone else who belongs to a fetish club to exit tonight. Every Dom in the place will see if you *are* wearing a bra and they'll know something is wrong. For all we know, someone out there could be involved in this shit. We've managed to keep this training secret to all but a select few, but that might change if you can't be bothered to follow simple instructions. No fucking way are we dropping the pretense because you don't want to jiggle. Are we clear?"

Damn it, she hated that he was right. "Fine, but why can't I have my panties? No one will know if I have them on but me."

"I'll know. You're riding with me when we leave. If I want to touch you, I want full access. You'll give it to me, and that's the end of the discussion. You're going to get used to it or they'll figure us out all too quickly at Fantasy Key."

"Do you always have to push me, every moment of every day? When we're undercover, do whatever the hell you want. But this, tonight, you're just pressing your agenda and probably getting some real thrill out of bending me to your will."

He stalked closer, wrapped his hand around her hip. "I'm always going to get a thrill out of bending you to my will. I'm just wired that way, baby. But I'm also going to make damn sure that you're ready for whatever command I throw your way once we reach that fucking resort. If you want to argue about it some more, then expect another spanking the second we hit my door."

"*Your* door?"

"Yeah." Logan cocked his head to the side. "You don't actually think that, after someone watched you submit to me tonight then left me a note threatening to kill you, that I'm going to leave you in that motel alone."

"I work for the FBI. I'm *not* helpless."

"I totally agree, but that changes nothing. You're not staying at that dingy little motel, even if I tag along. My condo is far more secure. No one will get to you tonight."

"Except you."

"Especially me. If you think I'm not going to spend these last few hours holding you and telling you how special you are to me before I have to pretend otherwise, you're lying to yourself."

"We've already . . . I mean, we've had sex twice today."

Logan merely smiled. "Third time's the charm."

Even as her mouth pursed mutinously, she blushed. "I admit that it's not terribly safe at the motel. But maybe I should stay the night at my stepfather's place and meet you in the morning. I need some space, Logan. I just don't think it's a good idea to be around you tonight."

Logan sent her an uncompromising stare. "You know that staying with me is the safest option. I don't like you being obstinate, especially when it potentially compromises your safety."

"I'm thinking about more than my physical safety, Logan. Seriously, I need peace and some time to come to terms with everything that's happening."

"Sorry. You get me instead. Take off the garments I've instructed. We'll stop by the motel, check you out, pick up your things, and go to my place."

Tara wanted to taunt him that he couldn't make her, but she had no doubt that he'd only pick her up and carry her out, regardless of how she felt.

"God, you can be such a bastard."

"Yep." He didn't even try to refute her. "But I'm the bastard determined to keep you alive and prove that I love you. Let's go."

All but snarling, she yanked off her suit coat and panties, then struggled out of her bra without taking off her shirt. She tossed everything at Logan—then gasped. Even the slightest movement of her silk blouse against her nipples sent a shiver through her. Quickly, the little buds hardened, stood up.

Logan noticed immediately and ran a thumb over one. "So fucking pretty. I can't wait to strip this off and get deep inside you again."

"Don't say things like that," she protested, but it sounded weak, even to her own ears.

Tara wanted him again, the force of her desire like a tornado swirling uncontrollably inside her. And it wasn't just the way he touched her; it was *him*. He alone commanded her body.

That was a hard realization, along with her growing awareness that her feelings weren't simply those of a girl pining for the first boy she'd ever loved, but a woman desperately infatuated with a man destined to get over her eventually and move on with his life.

If she called him on it, he'd only deny it. Logan could be a pit bull like that. He certainly had been in high school, and she hadn't been able to keep him. Extenuating circumstances aside, she doubted she'd be able to hold him now. Hell, she hadn't even been able to make Brad happy. How would she ever please a man like Logan for long? It was just the case throwing them together. He'd figure that out soon.

She swallowed down the crushing sadness, focusing on anger. It, at least, was safe.

"Just shut up and let's go." She stepped into her skirt and shoes, ridiculously aware of her nudity beneath her clothes, and headed for the door.

With every step, she bounced and jiggled. The silk lining of her skirt brushed the sensitive cheeks of her ass. Even her thighs took notice of the sudden stimulation. And those nipples that Logan had stroked hard again? They reveled in every sensual slide of the fabric, engorging even more. Tara gritted her teeth, wondering if she'd make it out to the parking lot without shoving his pants down and demanding sex. That would serve him right. She frowned. Or was that his plan?

With a sharp economy of movement, he locked up the cabinet, then followed her, locking the dungeon door behind him. In silence, they headed to the club's common areas, and Tara couldn't stop herself from looking around, wondering if the scum who'd murdered Logan's mother—and wanted to kill her—was watching her even now. Around her, the music thumped and bodies gyrated on the floor in the distance as others played out scenes full of their favorite kink. Logan himself continually scanned the crowds, looking for trouble. Thorpe and Bocelli, along with Axel and Jason, had all fanned around the room and were scanning the guests.

"If he's smart, he's long gone," she murmured over her shoulder.

Logan was right there with a hand at the small of her back. He bumped her side, and she felt the unmistakable outline of a gun. "If he's not, I'm ready."

Her FBI-issued piece was in her purse, tucked against her side. If there were danger, she'd be ready, too.

Quickly, Logan hustled her to the door. The anxiety that balled her stomach didn't start to unravel until they were secure in his truck and were backing out of the parking lot.

"What will happen to my car?"

"I'll ask Thorpe to bring it by my condo while you're gone."

So she'd have to retrieve it when they returned from the mission. "Why doesn't he just take it to Adam's house?"

"God damn it, Cherry." He turned to her with not just anger on his harshly angled face, but hurt. "Why are you trying so hard to avoid talking or thinking about our future after this mission? You're crazy if you think we don't have feelings between us to hash out when all this is over. You told your boss that we were going our separate ways afterward. That's bullshit."

"You made a deal," she objected, both thrilled and terrified that Logan seemed so determined to pursue her.

"Which you violated when you argued with me about your wardrobe choice five minutes ago, among other things. Since you pushed back, I'm coming after you. End of conversation."

"I don't understand you. I'm all for helping you move on from the past and—"

"So it's okay if I try to fuck you out of my system. I just can't try to love my way back into your heart?"

His ugly question made her wince. "You're totally misunderstanding me. I just don't . . . I don't want to get hurt again, okay?"

"Hurting and losing you the first time damn near killed me. I won't let it happen again."

Tara sat back in her seat, watching the sparse Dallas traffic slide by. It was warm, despite being nearly one in the morning. But the vibe across the seat was chilly.

Was Logan serious? He seemed so free with his feelings. Then again, he had been in high school, too. She'd spent so many years since then thinking he was a liar and a user. Knowing why he'd dumped her helped, but everything was happening so fast. Still, she couldn't deny that Logan had spent five celibate years. Missing her? It seemed so. She sighed, not certain how to process it now. She was exhausted.

"And I'm doing my best to believe you, but let me catch up. You've had twelve years to reconcile the reason for our split. I've had twelve hours."

"Patience isn't high on my list of attributes, but I'll do my best." Logan sighed. "You hungry, Cherry?"

The food would probably do her good, but she shook her head. "I just want to sleep."

Logan grunted, but said nothing else as he drove to her motel room. When she found the key at the bottom of her purse, Logan grabbed it, opened the door, then flipped on the light.

"Son of a fucking bitch."

Chapter Twelve

Nearby motel—
Saturday night/Sunday morning

TARA peeked around the bulging cap of Logan's broad shoulder and was stunned to find the dingy little motel room completely turned upside down.

On second thought, maybe she should have seen this coming. Bocelli had warned her that the asshole who had killed Logan's mother wasn't the kind to give up. Clearly, this guy had been watching her. As much as she wanted to believe that her room being trashed had been a random vandal's act, it felt like a maniac's rage. He wanted to scare her off.

The drapes had been half pulled from their rod and sat askew over the achingly clean window. Both pillows had been cut open, the stuffing bulging from threadbare cases. The sheets were stained with red paint. Her suitcase had been sliced in half and her clothing strewn everywhere.

Logan drew a SIG SAUER from his shoulder holster, barely hidden by a dark blue windbreaker. "Stay out here in the hall, right under the light, Cherry."

"Bullshit." She reached into her purse and pulled out her Glock, following him into the darkened room, and ignoring his curse.

A cursory examination of the room proved that whoever had

done this was long gone—but had left a wide path of destruction. Anger slapped her, and damn it, she felt violated. The last two days had been hell, and the pressure was only growing thicker.

Tara squeezed her eyes shut and smoothed out her thoughts. She couldn't let this get to her now when there was so much at stake. Darcy certainly wouldn't let some douche bag's breaking and entering interfere with her work.

Logan tore his cell phone from his pocket, then stepped a few paces away and started making phone calls. Tara did the same, figuring she'd better give her boss fair warning. Within ten minutes, the Dallas police arrived to investigate the crime scene. Thorpe and Bocelli pulled up right behind them.

As the detectives and uniformed cops shooed them outside, Bocelli unfolded his powerful body from Thorpe's Lexus and approached. "They're not going to find anything."

Logan nodded, fury simmering off him. "It's a warning."

They were right, and the very thought made Tara trembling mad. The man who'd killed Logan's mother had been here, prowling among her stuff, tearing the place up to scare the shit out of her. What would have happened if she'd returned alone while he was here?

She must have made some noise, because Logan wrapped his arms around her, easing her head to his chest. "Don't be scared, baby. I'm not going to let anything happen to you."

The sentiment was sweet, but Tara knew that was a guarantee he couldn't make. "I'm not as scared as I am pissed. This son of a bitch deserves to pay for everything he's done."

"He'll fuck up, and I'll be waiting."

"I didn't just hear you plotting vigilante justice." Bocelli shot him a tight smile.

Within a half hour, one of the detectives asked Tara to clarify the statement she'd given earlier, then suggested she take an inventory.

Nothing was missing, not even the diamond earrings she'd inherited from her mother or the sweet gold heart pendant she'd received from Adam during her breakup with Logan.

Tara tried not to let this break-in get to her as she packed up her scattered belongings. Logan had a roll of trash bags in his glove box, and she threw everything into a couple, thinking that, in the last forty-eight hours she'd packed up her entire life twice, once to leave a man, and now to tie her fate to another. Everything was changing so fast—the mission, her relationships, and her heart—that she struggled to keep up. Logan pitched in, right beside her, helping her sort and store her things.

With a warning to be careful, Bocelli left, Thorpe driving him away back toward Dominion. The police took a statement from the motel owner, who admitted that he had no security cameras. With a transient population at the motel, no one could say that any particular stranger seemed any more out of place than another. And in this part of town, no one saw anything, regardless of the truth. Logan could tell them about the note, but then they would take it as evidence. The cops wouldn't find anything. Logan preferred to keep the investigation in his own hands. He trusted Bocelli far more than the local P.D.

This was a dead end.

"C'mon, Cherry. You're about to fall on your feet. Let me take care of you."

Logan tied off her trash bags, then tossed them in the back of the truck before helping in her.

"I'm fine."

"I ought to spank your ass red for that lie."

She glared at him. "Because that's going to make me feel so much better right now."

"No, because I can't take care of you if you're not honest with me. When we get to Fantasy Key, clear communication will be critical."

Tara sighed. He was right . . . again. "Fine, yes. I'm exhausted. I couldn't eat dinner because I knew you had something up your sleeve tonight. The public submission and the sex made me hungry.

I've tried to push my apprehension to the back of my mind, but I'm afraid that when I get to the resort I won't be able to pull this off."

Or you'll realize you don't really want me.

Something she'd seen as inevitable even this morning now filled her with dread.

"See, was that so hard?" He started the truck and drove a few blocks, stopping at a twenty-four-hour greasy spoon.

"Eggs at two in the morning?" She shot him a questioning glance.

"It's better than my cooking."

"A killer just went through my belongings, and you want me to eat?"

"It beats the hell out of you fainting."

Logan exited and helped her from the truck. Tara shoved aside her discomfiting, arousing lack of undergarments. The clientele here didn't care. Within minutes, they were tucking into eggs and pancakes. Though it was ordinary food, Tara couldn't remember the last time something tasted this good. She'd been famished.

"Hmm," she moaned, closing her eyes as she savored each bite.

"Don't do that unless you want to make my dick hard," he murmured across the table.

"I'm just enjoying my pancakes."

"I don't differentiate. You make sounds like that, baby, and I'm dying to fuck you."

Tara didn't think he was kidding and couldn't handle another of his sensual assaults now. So she finished her meal in silence.

Finally, she pushed her half-empty plate away. "Oh my gosh, do they feed lumberjacks here?"

"Mostly truckers and drunks. Both can pack a hell of an appetite. You did good. Feel better?"

Whatever his true feelings, Logan took care of her. Tara tried not to read anything into it. After all, that's what Doms did. Even so, he made her feel as if no one else had ever been more important to him. She couldn't deny that turned her on.

"Yes. Thanks."

Logan caressed her cheek. "My pleasure. I look forward to the day you let me take care of you in all ways, all the time."

Tara swallowed against a new wave of shimmering heat. And not about to bite on that dangerous bait, she sent him a wan smile, then headed for his truck.

He drove them about ten minutes north, where the glittering lights of the city were just beginning to give way to a quieter area, and pulled into an assigned parking spot. After killing the engine, he paused for a long moment, clearly choosing his words carefully.

"This means a lot to me, having you here. I hope you'll continue to trust me."

Before she could reply, Logan scrambled out into the cool, humid night. She opened the passenger door, only to find him waiting there with open arms to help her down. With his big hands, he circled her waist and lingered. Tara's breath caught. Finally, he pulled away to grab the trash bags full of her belongings from the back and headed to a nearby door.

He lived in a well-lit, upscale complex with lush gardens and a water feature trickling somewhere nearby. The courtyard tile had hand-painted designs, and the stucco exteriors were a warm beige with chocolate and gold trim. Many of the residents had pots full of flowers or decorative wreaths hung to brighten their doors.

Logan's was bare.

From his pocket, he produced a set of keys and turned one in the lock. To the right, he flipped a metal lever, then pushed the pad of his thumb onto the flat surface that emerged. Finally, she heard a click, and Logan reached out to open the door.

Only to lean back against it, hesitation all over his face.

"I'm not in town a lot. Sometimes, when I am, I like . . . privacy." He swallowed. "I've brought girls here. A lot of girls."

His words were like a sudden slap, and Tara felt sick to her stomach, imagining him here with naked women wet and aching, bucking against his hand or mouth as they came at his command. But she steeled herself against the jealousy. She and Logan hadn't been together in years, and she had no say in how he'd spent his time. Still, the knowledge ate at her insides like acid.

"We're just here to sleep and regroup before we leave in the morning. We've only got a few hours to rest." She shrugged, playing nonchalant.

"To me, it's more. Just—" He sighed. "When we walk through my playroom, close your eyes, okay? Don't think about what's here. I want to take you where I've never brought any other woman, ever. I want you in my bed."

The words took her breath away, made her heart actually flutter. Tara examined her reaction; it made no sense. She already knew that Logan hadn't had intercourse with anyone else in five years, but she sensed that he wasn't talking about sex now. He was talking about sharing his space. Sharing himself.

She was terribly touched. "Why would you want that?"

"You don't ask the complicated questions, do you?" He held out his hand. "Come with me, and I'll try to explain."

Tara hesitated. Somehow, the idea of walking across his threshold, into the bedroom he'd never shared with a woman, felt symbolic, like taking the next step. She shoved the feeling aside, certain she was reading too much into it—until he stood there looking so uncertain.

And suddenly, she realized the truth. "You've been lonely?"

"For twelve fucking years without you, yes." He reached for her, anchoring his hand around her nape. "I've never wanted anyone else in my most personal space. I want you here. I want you now."

His pain compelled her to soothe it. No way she could say no. She put aside everything that had happened tonight, the danger and uncertainty of the future, and placed a soft kiss on his lips.

God, she'd been assuming that he merely needed closure or to work her out of his system. She'd thought maybe he was confused, nostalgic, had the chest-beating need to chase the one who got away—something. Until now, she hadn't really considered that he might truly love her, that he got her on some soul-deep level that neither time nor distance had erased.

How was it possible that three short months of friendship and the loss of her virginity had made such an indelible impression on him? It sounded ludicrous, but somehow it appeared that had happened. Maybe it was time to consider that he knew his heart better than she did.

Maybe she should truly entertain the notion that Logan might still be in love with her.

Hope surged, desire flared. Tara threw her arms around his neck, pressed her body to his against the front door, and layered a kiss over his mouth. He wrapped her tightly in his embrace, clutching the back of her blouse in his fists, and sinking into her mouth like a dying man.

When she moaned, he angled his mouth over hers to press his claim even deeper. His raw hunger sizzled through her.

Why did he affect her as no man ever had? Why did she wonder about his feelings, unless a part of her still loved him, too?

Not ready to face that possibility, Tara wrenched away. "Still want to go inside?"

Logan scanned her face, then the parking lot. "Inside would be safer. Come with me."

After opening the door again, he led her into a dark space. The moon slanted through the blinds as he disabled the alarm, then set it once more. Tara got a fleeting impression of hardwood floors and a wide room without a single sofa or chair. But as her eyes adjusted to the shadows, she saw a spanking bench, a St. Andrew's Cross, and manacles dangling from the ceiling beam. A collection of whips lined the walls.

"Oh God." The words slipped out.

He grabbed her hand. "You've already been on a bench and a cross, baby. You've been manacled from the ceiling. Nothing new there."

"The whips . . ." She backed away.

"They scare you?"

Tara nodded emphatically. "I can't take that."

"This sort of discipline may come up at Fantasy Key." Logan hesitated, raked a hand through his hair. "I wanted to give you the kiss of the whip next in your training, just in case."

"No."

"Cherry, you might not get that choice. What I do . . . it's not like the movies, where they're intentionally tearing flesh from bone. I wouldn't hurt you, not beyond the amount of pain that feels good to you. I'd only arouse you, I swear."

Her mind raced. "But whips draw blood."

"Only if they're meant to. With a light flick of the wrist and the right equipment, they just wake up your skin, make it tingle, like a good spanking. Physiologically, your blood rushes to the surface, stimulating your skin and—"

"Not tonight." Maybe never, but Tara knew she couldn't take it now.

Logan paused, then nodded. "You're right. Tonight, I just want to be with you. No pushing boundaries. Follow me."

At the far end of the living area, he opened a door to a masculine bedroom. It contained nothing but dark, modern furniture and black walls. Everything about it was impersonal, like a hotel room but with less warmth. The lone exception was the bridal portrait of his sister. He slept here alone? The room silently cried out his solitude, discouraged anyone from caring.

Until he grabbed her hand, tugging her inside with a watchful glance, and settled on the edge of the bed. "I want you here."

"I'm here."

"No." He tugged off his T-shirt, revealing his wide chest, heavily roped and veined arms, and abs that rippled when he patted the mattress. "Here."

Heat shafted her. How could she want him again? Why was it that she only had to be near Logan and she needed to feel his skin on hers, press her lips to the strong column of his throat, and spread her trembling thighs so he could work deep into her again?

He reached up, dragged his knuckles across her cheek, then over her suddenly tight nipples. "I know you've been through a lot today. Hell, the last few days. I see that you're confused and don't know where to turn, but I'll tell you where: *Me.* Turn to me. Lean on me, Cherry. I swear to God I won't let you down again. Just let me make love to you."

Resisting Logan was difficult enough when he delivered wicked words in a sexy rumble. This entreaty was twenty times harder to deny. He said that he wanted to help her—and clearly meant it. But he looked at her like she was the answer to his prayers, the medicine he needed to heal. Whatever had happened between them in the past, no way could she refuse him now.

Time to face facts: A part of her belonged to Logan and always would.

"Yes." Her hands went to the buttons of her blouse. Slowly, she slid the first button through its moorings, then the second.

Logan stopped her before she reached the third. "In high school, I had these fantasies about undressing you slowly and revealing that pretty pale skin a soft inch at a time before I kissed it all."

Her breath hitched. Back then, he'd frequently looked at her as if he had sin on his mind. Now, he looked even more wicked. And she knew how wonderful he could make her feel. Every time he touched her, he drove her to the shimmering brink of pleasure and built it into a towering swell of need. And with every kiss, instead of being less affected and working him out of her system, their connection reached deeper inside her, coming dangerously close to her heart.

How the hell did she fight that?

"Logan . . ."

"I'm serious." He slipped the third button from its hole, then caressed the top swell of her breast, moving up with a sweep of his palm until he eased the silk off her shoulder. He stood, leaned in, nipped at her neck with his teeth and a hot breath. "You really don't know how much I want you. But I'm going to show you tonight."

In the back of her head, Tara knew this was reckless. They should rest for the mission and start fresh. But with Logan's blue gaze searching hers through the shadows, she didn't care. She wanted him too badly. She didn't know where their relationship was going. Right now, it didn't matter. Only sharing this solemn, intimate moment did. She could fulfill the fantasy he had of making love to her in his bed. And she could revel in touching the boy she'd never forgotten, who'd become the man able to rule her body with a single velvet caress.

"Show me," she whispered, sliding her lips across his jaw until she reached his ear. "Touch me."

His eyes flared with heat as Logan wrapped his fingers into her hair, pulled her head back, and laid a soft kiss ripe with demand on her lips. Tara whimpered, wanting more. So he took her hand, leading her to the big bed with the black comforter and a mountain of pillows.

Then she noticed the padded manacles extending from the wall behind the headboard, dangling beside the posts, just waiting. For her.

Tara's heart started to race in a wild beat. Then Logan slipped free the final button of her blouse and shoved it down her arms. Even that soft touch made her shiver.

Before the silk slithered to the floor, he was there, hands cupping her breasts, thumbs rasping across her nipples, still sensitive from the cherry clamps he'd used on them earlier. Tossing her head back, she moaned.

"You're so beautiful, baby," he whispered.

Brad had told her that before. The difference was that Logan said it with reverence, his hands worshipful. She believed him.

He slid his palms down to the waistband of her skirt. With a twist of his fingers and a flick of his wrist, it slid down her hips and landed in a puddle with her blouse. Finally, he bent and slipped off her heels, massaging her arches as he set the shoes aside.

"You're going to spoil me."

Straightening, he smiled as he slid a hand over the bare curve of her ass. "That's my job, to see to your needs, to make you feel cherished. So it's working?"

Oh yeah.

Tara closed her eyes and reached for him, needing to touch him, craving more closeness between them.

Instead, Logan caressed his way down her arms, then took both of her wrists in his hands, pinning them together at the small of her back in a silken grip that held like iron. In this position, he forced her to arch, lifting her breasts to him. And he stared with hunger as her nipples hardened more, swelled.

As his free hand glided up her waist, closer to the aching mounds of her breasts, Tara became acutely aware of her helplessness, her vulnerability. Logan could touch her in whatever way he wished. She couldn't stop him.

With their gazes fused together, she lost herself to him. She panted, her nipples rising helplessly with every inhalation. Completely still, he watched, waiting—for what, she wasn't sure. The tension thickened between, crashed through her system, burning into her veins.

"Logan . . ." God, she didn't know exactly what she asked for, except relief.

His slow smile curled up as he dragged a finger down to her drenched folds and fondled her. "Patience, Cherry. I don't want to devour you in one bite. You're a treat to be savored."

Then he thrust a finger inside her, and Tara's pussy clenched around the digit, silently begging for more. Her skin tingled. She needed his hands on her, his cock deep inside her. That need skyrocketed when he withdrew his finger and slid it into his mouth with a savoring moan.

"Christ, do you know what it does to me to see you all naked and aroused, baby?"

Tara shifted closer, jerked her hips against his. She felt only a fleeting impression of his hard cock pressing against his leather pants before he gripped her hip and angled her away. "No rushing me."

"Then stop teasing me."

"What fun would that be?" Cupping a breast, he stroked the underside, brushing a thumb over her aching nipple. "Spread your legs, baby."

Tara did so without hesitation, dying for his next touch, trembling with anticipation.

"Good girl." He swiped a finger across her pleading clit once more, making her gasp. "You're so wet and you tempt me so damn much. I have to muster all my control to stop myself from throwing you to the bed and fucking you senseless."

"Don't restrain yourself on my account," Tara whispered as she rocked against his hand.

Logan pulled his fingers back and stared down into her eyes. "When I'm ready, I won't. But now, you don't have any control over this, Cherry. I say how. I say when. Don't forget it."

Without warning, he slid two fingers deep into her pussy, rubbing at that spot inside that sent her reeling, as he thumbed her burning clit. Already aroused, now his touch felt almost too sharp to bear. Tara gasped and clenched her fists, yearning to clutch his shoulders and rub herself against him like a cat in heat. But he still held her wrists in a steely grip at the small of her back, making her take his shattering touch.

He ramped her up so quickly, she could barely catch her breath. Tingles deluged her as the ache built between her legs to something dark, demanding her every sense, urging her to beg. Orgasm shimmered just within reach.

And he backed away again.

"No, Logan. Damn it!"

He shot her a harsh stare. "I told you, I'll grant your climax when it pleases me, baby. I'll fuck you when I think you're good and ready. If you're damning me now, there's still too much starch in your spine."

His steely words reminded her that, while he had a heart, he was also a big, very bad Dom. Not once since they'd started having sex had he truly unleashed that side of himself on her. Last night, he'd been tender, but desperate to have her. During her training with Xander, he'd been downright possessive. After the public submission, he'd inhaled her.

Tonight, Logan would utterly dominate. This was his fantasy, and his searing stare told her that he planned to live it to the fullest—while he drove her to the brink of sanity.

"Please, Logan. I need more." He'd left her so close to orgasm that her body burned. The air conditioner kicked in, but it didn't help. Instead, the air flow dragged a cool breeze across her nipples that sent her into a sensory tailspin. "I can't take this."

He dragged his fingers through her soaking pussy again, then swirled them around her nipples, coating them with her essence, making them peak harder. "You're strong, Cherry. Trust that, if you give me what I want, I'll give you what you need."

A basic tenet of any good D/s relationship. Tara tried to reassure herself with that fact, but with her body on fire, perspiration beginning to coat her skin, and a haze of need clouding her thoughts, she could only whimper. Submitting everything to Logan in the privacy of his bedroom, when it meant so much to him, when he had complete control of her every sensation, turned her on wildly.

"Can you do that?"

Honestly, she wasn't sure, but she feared that if she said no, he'd stop everything and leave her to burn. "Yes, Logan."

"Good girl." Slowly, he released her wrists. "Get on the bed."

Heart pounding, she did. Logan wasted no time in shackling

each of her limbs at the corners of the bed, spreading her wide open. Then, still dressed in his leathers, he crawled between her knees, sat back on his heels and looked his fill.

Her skin burned under his dark, unwavering gaze. Spread so totally, feeling vulnerable, her pussy seeped with need. She writhed and arched, lifting her hips to him. "Touch me."

"I told you, you're not setting the pace or making the rules. Forget that again, Cherry, and I'll have to punish you." His silky tone belied the hard glitter of his eyes. "I'd rather savor you, so totally open to me. I want you good and ready for every nasty thing I'm going to do to you."

At his words, her pussy clamped down. Empty inside, the aching hollowness consumed her, so acute it almost hurt.

Without warning, Logan bent and lashed his hot tongue across her pussy. She cried out and bucked up, the sudden jolt of pleasure stunning her. Tara wished desperately that Logan would cover her body with his, fill her with his cock, and take her hard.

Instead, he lifted his head, his face dark and intent in the mysterious shadows. "Ready to give me everything I want from you?"

"Yes! Take me. Anything. Everything."

Logan pushed a strand of hair from her face, caressed her shoulder, her breast. "Good answer. I'm going to lift your pussy and ass up, baby. I want them spread wide open for me."

His words thundered a dark desire through her as he slid a pillow beneath her hips, forcing her to tilt up. Her feet turned out, which spread her legs even more, exposing her completely. She fought to touch him, lure him closer, but he'd restrained her so thoroughly that she could only keep her legs spread and raise up to him in a silent plea he ignored.

With a feral smile, Logan slid a possessive hand over her mound. "Here, now, there's no training, just us. It's sweet to know that you like being at my mercy, Cherry. Too bad I'm not going to have any tonight."

He scrambled off the bed to tear off his leathers, then he approached her, his body taut, huge cock standing tall and thick. He glided a gentle hand from her shoulder to one breast, circling, but not touching, its tight nipple. As she gasped, arched, he moved down her abdomen, settling his fingers into her folds.

"I need to give you this dominant part of me, as much as I need you to submit yourself totally. I won't rest until I know that you truly belong to me."

When his gaze locked on hers again, every shred of the desire clawing at him reflected in his eyes. And determination. This was far more than sexual for him. He was playing for keeps.

Her heart turned over in his chest. An alternate thrill and panic rushed through her. What if she let her guard down and he broke her heart again?

What if he didn't and ended up loving her for the rest of their lives?

His eyes hardened. "You're starting to overanalyze this, Tara. Don't."

How could he know that, because he knew her so well?

"I'm giving you fair warning," he whispered, lowering himself over her body. "Tune out those destructive worries and just feel."

Logan captured her mouth with his in a kiss. The simple press of lips quickly turned devastating as his tongue prowled deep, exploring her mouth with a thoroughness that staggered her, leaving her in no doubt of his dominance. He left his stamp of possession on her swollen lips, letting her know that he would take any and every part of her as he wished. As she whimpered, he proved that she didn't want him any other way.

Tara felt herself slipping deeper into a well of desire with every stroke of his tongue against hers. She tried to press her body to his, but the shackles held strong. Instead, she threw herself desperately into the kiss, giving him every bit of her hunger.

Suddenly, he wrenched away and stared down at her, his eyes nearly black as he backed onto his knees and caressed his way down her body, leaving a trail of heat in his wake.

Then Logan settled himself between her thighs, and she quivered. Her heart pounded furiously as he held her gaze while he slowly bent to her pussy.

He lapped at her swollen, slick folds and opened her wider with the spread of his thumbs. "This is mine," he murmured. "It's always been mine."

Yes! The thought screamed through her brain, but she couldn't gasp enough air to say it.

"I'm taking it back, Cherry. Right now."

Nothing tentative about his statement or the torturous flicks of his tongue against her clit.

Heat spiraling, she bucked against the shackles. "Please, Logan."

He ignored her plea and continued with his slow seduction of her flesh, circling her clit with a measured precision that drove her mad. He knew exactly where and how to touch her.

Again, she lifted up, tried to make him taste more of her, but Logan slid his arms beneath her thighs and wrapped them around her body, hands pressing down on her hips. With her thighs now over his shoulders and his face buried between them, she couldn't move an inch.

"Tara, behave. You'll get what you need when I get what I want."

Again, he bent and resumed his slow devastation of her senses. And she could do nothing to stop him.

That knowledge sent an undeniable flare of heat bursting though her. He didn't just arouse her body, but gave her something she craved on a deeper level, something she'd never felt or imagined before. A connection, a give-and-take that she desperately needed.

Her moans turned more desperate with each heartbeat, the promise of sweet release looming closer. Her skin tingled, the sensation magnified as the air conditioner worked overtime, blowing cold air across her body.

Her hands fisted, and she clawed at her restraints. She gulped in huge breaths, tensed against the bombarding sensations as Logan's tongue lashed her clit again and again. Jolts assailed her with every clever lap. She couldn't breathe or think. A frantic scream scratched its way up to her throat and broke free as sparks erupted all through her body.

"Logan, I'm coming!" she cried out in the dark bedroom, breathless and throaty as her fingertips tingled, her blood turned heavy, and pleasure overtook her.

Climax held her in a ruthless grip. And Tara could do nothing but take it, succumb to its dark power. He moaned against her so-sensitive flesh, sending her higher and higher. She hadn't known a climax could be seemingly endless, but the merciless pleasure wracked her body as pulse after pulse rolled over her.

And still, he kept eating at her like a starving man.

"Oh! Logan. I can't stop." Her protest sounded breathy. "It's—oh . . . too much."

Logan ignored her and swirled his tongue around her throbbing nub in a long, unhurried stroke. "I'm not finished, baby. Come for me again."

"But—"

He lapped at her pussy again and again, silencing her. The heat of his mouth spread more fire across her flesh. Then he pressed his fingers deep, deep inside her until the tingling promise of another orgasm shimmered through her.

Tara arched, frenzied. She hadn't believed another orgasm was possible. Now, it was imminent. "Logan! Oh my . . . God. It's too big. I can't . . ."

She thrashed against the bonds, her shaking muscles pressing against his wide shoulders. He didn't budge.

"You can. You'll come for me."

Edict given, Logan lowered his head and resumed torturing her with destructive flicks of his tongue and erotic presses of his fingers.

No matter how much she bucked or pleaded, he showed no

mercy. Logan razed her with the inferno he built inside her, and she cried out over and over as he sucked her clit into his mouth continuously and moaned over her swollen bundle of nerves.

Shocked at the white-hot pleasure tearing through her, Tara tried in vain to pull on her bonds. But the electricity settled between her legs, sharpening the sensation in her nipples. Her empty pussy clenched in protest as the overload of need became too strong to endure.

Shifting helplessly beneath him, Tara screamed his name until she went hoarse. With that ruthless mouth, he continued to streak fire through her cunt, lapping at her, stealing her juices for himself, then humming in approval when her body gave him more.

Conscious thought slipped away until all she knew was Logan and the seething pleasure he forced on her. Each possessive swipe of his tongue stole more of her sanity until every muscle in her body seized up.

"Come!" he demanded.

No way she could hold her climax back. It swept over her, searing her. She screamed as her entire body succumbed to the brutal wave of pleasure that battered her.

His mouth turned gentle, his licks slow as she emerged from the pleasure high. Finally, he pulled away. With an exhausted sigh, she gave herself over to him completely.

The second she did, he lifted his head to watch her with feral blue eyes. "There's my sweet surrender. Now you're ready for me to fuck you."

Tara couldn't look away as he unfastened the shackles at her wrists and ankles. Exhausted, she let Logan move her like a rag doll onto her hands and knees.

"Grab on to the headboard until I tell you otherwise."

With a shaking sigh and a trembling body, she complied.

Positioning himself behind her, Logan grabbed her hips, aligned their bodies, and began pushing his cock inside her. She was so swollen, he had to shove his way in slowly, and she felt every inch he scraped down her pussy.

"Cherry . . ." He moaned as though pleasure agonized him while he pushed in deeper. "So tight."

Besieged by tingles that reawakened her flesh, she inhaled sharply and pushed back on him, taking him deeper.

"Be still." His voice shook, as if he was on the edge of his control.

Tara tried, but she couldn't stop arching, moaning, clamping down as he worked inside. Logan growled, then tightened his hands on her hips, forging in the rest of the way with one quick thrust.

Eyes going wide, she gasped. *Oh God.* Burned by every ridge and vein of Logan's cock, she mewled. Her broken cries seemed to drive him mad, because he nuzzled her neck and silently dismantled her sanity one frenzied thrust after another.

"I *need* to fuck you, Cherry. I've never needed a woman the way I need to possess you."

His words reached into her chest and squeezed. Tara felt not just desired, but cherished.

Logan wrapped his arm around her and latched on to her nipple, rolling it between his thumb and finger ruthlessly. "Take all of me, Cherry. Everything I give you."

He didn't just mean his cock, but all facets of him: his wry humor, his dominance, his caring nature.

His heart.

It was her last thought before he sank his teeth into her neck, pinched her clit, and set a wild pace that sent her soaring headlong into crushing pleasure again. He followed her down into the abyss of ecstasy that had her crying out as he flooded her with his hot release.

She'd definitely have to remember to take her birth-control pill tonight. But unbidden, the image of Logan as her husband, caressing her swollen belly as they awaited their child flashed through her mind. A fierce, destructive longing gripped her.

Tara closed her eyes as Logan lowered her to the mattress, then rolled them to their sides, so that he spooned her against his damp, heaving chest.

"I love you, Cherry. Having you here means the world to me."

She could hear that in his voice. Being here for him suddenly meant the world to her. Her head was filled with images of picket fences and cribs. Damn, was she falling for him . . . again?

Chapter Thirteen

AFTER barely sleeping all night, Tara awoke from her catnap and stretched, every muscle in her body feeling deliciously sore and used. When a girl felt this good, sleep was definitely overrated.

With a smile, she rose, padding her way over to the suitcase Logan had packed for her while she slept. He'd been very specific before leaving for the kitchen to toss together some breakfast: No peeking inside. If she wanted to add anything—no panties allowed—she was to leave the items on top. Tara wasn't sure she liked this rule, as if she were too stupid to pack on her own, but he'd sworn it was about expectation. Fantasy Key would expect her to have certain articles of clothing and other . . . items. And Logan wanted to surprise her with all the things he'd collected for her in the last few days.

Tara wasn't sure what to make of that. She was excited—but scared. Lord knows what a man with Logan's sexual leanings had packed for her.

Repressing a shiver, she brushed her teeth, showered, then changed into her street clothes, at least for now. No doubt, Logan would have her change those before they reached the resort. And no matter how unsettling all his concentrated attention felt, she had to allow it.

Gathering some of her toiletries, she set them on her suitcase. When she came across her cell phone charger, she dug the phone out of her purse to check the battery. Almost fully charged—but she'd missed a call from Adam.

Five thirty in the morning. He'd be up.

She dialed his number, wincing. What should she tell him about everything happening?

"Morning, princess. You're up early."

"Hi, Adam. Yeah, I am. There's been a change of plans." She drew in a deep breath. This part he wouldn't like, for sure. "I'm meeting with Bocelli in thirty minutes, then I'll be on a plane to Florida. There have been some recent developments in my case, so I can't wait to go until Wednesday. I should be home no later than Friday."

"You're leaving so suddenly?"

"You know how this job is. You did it for years."

Adam blew out a breath, clearly concerned. "Yes, but I thought they'd give you more time to prepare for your first assignment."

"I thought so, too. It didn't work out that way."

He paused, and Tara could almost hear him gearing up his arguments from the other end of the line. "Who's your partner for this mission?"

Her heart shuddered to a stop, then beat frantically. "You know I was assigned to York."

"I also know he's gone AWOL." When she gasped at his spying, he rushed to add, "Sorry. I still have friends in the Bureau, and—"

"You're checking up on me." And damn it, if that didn't completely piss her off. "I'm not a child."

"But you *are* a novice."

"You probably know exactly who Bocelli is sending me in with, don't you."

"I do," he admitted. "I got concerned when Brad told me that shithead user was training you. The fact that they're making you partner with him nearly sent me through the roof."

Tara huffed out a breath. "I can't get into this with you now. I have to go in a few minutes and—"

"You're putting yourself in a position to sexually and submissively serve the man who broke your heart. He's going to get inside your head and break your heart again. Just like last time, he'll say and do all the right things. Then, when you've fallen for him, he will rip you in two."

His words pierced her with cold fear and sharp pain. She was definitely having feelings for Logan again. If she didn't put the brakes on them, he'd soon have the ability to total her heart when she crashed.

But Adam didn't know everything.

"I'll be careful. But Logan had reasons for leaving me back then. Reasons he couldn't share with me until now."

"Yeah, so the piece of shit had a reason he's spent years spinning and learning to deliver perfectly."

Tara bit her lip. She thought Adam had Logan all wrong . . . but he'd said much of this to her at sixteen and, for years, it had seemed that he was dead right.

The night Logan had broken up with her, she'd found a beautiful heart pendant in Adam's car. When she asked him if she could have it, he'd given it to her and explained that he'd bought it for her, to serve as a reminder that her heart was fragile and deserved someone who would give it special care. From all of the belongings she'd packed up at Brad's house, she fished out that necklace and slipped it into her purse. She had a feeling that while with Logan over the next few days, she'd need the reminder.

"Guard your heart," he insisted. "Get in, do your job, get out, then get as far away from that son of a bitch as you can."

She couldn't promise that, not with the feelings she was having for Logan now, but she didn't want to argue with Adam, especially when he might be right. "I'll tread carefully and do whatever I need to, I promise."

Plane ride to Florida—Sunday morning

Bocelli's warning rang in Logan's ears: Don't appear to want Tara too much.

Logan knew he had to hide his need for her or this mission would blow up in their faces. But as she curled up against his side on the airplane, her cheek resting on his shoulder as she clasped his hand trustingly, he had everything he'd ever wanted. Too bad this situation wasn't that simple. Ending this mission safely had to take priority over his heart. That meant he had to shove aside his desperate urge to tie Tara to his bed again and master her body until she admitted that she still loved him. And she did; he was almost certain of that.

He itched to get some stamp of ownership on her, not so that Thorpe allowed him to keep his membership at Dominion—although once they were together and Logan met Thorpe's conditions, he had a feeling that he and Cherry would play there sometimes—but because he *needed* to make her his. And he was desperate to be hers.

Getting these sick freaks who abducted women and made them slaves had to come first. Then he'd deal with the fucker who had killed his mother and now threatened Tara.

But one way or another, Logan vowed that Tara wasn't getting away from him again.

As the flight landed, she jarred awake, blinking at him from behind fluttering ginger lashes, her expression sleepy and trusting. Just like that, she made him hard again.

"Are we here?"

"We're in Key West." He dropped his voice to something barely above a whisper. "Once we step off the plane, Fantasy Key's van should pick us up. From that point on, we'll have to stay in character. I'm going to be a son of a bitch, and you're going to have to obey. I'll apologize in advance and tell you that, for the most part, this isn't me."

She bit her lip. "I just hope I'm ready to handle whatever comes my way."

"Whatever you do, keep hold of that little temper of yours. Think about how every response will look to others."

"What about that VIP room Bocelli told us about this morning? If women are being 'auditioned' there, like he suggested, it's important we find our way in quickly and often."

"Once we determine who sends out those invites, we'll work on him. For now, be on your best behavior. I'll be on my worst. If we do this right, this scumbag should come after you."

With a shaky nod, she rose and grabbed her carry-on luggage as the other passengers filed off the plane. Logan knew she was nervous. Hell, he was, too. His missions mostly consisted of timing, precision, and blowing the head off of some terrorist motherfucker. When he engaged in combat, he usually knew exactly who to target. This would be different, especially since he had to protect Cherry first and foremost.

Logan stood behind her, staying her from stepping into the aisle by wrapping an arm around her waist and pulling her back against his chest.

"Nothing I'm going to say or do here publicly is any reflection of how I feel about you. I need you to know that."

Tara swung her gaze over her shoulder, meeting him head-on. "I know. And I asked for this assignment. I'm trying not to be scared."

He planted a soft kiss on her lips. "It's natural. Just remember, lean on me when you need to. I'll take care of you."

"This is *my* job." Her mouth set in a stubborn line. "I need to do it."

"We're a team," he reminded her darkly. "Don't play hero all by yourself."

Cherry gritted her teeth as that independent streak asserted itself. "If we're a team, you need to remember that I have a role here besides kneeling at your feet."

Fuck, she was right.

"I'll try to keep my inner caveman at bay," he quipped and reluctantly released her, following her, luggage in hand.

Once they'd deplaned and worked their way to the baggage claim, they found a driver in a black suit, his dark hair tucked under a cap, carrying a sign directing people to Fantasy Key.

It didn't take long for their checked luggage to come off the carousel. Logan grabbed it and turned toward the driver, whispering to her, "Showtime . . ."

She nodded nervously.

"Deep breath," he demanded in a low voice.

She complied, slowly relaxing.

"Better," he praised, then directed her to the driver, who watched them carefully with dark eyes.

"You're heading to Fantasy Key?" the driver asked. He wore a small nametag that read JORDAN.

Tara started to reply. Logan cast her a sharp stare. Instantly, she closed her mouth.

"Yes. Logan Flint," he said, using the name Bocelli and the FBI had used when making their reservations at the resort.

Jordan set the sign at his feet, then glanced at the notepad he'd tucked into his shirt pocket. "Very good. And your submissive is Tara Cabot?"

"Yes."

"May I address her?"

Logan paused. Even the drivers observed protocol. Serious stuff . . . "Sure."

"Excellent." The thirtysomething man, now giving off a definite Dom vibe, turned to Tara. "Do you need help with your carry-on bag?"

Helping Tara should be Logan's own right and responsibility, but Jordan had a job to do. Normally, Tara would prefer to make her own decisions, no doubt. In this case, she made a small production of glancing at him, as if seeking permission. She was definitely on her game.

"Answer him," Logan demanded.

Something about Jordan bothered Logan, probably the way he looked at Cherry as if he'd like to eat her whole. If they'd been traveling to this resort for real, he would have rescinded the driver's permission to address Tara and growled a warning. But he had to play indifferent.

"Yes. Thank you for your help." Tara rolled the pull-along in Jordan's direction.

The driver took it. After Logan declined help with the rest of the luggage, they followed Jordan to a sleek black sedan.

"You're the only guests who've arrived on this flight, so unless you need to make a stop in town for anything, we'll be on our way."

"No stops necessary." Logan just wanted to get there, find Tara's missing friend, and get out, hopefully after nailing the degenerates who farmed victims from a resort intended to celebrate what should be a deep and sacred power exchange.

"You'll be with us for three days?" Jordan asked.

"Maybe four, as my schedule allows." They'd left themselves a bit of wiggle room, in case they didn't complete their mission objectives right away.

Jordan glanced at Tara in the rearview mirror. "Do you require anything before we arrive? There are cold bottles of water in your cup holders. I also have a few snacks, if you'd like one."

Logan clenched his fist. Jordan didn't need to ask Tara those questions; a good Dom took care of his sub, and Logan had already persuaded her to both eat and drink something on the plane. But the driver was interacting with Tara, gauging her interest in him. As much as it chafed, Logan played his role and glanced out the window in seeming disinterest.

He'd rather pound Jordan's face.

"No, thank you," she said softly.

"Very well. Mr. Flint, we're aren't far from the dock. We'll take a twenty-minute boat ride to our private island. We have a dressing area there. You'll have the opportunity to change her clothes. Submissives are not permitted to wear shoes unless scening, house rules."

Already this place felt strange. The rules were definitely more lax at Dominion and put more control in the hands of the individual Doms. He had an inkling there would be more surprises once they arrived at Fantasy Key.

"Can you tell me a bit about what we can expect after arrival? I would like the opportunity to rest and speak with my slave in private before engaging with others."

"After check-in and orientation for all the new resort guests, in which we'll review the basic rules, there will be time to rest. After dinner, you'll be escorted around the various play areas, then asked to scene for your guide, to ensure you're capable of following the resort's rules."

"Guide?"

Jordan smiled smugly in the rearview mirror. "Me. We were short a driver today, so I volunteered, but I'm your dungeon master."

Just fucking perfect.

Logan looked out the passenger window again, restraining the urge to pound Jordan's face. Beside him, he felt Tara slip her hand in his. He didn't dare look at her now; his expression would reflect possessiveness and need. But he squeezed back before releasing her.

The minutes slipped by until they reached a small marina with a speedboat tethered to the sun-washed dock. Jordan handed Tara a life jacket and helped her put it on, his hands lingering when they shouldn't, before directing Tara to a shaded overhang with a smile. "To protect your fair skin, sweet sub."

Tara did the perfect job of looking flustered and slightly flattered by his attention. On the inside, Logan seethed and almost choked, trying to restrain himself from beating the shit out of Jordan. Instead, he had to wander to the front of the boat and pretend interest in the big blue ocean. When really, water wasn't that beautiful to a SEAL; it was just a place to get the job done.

Long minutes stretched, and he resisted the urge to look back at Cherry. He heard their guide's low-voiced murmur to her. Her reply sounded breathy and small. The good news was, if Jordan had any say in which female guests were singled out for auction, Tara stood a good chance of being picked. For that reason alone, he pretended not to pay them a lick of attention again until they docked on the private island.

Logan tossed a few bags Jordan's way, keeping his own carry-on close. Besides having a satellite phone and his laptop inside, he also had Cherry's change of clothing. Idly, he wondered how she was going to feel about his selections, but nearly any reaction would be worth this view.

The fact that Jordan would see, too—and likely wet himself—set Logan's teeth on edge. But he couldn't let jealousy derail him. Instead, he herded Tara to the private cabana, not terribly surprised to find it more like a spa without the attendants. With Tara's help, he scanned the room for any listening or recording devices and, thankfully, found it clean.

Leading her to a padded table in the middle of the room, he laid Tara down, then pulled up a chair, settling close to her face. Her doe-soft eyes reflected a mixture of apprehension and determination. She'd see this through, no matter what.

"Now it gets tougher, Cherry. We have to play like this is for real."

"I thought we were."

Logan paused. "If you were truly any Dom's submissive, he would have already made modifications to your dress. And to your body."

She rolled her eyes. "I figured you'd put me in some get-up, but I can't reduce the size of my ass. I've tried. It's just big."

"It's luscious," he corrected. "I adore it. That's not the issue. Before we leave this room, you need to be comfortable with two changes."

Reaching into the bag at his feet, he pulled free a bundle wrapped in tissue paper, set it on the counter behind him, and removed the tags. His hands shook. Tara was going to look gorgeous, and he wished to fuck that he didn't have to share the view with anyone.

"Logan?" she called from behind him.

"You'll be dressed submissively, Cherry." Of course, he didn't tell her that if he had his way, if he could persuade her to the altar, she'd always be dressed submissively in the privacy of their bedroom. "Which is to say, barely dressed at all."

"Yeah . . ." She sounded breathy.

"Good. One last change." Logan sat in the chair by her side again, landing a hand on her thigh, then gliding his fingers up, up, up until he covered her mound. "I've got to shave you."

She gulped in a deep breath, then sent him a shaky nod. "I suspected that."

Pride swelled in Logan. She'd taken it well. In truth, he preferred her fiery red pussy, but it would be exciting to see her completely bare.

"I can do it myself." Tara eased up on her elbows, looking around for a razor.

Logan shook his head. "It's my privilege and my right. Lie back."

She stared, clearly stunned. Logan gazed back, unblinking. He knew the second it dawned on her that he meant those words. In the next instant, she licked her lips and lowered herself to the table again.

Pride speared him as he turned to the counter behind him and found the necessary tools. In moments, he brought over a warm washcloth. "Spread your legs wide."

She hesitated. "That's your Dom voice."

"And you'll be hearing it a lot for the next few days. This is probably one of the few personal acts we'll have between us while we're here. I want this."

Within seconds, she opened to him, parting creamy pale thighs, slowly revealing that silky red hair that hid all her sweet pink secrets. Just looking at her made him want her with something bordering obsession.

Swallowing down his lust, he set the washcloth over her cunt, softening the skin and hair. In the cabinet beside him, he found a can of shaving cream and a fresh disposable razor. He lifted the washcloth from her flesh, gratified to see it soft and rosy, then he slathered the foamy white cream on top. With extreme concentration, he drew the razor across her mound, down her vaginal lips, then ordered her to flip over and get on all fours. Before she had time to question him, he'd swiped more shaving cream between her cheeks. She tensed and tried to clench against him, but he held her open to shave away the wisps of hair, then wiped her clean. He finished off by rubbing her top to bottom with soothing lotion.

"God, that's embarrassing," she groaned.

"Really? I'm turned on and can't wait to do it again tomorrow. Get on your back."

She complied slowly. "Logan, this is happening so fast. I'm used to having the opportunity to talk things through with you."

And her tone indicated that she felt uncertain about this total imbalance of power. "You could have used the extra training, but with the changes in the situation, we didn't get to progress further. You're going to have to trust for me. When we can't openly communicate, that's all we'll have. Now spread your legs again."

Slowly, with trust in her eyes, she opened to him, her pussy completely bare. It nearly brought him to his fucking knees.

Unable to help himself, he swiped a thumb through her slit. She was soaking.

He settled the digit over her clit. "You like it when I go all Dom on you."

"It's a little annoying and frustrating sometimes." She raised her chin in challenge.

"Probably, but it still makes your sweet little pussy wet." And Logan loved that fact. He cocked his head and stared as a thought occurred to him. "Did you ever realize before being with me that you're submissive?"

She closed her eyes, looking away, almost like she was ashamed. "No."

Fuck shame. "Look at me."

Tara did, then sighed. "No. Bocelli told me my profile indicated that, and I . . . thought he had a screw loose."

Whoever had compiled her psychological profile had been dead-on. The Feds weren't the only perceptive folks out there. Other men had crossed paths with Tara and certainly figured her out, too. And Tara's sweet nature had probably turned them on, damn it.

Too bad. She was his right now, and if he played his cards right, always.

He reached for the tissue-paper bundle, untying the silken red bow around it with a single pull. He fished inside for the thong and handed it to her.

Cherry stared at the little scrap of transparent flesh-colored fabric like he'd lost his mind. Then she shifted her weight and heaved out a breath. "Wow, nothing says 'see my wide ass' quite like this little garment."

He'd had enough denigration against her luscious backside. Wrapping a hand around her neck, he yanked her closer, bringing her crashing against his chest. "Not another negative word about yourself or you'll answer to me."

"You're serious?" She blinked.

"Damn straight. And I could tell you all day long how fucking sexy I think you are, but you won't hear me. I'm hoping this will help you figure it out and keep your cover. Put it on."

She fingered the garment, then nodded. "Okay. If anyone laughs, I'm punching you."

Logan couldn't help it; he grinned. She snuck under his Dom persona and warmed his heart. He couldn't resist planting a sweet, slow kiss on her lips. "You can try."

"Bully." She stuck out her tongue playfully.

Then she donned the thong and looked down. "Oh, come on. Seriously?"

Logan nearly swallowed his tongue. "Yes."

"There's a big bow down *there*, which would be fine if it covered something. But instead, I just look like some X-rated present."

"Yeah." He grinned. "I wish we had time to—"

"But we don't, perv. As it is, Jordan is probably wondering what's taking so long."

"Fuck Jordan," he said automatically.

Tara wrinkled her nose. "Pass. Something about him seems . . . off."

"Good instinct, Cherry. I'd bet my last dime that guy is seriously bent."

Logan turned his attention back to the tissue paper bundle in his hand. And now for the next adornment. He got even harder just thinking about it.

Without preamble, he bent and cupped one of her breasts, sucking her nipple into his mouth, nipping it with his teeth. Tara gasped, arched to him. God, he could do this all day. And someday, he would.

When the nipple turned hard and began to swell, he eased back and pulled the first of two metallic ornaments from his hand. "These are nipple huggers. Watch."

He parted the delicate object at the tiny hinge, then settled it around her nipple, tightening the thin wire beneath until it encompassed the little taut bud securely. Stepping back, he surveyed his handiwork. And damn near came in his pants.

The fragile silver, shaped like petals, unfurled around her rosy-brown nipple, which now looked like the flower's lush center.

"Perfect," he murmured as he bent to repeat the process with her other breast.

As soon as he finished, she shifted her weight from one foot to the other. "They're tight."

"They're supposed to be, but you'll be able to wear them all day without issue."

She nearly choked. "All day?"

"Yes. Walk across the room and back for me."

Since the little bathroom of this spa wasn't terribly big, three steps took her toward the slate tiled wall. When she pivoted back, her eyes had gone wide and stunned.

"Oh my gosh . . ." Tara turned her shocked stare on him. "I suspected it turned me on . . . but I'm so wet."

He smiled indulgently. "Exactly."

"And you knew that. You really are a perv."

"Amen. Here's the last bit of your outfit."

Cherry took the little top he extended her way with a reluctant stare. "It's totally sheer."

"Yeah. Isn't it awesome?"

She socked him in the arm with a half-hearted punch. "I'll freeze to death."

"Baby, it's summer in the Keys. You won't get cold." He cupped her face in his hands. "You're going to do great. And remember, just because I'm not looking at you doesn't mean I'm not dying to."

"You don't have to keep reassuring me."

Yeah, he did. Logan had a bad suspicion this could get painful for both of them.

Carrying her old clothes, he led her out the door and stiffened when Jordan locked his gaze on her.

Somehow repressing his violent instinct, Logan backed away and let the creep help Tara into the car. Within minutes, they were pulling up to the resort, a huge white building designed with a cottage motif that spanned the length of a private beach. The ocean lapped gently at its edges. All around, private cottages soaked in the afternoon sun. The whole thing reeked of money and exclusion.

Jordan climbed from the car and opened the door for Tara, holding out his hand. He'd said the pretty boy could talk to Tara, not touch her. And damn it, Logan knew he had to pretend not to care. The next three days were going to be pure fucking torture.

Fantasy Key—Sunday afternoon

Their seemingly eight-handed driver escorted them to a side door, which he unlocked. The door gave way to an air-conditioned meeting room just inside the resort. Jordan palmed Tara's hip as he helped her inside, and Tara repressed a shiver. Hopefully, her contact with him would be brief over the next few days. Logan had done a good job hiding his irritation, but she'd felt his livid fury under the surface. She smiled to herself.

When Jordan excused himself for a moment, Tara scanned the room. She hadn't expected the lobby since they'd entered from the side. What she saw instead was tuxedoed waiters circulating with platters of fruit and cheese, ornate quiches, crab-stuffed mushrooms, and champagne. Tara desperately wanted a glass to calm her nerves, but Logan declined on her behalf when a young waiter passed.

A few other guests milled around. Tara stared at them—a motley collection of Doms and Dommes, most tagging a submissive or two along who were often dressed far more scantily than she. A few submissives had come alone.

Logan surveyed their surroundings, too. "You see anything interesting?"

She frowned. "Yeah. See the submissive talking to Jordan, the one in the latex corset with her boobs hanging out?" she whispered.

He shot her a wry glance. "Sort of hard to miss her. She's really working it."

"Totally, but notice how she's greeting Jordan like an old friend?"

"Or flirting up a storm."

Tara shook her head. "I don't think so. Most every sub looks a bit apprehensive, like they're not sure what to expect next. She doesn't.

And she keeps glancing at the door on the other side of the room, like she's expecting someone to enter from that direction."

After a watchful minute, Logan nodded. "You're right. But she might work here. We know from Xander that they employ Doms to top the single submissive guests. Maybe the reverse applies."

"Possible. But I think she may be our best bet to start getting the lay of the land."

"Agreed." Regret crossed his face. "I'd really love to touch you now, but it doesn't serve our purpose. So, this is where I'm going to pretend to strike up a flirtation with the little sub. You hang in the corner and see if Jordan comes your way. He may chat you up once I'm gone."

Tara didn't like that idea at all, but she'd come to Fantasy Key to investigate. "Agreed."

Logan nodded, his eyes already across the room on the other woman. And her large, enhanced breasts with the bloodred teardrop crystals hanging from her pierced nipples.

In the corner, Tara did her best impression of a sub who had been relegated to the back burner by her Dom. She dropped into a slave position, head down, and waited. A collection of boots—both men's and women's—wandered past. Tara felt eyes on her, scanning, accessing. One man even walked a circle around her. She tensed, blocking out the feeling of being alone and vulnerable in front of a stranger. Looking up or telling him off would be seen as a punishable sign of disrespect.

"You're not collared, pretty sub. You have a lovely ass," the deep voice said from just behind her, near her ear. "Do you have a name?"

Answer? Don't answer? Before she could decide, a familiar pair of loafers came into view.

"This sub is spoken for," Jordan told the other Dom. "I'll advise her Master over there"—Tara looked up through the fringe of her lashes to see him point—"that he must clearly mark his property or be prepared to lose her."

The Dom stood closer to Jordan. "If he's not claiming his terri-tory, perhaps there's a reason. And he looks rather busy with another sub."

Tara risked a peek across the room at Logan—and jealousy stabbed her heart. He looked at the virtually topless blonde as if she fascinated him. She spoke, eyes drifting down for a second. Logan leaned close and ran a knuckle under her jaw, then over the swell of her breast. Before Tara could stop it, she gasped.

Jordan stepped into her line of vision. "Did your Master leave you here?"

"Yes." She willed herself to lower her gaze, and stared hard at the green-and-gold-patterned carpet. Logan was doing his job, she told herself. Yes, but did he have to look so enthusiastic about it?

"Are you being punished?" Jordan asked.

"No."

"No, Sir?" he corrected her.

She brought her full focus back to Jordan. With Logan seem-ingly otherwise occupied, was the dungeon master trying to estab-lish a rapport with her? As much as he raised her hackles, getting in good with him would help their cause.

"No, Sir," she repeated, doing her best to sound breathy and chastised at once.

"Look at me."

Immediately, she raised her gaze to his. Without the driver's cap, he was almost too attractive. Sharp bone structure, a lean swimmer's sort of body, dark hair with a hint of curl around his ears and just tousled enough to make him look like he could find trouble and be happy reveling in it. Very Abercrombie. Something about him chafed at her instincts.

"Very good." He glanced at his watch. "We have a few minutes before the orientation begins. Would you like a little bonus tour?" He lowered his voice conspiratorially. "You won't see this part of the resort unless you're invited."

The VIP area? If that's what Jordan meant, it would be an awesome break for her case. She glanced back over at Logan, trying to catch his attention. He didn't veer for a second from Miss Plastic Double-D Cups.

"You won't be gone long enough for him to miss you," Jordan promised, sidling closer.

In fact, every time she acted a bit shy and overwhelmed, he seemed more interested. She'd noticed it on the boat and again just now. So she played the reticent card by looking down once more and angling her shoulders away from him.

"He might get angry. I don't know . . . Sir."

"Hmm," he moaned very near her ear, like just hearing that word on her lips turned him on. "If he's angry, I'll talk to him, let him know I led you away."

In truth, she didn't want to go anywhere with Jordan. She could feel his lascivious gray eyes scanning every inch of her flesh, lingering especially on her nipples. But turning him down now might mean the opportunity would never come again.

"A—all right. Thank you, Sir. I'm very curious." She tried to sound breathy and flattered.

Jordan reached for her arm, grazing the side of her breast with his long fingers. She gasped, and he chuckled in her ear as he guided her out the door. "I'll bet you're a very curious pet. There are many things here I'd love to show you."

Tara didn't have to pretend to shiver, though she hoped he'd interpret it as excitement.

As they neared the door leading deeper into the resort, Logan cast her a sidelong glance, even as he all but buried his face in the blonde's neck. The other sub looked flushed and she swayed toward him like she was ready to lie down and spread her legs.

Shoving the feelings of betrayal down, Tara let Jordan lead her out of the room. She and Logan were assuming identities and behaving like those characters for this case. But as she nibbled at the side of her cheek, Tara felt old insecurities sneak back into her head. The sub Logan flirted with reminded her so much of Brittany Fuller from high school, the girlfriend he'd taken to bed both before and after her.

Logan had told her just this morning that he loved her. But in the past, love had never equated with being faithful for Logan. He'd left her to protect her before, yes. But had it really been necessary to punctuate their breakup with an exclamation note by fucking Brittany at a party that night and letting the whole school know? Granted, he'd been celibate these last few years, but what if she'd "cured" him of that so he could now move on with someone else? Even if he didn't really want this blonde, would he take her to bed in order to wheedle information from her? Did he want to?

"You're thinking awfully hard, little sub. Understandable since your Dom isn't here to do it for you."

Blech. Did he really just say that?

"So let me help," Jordan continued on. "There's nothing to worry about. If you aren't getting the proper attention from Logan, I'll make sure you receive it. I would love to take you under my wing for the duration of your stay."

Yeah, how often did he use that line? He probably had success with it or he wouldn't be using it now.

She forced a smile, fluttered her lashes, and looked away demurely, holding back the urge to vomit.

Jordan looped an arm around her shoulders. "So sweet. You haven't been submitting long?"

He phrased it like a question, but clearly he knew the answer. Tara jumped to mental attention. Jordan was a Dom—and clearly a smart one. Unless she wanted him to figure her out and get suspicious, she'd better stay on top of her game.

"No. Master Logan is my first Dom. I'm trying to learn, but I fear he's . . . losing interest in me."

A nice add to their cover story. Jordan instantly took the bait.

"I won't let you spend your time here alone." He picked up the pace down a long hallway, then used a key card to enter an elevator to a higher floor. Inside the car, Jordan caressed her hips with his thumbs, and Tara felt his breath on the back of her neck as he nestled his hard cock against her ass. It was all she could do to stand there and let him touch her.

When they emerged into a hall, it was empty, except the super-plush decor. Tara stopped in alarm. For all she knew, Jordan was taking her to a deserted part of the resort to abduct her now. It's not like she was wearing a gun with this getup—something she intended to talk to Logan about if she got free.

"We're almost there, sweet sub."

"I—I'm afraid." She kept playing her shy almost-virgin card. "Where are you taking me?"

He grabbed her chin and forced her to look at him. "The VIP room. It's a very special place where your fantasies can come true. Would you like that?"

Tara's stomach jumped. This definitely was a break, and she needed to stay in Jordan's good graces.

"Really? Yes, Sir."

"Look." He led her down to the end of the hallway, then used his key card to access a set of double steel doors. After they clicked open, he shoved them wide.

Before her was a BDSM heaven—or hell. Three naked men stood around a flushed brunette who was bound and blindfolded. Tara tried not to let her jaw drop as they each took turns feeding their cocks into her mouth or pussy. Her tight breasts bobbed with every thrust.

"Does that excite you?"

It was titillating and repelling at once, but she played along. "Oh my . . . yes."

"This slave's fantasy was to experience complete submission to strangers while her Dom watches. I think they're both enjoying it."

With a glance across the room, Tara spotted an older, very ur-bane man lounging in a recliner, watching the scene with a faint smile as he sipped a glass of brandy. In the chair beside him, another man watched. He looked more official, and she realized he wore the same black garb that Jordan did, emblazoned with the resort's logo in turquoise on the front. He also wore a matching tie. Another dungeon Master? Someone higher up the food chain?

The man looked her way, sized her up. Tara had to resist the urge to take a step back. When Jordan glanced at her, it was like he sized up a sex object he couldn't wait to get his dick into. This man looked at her like a commodity he couldn't wait to exploit.

The brunette across the room gasped, then screamed, as if she were in pain. Tara swung her gaze across the room, stunned to see the sub, now bent at the waist, taking the cock of yet another man, this one wearing a latex hood. His penis was blue at the head and enormous. She'd never seen equipment that large on any guy. And he was ruthlessly shoving it into the woman, between her legs that had been tied obscenely wide apart.

Tara stiffened.

"So innocent." Jordan laughed. "She wants this. She enjoys the struggle of taking a man this size."

Seriously? Given how painful it looked, she couldn't imagine why. And the woman was going to fail. Though the man pounded away at her, at least three inches of his cock remained outside her body.

The woman's well-dressed Dom rose and doffed his dark blue blazer, sauntering across the room. He lifted her head to him by fisting a handful of her hair and yanking.

"Do you like it, slave?"

"Yes, Master. Thank you, Master."

"Take more of his cock. You've got inches to go."

The words alone nearly made the woman come, given the way she gasped and moaned. The man behind her shoved more of his dick in her pussy. She screamed again. Her Dom angled her head toward the man to her left, who rapidly stroked himself, then came in her open mouth.

"Swallow," her Dom demanded.

She did, then groaned again when the other two men around

her, also masturbating, came in fluid strokes across the smooth olive skin of her back. As they did, she arched and stuck her butt out. The stranger with the huge cock thrust even deeper into her pussy, until most of it disappeared. Then her Dom settled his fingers on her clit.

"You want to come, slave?"

"Please, Master. Please."

"You have my permission." He rubbed furiously between her legs as the hooded stranger shoved into her. The brunette's mouth opened in a silent O for a long moment. She closed her eyes, focusing. Then she screamed loudly, her entire body convulsing as the hugely hung stranger groaned in release.

Tara let out a breath. It was a scene she wouldn't want to participate in, but the submissive had clearly enjoyed herself. And that freedom of self-expression appealed to Tara.

"Very well done," the man with the emblazoned shirt and the tie said, clapping. "Was the scene to your satisfaction?" he asked the brunette's Dom.

Surprise poked at Tara. That voice sounded familiar . . .

"Yes. Thank you."

The two men shook hands, then the Dom unclipped his female, wrapping a gentle arm around her, before he grabbed his jacket, and helped her out the door.

The second they'd gone, the other man turned his attention to her. "And who have we here?"

Tara frowned. Yes, she'd definitely heard that voice before. His face wasn't familiar at all, but his voice—mellow, with a used car salesman flare—she knew. But from where?

Damn, she couldn't place it.

Jordan shoved her forward. "This is a new little sub whose Dom is . . . otherwise occupied. Her name is Tara."

The man stuck out his hand. "I'm Lincoln Kantor, the resort's manager. Welcome to our VIP room. I think you'll enjoy it here."

Chapter Fourteen

"WHAT did you find?" Tara whispered to Logan after Jordan and Mr. Kantor escorted her back to the orientation, all smiles and attentiveness.

The two of them were a one-two punch of pure wrong.

A quick glance around the room proved that Logan's little slut bunny had gone, and he stood alone, arms crossed over his massive chest. He didn't have to pretend to be angry.

When she reached his side, he wrapped his hand around her arm and dragged her to the back of the room. "Where the hell did you go?"

"The VIP room. I met Fantasy Key's manager." Tara nodded at Kantor, who stood at the front of the room, reaching for a microphone. He looked distinguished with this tall, almost scholarly build, his hair more salt than pepper. "That's him."

"Hello, everyone. Welcome to Fantasy Key," Kantor said into the microphone, wearing a friendly, perfectly fake smile.

Everyone clapped. Jordan stood beside his manager, scanning the crowd. His gaze found her and lingered. She played shy and looked down.

Logan lingered close to her during the orientation, which was a general overview of the resort's rules, meal times, dungeon hours, and etiquette. Tara listened with half an ear, bursting with everything she'd learned earlier, trying to process it all.

The second Kantor walked off the stage and started shaking hands, Logan grabbed her by the arm and thrust her out the door and down the hall.

Tara dug in her heels. "Where are you taking me?"

"Our room. We have two hours before dinner and play time."

They were here to work a case, so they needed to make use of every free second. "Great, but could you slow down? Unlike you, I'm not six-four."

Cursing under his breath, Logan slowed his step. "What did you see in the VIP room?"

"Some hardcore stuff." She explained the scene she'd witnessed. "And in case you didn't notice, Jordan was very interested in me. As was Kantor."

Logan scowled. "They were so obvious, they might as well have been wearing signs. And either Kantor is a piss-poor manager, or he knows *exactly* what's happening under his roof."

She agreed with that assessment. "I'm betting on the latter. He's creepy with a capital *C*. The weirdest thing? I know I've heard his voice before. I just can't place it."

He snapped a laser-sharp stare in her direction. "You're sure?"

"Positive. I just wish I could remember where . . ."

"Keep working on it." Logan clenched his jaw and grabbed her elbow. His strides picked up pace again as they turned a corner.

"Seriously, slow down." She jerked her elbow from his grasp. "What are you so pissed about?"

"Pissed, worried, out of my mind . . ."

Logan didn't stop again until he found their room and used the key card to push her inside the door. He slammed it behind him. "Strip."

"Excuse me?" Tara's brows shot up and her jaw dropped. He wanted to play games? Even as a first-time field agent, she knew they had to sweep the room for bugs. It was standard protocol.

"Take everything off except your nipple huggers. Now," he growled.

"Fuck off," she growled under her breath, pointing around the room, then to her ears.

With a curt nod, he tore around the room, looking in crevices and crannies, upending pillows, lifting lamps, uncovering bare walls behind pictures. Tara joined in, searching the room.

Suddenly, Logan stiffened, then set the remote control back on the desk. "Come with me, slave."

As he dragged her to their luxurious bathroom, her mind raced. He'd found surveillance equipment in their room. Was every suite in this place equipped in that way, as a part of some standard operating procedure? Or had she and Logan been discovered before they'd even stepped foot on the island? Shit. If so, what should they do next?

Inside the dazzling bathroom, natural stone tiles blended with glass accents in earthy colors. Soft lighting, fluffy towels, and a sinful shower with six heads waited. Logan flipped on the faucet full blast in the huge stall. A muscle ticked in his jaw.

"Last warning. Strip or else."

This was the only way they could talk freely. Their voices would be obscured by the spray.

Tara swallowed and complied, pushing the little top's spaghetti straps down her shoulders, then peeling the sheer material off her body. Logan ate her up with his gaze, his face growing intent, his eyes fierce, predatory. Her breath stuttered.

Then he backed her against the wall and shoved the thong down her legs with a growl. Flinging the little garment aside, he rose and covered her body with his own, the muscled slabs of his chest and sinewy arms eclipsing her. Notching his hard cock right between her thighs, he tore off his own clothes. Then he fused their mouths together with a dark hunger that sent her reeling.

God, they were here to do a job, and she was exhausted after the last forty-eight really eventful hours, but the second he kissed her, all that fell away. Only the mind-stealing sear of desire and the desperate need to feel Logan inside her remained.

Tearing his mouth away, a muscle in his jaw ticking like leaving her for a second pissed him off, he tossed her into the shower and closed the clear glass doors behind him.

Tara frowned. "Logan, I—"

"Our room is bugged," he spat out matter-of-factly.

"I guessed as much. Why?"

"I don't know. I'm damn worried that means someone already knows who we are and why we're here. As much as I hate it, I'm wondering if we should bail."

She shook her head emphatically. "I can't walk away from this assignment without proof that we've been made. I can't leave Darcy . . . I've got to find her before Thursday, when intel says they'll take her out of the country." To film the snuff piece that would end her life.

"Fuck." He sighed. "I knew you were going to say that. Fine, but if we want to talk, we'll have to do it here or turn up the music really loudly in our room and whisper."

"I understand."

"Do you?" He dragged her against his body as hot water pelted them. Steam rose all around. "This place is teeming with sick fucks selling women to abusers and rapists around the world who might be on to us, and you have to ask why I'm uptight when you disappear? I swear to God, Cherry, I should give you the spanking of a lifetime. Don't you dare leave my side again in this place without telling me where you're going."

That raised her hackles. She wasn't helpless. "Do you act this way with the other SEALs? No, you trust them to do their jobs. Trust me to do mine. I'm a federal agent, if you'll recall."

"Yeah, one without a gun, Bureau backup, or experience."

Eyes narrowed, she let him have a dose of the fury brewing inside her. "Well, when I left before the orientation, you looked far too busy to interrupt."

"God damn it, I only talked to Allison. Like you suspected, she's been here before."

"Allison, is it?" Of course they were on a first name basis. "You work fast."

"I was pumping her for information."

She put her hands on her hips. "I'll bet you were."

Logan raised a dark brow at her and said nothing. Tara realized that she sounded like a jealous shrew. He was doing a job; they both were. She couldn't bring her emotions in the middle of this.

Tara drew in a deep breath. "Sorry. I'm on edge."

"I'll take that edge off." He sent her a sideways smile. "If you're good and obey me."

Her heart skipped a beat. Her pussy clenched. Tara shoved her reactions aside. "What did *Allison* say?"

Logan reached for the soap and rubbed it between his big palms. "That she was friends with Laken Fox, the dead girl pulled out of the ocean a few days ago. She said that it's against the rules to exchange personal information with other guests, but she and Laken did it anyway and became friends. Allison came this week because she was supposed to join Laken. Now she can't find her friend and doesn't know why. Apparently, the woman wrote Allison last week to say that she'd returned to Fantasy Key and met a great Dom."

"Jordan?"

Logan shrugged. "Maybe. Allison is worried."

"She has every right to be. If Jordan is the one who targets our vics, he definitely has access to the VIP room. No one batted an eyelash when he walked in with me. But Kantor sure sized me up."

"I'll watch him. You get Bocelli digging deeper into both of them. We'll come up with a plan to figure out Jordan's role in this together. Understood?"

There was his Dom voice again. He wasn't speaking to her as an operative or a partner, but as a Master. Tara knew she shouldn't, but somehow that voice made her shiver and melt.

"Yes. We should be working together and—ah!"

He cupped her breasts with his soapy hands and thumbed her incredibly sensitive nipples. Bracketed by the delicate silver jewelry, they stood up, had swelled, and every brush of his skin against them had her gasping and holding on to him.

"Good. Not another word."

"But—"

He cut her off by lifting and spinning her until she was directly beneath the warm spray. The soap ran down her body until only water remained in rivulets. Logan began to catch them with his tongue, the shower running down his face as he sipped at her breasts and lapped at her tight, aching nipples. "So fucking gorgeous, Cherry. I love eating at these. I love eating all of you."

Tara nearly lost her mind. Tingles multiplied and sizzled, firing her blood, burning hotter with his every word until he nearly shut down her brain.

He wedged his feet between hers and nudged her legs apart— and she was too far gone to object. Her stomach pulsed as he covered her mound possessively with his palm, fingers sliding into her slick folds.

"It's so sexy how wet you get for me."

She was still catching her breath when he lifted her body against his, arms straining, veins bulging, as he forced her legs around his waist and flattened her back to the wall. She hissed at the cold surface between her shoulders and the inferno of his flesh over her breasts. Heaven and hell all in one.

And she wanted it, him, throwing her arms around her neck as his cock bobbed between them, steely and thick and impossible to resist.

He bent, positioned himself at her entrance, and tried to impale her in one savage thrust.

"Take me," he panted against her jaw, then covered her mouth with his.

Logan gripped her hips and pushed her down on his cock as he arched, trying to shove more of that fat blue head and those unyielding inches into her. She gasped against his lips—and he used the opening as an opportunity to thrust his tongue deep.

Tara couldn't feel, hear, see, smell, or taste anything except Logan. He overtook every sense, wrapping himself all around her with his strength, his conviction, his seduction. She'd had "just sex" before. This was far more.

With a whimper, she wriggled, trying to take all of his hard stalk. He cursed, eased back a fraction, then plowed so deeply into her body, her head fell back against the tile with a scream.

"That's it, Cherry. Take every inch of me, sweet girl. Yeah," he rasped into her ear as he stroked into her again, easier with each spine-tingling plunge. She softened to accommodate all of him.

"Logan." She grabbed frantically at his hair. "God, you fill me up. I've never felt so alive."

His lips razed across her jaw. "I'd been dead for years until you came back. Don't leave me."

Never, a voice inside her cried.

But was it really that simple? Could they simply resolve to be together? Her stepfather would oppose it. More important, they still had trust issues to bridge. In her head, she knew why Logan left her in high school. But for her heart, letting go of the pain and believing that he wouldn't hurt her again wasn't a matter of pure logic.

But when she was in his arms, like now, when he couldn't seem to get close enough, she felt adored. Like the only woman in his world.

Logan cupped her, lifting her closer as he nipped her lobe and whispered to her. "You're so beautiful, baby. I dreamed of you. Wanted you. Fantasized. For me, it's always been you."

And with every word, he forged deeper inside her slick, swelling pussy, scraping against her sensitized flesh. When he was like this, it was so easy to crave him, care about him, impossible to remember any reason she shouldn't.

"That's it, Cherry. Get all tight on me." He slowed his strokes, lingering over the one spot designed to send her soaring.

"Please, Logan!" she dug her nails into his shoulders, feeling her world tilt out of control.

"It's right here, baby. Let me give you what you need." He grabbed her tighter, ground into her, against the spot that ached most.

That was all she had to hear. With his voice mingling with her racing heartbeat, and their bodies moving as one, pleasure rushed her. Overwhelmed by the sensation overtaking her body and Logan shouting her name, she reveled when he followed her into the rush, coming inside her in a hot, liquid release.

Long moments and hard breaths later, Logan set her on her feet, then braced one hand on the wall above her shoulder for support. He nuzzled her neck as he panted, "I can't stop fucking you. You're killing me."

Her legs felt boneless, too. Still, she teased, "You're complaining?"

He lifted his head, even with water plastering his hair to his forehead, he was the most heart-stopping man she'd ever seen. The thick, black fringe of his lashes framed blue, blue eyes that sparkled with sudden mischief. "Hell, no. If I die from having too much sex with you, that's the best possible way to go."

Tara rolled her eyes, but couldn't wipe the grin off her face. Until she began washing up. No missing his semen leaking from her sex. And she wondered again why she'd held her birth-control pill in her hand last night . . . then elected not to take it. She wasn't sure she trusted him entirely, but she wanted him so badly, wanted to tie him to her always. Swept by the rightness of the image of her holding his son or daughter.

He watched her intently, almost as if he knew what she was thinking. Given their intense connection, it was possible he did.

"Cherry, did you take your pill last night?"

It would be so easy to lie and say she forgot, but she wasn't a coward. "No."

His smile dazzled her. "You're making me hard all over again. I want you committed to me. Tell me you haven't thought about the future and kids. I have. I've been thinking about that a lot, about little girls with red hair."

A big part of her wanted to throw caution to the wind and admit that she'd thought about it, too. But she hadn't come to Fantasy Key to hash out her personal life. She'd be here a few days at most. They could sort all this out afterward.

"Logan, I can't think about the future now. My mission here is to find Darcy and arrest her tormenters. After that . . . we'll talk. It's not as simple as me getting over the past. Adam is my only family, the one who'd walk me down the aisle. And he hates you. We can't pretend that being together would be easy."

It wouldn't. And not preventing herself from getting pregnant didn't sound smart, but she'd looked at the little tablet and the glass of water—and just couldn't bring herself to swallow them. What did that mean?

"Being with me would force hard choices on you. I understand that and I wish I could change it. I can only say that, if you choose me, I'd do everything possible to not make your regret your decision."

Whereas Adam would try his damndest to come between them. He might not be worried anymore that Logan was only after one thing, but he'd never forgiven Logan for breaking her heart. "But that isn't our only obstacle. You're still a SEAL, barely ever home and—"

"I can say the word tomorrow and have a position as a BUD/S instructor in Coronado, California."

An instructor? He'd be in one place, no more missions? "Would you be happy being sidelined?"

"I like the teams. Hell, I've loved them. But I love you more."

Tara blinked. Of all the things she'd expected him to say, this wasn't it. She stared—and couldn't deny that his words touched her. Tears stung her eyes. "I couldn't make you give up something you love for me."

"You're not *making* me. I'm volunteering, totally willingly." Before she could open her mouth, he laid a finger over her lips. "Think about it. I know we have a different agenda right now, but when this is over, okay?"

Didn't she owe them both that much? Whatever they had between them had long since stopped feeling like merely bringing closure to their shared past. This now felt more like a possible future. As much as her heart embraced that, she couldn't deny that Logan still scared the hell out of her.

Silently, she nodded as he cut off the shower.

He kissed the tip of her nose, then stepped out onto the cool tile and handed her a towel. As she dried off, he wrapped his own around his waist, and checked his cell phone. "Damn, only thirty minutes before dinner. When the hell are they going to bring our luggage?"

Other than his carry-on with the sat phone and laptop, he had nothing. Tara had only a few toiletries.

No sooner than he spoke the words, then a knock resounded through the room.

"Porter," the man from the other side called.

Logan secured the towel around his waist, then shut the bathroom door to shield her before he answered the door. Tara peeked through the crack as he wrenched the door open and found their luggage sitting by the portal.

With a frown, he carted the suitcases inside. Tara knew what he was thinking. If the resort's management only intended to x-ray luggage to ensure no one brought weapons into the resort, as they said, why was their luggage so delayed? There hadn't been a ton of guests at the orientation—maybe twenty—and the resort wasn't that big. She bit her lip. Something definitely wasn't right.

Something like Fantasy Key already knowing that she and Logan had come to take them down.

Maybe it would be wiser to abort this mission, but she refused to leave Darcy to certain death, not while she could still save her friend. The suspicious look on Logan's face said his thoughts were chugging down the same track.

"Open the suitcase I packed for you." *Make sure everything is untouched.* "Get dressed in the beige silk. No bra. No panties. Quickly. We're pressed for time."

He lifted her bag onto the bed, then did the same with his duffel. Tara unzipped hers, and frowned. Most of the scanty, unfamiliar garments Logan had chosen for her were still folded and neatly stacked. Even the little bit of jewelry she'd brought with her was still in place. But everything looked a bit displaced, out of order, more than the normal settling that occurred on an airplane.

Beside her, Logan unzipped his gear. Almost instantly, he stiffened. His luggage had been tampered with, too.

But he forced a smile, then turned to her, kissing her cheek. "Be quick. We'll talk on the way to dinner."

In the hall, where electronic ears probably weren't monitoring them. Was there any chance that the resort listened in on all their guests as a habit? Or did he worry, like her, that someone at Fantasy Key already knew they had the FBI in their midst?

Fantasy Key—Sunday night

As they walked from the dining room to the dungeon, Logan glanced again at Cherry—and damn near lost his mind. Hell, he'd been distracted the moment she'd donned the dress.

He'd known when he'd picked it out for her a few days ago that she'd look spectacular in it, but he hadn't expected being so hot for her that he couldn't eat, couldn't do anything but stare at the way the soft, sheer fabric clung to her breasts. Scooping low in the front, elastic cupped the sweet mounds beneath, while the garment showcased her gloriously stiff nipples, still encased in the nipple huggers. Every time she moved, they brushed the material. Her little gasps and groans told Logan those pretty little buds were all fucking kinds of sensitive—and the knowledge had him so damn hard.

Even though he'd fucked her barely an hour ago, the need to

work his aching cock deep into that narrow, clasping pussy of hers right now obliterated nearly every other thought.

The dress hung in a straight line from just beneath her breasts, but the main hallways of Fantasy Key were well lit. The glow from nearby sconces slanted through the sheer fabric, perfectly revealing the smooth mound of her cunt and the lush globes of her ass.

The shitty part? He wasn't the only one looking. They'd barely taken two steps into the dining room before Jordan had fallen into step beside her and reminded him that their safety demonstration scene must be held before they'd be allowed to use the dungeons freely.

"I can't believe the little asshole reserved us a time at the spanking bench without even consulting me. He's trying to usurp me to get to you," Logan growled. "I want to wring his fucking neck."

"You can't. You're not supposed to care, remember?"

He scoffed. "I'm not letting you out of my sight again. Period."

"As long as we stay in the more public areas, I should be fine. If he invites me back to the VIP area, we'll put a plan together. I got his attention, and that's a good first step."

As Tara had all through dinner, she fingered a dainty pendant that hung from her slender neck. The little gold filigreed heart was nestled right in the hollow of her throat, suspended by a thin gold chain, so short it could almost pass for a choker—or a very pretty collar. It looked familiar.

He leaned in, frowned. "Where have I seen you wear that before?"

"The day we . . . split up. I don't wear it that much anymore, but I did tonight because while I was kneeling in the orientation room earlier while you chatted up Allison, another Dom approached me and mentioned that I looked available because I don't have a collar. I thought this might work in a pinch."

Good thinking on her part. "It doesn't look like a collar, per se, but it's close enough that others will wonder if it's intended for that purpose and steer clear. Our situation here is complicated enough without having other creeps chase after you. So, you ready for this demonstration?"

She shrugged. "The basics didn't sound hard."

"No, but it's their public way of weeding out the total amateurs who could cause problems. This way, they keep as many people as possible safe."

"Yeah, while trying to decide which subs to kidnap and sell off to oil barons and Internet billionaires in obscure countries."

"Exactly."

In the dungeon, the lighting was much lower, but the fabric of Tara's dress was so sheer he could still see the outline of her labia and the crack of her ass, not to mention the hard nubs of her nipples poking the front until he could barely look at anything else.

It was almost a relief to reach the spanking bench—except that Jordan awaited them, devouring her with his gaze.

"Welcome to your safety scene." He gestured to Tara to make her way onto the padded bench. "What is your safe word?"

Tara knelt on the red leather and sent Logan a sly grin—and made his heart tumble in his chest. Their private joke and the deeper meaning behind her safe word roused every primal part of him until he wanted to scream, *Mine!*

"It's *Romeo*," she said finally.

"That's acceptable." Jordan turned to him. "Her hard limits?"

Crap, they'd never had the opportunity to actually discuss these. He'd been too busy fucking her to ask. Shit, he hated to miss details, but now he had to wing it. "Cutting, branding, piercing—anything permanent. No bodily functions, blood, or breathplay. And no sex with multiple partners or strangers."

With that, it should be very clear to Jordan that he wasn't getting a piece of Cherry.

"Is this a full and complete list, sub?"

Tara looked at him, as if seeking direction, then she nodded. "What he said, Sir."

Hearing her call another Dom "Sir" bugged the shit out of Logan. It bugged him more that he couldn't do a damn thing about it.

Jordan nodded. "Her soft limits?"

"Hot wax and anal." Logan stroked his chin, trying to think of limitations that would inhibit the dungeon creep's ability to steal her away. "She doesn't like being blindfolded or gagged."

"Duly noted. Anything else you'd like to add, sub?"

She shook her head.

"Very well. Let's see how you use the equipment." He gestured to the spanking bench.

Logan attached cuffs to her wrists, then clipped them into the restraints on each side of the apparatus. She sent him a nervous glance. He wanted so badly to reassure her that he wouldn't leave her side and would act as a buffer between her and Jordan, but he couldn't give her more than an encouraging glance. He finished with ankle cuffs and a spreader bar.

As he straightened up, Jordan handed him a four-foot single-tail whip. "I presume you know how to use this and find it acceptable?"

"I know how to use it, though I prefer a six-footer."

Jordan scowled. "They're unpredictable."

Logan smiled. "Unpredictable is what I do best. But in this sub's case, I must add whipping to her list of soft limits. Spanking by hand or crop in small doses, yes. Whip or cane, no."

"You're bringing along a soft little sub." The dungeon master's tone held a note of contempt that made Logan want to pound his face.

"That's exactly the way I like her."

"She'd be a better sub with her horizons expanded. While she's here, we should work on that."

We? As if Jordan had any rights or say-so over Cherry? If Logan wasn't playing a part for this mission, he'd open up a huge can of badass on this pretentious little fuck and let him know unequivocally that he had no part in her training or her life.

"Maybe," Logan forced himself to say.

Jordan could barely tamp down his superior smirk. "I'll think on it and map out a plan."

And I will shove your balls down your throat and make you thank me for it.

A big leather-clad Dom wielding a whip and wearing a mask ran into their scene, exuding an urgency that immediately put Logan on alert. "Master Jordan, there's been a fight in the orgy room. It's turning into a melee. Mr. Kantor sent me to find you."

Concern washed over the dungeon master's face. "Damn!" He took in the monogram on the new Dom's shirt. "Stay here with these two. They aren't to leave this scene until they've completed their safety drill."

"I've got it. Go!"

Jordan dashed off like his ass was on fire, so Logan turned to the masked dungeon monitor. "Look, we were nearly done, and I've been studying and practicing this lifestyle for nearly ten years, so—"

"No shit, Logan." The stranger ripped off his mask.

Shock blanched Logan. "What the fuck are you doing here, Xander?"

Chapter Fifteen

"Great to see you, too," Xander shot back.

Logan's mind raced, trying to reconcile seeing his buddy in the middle of his mission. "Did Bocelli send you after all?"

"Nope. He'd probably kill me if he knew I'd come, but the more I thought about it, the more I realized I could help. I know this place. Everyone who works here signs a contract that prohibits you from saying anything about any guest to anyone, other than staff. That fucking thing is tighter than a straitjacket. You're not going to learn jack shit from any employee if you don't have an in. Which is why I begged for my old job back, and what do you know? One of their resident Doms met up with an unfortunate hiking accident just this morning. Broken ankle; he'll recover. But they needed *someone* to fill in." He grinned.

With a shake of his head, Logan leaned in and murmured, "We're probably not going to get any info, anyway. The remote control in our room had a bug placed inside and our luggage had been searched. Unless you're going to tell me that's standard operating procedure here, then I think they knew who we were before we even walked in the door."

Xander recoiled. "It's been a few years since I worked here, but that isn't the SOP I remember. I mean, yeah, they search the luggage to confiscate any video or audio recording equipment. They started that after a high-profile blackmail incident a few years ago. If Bocelli had given you all the literature they send once you book your reservation, you would have read that. But bugging the rooms . . ."

Because it really didn't make sense. Why spy on all their guests? Though a small, exclusive resort, there was no way that they could listen to all those conversations at once or even record them for later playback unless they hired a whole staff twenty-four/seven. And why bother?

Logan piped up, "There's only one conclusion, man: Someone at Fantasy Key knows why we've come."

"Not necessarily. Even a few years ago, some of the staff liked to abuse their powers. They'd electronically eavesdrop on certain guests they found . . . intriguing."

As Jordan had certainly found Cherry. That conclusion was disconcerting, but more palatable than someone nefarious knowing that he and Tara were here on behalf of the FBI to break up their sex slave ring.

"It's possible, but I can't prove if it's that or something else. Until then, it's better to work off the assumption that the listening device was more suspicious than lecherous. For that reason, you need to act like you don't know me. Pretend to run through the rest of this safety scene and we'll meet up after."

With a nod, Xander made a production of covering the checklist again, then signing off and handing a copy of the form to Logan, who took it from his pal. On it, he'd written:

Meet me on the east beach in ten.

"Thanks."

Xander looked around to see if anyone was watching, but the room wasn't very busy yet, and everyone seemed to be going about their business. "I'll see what I can find out." Then he spoke up again.

"Play safe. Be sure to find a member of the staff if you need any help or have any questions."

With that, he walked off. Logan leaned over to Cherry, who'd remained surprisingly quiet during the exchange."

"Did you hear all that?" he asked, leaning to whisper in her ear.

"Most. The music is a little loud. I heard Xander say why he's here, but don't you find his presence a little suspicious?"

If he were anyone else, Logan would wonder what kind of shit he was up to. But Xander had always been unpredictable. His buddy was more than a little closemouthed about himself, but Logan knew he came from money—so much of it that bankers had to physically count the number of zeros in his family's balances. Though smart as hell and go-getting when he wanted to be, Xander had never held a real job. One thing Logan did know: The man never liked to miss out on the action, especially if he could make mischief right in the middle of it.

"No. It's just Xander being Xander. But we'll have to watch him. If he's decided to help us, he'll throw caution to the wind."

"Which could be destructive for us all." Tara frowned as Logan unclipped her cuffs and removed them. "What are you doing? Aren't we supposed to scene?"

"It's optional right now. I'd rather take a walk on the beach."

* * *

SOMETHING about the look on Logan's face told her this walk was more important than establishing their dynamic as the obedient sub to his indifferent Dom.

"All right. Lead the way."

No one's head turned as they slipped out the door, through the lobby, and out a side exit. Past a small parking lot full of resort vehicles and a foul Dumpster, they followed a stone-laden path between a few palm trees, away from prying eyes, toward the sound of waves breaking.

As she felt sand beneath her toes and smelled salt in the air, Logan grabbed her hand and held it in his. The moon hung heavy and surprisingly bright, and Tara wished for one moment that she and Logan were here for romance, without a care in the world.

But she needed to put frivolous wishes aside and focus on saving Darcy. Tara wondered if her friend even knew she was scheduled to die horrifically in a gang-rape snuff film in a few days. She tensed, gripping Logan's hand.

"You okay?"

Now wasn't the time to break down. "Trying to keep it together. Why are we out here?"

"Xander wanted us to meet him. No idea why. Like everything he does, we'll have to wait and find out when he deigns to tell us."

"Ouch," Xander said suddenly, emerging from behind a little cabana, then winked at her. "I try to help out and this is the thanks I get from my old pal, despite providing one of the few places on the island that I know isn't covered by surveillance. And for arranging Freddy in maintenance to get you a new remote for your TV that isn't bugged. Sheesh. How are you, gorgeous?"

Tara couldn't help but grin. He was incorrigible. "A little stunned to see you."

"No way I was going to miss out on this action. Got anything yet?"

She and Logan exchanged a glance, then he gestured to her. It touched her that the big, bad Dom was willing to step aside and let her lead. Yes, it was her case, but Logan could have made her bow to his greater experience, if he'd wanted to push it.

"Not much. It's all hunches so far." Choosing her words carefully, she told him about her episode with the dungeon master and the manager just before orientation. "But other than Jordan being stalkerish and Kantor taking stock of me like a product, I've got nothing."

Xander nodded. "I still have friends here, some of the resident Doms, wait and security staff, bartenders. Kantor took over for my old boss, Ms. Newmann, after she was abruptly fired. The rumor mill said the reclusive owner caught her skimming money."

"Anyone know this reclusive owner's name?" Tara asked without a lot of hope. If the FBI hadn't been able to figure it out, chances were Xander didn't know squat.

"Not me. If Newmann knew, she didn't share. Anyway, about six months ago this mystery owner brought Kantor on board. No one likes him. I mean, *no one*."

"Six months ago," Tara said. "About the time girls started disappearing."

"I doubt that's a coincidence," Logan drawled.

"Which means we should assume that, whatever is going on, he's in on it."

"Pretty safe assumption, I think. I met the guy earlier this afternoon. I didn't like him, and vice versa. But I knew that, being short a Dom, he was in a bind. Being beholden to me clearly pissed him off. I think he's definitely worth looking into."

"Did Bocelli have any information on him?" Logan asked her. "Did he brief you about him at any point?"

"Yeah, early on, we got a file on most of the management. Kantor's is sketchy and says nothing out of the ordinary. He came from an upper-middle-class family in New Jersey, went to Princeton. By all accounts, he's a smart guy."

"With all the personality of a bleeding hemorrhoid." Xander grimaced.

Tara couldn't not laugh. "The rest of his background is nondescript. He's been working at hotels his whole life. Married young. Divorced after three years. No kids. No girlfriends, no glaring debts, no ties to any sort of criminal activity. On the surface, he looks perfect."

Logan shook his head. "We don't have to prove why Kantor is neck deep in this shit, just that he is."

True, but . . . "To do that, we've got to get closer to him."

That realization creeped her out.

"I think you should try the easy way first," Xander suggested.

Tara raised a brow at him. "Oh?"

He fished in his pocket for a ring of keys, rifled through them, then pulled one off and handed it to Tara. "The key to the desk in the manager's office. It should still work. All the other keys I've tried today have."

"You kept these from the last time you worked here?" Logan asked, arms crossed over his chest.

Xander grinned. "Let's just say that Ms. Newmann liked me, and I made sure she was a bit . . . distracted as she made her way through the employee exit process."

"Why would you do that?" Tara couldn't understand it. "Why keep keys to a resort you're no longer working for?"

"I come and go from this place a lot. I like to keep my options open."

Really? Tara frowned. At first, she'd been willing to take Xander on good faith because Logan had vouched for him. Now? It seemed a little odd that he would upend his life in Dallas to follow them back to his old job simply to "help out." Who did that?

Still, she closed the key in her fist. "All right. We'll investigate Kantor's office, see what we can find. How do we get down some of the restricted hallways? I know they require a key card."

"I'll swipe one from a maid and have someone give it to you during lunch. Kantor will do another orientation tomorrow at the same time. That's a good time to prowl through his office. I'll make sure the maid is too busy to miss her access card before then and create a little diversion on the other side of the resort as the little meet-and-greet is ending, just to make sure you get enough time. Newmann wasn't big on computers, and kept everything of interest in the safe in the floor under the Persian rug by the window. In case Kantor hasn't changed the combination, here it is." He handed Tara a scrap of paper. "Keep me posted."

She stared at Xander, trying to decide if he was really just a bored rich boy in search of adventure or if he was the wolf in sheep's clothing. Unfortunately, she'd have to play along to find out.

"Thank you."

As if he'd guessed her thoughts, Xander nodded coolly. "No sweat. But before I leave, just ask yourself if I seemed like a dishonest slime at any time Logan let me touch you."

No, he hadn't. Pushed the boundaries, yes. Done whatever he could to yank Logan's chain, absolutely. But he'd never crossed the line. Still, if he were involved in this terrible human-auction scheme, he would have been nice to her from the get-go.

Tara made a mental note to ask Logan a few more questions about his buddy. Because Xander being involved in this sex ring would certainly explain why their room had been bugged and why he'd unexpectedly come to Florida to cozy up to them. On the other hand, why would a billionaire's heir need money?

"Of course."

Logan looked between the two of them with a frown. "What do you know about Jordan?"

"Besides the fact he's a serious sadist, not much. That dude gives Doms a bad name."

That had been her impression of Jordan. Just *ick*.

"I hear he hasn't been here long, maybe six weeks. What's odd is that he came from nowhere and didn't have to do any time as a dungeon monitor. Kantor just moved him ahead of all the resident Doms and made him the dungeon master. He told some others that he was from Phoenix, but I've got friends who live there. I called around. No one's heard of the guy."

Since BDSM could be a small community, if Xander was telling the truth, it was definitely fishy. "I'll contact Bocelli and ask if he can look into our friend."

"Good thought," Logan said, then addressed Xander. "Our top initiative is to rescue Tara's friend Darcy. Hear anything about her?"

"Not yet. I'll keep my ear to the ground."

Fantasy Key—Monday afternoon

Tara's waiter delivered her plate of tropical fruit salad and iced tea. "Will there be anything else?"

She shook her head. "No, thanks."

"Your entrees should be ready shortly. Until then, Master Xander asked me to deliver something to you, which you'll find under your plate. His instructions were take it discreetly at the end of the meal, not before."

The access card. She gazed across the table at Logan, who merely nodded at the waiter. "Thank you."

The tuxedoed man nodded, then turned on his heel. Tara ached to look under her plate for that little plastic card, but refrained. Too many eyes here could see too much. She'd wait until people left.

"I told you he'd come through," Logan pointed out.

Xander had indeed done exactly as he'd said he would, but she still didn't quite understand his motivation. He hadn't seemed close enough to Logan that he would risk his life, but that was exactly what he was doing. Tara hoped like hell that Logan himself wasn't being duped by his pal.

She shrugged. "We'll see."

"He's not going to betray us, Cherry. Believe me."

Like every day since her teenage heartbreak, she found trust difficult. "There's a lot at stake here. You're asking me to rest the outcome of my mission on your instinct that he's honest."

"If the shoe was on the other foot and you asked me to trust someone I didn't know, I would. No questions asked."

Tara winced and forked in a bite of pineapple to stall her reply. She'd like to call bullshit, but he meant that. Nor was it fair to hold their past against him since he'd left her to protect her. But when he'd cast her aside, it had frozen something deep in her core. She hadn't allowed anyone to breathe warmth and life into her again.

Logan was on the verge of melting those walls around her heart. And it scared the hell out of her.

"I'll try. It's just not easy for me."

Logan put down his fork and leveled a direct stare at her across the table. "When are you going to trust me again?"

It was a fair question—and a painful one. "I don't know."

"That's why you don't want to talk about our future. You don't trust my sincerity."

He was right; she couldn't picture him sleeping beside her every night, much less slipping a ring on her finger. It had been a fantasy for years, that he'd come back still in love with her and want her for the rest of their lives, have some perfectly plausible explanation for ripping out her heart and forever killing her adolescent ability to love with her whole being. But now that he'd returned with a noble rationale for their breakup, claiming she was still the only woman in his heart? Tara *ached* to believe it. She just didn't know how to after twelve long years.

But she couldn't quit trying. If he really did mean it, she needed to find a way to embrace him before her doubt ran him off again.

"Give me a little more time, when we're not in the middle of . . . all this." She pushed her fruit around on her plate.

Logan hesitated. "I know you've endured a lot these past few days. I also know that I put you through hell in the past. But that was then. In my youth I allowed something to come between us that I'd never allow today. Just keep trying to trust me with more than your body, Cherry. I swear I will never give you any reason to regret it."

Hearing that sincerity from such a dominant, ferocious man undid something inside her. Deep inside, she knew he was right, and that if she didn't want to be alone again, she was going to have to figure out how to close the door on their past and move forward.

Their waiter returned and smoothly replaced the fruit plate with her chicken before she could even see the access card on the table. Then he left Logan's fish in front of him.

"How does everything look?"

"Excellent," Logan said impatiently, clearly wishing the waiter would leave so they could finish their conversation.

"Very good." The waiter reached on the cart behind him and produced a silver jug of iced tea. "According to Xander, you'll need to leave in ten minutes. He left service-crew uniforms in your cabin. You'll have approximately five minutes to find Kantor's office on the top floor, then another five inside. Ten at most. Trash the uniforms when you've finished. He'll be back for the card later this afternoon."

"Why are you helping us?" Tara couldn't help but ask. She still wasn't exactly sure it was smart to put her faith in Xander, despite Logan vouching for him. Trusting their darkly handsome waiter, whose name tag read CHAZ, wasn't any easier.

He produced a pepper mill with a bland smile. But his eyes were alive with hatred. "Laken Fox had just become mine, and she returned here to be with me. Kantor was the last person known to see her alive, and his excuses are bullshit. I want that son of a bitch nailed to the wall."

Good answer.

As another waiter sidled by and stared, he removed all expression from his face. "Have a good afternoon."

With that, he was gone. Tara immediately went into mission mode. "Eat what you can quickly."

They both shoved down a few bites of protein and vegetables. As the other guests filed out of the dining room, she lifted her plate aside with one hand and swiped her napkin beneath with her other. The little plastic card fell in her lap.

"Let's go."

* * *

AT exactly two o'clock, Logan and Tara, dressed as maintenance workers in the outfits Xander provided, let themselves into the secure hallway on the top floor. He pulled his cap low over his face and pushed an empty trash can, just in case they were on surveillance.

Cherry did the same, ensuring her hair was tucked beneath, as she shoved the vacuum over the garish, resort-style carpet.

The access card clicked, and they moved into Kantor's office. Logan looked around for surveillance equipment and didn't see anything obvious. Still, they had to be cautious.

Per the plan they'd developed as they worked into the gray zip-up maintenance jumpers, he moved immediately to the safe beneath the ornate rug of red and gold near the window. It opened up with the combination Xander provided.

Logan pushed aside a stack of cash and stared at the thick section of DVDs tucked inside. He flipped through them quickly. None had any sort of writing or markings, so he'd have to put them back for now. He couldn't afford to take them and have them be missed.

Next, he found a set of accounting ledgers, which meant these were likely the real books, and Tara would probably find the doctored set in Kantor's desk. A quick skim proved this place brought in a more-than-decent take. But it was the pages devoted to "product sales" that caught his attention. Here, they recorded a staggering fucking fortune in the millions. There was no way their little shop of BDSM gear and other assorted perversions downstairs was bringing in that sort of money. The "products" they sold had to be human, but each of the ledger entries was marked with nothing more than a number. The first sale took place approximately six months ago. The latest was pending for Thursday.

Extracting a little camera, he took pictures of multiple pages, zeroing in on the most suspicious, then shoved the books back into the safe.

He checked his watch. "Four minutes."

"I'll be ready," Tara said.

Damn, he was proud of her. Despite this being her first mission, she was performing well under pressure. They could very well be risking their lives, and she didn't trust Xander, but she wasn't letting the stress get to her.

Logan poked his head into the safe again but found nothing

more of interest. Locking up, he replaced the carpet on the hardwood floors, then went to Cherry's side.

"Got anything?"

"It took me a minute to hack into his computer, but I'm in now and downloading everything onto a flash drive. I imagine it's all encrypted and password protected so that will take a while. Here." She shoved the desk key into his hand. "Look around."

Without a word, Logan opened up the desk, poked around in drawers and files, not sure what he was looking for. In the back of the lateral filing cabinet, he found something long and rolled up. Logan spread them out across the desk.

"I've got the blueprints of this place. Shit, there's a dungeon under the resort, and not the kind we play in."

Tara pulled her gaze from the screen, her brown eyes saucer-wide. "They could be holding Darcy there. We need to get inside ASAP."

"That could be easier said than done. Let's talk to Xander, see what he knows."

"This is my mission, not his."

"Hasn't he gotten us this far?"

A little beep sounded and she pulled the flash drive out of the USB slot, her mouth pursed in anger. "We're not out of this office safely yet. For all we know, we've walked into a trap."

As if on cue, they heard footsteps in the hall. She bit her lip, then mouthed *Kantor*?

He shrugged, then motioned her under the desk. Tara put the computer to sleep, then shoved the vacuum into the corner, next to the trash can. They ducked down just as someone entered the room.

"Who left this fucking trash can and vacuum? Lazy bastards . . ."

A cell phone rang.

"Kantor," the voice barked, then paused. "You're sure he's dead?"

Logan's brain raced and his instincts went on alert.

"Excellent. I'll be down to the Pit to help you dispose of his body. And next time? I need better background checks on all incoming employees."

Tara pressed a hand over her mouth, clearly coming to the same conclusion Logan was. Had they somehow found out Xander helped them and killed him for it?

Just then, the office door opened again, and a woman stuck her head inside. "Sir, there's a kitchen fire. It's spreading quickly. We've called the fire department."

"Fuck!" Kantor snarled. "I'll call you back."

With that, he slammed out the door.

* * *

TWENTY minutes later, Tara and Logan were safely back in their room. Logan tried to call Xander twice as he checked the new remote Xander had arranged. But his phone went to voicemail both times. Panic started eating at Logan's gut. Other than his brother, Hunter, Xander was the best friend he had. He couldn't be dead, god damn it.

Cherry emerged from the bathroom, taking the elastic band out of her hair. She looked at him with concern in those sweet chocolate eyes, then made her way to him, kneeling in front of him, taking his hands in hers.

"I know you're worried."

Logan stared at the remote control.

"We can talk freely. I just checked the rest of the room."

He nodded miserably. "How can I not be concerned? I feel responsible. We had so little to go on with this case, and Xander seemed able to give us exactly the help we needed. But he isn't trained for this shit, and I should have remembered that."

Tara kissed his cheek and squeezed his fingers. "You know, this is one of the things I always loved about you, your ability to care. You were never too macho to be worried or help someone. Please don't let your worry eat at you. For all you know, he's laying low or found something else for us to check."

"You believe he's on our side now?" Logan wanted her to trust him so badly, the ache was a hollow craving deep inside him. He swallowed, fingering the delicate heart-shaped choker at her throat. Unlike the heart in her chest, this one he could touch easily, hold in the palm of his hand, protect and adore. She'd give him this one, if he asked. He wished like hell that she'd gift him with the one that mattered most.

"Obviously if they've hurt him, he's not on their side, but we don't know that anything like that has happened." She sent him a compassionate smile that only made his chest tighten more. "You believe Xander tried to help us, and for your sake, I want you to be right."

He closed his eyes. Her words hurt, but even though she couldn't quite trust, the fact that she was willing to comfort him meant so much.

No way was he letting this woman slip through his fingers again. When they left here—if they left alive—he'd move heaven and earth to unmask the motherfucker threatening her and silence him forever.

"You going to be okay?" she asked softly.

Compartmentalize. It was something he did well on missions. Having Cherry here was messing with his head some. He needed to focus on getting the job done.

"Fine. We'll see Chaz in a few hours. Maybe he knows what's happened to Xander."

Tara held up the access card they'd used to sneak into Kantor's office. "Or maybe he'll come by himself for this. In the meantime, I need to ship all the data we collected to Bocelli and let the analysts plow through it."

"Yeah, if we tried ourselves, it would take days."

"That we don't have."

Logan didn't have days left with her, either. Two at most. Forty-eight hours was not a lot of time to mend broken trust and allay all her fears. If he had weeks or months—years, even—to prove his constancy and devotion, he'd use them. But he had two fucking days before she might be out of his life again forever. Dominion had been his lifeline for years, but losing his membership and status there was nothing compared to losing Cherry. As a teenager, he'd dealt with the loss of his mother. As a man, he wanted that tight family unit again. He wanted to create one with Tara. By not taking her birth control pill, it told him that at least some part of her subconsciously wanted that, too. What would it take for her to give him a chance?

She turned away to prepare for the data upload. Logan handed her his digital camera so she could upload those images, wishing he had the answer to his question.

With a sigh, he sat back on their bed and pulled out the photo he kept in his wallet of his family. This had been their last Christmas together. Hunter hadn't had his driver's license for long and had nearly killed everyone in the car on the way to the photographer's. At six, Kimber had been the only one whose life hadn't flashed before their eyes. They'd all been fighting like dogs when they walked in— then his mother had burst out laughing. Everyone else had joined in for one of those priceless moments of family harmony captured as the photographer had snapped the picture.

A few months later, his mother had sought a divorce. She'd been murdered a year after that. His father had spent a decade and a half as an angry recluse. Hunter had been so bitter that Mom had left— and Dad had let her. He really hadn't spoken much to either of them until Amanda Edgington had been cruelly murdered. By then, it had been too late.

Logan had never understood his brother's behavior. Whether she'd remained married to his father, Amanda had always been and would always be his mother. He still missed her. She'd had a soft spot for him, and he'd milked it as a kid. Times like now, he also missed her sage council. He wished she could have spent more time with Tara, given him some insight to the female mind. In fact, the day he'd found Amanda's body, Logan had gone to see his mother to tell her that he was in love.

Everything in his life came back to the fateful day that had changed everything.

Logan rubbed his thumb over his mother's image. He hated the thought that, if he managed to convince Tara to trust him again with her heart, his mother wouldn't be there to see him get married, have children, grow middle-aged with the woman he loved. Another fucking hole in his heart.

As he stared at the photo, a bit of gold caught his attention. He pulled it closer to his face, staring hard. He wondered if his eyes were deceiving him.

They weren't.

"Okay," Tara said as she rose from the laptop, fingers clutching the heart pendant. "Data is uploading. It's going to take a while."

Now he knew why that little charm was so fucking familiar.

On wooden legs, his heart pounding, he rose and crossed the room.

"What is it?" Concern spread across her face.

He swallowed, trying to moisten a suddenly dry mouth. When he got close enough, he nudged her hand aside, cradled her heart pendant in his fingers, and turned it over. Exactly where he expected to see it, Logan spotted a familiar little dent in the gold.

"You keep looking at that. Are you worried that Brad or some boyfriend gave it to me? It isn't like that. I've had it for years. My stepfather gave it to me—well, I found it, and he said that he'd intended to give it to me—to serve as a reminder to be careful with my heart."

"When?" he barked the question at her.

"Sh-Shortly before we broke up."

"How shortly?"

"The night before."

Logan could barely control his rage. All this time, he hadn't understood . . . He still didn't know why—but he'd find out. At least he now he knew who. But one thing he knew as well as his own name: Tara could only be wearing his mother's necklace if Adam had ripped it off of Amanda's broken neck while killing her.

Chapter Sixteen

THE enormity of his realization made Logan stumble back to the bed. Almost blindly, he sat, thoughts whizzing through his head. Maybe there was another explanation. Maybe the killer had taken it off his mother's neck not as a trophy, but for its monetary value. Maybe he'd pawned it. And maybe Adam had simply purchased it.

Maybe. But that was a pretty big coincidence.

His mother's murder had been a crime of passion, not greed. That necklace wasn't worth more than a few hundred dollars and had been the only item missing from Amanda's apartment. The killer had left her old wedding rings, worth thousands more. The police—along with his father—had watched the local pawn shops for the pendant, but it had never appeared. Besides, upscale Adam had always loved his little princess. Why would he buy her a token at a pawn shop?

Of course, Adam Sterling hadn't actually given it to Tara; she'd found it. And he'd let her wear it. Had she stumbled onto Adam's trophy from the kill, then he made up a story about buying the necklace to remind her to guard her heart so Tara wouldn't get suspicious?

If that was the case, if Adam was the real killer, that also meant he'd threatened to kill his own stepdaughter—more than once.

But why? True, Adam had never liked him, had bullied him about leaving Tara alone almost from the beginning. He'd ignored her stepfather. If Cherry hadn't wanted him, he would have respected her wishes, but he'd refused to let Adam make that choice for her. Suspecting it would finally have an impact on Logan, had the asshole threatened Tara instead? Had he been afraid that Logan would see the necklace around Tara's neck and guess the truth? Why not just make up some other excuse so that Tara didn't wear it? It probably gave the egotistical bastard a sick thrill to know that his princess wore the key to solving the murder around her throat, and because he'd split them up so effectively, Logan would never know. Fucking bastard!

Then came the biggest question: What motive would Adam have for killing his mother in the first place? She'd been a good teacher, involved with her students' lives to the point that she'd led a weeks-long effort to find one of her runaway students.

"What is it?" Cherry darted to his side, wrapping an arm around his shoulder.

Logan looked into her worried face. What the hell was he going to tell her? She didn't trust him about Xander, so how could he possibly tell her that he suspected her own stepfather, the only stable parent she'd really known, might be a killer?

He couldn't—at least not now. Not only could he not prove anything, now wasn't the time to mess with Tara's head. They were here to find Darcy, stop the sex ring, see if they could nail the elusive owner of this house of kink gone wrong. He needed to strengthen his bond with Tara now, both to solidify their partnership on this mission and to build a foundation for their future. Accusing her stepfather of being a cold-blooded killer without adequate proof wasn't going to help his cause.

Scrubbing a hand over his face, he sighed and grasped for the first excuse he could think of. "Just worried about Xander."

Tara frowned. "Then why the twenty questions about my necklace?"

She never had let much slip past her, but he wished she would now.

"Sorry. Bunny trail. Guess I worried that Brad had given it to you, and that you were wearing it because you still had feelings for him," Logan mumbled. "I need to get my head on straight."

"I don't love Brad."

Inside, he rejoiced . . . until he realized that didn't necessarily mean that she was willing to admit that she loved him. And even if she did, now there was a whole new obstacle in front of them. Fuck. No way was he leaving Cherry alone with Adam again, but he also had no way of keeping them apart without telling her about his suspicions. Since he couldn't prove it and she didn't trust him, where would that leave him?

"Knowing that makes me really happy, baby." He kissed her softly, hoping like hell it wasn't the last time. "Stay here. I'm going to see if I can find Xander. Use the sat phone to check in with Bocelli."

Tara grabbed his hand. "You seem really upset. Please be careful."

Everything on her sweet face said that she cared—deeply. He'd never loved another woman in his life and knew that he never would. What the hell was he going to do if his suspicions were right?

"You be careful, too. Don't go anywhere. Don't open the door for anyone."

With her nod, Logan slipped out. At some point, he had to get a call out to his dad, tell him what he'd discovered, see if someone on the Tyler P.D. would reopen his mom's cold case, get the latest threatening note he'd received at Dominion into their hands. He needed to ask the Colonel if he could think of any reason that Adam would want Mom dead. And he needed to figure out when and how the hell he was going to approach Tara about this—while keeping her safe.

Because, above all, that was his first priority.

* * *

TEN minutes after Logan's departure, a knock sounded at their door. Tara jumped, fearing that Jordan had been waiting for an opportunity to get her alone. He'd been eerily absent since last night. Or worse, that Kantor had somehow discovered that they'd broken into his office and had come for retribution.

Taking a taper out of the decorative candlestick on the nightstand and cursing the fact that she'd been unable to smuggle a weapon onto the island, she gripped the candlestick behind her back as she opened the door. But it wasn't Jordan or Kantor standing on the other side.

"Xander? You're okay." He looked mussed and slightly heavy-lidded but unharmed.

"Yeah. Why wouldn't I be?" He sauntered in.

"We overheard Kantor say they'd killed a man and to screen the employees more carefully. When we got back and Logan couldn't find you, he freaked out."

The bad-boy Dom repressed a smile. "That's actually kind of sweet, but I'm fine."

Clearly. But if Xander hadn't been their victim, who had?

"Why didn't you answer your phone when Logan called?"

"I had to occupy Marciela so she wouldn't notice that her access card was absent."

"Occupy?"

A very wicked grin crossed Xander's face. "Do you have it?"

Dear God, he'd slept with one of the maids to swipe her access card? Wincing at the thought, Tara set down the candlestick and fished the card out of her back pocket before handing it to him.

"Were you going to hit me?" He didn't look intimidated in the least.

"If I had to. All of today's shit has made me a little jumpy. Kantor almost found us in his office. If it hadn't been for that kitchen fire that sent him running . . ."

"I'll have to pay Alfredo his hundred bucks. Sounds like he performed on schedule."

That implication flattened Tara. "You paid someone to start that fire?"

"I knew Kantor was going to need a well-timed distraction."

Tara stared at Logan's friend. He'd made the entire search not only possible, but run smoothly. They weren't out of danger yet, and until Bocelli's analysts had sifted through the data, they wouldn't know if their break-in had accomplished anything. But without Xander, they certainly wouldn't have had that opportunity.

"Thank you."

"You're done being suspicious?"

She shrugged. "It just— Your reasons for helping didn't seem . . . obvious. It's not your problem or your fight."

"I need a reason to not want women to be sold as sex slaves to monsters likely to abuse or kill them?"

"I hate to sound cynical, but most people would give a great big 'awww' and say that the girls would be in their prayers or tell us to nail the bastards responsible. They wouldn't go out of their way to help, much less uproot their whole lives."

"I can afford to do more. I don't have a job or the need for a paycheck holding me back." He wandered over to the plush easy chair in the corner. "I don't have anyone who loves me worrying. Getting involved was easy and had minimal impact on my life."

"Unless you're caught and they kill you."

Xander raised a dark brow. "Kantor's not stupid. He knows I come from a very wealthy family and that there would be a lot of questions if I disappeared or died here. He won't want that wrath raining down on his head. Now, will he make my life uncomfortable in the hopes that I go away? Sure. And I'll let him when you don't need my help anymore."

Wow, Xander had it all figured out. Tara had to give him credit. He seemed to be on the up and up. Perhaps she should have trusted Logan's instincts . . .

"I guess I was wrong. Sorry if I offended you."

"It's not the first time someone has mistaken my motives." He shrugged. "But Logan is a really good friend—one of the few I trust—and you're the woman he loves. He'd do anything for you, so I'm going to do the same."

When he put it like that, Tara felt almost ashamed about how suspicious she'd been. Ditto for how much difficulty she'd given Logan since he'd become her trainer for this mission.

"I'm not sure what's up with us, but I should probably thank Logan for all he's done to help me through this mission and educate me so I could stay safe. And as much as I was pissed off at the time, I should probably also thank Mr. Thorpe."

Xander frowned. "Mitchell can be a real asshole. Don't make the mistake of thinking he's a nice guy. The FBI paid him to get you trained."

"Yes, but when I screamed my safe word, he must have known that I was more angry at Logan than genuinely afraid. Even though I all but begged him to give me another instructor, he didn't deviate. I wouldn't have done as well with anyone else."

Looking distinctly uncomfortable, Xander leaned forward. "Thorpe didn't do that for you, sweetheart. He did it because Logan made him."

"How? I can't picture Thorpe bowing to pressure from anyone."

"Doms can be victims of their own rules sometimes. When you screamed your safe word, well . . . a rule is a rule, and he was going to reassign you until Logan came in and threw one of the club's own rules in his face, the prior claim clause. Mitchell didn't have a choice but to give in. He gave Logan seven days to either collar or marry you, or he'd have to give up his membership."

Xander's words hit her like a blow to the chest. After the initial impact, a dozen thoughts crashed through her head: He'd made a *secret deal* to stay with her. Because he truly wanted her? But why not just tell her about his "prior claim"? Why be underhanded?

They weren't sixteen anymore, and she desperately wanted to believe that Logan had entered into this agreement with Thorpe because he wanted to keep her safe, at the least. The fact that he'd left her in high school to protect her proved that he cared about her well-being. But was it more than that? Had Logan put himself in the position to be her trainer, come hell or high water, because he'd known that he could teach her what she needed to know? Or had

Logan used the week Thorpe had given him as a way to keep her with him because he wanted to win her back? She didn't want to think he'd kept the truth from her just to hurt her, not after all his tenderness and his avowals of love.

But he hadn't said a word about any such bargain. He hadn't let on for a second of their time together that he had more on the line than his heart and their future.

"Shit, I shouldn't have said anything." Xander winced. "Forget I mentioned it. Damn it, you look pissed."

Yes, very much. He'd plotted to change the course of her mission—and maybe even her whole future—without consulting her. Did he think that she was a pawn in some fucking game?

But underneath, Tara was somewhat touched that he'd risked his membership at a club that was vitally important to his psyche to either keep her safe or win her heart.

Xander stood. "I think I'll leave now before he returns and realizes that I've screwed the pooch. Go easy on him, huh? Bye!"

Tara barely got her mouth open before Xander was out the door. She tried to talk herself out of this weird sense of both tenderness and betrayal. Did he really have anything but her best interests at heart? Probably not. But damn it, if she was as important to him as he swore, then why didn't the bastard just *talk* to her? Why did he continue making decisions without her input?

She might have let him top her in the bedroom, but there was no way she'd let him top her in life. And as soon as he returned, she was going to make that absolutely crystal clear to him.

* * *

LOGAN dashed back to the suite he shared with Cherry, anxious to return. Since he'd run into Xander and seen for himself that his buddy was in one piece, he prayed the same was true of her. Xander had said she was fine, but until Logan saw her, held her, he'd worry.

Stuffing the key in the slot, he shoved the door open and found Tara pacing. Relief poured through him. Worrying about Xander had made him edgy, as had breaking into Kantor's office. Hell, the fact that Jordan hadn't pursued Tara all day even made him edgy. The slimeball had slobbered on himself, drooling all over Tara when they'd arrived at the resort. Logan had been certain that he'd soon issue them an invitation to the VIP room as a means of testing her out. But they hadn't seen or heard from Jordan since he'd hurried away from their safety scene last night, and that was feeling mighty odd—along with their formerly bugged remote. Xander had asked the maintenance guys to stash it in another guest room. Logan had to hope that no one noticed they were hearing someone else's conversations.

Something was definitely fishy. If the management here at Fantasy Key knew that Tara was FBI, it was in their best interest to lay low, not do anything to raise red flags and invite further investigation. But being stonewalled frustrated the hell out of Logan. Time was running out to rescue Darcy and capture these predators.

"I found Xander," Logan said into the odd silence. "He's alive, though at the moment, I'd like to kill him myself."

She nodded coolly. "He stopped by and picked up the access key."

Tara's mouth was a thin, angry line. She leveled a dark, brittle stare at him.

Logan frowned as he closed the distance to take her in his arms. She backed away. All his warning flares shot up.

"What's wrong, Cherry?"

Fiery hair clinging to her shoulders, she paced, not bothering to hide her agitation. "Forget it. We don't need drama right now. I'm working, and we're supposed to be saving Darcy."

"Yeah, but if something is bothering you, I want to know about it. We'll communicate better if you do. Tell me." He reached for her hand.

Tara jerked away. "Bocelli said he'd get back to us on the data. He'll have to do some digging on Jordan. Still no progress on the identity of the resort owner. That's not surprising. The FBI has been trying to untangle the legal paperwork to figure out who really owns this place, but it's like a labyrinth. Do you think he's here?"

All relevant stuff, and if she were anyone else, Logan would leap on the change of subject. But since he wanted to spend the rest of his life with her, if something was upsetting her, he wanted to get to the bottom of the issue and fix it.

"If he is and he's smart, he's posing as a guest or other employee. Otherwise, it's too incriminating. So our best shot at learning his identity is the information we pulled off Kantor's computer and the analysts back in Washington, D.C., wading through all the dummy corporations and DBAs until we find this guy. But that's not what's bugging you. Spit it out."

She paced, fists clenched. "I don't think waiting is the answer. It's taking too long. Darcy's time is running short. I need to talk to Adam."

Logan's blood ran cold. "Your stepfather?"

"Of course." She scowled, as if that was obvious. "He's former FBI, and I told him a bit about this case before we left so that—"

"You *what*?" He charged toward her. "Does he know that you're here?"

Tara lifted her chin, daring his anger. "Yes."

"With me?"

She hesitated, then admitted reluctantly, "Yes."

Fuck! He'd assumed in bringing Cherry to Fantasy Key that his mother's killer couldn't touch her here. But Adam Sterling was now a wealthy man with former FBI connections. If anyone could do her in under this kind of security, it would be Adam.

"You're *not* calling him."

She bristled. "Despite what you think or want, you can't tell me what to do. If I want to talk to my stepfather, I will."

He shook his head, staring at her with a silent vow to do *anything* to enforce his will. No way was she giving that dangerous bastard more access to her or any more information that might help him to harm her. But he didn't want to put more wedges between them now, before she wholly trusted him.

"You won't. Bocelli wouldn't want you to. Neither do I. Technically, Adam is no longer FBI." It was a good excuse, thank God.

"You never have been, yet here you are." She scowled at him, mouth gaping open with confusion. "What is your issue? Adam can help us. I told him about the case because he has so much experience."

"And you didn't tell me this earlier? Why the hell not?"

A blaze of fury suddenly darkened her eyes. "Don't you *dare* go there. If one of us is keeping secrets, it's you. Or were you going to tell me about your little bet with Thorpe?"

Logan closed his eyes. *Fucking Xander.* Why would he tell Cherry about that? She was taking it the wrong way. "It wasn't a bet; it was a last resort. You're not a game to me, but Thorpe was going to assign you to another Dom. Enacting that club rule was the only way I could prevent that."

Tara didn't look moved. Instead, she crossed her arms over her chest and raised a ginger brow. "Except talking to me. If you had, we might have been able to work it out. If so, I would have told Thorpe that I didn't want anyone else near me."

As many times as he'd tried to tell her about the reasons for their breakup, she was going to pin this on him? "Baby, I could have talked to you all day. There was no fucking way you were going to give me an inch at that point. I threatened your safe little world and that heart you've been trying so damn hard to protect from me."

A flush crawled up her fair skin. "Look, you left me at sixteen because someone had threatened me. I get that. But instead of talking to me about it, you made the decision to leave me."

"I kept quiet for your safety."

"Maybe, but you didn't learn. You waltzed back into my life and bet Thorpe that you'd collar or marry me in a week, again without talking to me."

"Collar *and* marry, just to be clear. And I explained my reason to you. Do you need me to repeat it?"

"Yeah, you explained *after* I caught you, not before you made the deal. Why, so you'd have extra time to ensnare me. Why not just come clean when you dealt with Thorpe?"

Logan felt his ire mounting. He wasn't perfect, but he'd always had her best interests at heart. "I don't think I ever made any secret of the fact that I love you and want a future with you. What I said to Thorpe is irrelevant between us."

Tara looked like she was about to cry, but blinked back tears. "But you didn't ask if that's what *I* wanted."

"You're still clinging to your pain, like it's a life jacket, so that you don't let yourself love me back. Please, baby, don't do that. I know I hurt you. I'll apologize every damn day if I have to. But I want you to push past the fear and think about our future. Deep down, you trust me with your body and your safety, or I wouldn't be here now. I have to believe that your heart can't be far behind."

She paled. *Bull's-eye!* Now if she'd just stop being stubborn, picking fights, and admit how she felt, they could move forward.

"So when does your deal with Thorpe expire?"

He clenched his jaw. Where the hell was she going with this? "Thursday night."

"In less than three days?"

"Yes."

"I hope you're prepared to miss strutting down Dominion's halls in your leather pants, because if you think for one damn minute that I'm going to stand here like a brainless twit while you decide my whole life without ever once asking me what I want, you're out of your fucking mind."

So quickly that she had no time to scramble away, Logan grabbed Cherry's wrist and pulled as he backed onto the bed and threw her facedown across his lap. Without pause, he slapped one firm cheek of her ass, barely covered by one of those little sheer dresses. She gasped, and before the sound even died, he smacked the other cheek.

"I don't like you throwing out f-bombs. Do it again, and I'll spank you more."

"Fuck you!"

"Cherry, Cherry, Cherry . . ." He sighed with regret.

Even so, he couldn't deny that this feisty side of her had him revved up. She wanted this spanking—wanted him—but her fear and her pride wouldn't let her admit it. She was angry, and maybe she had every right to be. Maybe he should have handled his invocation of the club rule differently, told her in advance of his plans, and given her the opportunity to resolve it without involving Thorpe. But she would have only freaked out. She'd still been engaged to Brad at the time. She hadn't been ready to hear that he wanted a lifelong claim on her.

But he'd concede that maybe he should have told her sometime between then and now.

Because he'd said he would, Logan whacked Tara's ass twice more and held down her squirming form, trying desperately not to think about how badly he wanted inside her.

Damn. He'd bet she was dying to call him twenty kinds of asshole and let loose on him, but the spanking had curbed the worst of her tongue. They both needed to be a bit more calm.

The moment he let her up, she jerked to her feet, rage spitting from her eyes. "Don't do that again. I'm not one of your club bunnies, waiting around for your discipline."

"Don't discipline you?" He stood slowly, walking toward her, crowding her personal space, almost proud when she stood her ground. "I came back into your life because I'm a Dom. Guess what? I'm still a Dom. I'm always going to be one. And I'm going to bet that, even though you're spitting mad, your pretty little pussy is dripping wet."

She gasped in an offended breath. "That's low."

"But true."

Suddenly, she cocked her head, tightened her little fists, and glared at him through eyes narrowed with purpose. *Uh-oh.* What the hell was going through her head now?

"Okay, so I'm wet. I admit it. Just because you get me hot doesn't mean that you get to decide the rest of my life. I won't let you use my desire against me."

Is that what she thought? Hell, he adored Cherry because she was smart and compassionate, kind. She showed the world a roaring tiger willing to fight for injustice and those weaker, but underneath that front, she was vulnerable.

No matter what he did, he managed to push her buttons. She put protective walls between them. Yeah, he could stand here and argue with her. He might actually win the battle. But he was in this fight to win the war. If that meant that he needed to back off and let her have more control, he'd do his best to stifle his need to dominate and give it to her. Because at the end of the day, he wanted her by his side because she wanted to be there. Not because he'd coerced her.

"Then help me. I keep fucking this up, and that's not my intention. If you think I'm trying to use your desire against you to decide your life, then take control. I'll step back. If, after this mission, you tell me to go away, then fine. I'll go away and I won't come back."

Tara recoiled, her brown eyes wide and startled. Her mouth gaped open, but silence followed for a long moment until she finally said, "Thank you."

"But not until I'm convinced that you know the difference between me trying to lead you around by your pussy and me trying to bond your heart to mine, Cherry. When I'm sure you know *exactly* how much love you'd be giving up, I'll give you all the space you want."

With an angry jerk he hoped to hell communicated that he meant business, Logan tore off his shirt.

Chapter Seventeen

WITH unblinking eyes, Tara watched Logan peel the tight black T-shirt from his body, revealing an incredible work of masculine art to her slowly. Her helpless gaze caressed the bulges of his shoulders, lingered on his meaty biceps, devoured the tight slabs of his pectorals, widened at the sight of his rippling abdomen above low-slung jeans. And the sight of that tattoo crawling up his ribs in Japanese transfixed her. Though it had to have hurt like a bitch, it was oddly beautiful on his bronzed skin.

It didn't matter how many times she looked at Logan. Each and every time, she melted. Her heart stuttered. Her blood warmed, while her fingers itched to touch him all over. Now his gaze snared her attention. Stark and midnight blue, that stare he locked on her rooted Tara to the spot with its intensity and savagery. He was like a powder keg. Tara had a suspicion that she'd already set him off and that his fuse was burning down toward the inevitable explosion.

He reached for the snap on his jeans and flicked it open. Tara's gaze darted down nervously as anticipation sliced through her. She shivered, swallowed.

"Nervous?"

"You won't hurt me," she stated with a lift of her chin.

"Ever," he vowed. "That doesn't mean I'm going to go easy on you, Cherry."

That fact was stamped all over his demanding stare. She backed up a step.

His low laugh resonated through her, daring, challenging—sexy as hell. "Going somewhere?"

No. Behind her a step, two at most, Tara knew she'd find her back against a wall. But in front of her was two hundred pounds plus of determined male willing to do whatever necessary to make her whimper, beg, and surrender.

The prickly part of her nature reared up. He wasn't going to pleasure her into giving up her anger. At least not yet, damn it. She had a point.

Because sometimes the best defense was an offense, Tara crossed her arms over her chest and put on her best glare. "Why are you trying to intimidate me?"

Logan shook his head. "Baby, I'm just trying to get you to keep still so that we can . . . chat. Believe me, I'd rather not play games."

"I'm not. You are. I'm trying to tell you how I feel and—"

"I heard you. You're pissed because I don't tell you everything. Got it. So now I'm trying to communicate." He shrugged. "If you're sure you're ready, I am."

As angry as she was, as much as she felt a tinge of worry that she'd pissed off the big, bad Dom inside him, she couldn't very well tell him that she wanted to know everything, then refuse to hear him. "I can handle it and I'm listening. Shoot."

"Kneel."

She raised a cool brow but her heart stuttered. "Excuse me."

"You said you weren't playing games. Don't start now. You heard what I want."

"Why? You're playing domination games with me."

He shook his head. "If you extend me trust, baby, I'll puke up every dirty little secret I have."

And all she had to do to hear them was kneel. That went against her independent grain. On the other hand . . . she had an image of him, towering, ruthlessly male, demanding, cradling her head in his huge palm as he guided her lips to all the hard inches of his thick cock and told her to suck. God, why did that arouse her?

No, she'd play it his way for now, but as soon as she got on her knees, she wanted answers.

He trapped her gaze in his as she slowly went to one knee, then the other, then sat back on her heels, her palms sweating, and held her breath, feeling like a concubine waiting at her master's feet for his pleasure. And that feeling didn't bother her in the least.

"Good girl." He touched a finger to her cheek, then reached for his jeans again.

She jerked away. "Don't patronize me. Stop this head game you're playing and talk."

"I'm just communicating. Watch . . ."

The gentle hiss of his zipper lowering filled the quiet room. Tara's heart began to career crazily, and she sucked in a breath to calm herself. But as he lowered the denim over his hips, revealing the fact that he'd been commando underneath and that each and every inch of him was velvety hard and standing straight up for her, she couldn't stop her gasp.

"I want you to get a good look at this . . . Cherry."

She frowned. Logan had called her that a thousand times, but this time was somehow different.

Before she could question him, he reached to her side and yanked the desk chair beside her, bringing it close. He watched her with a dark stare.

"What do you have on the inside of your left thigh?" he demanded.

"A—a birthmark."

"Sit back, lift your skirt, and spread your legs so I can see."

Tara paused. Not because she didn't want to, but because she did. "How is this getting us any closer to whatever truth you want to tell me?"

Logan raised a brow. "Remember trust?"

With a sigh, she complied, rocking onto her backside, easing the sheer skirt up her thighs, and parting her legs. Logan zeroed in on her pussy, and instantly she felt her folds go wet. As he crouched between her legs, her sheath tightened, spasmed.

Slowly, he glided his finger up her thigh to her birthmark. "I never forgot this little round reddish mark of yours. That day in my bedroom that I touched it, tongued it, I decided it reminded me of a little cherry. After I'd broken things off, that sweet spot was burned onto my brain. It killed me that I couldn't touch yours, so . . . See what I got."

Logan stood and lifted his left foot onto the chair. At first, she couldn't look past all the inches of his swollen, hungry cock and the swing of his heavy testicles. Then he pressed his finger to the inside of his left thigh. In the same spot in which she had her own birthmark, he'd had something tattooed into his skin. She knelt, leaning in to peer closer, then realized exactly what it was.

Shock pinging through her system, she bounced her gaze up to his. "A cherry?"

"Got it the day I turned eighteen. I still loved you. I was drunk and alone and miserable, and the only thing I wanted was to brand myself with you."

Oh. Dear. God.

Shock reverberated down her system, jarring open the floodgates she'd been hiding her emotions behind. They poured out in a warm gush that inundated her chest.

All these years between them, lost. She'd been trying to muddle her way though and had been doing a lousy job. She'd thrown herself into school, then into a career, all the while wearing her anger at him like armor. She'd dated some, never quite sure why no one ever suited her, why she always felt restless and uncomfortable when other men touched her.

Now she knew. She'd been fooling herself for over a decade. Finally, the truth was crystal clear.

Tears sprang to her eyes as she touched one finger to the little shiny red cherry on his muscular thigh, transfixed by the slightly paler skin here, the dark dusting of hair around it. "I didn't know."

"So I'm telling you now. These are the last of my secrets, and I want you to know them."

Their gazes met again, and she felt the solid warmth and never ending flow of his love reaching out to her heart, thawing that terrible numbness she'd shoved on herself in the hopes that she'd never hurt again. His blue stare lasered in on her, gently but firmly letting her know that he wouldn't accept her hiding from him anymore. That suited Tara. She didn't want to.

She braced one trembling hand on his thigh, then reached up to finger the tattoo running from his hips, up his ribs, ending under his arm. "And this?"

He swallowed, unblinking as he met her gaze. "Japanese for 'Tara forever.' "

Her eyes slid closed. Xander had told her days ago to find these on his body and ask him what they meant. She'd been distracted. And if she was honest, a little afraid. Now . . .

Tears spilled down her cheeks. She didn't have to ask why he'd done it, nor could she claim that she didn't understand. He loved her. He'd said it. He'd come here to help and protect her, instead of spending his leave with family and friends. He'd imprinted that fact on his body, creating his own temple where he could worship her. In his own way, he'd been largely faithful to her, especially over the last five years. During that time, she'd deceived herself into believing that she'd moved on with life and that she was okay. Logan had remained steadfast to his pain, not trying to deny the festering hurt, but rather incorporating it into his life, honoring what they meant to one another.

When he brushed the tears from her cheeks, his tender caress wrenched her heart.

She blinked up at him, touched down to her soul. "I d-didn't know."

"You weren't supposed to." He kicked his jeans aside, leaving himself naked, and helped her to her feet. "I've been on some of the most dangerous missions the navy has doled out in the last ten years. Iraq, Afghanistan, tons of third world shitholes. I never worried. I knew my role, knew I was good at my job. I went in, did what I needed to do, and got out. I even woke up in the desert once with a viper's fangs about six inches from my face. My heart may have raced a little then. But I was never truly afraid of anything until you came back into my life and I realized how much I still loved you. Knowing that you could utter one Shakespearian character's name and walk out forever scared me more than anything, ever."

She bit her lip to hold in a sob, clutched his shoulders, and looked right into his eyes. "I love you."

Logan stepped close, eliminating her personal space and pressing his body against hers. His hands trembled as he grabbed her face. With his jaw clenched, his stare delved deep, past her eyes, right into her soul. "Say it again."

The tears took over again, blurring her vision of Logan, but Tara felt him all around her, somehow inside her. She might not have any visible tattoos to remind herself of him, but he was indelibly imprinted on her heart. "I love you. I don't think I ever stopped. I tried everything I could think of to cut you out of my heart." She shook her head. "But you were always there."

Pain tore across his face. "That night I came to your house a few years ago?"

God, *that* night. "And I slammed the door in your face. I'm sorry. It was like you had a sixth sense. I was just getting together with Brad, thinking that maybe he'd be different and that I could love him. We'd planned to . . . spend that night together for the first time."

She swallowed, wishing she didn't have to give him such a truth, but if he wanted it, Tara wouldn't hide.

"Did you?"

"No. Seeing you, even for two seconds, flipped some sort of

switch in me. As soon as I saw you, I finally felt the excitement, yearning, and need I'd been trying to manufacture with someone else for
years. It only took me a second to realize that you gave me everything
I'd been searching for, and you didn't even have to speak a word. I got
angry. Then I panicked. I knew Brad would see it all over my face. So
I slammed the door, told him that I wasn't feeling well, and sent him
home."

He pulled her face closer, whispering against her lips. "I wish to
fuck I'd had the courage to knock on your door each day of every
single leave home."

Fresh tears scalded her cheeks. "You would have worn me
down."

"No, Cherry. I would have loved you. Christ . . ."

Logan pulled her tightly against him, wrapping his arms around
her, burying his head in her neck. Tara felt him everywhere, his heat
all over her, his love running through her, his need simmering in her
veins.

Gently, she pulled away, then took his hand and led him to the
bed. "Love me now?"

He yanked the dress from her body, then tumbled her down
onto the mattress, covering her body with his. "Every day for the rest
of your life, if you'll let me, Cherry. Marry me?"

Tara thought her heart would explode. After everything they'd
been through, all the years and distance, life experiences and heartbreak, they were going to be together—where they belonged.

Tears spilled over again as she nodded. "I would love that more
than anything."

Logan's smile dazzled her, and the genuine warmth and happiness in his eyes was infectious. In that moment, Tara felt deep down
that they'd finally overcome everything. As soon as they finished this
mission, they could plan a wonderful, perfect life together.

With one hand anchored on her hip and the other wrapped
around her nape, Logan began sliding into her body, feeding her wet
pussy one slow, hard inch at a time. The friction of his cock sinking

into her clasping sheath charged a whirl of tingles through her, lighting up something that went heart deep.

"I'll take good care of you, baby. And I'll always love you," he whispered against her mouth. "It may not have been the most romantic proposal you've ever received, but it's the most sincere."

"It's perfect," she whispered, then covered his lips with her own, tangling his tongue with hers as if she could drink in every part of him and keep him with her forever.

As he pressed deeper, Tara's need to have all of him surged. She lifted and wriggled, head tossed back. Logan kissed her exposed throat and ground his hips to her, detonating a new flurry of sensation through her.

They weren't just joining bodies, and she knew it. Felt the tendrils of the fragile love they'd both clung to over the years thicken and grow, curling around them with every sweet, slow glide deep inside her. With every thrust, she panted out her pleasure, then held her breath as he withdrew, waiting for more of the sweet ache to ramp up to the explosion she needed to feel all the way down to her soul.

"Will you trust me, Cherry?" His gaze pleaded with her, saying what he wouldn't.

She didn't know exactly what he sought, but in that moment, it didn't matter. Whatever he did—whatever he wanted—would give her pleasure.

"Yes. Always."

His smile of joy was almost blinding as he slowly kissed her, their lips and breaths entwined reverently. Then withdrew from her.

With a gentle nudge, he rolled her to her stomach, disappeared for a moment, then returned to the bed.

"We're going to take this slow and gentle, baby. I only want to make you feel good. If you don't like anything, just tell me."

Tara had a pretty good idea what he wanted, and her heart skipped. "Hmm. You don't sound much like the badass Dom now."

He laughed and pressed a kiss to her shoulder. "Now that I've got a lifetime to unleash that side of myself on you, I can afford to take it slow. Trust me, you'll see the badass again. But right now, there's nothing more important than simply sharing this moment with you."

Joy welled up in her at his words. He wanted to connect them together in body now. In heart. They'd soon do it legally, in the eyes of God and man. And someday, if they hadn't already, they'd create life together. And live all their days side by side.

The fact that happiness—that Logan himself—was finally in her grasp made her urgent to have him now that he was finally, truly her man. "Hurry."

His warm palm glided down her back, over the curve of her waist to cling to her hip. "I want you to belong to me in every way. Will you let me try?"

Before she could answer, she felt a cool drizzle of liquid slide in the crevice of her backside. Then he penetrated her there with one finger, silently telling her exactly what he sought.

Tara gasped as her body swallowed him up, clamped down, and sent jolts of sensation pinging all through her body. "Yes."

"You like that?"

The plug he'd used on her previously had been sexy, awakened nerves she hadn't realized she possessed. But his fingers, with their warm skin and gliding movements, were something else altogether. She nodded. "More. Please."

Logan leaned across her back to whisper in her ear, "Like this?"

Then he withdrew completely, only to enter her ass again with two fingers, scissoring them apart, stretching her. This time, her body clenched, her skin burning. The utter intimacy of the act, as if he found every part of her worthy of attention, as if he loved and accepted every part of her and wanted to claim her wholly, encouraged her to take a deep breath, relax, and give him everything he wanted.

"Yes!" she cried out.

His fingers dug into her hip. "Even now I can see your fair skin flushing, baby. There's nothing more beautiful than your acceptance. Can you take more?"

For him, she could take anything. If it pleased him, if it brought them closer together, she'd endure anything.

But this electric touch lighting up her whole body told her this wouldn't be something she'd have to bear through, but a sizzling pleasure she could only hope to survive.

"Give me everything, Logan."

He moaned against the sensitive skin of her neck. "When you say it like that, Cherry—God, it turns me on."

Tara felt that in the next moment when he pressed his hard cock against the cheek of her ass, then eased his fingers past her rosette again. One, then two . . . until he added a third. The burn intensified until her skin seemed to be on fire. She hissed in pleasure and thrust back, gyrating to impale herself deeper.

Logan stilled her with a firm grip on her hip. "Easy, baby. We're taking this slow. I want this to go down as smooth as possible."

"I'm ready."

"Soon. Be patient."

She moaned in frustration, then cried out when he pressed his fingers deeper into her backside. "Now!"

"Do I have to drag out the ropes and discipline to make you behave?"

Someday—probably soon—he would. Tara could picture herself bound helplessly to his bed while he tormented her body slowly, mercilessly, until she begged him to fill her anywhere, everywhere.

Today, she understood his need for a gentler approach. They were mutually acknowledging not only pleasure, but the bond of their love for one another. Every touch felt profound.

With firm, slow strokes, he thrust his fingers deeper into her backside, spreading tender kisses across her back. "How's that, Cherry?"

Heavenly. She whimpered at those thick fingers inside her. She felt invaded and somehow conquered—yet still loved. Logan was opening her up to one of the most intimate acts possible, yet with every word and deed, he treated her with care, mindful of her pleasure and pain. And there was a bit of both that blended together to saturate her with startling pleasure.

He stilled. "Answer me."

"So good," she moaned.

"When I get inside you, it's going to sting, maybe even hurt a bit."

"I want to give myself to you, please you."

Logan leaned across her back, wrapping his arm around her to caress her belly. "The beautiful submissive I've always wanted inside the perfect woman I'll always love. I feel humbled."

Bliss exploded through her heart, then magnified as he glided his hand down her belly, settling it possessively over her mound. As one of his fingers slid between her slick folds, grazing her clit, Tara eased her head back on a slow groan.

Logan dropped his chin over her shoulder until they touched cheek to cheek. The rough coolness against the fever heating hers flared more need inside her, spinning a heavy ache all through her blood. She arched, melting into him.

"I feel so desired," she whispered.

With a gentle withdrawal, Logan removed his fingers from her backside, then spread more lube over the tender area. He disappeared for a moment, and Tara listened to the sounds he made around the room—the opening of a drawer, then ripping of cardboard, the clink of plastic. Vaguely, she wondered what he was doing, then decided it didn't matter. Whatever he did was for her greater pleasure, their heartfelt connection. Eyes still closed, she smiled as he made his way back to the bed and the mattress behind her dipped under his weight.

"You *are* desired, Cherry. I've always wanted you." He aligned himself behind her, hand curled around her hip, and fit the bulbous head of his cock against her rosette. "I will always want you."

A gasp replaced her reply as he eased into her, one slow torturous inch at a time. Her flesh stretched. The burn returned. Logan was not just longer, but thicker, and he paused when the tight ring of muscle there resisted his entry.

"You're going to be okay, baby. Take a deep breath for me. That's it. Relax. Good girl. Now arch your back and push out."

She did so as he used his hands to spread her cheeks apart, opening her even wider just for him. As he pushed forward, she braced herself, willing him past the constriction to fill her deep.

"Damn, this is so . . ." He groaned. "Fuck, you're so tight. The sight of you taking me here is killing me. I want all of you. Relax for me a bit more. Keep pushing out. Yeah." The sound was a long moan.

Then with a last push that flared her full of searing pain, he slid past the fist-tight muscles and sank inside her.

A whole new explosion of sensations opened up to her, the deeper he sank. The burning no longer lit her skin, but fired her muscles, igniting her very core. Having him in her pussy was always a pleasure that she could barely put into words, but this felt somehow more intimate, their connection so wordless yet absolute. Everything about the hushed whisper of sheets blending with their mutual moans, in rhythm to their slow, synchronized thrusts felt sacred.

Finally, Logan slid completely home and wrapped one arm tightly around her, as if he never wanted to let go. "We'll take our time because I'd never want to hurt you. I don't know how long I can hold out against this kind of pleasure, but I want you to feel utterly filled and fulfilled. So I need you to take everything I want to give you, Cherry."

He flexed his hips, pressing in just a bit deeper, making her gasp. Making her need even more.

"I will, Logan," she gasped. "Whatever you want."

He hugged her tighter. "Thank you for your trust. Spread your legs a bit wider. Perfect."

Suddenly, something cool and slick probed at the entrance to her pussy, then forged inside, up, up, up, filling her until she thought she'd burst. Then a buzzing sounded between them—and massaged every nerve lining the walls of her pussy.

With Logan in her ass, her sex had less space to accommodate the vibrator, and Tara felt every twitch of both toy and man. He held the vibrator deep inside her, its flared tip against her cervix, the outer wings stroking across her swollen clit, as he slowly shoved deep inside her rectum in a slow glide that had her holding her breath.

The air smelled of her arousal. Her desperate moans began to fill the air as he awakened every sensation in her pussy, her ass, and those tingles tightened into an ache that sent her thrusting back against him in a silent plea for more.

Never had she felt anything so consuming. When she fell off this edge of need, it would be into a chasm of pleasure unlike any other because it involved her whole body, her whole heart. And the man she loved would go with her, well pleased with the knowledge that she would do anything with or for him because she trusted him completely.

Behind her, sweat broke out across his chest, mixed with the fine sheen of perspiration slicking her back. Again he plunged into her, driving harder. Urgency tightened his fingertips, which held her still and at his mercy while he fucked her with that vibrator and his thick, unrelenting cock.

Blood rushed into her clit and the nerves around her rosette—everywhere he touched. The heartbeat surpassed her hard breathing in her head until all she could hear was the roar of her blood rushing. The sensations tightened, began to converge. Tara sobbed. Logan was going to overwhelm her, and she welcomed the chance to completely surrender. He would know then how totally she belonged to him and always would.

"Your back is flushing rosy," he panted. "Your ass is so tight on me, baby. You ready to come?"

"Yes!" She barely managed to find the breath to sob out.

He shoved the vibrator in another quarter inch and pulled it right against the front wall of her pussy, so it pulsated against that sensitive spot behind her clit, even as the exterior wings feathered over the screaming little bud.

"Take me!" he shouted and plunged into her over and over as fast and deep as he could.

Sensations multiplied, unrelenting. Every ache he created in her pussy, clit, and ass all united to create one huge supernova that had her screaming and fisting the sheets, crying his name, as her body burst with the most white-hot, sublime pleasure she'd ever experienced.

His breath heavy in her ear, he began to moan, short, frantic sounds as he pounded inside her with one long stroke after another. Then he loosed a long shout so anguished, it was as if pleasure had ripped it from his soul.

"Cherry!"

Tara took him, bucked with him. Still not finished with her first orgasm, it stretched into another as she felt the splash of his hot release inside her.

As their movements settled, stilled, he pulled the vibrator from her pussy and turned it off. The only sound in the room now was their harsh breathing as he collapsed to the bed on top of her, still buried deep in her ass.

"You are incredible," he whispered.

She turned her head, and he kissed her temple, her cheek as she murmured, "Hey, you stole my line."

He palmed her head gently. "I meant everything I said. I love you. I want to marry you."

Their lovemaking had suffused her with an inner glow already, but it brightened even more at his words. "I meant what I said. I love you, too. I will marry you." She smiled. "Let's get this job finished and get on with our lives."

* * *

GET on with our lives.

That handful of words doused Logan with a bucket of water, robbing him of the most vivid euphoria he'd ever experienced in

Tara's arms. Every muscle had been relaxed, his mind cleared of all
but happiness and the love that would fill their tomorrows. The getting on with this job part of her speech didn't disturb him. He looked
forward to that. Getting on with their lives even more so.

But Adam Sterling stood between them. Again.

Fuck!

His mind jolting back online, he rose, padded to the bathroom,
and started the shower. What the hell was he going to do? Thoughts
chased each other in his head. Tell Tara his suspicions about Adam
being his mother's killer because he'd promised he'd keep no more
secrets from her? Or wait to tell her until he had something more
than circumstantial evidence and a gut feeling? He'd like to . . . but
once they made their way off this island, Adam would be waiting. If
the fucker had in fact killed Amanda and threatened his own stepdaughter multiple times, then Logan couldn't risk Tara being alone
with him ever again.

Suddenly, he felt a soft hand on her shoulder. "You're already
thinking pretty hard."

Tara was supposed to be focused on the mission now. This would
only mess with her head. And cause a potential rift between them
just as they were truly connecting. But he'd lost her once because he
hadn't come clean. History could have easily repeated itself today, if
she hadn't been forgiving. Logan knew better than to risk it a third
time.

The warm smile that curled her lips fell. "Something's really
bothering you. What's wrong?"

"Get in, Cherry." He helped her into the shower, avoiding her
concerned expression as he climbed in after her.

Closing his eyes, he took hold of her face and pressed his lips to
hers reverently. He never wanted Tara to doubt his love for her again.
Whatever he said, he did so out of caution and devotion . . . though
she might not see it that way.

She pulled away. "Logan, you're scaring me."

He finally looked at her. "I want you to listen to me with an open mind because I know what I'm about to say will be hard for you to hear. Remember that I would never intentionally hurt you again."

Apprehension skittered across her face. "O-Okay."

Logan clutched her against him, praying that she understood his good intentions and that this wasn't the last time he held her. "Your stepfather killed my mother."

Chapter Eighteen

TARA stared at Logan, her brain replaying his words over and over. They simply wouldn't compute. He had to be wrong. "No. That's not—no."

She tried to thrash out of his embrace. The water from the hot shower should have made her skin slick enough to slip away.

Logan held tight. "Cherry, listen to me. That necklace you're wearing was my mother's."

"You're wrong. Adam gave it to me."

"You said earlier that you found it."

"I did, in his car, but he said he'd bought it for me."

With a shake of his head, Logan gripped her tighter. "Listen. He kept the necklace as a trophy from his kill. And you found it, so he told you he'd bought it for you to ward off suspicions. But I know that necklace. My father had given it to my mother in a last-ditch attempt to tell her that he cared. She must have been wearing it when Adam killed her, since the police found a thin abrasion around her neck. The medical examiner said it was consistent with something thin and metallic being ripped from her neck. This necklace was the only item missing from the crime scene."

Tara flinched as she pictured Logan's mother dead—and that he'd been the one to find her. "That doesn't prove my stepfather took it. I—if your dad bought it for your mom around that time, m-maybe my stepdad also bought one. If they were for sale at the mall or something—"

With a big hand, he grabbed hold of her pendant and turned it over. "This dent on the back, right here." He pointed. "Did you ever notice it?"

How could he know about that? "Yeah, after I'd been wearing it for a while. I always assumed that I'd accidentally slammed it in my jewelry box or set something on it."

Logan clutched it in his fist. "My sister's pet parrot bit it. I remember Mom crying when she realized the stupid bird had damaged the gold."

Stomach plummeting to her knees, Tara listened as the steamy water pelted her back in a hard sting. His accusations were even more merciless. Denial clawed down to her bones. "That doesn't mean it's the exact same dent. Because it's gold, it's somewhat f-fragile and . . ."

With a growl, he grabbed her shoulders. "I know this is hard to accept, but I'm telling the truth. My mother's necklace disappeared at nearly the same time you found one exactly like it, with the exact same damage. If your stepfather killed my mother, then he threatened to kill you, too."

"He would never!" Tara wrenched away. "That man took me in when he didn't have to. He raised me from the time I was twelve. He cared for me even before my mother died. I can't believe he'd—" She shook her head. "No."

"Threaten to kill you? If you wearing that necklace around me could implicate him as a killer and send him to prison from first-degree murder for twenty to life, hell yeah, he'd threaten you. Even before he killed my mother, he tried every way possible to separate us without success. But once you'd found that, he had to step up his game to keep me from ever seeing it, Cherry. Or I would have known. Even if he'd gotten rid of that necklace, he couldn't have me around in case some other tell gave him away."

Tara stared, blinked. She heard the words, heard the logic . . . but just couldn't wrap her head around the idea that Adam had killed anyone in cold blood or threatened to do the same to her. "I—it just . . ."

"I know it's hard to take in, but I'm not making this up." He slammed a fist into the shower's tile wall. "I'm almost positive that the son of a bitch killed my mother. We all suspected that she'd been seeing someone. Think back. Was Adam dating then?"

Frowning, she searched her memory, but the shock made her hazy. "I don't know. Adam dated quietly. I never paid attention."

"Maybe their relationship went sour."

"Adam had dated before and ended relationships amicably."

"Okay, so something else went wrong. But he killed her; I'd bet my god damn life on that."

Tara wrapped her arms around herself and trembled under the hot spray. "Why are you dumping this . . . theory on me now?"

He pressed tight lips together. "I just figured it out today, and you don't want me keeping secrets from you."

She blinked, trying to absorb all the shock. "You were staring at my necklace."

He nodded and caressed her hair, fastened his hand around her neck. "Cherry, when this mission is over, I can't risk having you near Adam. He knows you've been with me. The son of a bitch may make good on his threat to kill you. He won't risk me figuring out that he killed my mother."

God, his words were pressing in on her like a vise. She covered her face with her hands, still trying to process his accusation. He slung everything at her so damn fast. "Logan . . ."

"Don't start with that apologetic tone, Tara, like you're going to blow me off. I'm asking for your trust, as your fiancé. As your Dom. I would *never* want to see you hurt."

"I know you're not trying to be malicious." She shook her head. "You believe what you're saying. But . . ."

Logan looked like he was grasping for patience. "Promise me this: don't put yourself in the position to be alone with him again until I can get this taken care of."

Taken care of? As in . . . "You're going to try to have him put away?"

"If he committed the crime, and I can prove it, yeah. He killed a woman who was barely forty and left three kids without a mother. Shouldn't he pay?"

Tara blinked. If what Logan said was true, yes. "Adam is former FBI. One of the good guys. He's not a killer."

Frustration crested over his features as he backed away. "We'll wait and see."

* * *

AS soon as they stepped from the shower, Logan was relieved to hear the sat phone chirping. At least it would give them both something else to focus on. He pressed down his disappointment. Her reluctance to believe him was a blade in his heart. All the trust he'd been trying to build with her, where the fuck was that? Yes, he was asking for a lot, but she could at least try to believe him?

Tara charged over to the phone. "Jacobs."

Once she'd given her security code, Logan could hear the male voice muffled on the other end. In between, she said a lot of "yes, sir" and finally, "we'll get on that."

Within three minutes, she pressed the button to end the call, then heaved a huge sigh. "Some of the data has been processed. Still no identity on the mysterious owner of Fantasy Key. In all the files, he's simply referred to as 'Sire.' The analysts were able to find coded references on Kantor's computer about the slave auctions. The next one is set for Thursday at eleven p.m. The 'product' is being held in the Pit."

Logan filtered through the information. "The 'product' being Darcy?"

"Yeah." She shivered, and Logan knew she feared for her friend. "The Pit likely being that dungeon under the resort we found on the blueprints. We need to get down there today, see if there's a way to break Darcy out. If so, I can talk to them about arresting Kantor, at least. His fingerprints are all over that computer and his user ID is attached to the files. He's guilty as hell."

"He is, but I'm sure the Feds want Sire. If we go in too soon with guns blazing, what are the chances we'll get him? He'll turn tail and run, then set up shop elsewhere."

"I know." She tossed her head back and stared at the ceiling, uncertainty and anxiety clearly pressing down on her. "But I can't let Darcy be sold off—"

Logan wished he could do more to set her at ease than talk. "Let's see if we can find someone who can identify Sire. If they don't know his name, I have to believe that if he's running a business, he's been here at some point. Someone must have seen his face or know his identity. I'll ask Xander to poke around. We'll do everything possible to nail this bastard."

She nodded absently, her mind already turning. In spite of the furious pace of the bombshells coming her way, his Cherry was doing her best to press forward. Again, his pride in her bravery, her intelligence brimmed over. As much as he wanted her blind faith, dealing with the shock of his accusations against Adam would take time; no one could be expected to believe that a beloved family member was a stone-cold killer without proof in a matter of minutes. But she would do anything and everything to both save Darcy and salvage the other mission objectives. Her first objective was to save her fellow agent. The FBI didn't leave their own behind. Then she had to catch a killer.

"I think I have an idea." She bit her lip, still gelling her thoughts. "But I need to talk to Xander. We'll need his help."

Logan pulled out his phone. "I'll call him now. We'll figure this out, baby. We'll get Darcy free."

And he'd prove to her that her stepfather was a dangerous son of a bitch—while keeping her well loved and safe. Somehow.

* * *

TARA pushed fruit salad around her plate, avoiding Logan's glower.

"I don't like it," he growled.

"Got a better plan?"

He didn't, and she knew it. They'd been over everything when they'd consulted with Xander. They needed access to the Pit. They suspected that Kantor and Jordan had it. Kantor was damn hard to pin down, but Tara knew exactly how to get near Jordan, even if the dungeon master had been oddly stand-offish since their first day on the island. That man wanted her, and she could use it to her advantage.

Logan sighed. "You're pissing me off."

"Doubt it will be the last time in our lives." She tried to smile at him.

"Probably not."

He pursed his lips together, and she knew he was thinking of all the danger, worrying about her, maybe even brooding about what would happen when she got home and saw Adam. Frankly, that worried her, too. It didn't seem possible that her stepfather was a killer . . . but Logan seemed so convinced. While he was trying to prove Adam guilty, maybe she could get the real story on the necklace and show Logan that someone else had murdered his mother. Her stepfather and her fiancé were never going to be great friends, but she'd like at least a little harmony on holidays, especially for the kids' sake.

She blinked. Kids. Wow. Thinking about having them with the man she'd always secretly, deep down loved was magical, a sparkling fantasy she'd never expected to come true. Logan would make a great husband and father. And she'd get to share all the love, passion, and joy with him—just as soon as she rescued Darcy and got off this damn island.

"You'd better eat, Cherry. You're going to need your strength." A sensual threat threaded his low, growled words.

She repressed a shiver. "You're trying to scare me."

"No. I'm stating a fact. And I want you wet."

Tara couldn't help it; her womb clenched. "I'd ask if all you think about is sex, but that would be a stupid question."

"When you're near, I give a full point-one percent attention to other concerns."

He tried to grin, but it wasn't quite real. Her heart ached for him. She knew her lack of faith in him about his mother's killer upset him. It hurt her to disappoint Logan, but she needed time to work through this, prove Adam's innocence. Then they'd talk it all out.

"Do you need anything else?" Chaz stopped by their table and began collecting their half-empty plates. "Dessert?"

"Not for me." The idea of eating anything else turned her stomach.

"No thanks," Logan murmured.

Chaz regarded him with pale, tormented eyes against his olive skin. "At your three o'clock, see the empty table."

Logan glanced out of the corner of his eye. "Yeah."

"Allison, Laken's friend, was assigned to that table until her departure on Sunday. Jordan lured her to the VIP room last night. I haven't seen her since and I haven't been able to reach her."

Tara's blood froze in her veins.

"Her room attendant is a friend of mine," Chaz went on. "She said Allison didn't sleep in her bed last night. Allison knew I was concerned after Laken's death, and she was completely freaked about her friend's murder. She wouldn't have left without telling me."

"We'll look into it," Tara reassured.

With a tight nod, he turned and left.

"I'll bet Kantor is also involved in Allison's disappearance," Logan muttered.

Tara nodded, holding in a curse. "I'm guessing he's the brains on site. He and Jordan probably needed more 'product' for Sire to replace Laken."

Logan grimaced. "If she'd been sold before her death, yes. Allison already told me that she and Laken had bonded because they were both looking for the perfect Dom and didn't have a lot of family. So no one to miss her for days and days . . ."

Not what Tara wanted to hear. "Tonight, as our plan goes down, keep your eyes and ears open."

"I will." Logan nodded. "But I still don't like any of this."

Tara didn't either, but time was running short and with another woman gone, their options were frighteningly thin.

* * *

SOMEHOW, someway, Tara had to separate Jordan from his all-access key card for her plan to work. No one was getting into the Pit without it.

She'd offered herself up as the sacrificial sub, but it took Tara an hour to spot Jordan in the public dungeons, now dressed in leather pants. Amid the crack of whips and the cries of pleasure/pain, he tried to give off the all-American-hero vibe with his winning smile. He'd spiced it up with a bit of badass, punctuated by the barbed-wire tattoo around one of his biceps and his gym-cut abs rippling between peeks of his black leather vest, sans shirt. But his eyes were cuttingly shrewd. Tara sensed this guy was seriously bent.

She shoved back the urge to shake as she wandered past him wearing next to nothing, putting on her best little-girl-lost face as she watched a middle-aged Dom tie his female sub up to a rack with a series of complicated knots that framed her breasts and thighs, rubbing her nipples or clit whenever the sub moved. Tara didn't have to fake her eyes widening.

"That's Shibari, little sub. Japanese rope bondage. What are you doing wandering around here without your Dom? Did he leave you again?"

Tara pretended to look down, clandestinely checking his belt for anything attached and his pockets for any flat areas.

"Yes, Sir. He said he was going for water over thirty minutes ago."

Disapproval poured off him, but he softened it with a caress of his finger down her cheek. Willing herself not to flinch as he settled his knuckle under her chin, Tara allowed him to lift her face.

"He doesn't understand the treasure he has in such a sweet sub. You know, Tara, other Doms would welcome the opportunity to care for you."

Her heart picked up speed. Was this the first step in separating a vulnerable sub from her protector, pointing out his faults and trying to convince her that she could do better?

"I—I don't think he cares for me very much, Sir."

Jordan frowned, then held out his hand. "Come with me. We'll talk."

Crap! She couldn't go anywhere alone with him. Too dangerous. What if Logan and Xander couldn't follow?

Fearing that she'd overplayed her hand, she cast her eyes down again. "Master Logan told me not to wander from this area."

He grabbed her hand. "So sweetly obedient. Such a shame . . ." He sighed. "There is a sofa against the wall. That's not too far."

Tara breathed a sigh of relief. It was a bit shadowed for her comfort, but even without a weapon, she was well trained in self-defense. Logan and Xander could still see her. They'd step in if anything went seriously wrong.

With a nod, she followed. He settled himself on the sofa, then patted his thighs. She hesitated.

Jordan scowled. "I won't punish you—yet. You merely look like a sub in need of comfort, and my job is to provide all guests on the dungeon floor what they need."

The slime was stretching the privileges attached with his authority, but she did her best to look understanding.

"Master Logan might paddle me if he sees me . . . but I could use cuddling."

Tara tried not to cringe as she climbed onto his lap and let him put his arms around her. Beneath her left buttock, she felt something flat and hard. With a wriggle, as if trying to get more comfortable, she scooted off the item, only to see a hook at his belt his vest had previously hidden. From there, a thin silver chain dangled that disappeared into the pocket of his leather pants. *Bingo!*

"Thank you for holding me, Sir," she whimpered. "I was feeling very alone."

Probably a little too forward for someone she'd bet liked to crush girls under his feet, but he took the bait enough and tightened his arms around her. She forced herself to go limp against his chest, swallowing down bile as she thrust her hands under his vest, near his waist. The move put her breasts right in his face, and Jordan didn't miss an opportunity to ogle.

Willing her hands not to shake, she thrust her breasts forward and slid her hand to the hook on his belt. She pretended a big sigh, which lifted her cleavage as she thumbed the hook off of his belt loop.

"You are very soft, little sub."

"Thank you, Sir."

She tried to think of something to prolong the conversation without arousing his suspicion. In case he suspected she was law enforcement, she couldn't ask for a tour of the VIP room or say that she'd hoped to see him again. Instead, Tara took a softer approach.

"I don't know why I can't keep Master Logan's attention," she pretended to cry softly, wrapping her fingers around that thin little chain affixed to what she hoped was his access card in his pocket.

"It baffles me." He brushed the hair from her face. "Kantor asked me to steer clear of you, but I can't. You're a treat to be savored."

Tara froze. Why would Kantor do that unless he was suspicious? And why would Jordan tell her unless he was out of the loop? That was a puzzle to solve later.

For now, she wriggled again on his lap, trying to disguise the slow pull of the card from his pocket. It inched up, a corner sticking out, but with him sitting, she had no way to extract it cleanly.

She gave the prearranged gesture above Jordan's head. Within seconds, Logan's heavy footfalls came barreling toward them. With

a glance over her shoulder, she saw him charging like an angry predator bent on tearing apart a lesser male for daring to infringe on his
territory. She didn't think that terrifying expression was totally man-
ufactured.

Tara scrambled off Jordan's lap. As he stood, she tugged the card
free of his pocket. She yanked it behind her back, holding her breath
as Jordan looked down with a puzzled expression. He'd felt her free
it. *Shit!*

At that moment, Logan came to her rescue, advancing on the
dungeon master with blazing eyes and an accusatory finger. Jordan
merely puffed out his chest and tried to look intimidating.

Per their plan, Logan shoved her behind his back. With a clan-
destine movement, she slipped the key card into his back pocket.

His posture remained in angry barbarian mode. If this wasn't an
act, she suspected Logan would be forcing a big come-to-Jesus down
the dungeon master's throat. This wasn't doing much for Logan's
disinterested image.

"Never put your hands on my sub again."

"She was alone and needed reassurance. I provided it in your
inattentive absence."

Logan's entire back tensed. "The way I treat her is none of your
business. Perhaps I was disciplining her."

"Were you?" Jordan raised a brow.

"None of your business. Don't interfere again with my property.
She needs a good punishment, and I'll give it to her."

Tara had to bite her lip to keep her jaw from dropping. *Property?*

As Logan whirled and dragged her toward a nearby St. Andrew's
Cross, she didn't have to pretend too hard to drag her feet. Yes, this
had been her idea . . . but that didn't mean she liked it.

"Don't go tense on me, Cherry," he muttered. "You're going to be
fine."

All she had to do was trust him.

When they reached the cross, Logan stopped, adopted his most stern expression, eyes narrowed on her. "Why am I punishing you, slave?"

Oh, his Dom voice. It should intimidate her a bit, but he just made her melty. "F—for wandering away from the spot you left me, Logan."

"And?"

Tara did her best to look agitated and uncomfortable. Jordan hadn't followed, but he was watching. She felt his gaze crawling all over her. "Sitting in Master Jordan's lap."

"Taking the comfort you did not have permission to receive, yes. Face the cross."

She did as instructed, shivering inside.

"Strip. Fold your dress neatly and hand it to me."

Taking her clothes off in public. Tara tried not to wince. Granted the cross leaned against a wall, so no one would see her breasts or her pussy. But the entire room would see her fleshy ass. Logan liked it, but she still felt ridiculously self-conscious showing a group of strangers the part of herself that she liked least.

"Slave, you've been given an order. Do it now, or I add more punishment."

Blowing out a shuddering breath, Tara reached for the strapless dress and pulled it down. The elastic expanded over her breasts, collapsed again at her waist, flared over her hips, then slithered to the ground, leaving her completely bare.

Logan caressed her backside, lingering to cup the lower curve as he thumbed the slope. "God, I love your ass," he muttered for her ears only, then nudged her to the cross, forcing her to raise her arms.

All too soon, she was secured to the giant wooden X. Logan selected a whip from the nearby wall—and she swallowed. They hadn't talked about how he'd punish her. She'd assumed he'd find some soft crop or use his hand, but this whip was nearly as long as his entire body. With a flick of his wrist, he sent it flying through the air, testing its weight. Her heart drummed against her chest.

At the first snap, she jumped, gasped, then looked over her shoulder. Logan looked frighteningly proficient with the long whip as he sent it flying through the air again.

Tara closed her eyes. She could do this. Logan wouldn't really hurt her. All she had to do was trust him.

Jordan wandered closer.

On cue, Xander sauntered into the scene under the guise of dungeon monitor, just to the left of the cross, and gave her a reassuring nod when Jordan was watching Logan with the whip.

"Count for me, slave," Logan demanded.

Her entire body tensed as she waited for the first horrific blow.

"Wait," Jordan demanded. "This is one of her soft limits."

"We've been working on it."

Jordan cleared his throat. "Even so, we don't recommend discipline with a six-footer."

"I'm more than able to give my sub the punishment she needs. *Stand aside*," he growled.

"I'll be watching." Jordan glared in his direction. "One false move, and I'll step in."

"Relax," Xander whispered to her. "It'll hurt more if you don't."

Tara forced herself to exhale and release as much tension as she could. Then Logan struck.

He laid the whip directly across the fleshiest part of her ass. The leather almost caressed her. A slight sting followed, then gently dissipated, leaving behind the haziest of tingles.

She gasped. "One."

Before she'd taken another breath, Logan brought the whip down again, this time cradling the tender undercurve of her buttocks. The strike was a bit harder, the sensation stronger. As before, as soon as the whip lifted away, a soft nip dissolved into a mellow glow.

To her shock, she wanted more.

Wriggling, Tara struggled against her bonds. She was supposed to hate this. For their plan to work, she had to publicly scream her safe word. Instead, Logan was only proving how wonderful he was at making her embarrassingly wet.

"Count, slave. If I have to remind you again, we'll start at the beginning."

Pretty please.

She kept the thought to herself and forced a tremble to her voice. "Two. No more . . . Please."

"Liar," Xander whispered. "Someone's got really hard nipples. Did I ever tell you that I love the way you flush when you're aroused?"

Tara shot him a dirty look, and she could tell he held in a laugh.

While she was distracted, Logan flicked the whip at her again, this time across the top of her ass to wind around her hip.

Okay, that actually stung more on the pain than pleasure side. She hissed, tensed, promised she'd tell Logan off for that shit later.

Then the pain faded into a bevy of furious tingles dancing under her skin. Warmth sank into her muscles. The feel of it was nothing short of dazzling.

"Three," she panted.

"I'm going to make these last two really count, slave. No complaints. You've earned this punishment."

Tara nodded, trying to bring her breathing back under control, cool down the hot ache ramping her body up. Damn it, she'd let herself get carried away in the moment with Logan, in the trust they were building. She was gleefully drowning in her love for him.

But his accusations against her stepfather were a shadow between them.

The thought had barely crossed her mind when Logan struck again with the rawhide, this time making a vertical strike down her right cheek. That blow more than stung prettily and brought the blood to the surface skin of her ass. It actually hurt.

Her entire body tensed. Whipping like that she didn't want, and he still had another lash to give her.

Panicked breathing set in again. Even though Logan was supposed to scare her, the fear started jacking up her system and messing with her head.

"Pretty welt," Jordan commented. "I'll bet she looks good with a truly red ass."

"Yeah. She needs a matched set," Logan said loudly. "Maybe a sore backside will keep her off other Doms' laps."

He cracked the whip in the air again, and fear became an icy-hot panic flaring through her veins. Tara knew in her head this was all for show, but her right cheek still throbbed, and they had a plan to set in motion.

"Romeo!" she screamed.

Logan ignored her and laid the whip vertically across her left cheek, not quite as hard as the previous lash, but enough to have her gasping again, *"Romeo!"*

"No wimping out of this punishment, slave. I'm not hurting you. You get one more for interrupting me."

"Stop," Jordan said sternly. "Continuing after the safe word is against club rules. Let your slave off the cross and provide proper aftercare or I'll see to her myself."

"You don't interfere with my slave," Logan roared, then laid the whip across her thighs.

This was another gentle stroke, almost a caress, but Tara pushed past the pleasure and played her part with an Oscar-winning scream of pain and terror.

"Enough!" Jordan roared.

A scuffle and what sounded like a punch or two later, Xander left her side with a muttered, "Keep him busy as long as you can." Then he was gone.

"Take this asshole to Kantor's office and wait with him," Jordan said to Xander. "I will see to the slave, then meet you there." Then he addressed Logan with a growl. "Mr. Flint, it will be my pleasure to personally escort you off the island."

Tara's heart pounded as Logan put up a staged struggle with Xander, whom he allowed to overpower him eventually. By the time Jordan released her from her bonds, the other two men were gone.

"Are you all right?" he whispered, her dress thrown over his arm. He sounded like he genuinely cared.

She didn't have to pretend too hard to shake. The adrenaline was draining from her system, leaving her a shaky mess. Her legs nearly gave out, but Jordan was there, supporting her as he hurried across the floor, toward a locked door.

Tara wanted to resist going anywhere too private with him, especially naked, but her job was to distract him. Putting up a fight now would only either make him suspicious or angry.

"I'm sore, Sir."

"Your first whipping?"

She nodded as he eased the door open and helped her inside. As he flipped on the overhead light, a flare of white brilliance from the overhead bulb nearly blinded her. After a quick glance of a cot, a cabinet, and a small desk with a phone, she squinted her eyes shut against the brightness.

Jordan helped her to the cot, urging her onto her belly. He cupped the uninjured part of the right cheek of her ass, and she tensed. Having him touch her felt wrong.

"They really are pretty welts, but a bit painful until you get used to them. Let me doctor you up."

Pretty welts? Yuck. "Thank you, Sir."

She laid still and tolerated his ministrations, then docilely allowed him to enfold her in his arms. Kantor stopped in as soon as Jordan radioed. Tara told the manager her story haltingly, wasting as much time as possible. The longer she kept them occupied, hopefully the more time Logan and Xander had to investigate the Pit. She just hoped that Kantor didn't know her cover—and kill her for it.

* * *

USING the access card Tara had swiped from Jordan, Logan let Xander grip his wrists behind his back and lead him into the Pit. Worry bit into his gut for Cherry. She was capable of taking care of herself, but naked, she had no weapon. No way to fight off Jordan if he decided to make a move—or Kantor, if he chose to make her a "product."

Just outside the door with a small square window, a guard inside a station, surrounded by radios and video monitors, questioned them via intercom, "What?"

Xander pressed the button and leaned in. "Jordan asked me to bring this troublesome one down here."

Assuming that Jordan had the authority to bring someone down here had been a gamble. But since the access card had gotten them down the elevator and into the long hallway, Logan had to assume his name would get them deeper inside the Pit.

"A *male* prisoner?" Logan heard the guard's scowl and suspicion.

"He's unruly." Xander sounded like he was straining to keep him subdued, so Logan played along with a little struggle. "Jordan wanted him separated from the rest before he hurt someone else. Help me out here."

Sending a prayer upward, Logan hoped that making a scuffle now would prevent the guard from calling for Jordan or other backup. So he thrashed again, pretending to fight Xander's hold.

Finally, the guard sighed and ordered gruffly, "Put him in the second cage."

As soon as Xander opened the door, they wandered into a cold, humid cave—with modern conveniences. Security cameras monitored all the movement inside. Low, recessed lighting shone softly from above, illuminating a row of ten rectangular silver cages, lined up one after the other. The first one held an unconscious brunette Logan knew wasn't Darcy. He prayed she was only sleeping. The rest of the cages sat empty.

Shit! Was he too late?

Logan itched to look around more, find out if there were hidden areas to the Pit, but it would have to wait a few minutes until Xander could get in place.

Yanking the door of the appointed cage open, Xander shoved Logan inside. As he pushed the door closed, which should have engaged the lock, he slid a piece of thick putty he'd swiped from the maintenance folks over the mechanism.

"Jordan will be back for you," Xander warned loudly, then turned and headed to the guard station. All he could do now was wait for the charming bastard to work his magic.

He pretended disinterest as Xander jaunted up the stairs to the security booth. The guard, distrustful at first, refused to let him in. But within ten minutes, the uniformed man had opened the door and was yucking it up with Xander like they were old pals. While the guard was busy slapping his knee and chortling, Xander slipped some contraband narcotic painkiller he'd stolen from the resort's medical facility into the guy's coffee.

In minutes, the guard was slumped against his desk, out cold.

Logan raced out of the cage. Xander met him halfway and handed him the key and a semiautomatic he'd smuggled onto the island. "Heads up. Ruben, the guard, says that Sire actually arrived on the island an hour ago. He's *here*, in the next room."

Seriously? Adrenaline charged his system into hyperdrive. Fuck, he wanted to nail this son of a bitch. After his mother's death, any prick who preyed on women deserved to be a dead prick, and Logan would be more than happy to help make that happen.

"Let's get him."

"Yeah." Xander raced to the sleeping brunette in the first cage. "Go. I'll check her. Hit the office first and view the security feed. A few of the cameras point to a location I don't know. Hell, none of this 'Pit' area is familiar, but there's nasty shit going on wherever those cameras are pointing."

With any luck, he could catch a glimpse of Sire, maybe even get him on film.

With a nod, Logan turned and jogged past a wide steel door that made up almost an entire wall. The shiny shiver panel had a key swipe beside it.

From the other side, he heard a distinctly female scream.

Logan's first instinct was to race in there and start kicking some ass, but he forced patience. It wouldn't help the woman to go in there half-cocked and unprepared for who- or whatever he had to fight. And give Sire any opportunity to escape.

With a quick jog to the security station, Logan shoved the slumped guard aside and stared at the rows of video monitors before him. There had to be three dozen total, covering angles all over the resort. He could see the dungeon where he'd whipped Cherry earlier, but that station was in use by others now. Tara was nowhere in sight.

Tamping down his panic, Logan forced himself to breathe and stay focused on the plan, on finding Sire. He scanned the bank of three other monitors off to his right, one depicting an image with a corrugated-steel door in the background. Two submissives had been chained naked to the cave wall. The first, a blonde with short, wispy hair, was being whipped mercilessly with a crop. Darcy? Perhaps. From the back he couldn't tell. The other prisoner knelt at the feet of a dungeon monitor he recognized, tears streaming down her face. Her enhanced breasts bobbed as the bastard shoved his cock down her throat. When her tormenter stepped back for a moment, Logan got a good look at her face. Allison.

Xander raced into the booth. "The brunette says she's being punished by her Dom and doesn't want to be removed."

Logan bit back a curse. "We'll come back for her."

He had to save the women clearly in peril and search for Sire before he worried about the other woman. Since he didn't see another male in the image, Logan feared Sire had already left, but he could hunt. Then he'd find his way back to Tara. With the slaving mastermind roaming the island and her alone with the management, every minute they were apart was another minute that ratcheted up his fear.

"Let's go," Xander directed.

Just before he turned to leave the security booth, Logan glanced at the feed from inside the secured area of the Pit. A hidden door opened, and what he saw next made his blood freeze with sheer, blinding terror.

Chapter Nineteen

LOGAN stared, his mind racing, trying to comprehend exactly what he was seeing. *Holy son of a bitch!*

Adam fucking Sterling, Tara's stepfather, stood ogling the two bound women as Allison had her mouth raped by a resort employee. The other sobbed, chained against the wall, her ass a throbbing red. The bastard barked something at her, and Logan damned the fact that he couldn't hear any audio with the images. But Adam spoke a universal language when he picked up the crop at the woman's feet and ruthlessly swatted her ass again. The poor girl's shoulders shook harder as she did her best to curl into herself and escape.

"C'mon, man!" Xander tugged on his arm. "The one in the suit could be Sire. We've got to get in there and save the women before something bad happens to them."

Just like that, the pieces of the puzzle snapped into place. Before her death, his mother had organized a neighborhood effort to locate a missing teen. Sterling, with his law enforcement connections, would have had access to the investigation. Maybe Amanda had gotten too close to the truth. Since Adam had killed his mom so brutally, Logan knew the bastard was capable of most anything. That he was in the Pit, now fondling the "products," told him that if the man wasn't

Sire, he was up to his neck with the bastard in human trafficking. Rage screamed through Logan's brain, and he wanted to kill Adam Sterling.

And when Tara learned all of this . . . Logan almost hadn't wanted to be right about Tara's stepfather, for her sake. If his assumptions were right, Sterling's involvement in this sex ring, in Darcy's abduction, was going to absolutely crush her.

Cold fury swept over Logan as he pulled the semi-automatic from his waistband, checking the ammo clip. "The fucker in the suit is mine."

Xander studied him with a nod. "I'll mop up the other one."

As soon as they rounded up these two, he'd have to get to the sat phone, call the Feds, get them in here to start making arrests. They already had a small team waiting after conferring earlier today, so they could swoop in and arrest Kantor, Jordan, and Sterling—if he was still alive.

"Any other guards in there?" Logan gestured to the cameras that captured Adam Sterling's face in crisp black and white.

Xander shook his head. "There were two earlier. Now I only see one."

A lucky break, except that meant there was a handy exit inside that room. He had to hustle now.

Logan ran out of the guard station, Xander following on his heels. He grabbed the key card and swiped it through the device. Surprising them wasn't possible with the clanging metal door announcing their arrival, but he backed against the adjacent wall, gun drawn, hoping to draw the guard out. If they could take him out quickly, Adam Sterling would be all alone with Logan and his wrath.

As the door clattered up, and the dungeon monitor pulled out of Allison's mouth and wandered out of the cramped holding area, zipping up his leathers and looking mighty pissed. Xander glanced at Logan, who stood on the other side of the door and mouthed, *Go.*

With a nod, Xander pushed away from the side of the cave and met the other dungeon monitor. Logan peeked around the corner.

When he recognized one of his own in the uniform of the Fantasy Key dungeon, the guy relaxed slightly. "What's going on?"

"Jordan sent me to check on things."

The other man raked a hand through his blond waves, blue eyes narrowed. "You're the new guy. When did he let you in on this?"

"You haven't been here long." Xander leveled the statement at the other Dom as if it was obvious.

"A few months."

"Yeah, I worked here for years before. Took a break for a bit, but I'm back. Of course I know about all this."

"Oh." He frowned. "Kantor didn't tell me."

"Kantor doesn't tell anybody shit." Xander rolled his eyes.

"Yeah!" the other man agreed. "Like we're not important. Without us, how would keep the pussy subdued long enough to make money on it?"

"Good point. So, the girls are okay?"

"Jordan is a suspicious asshole. I didn't fuck them. You tell him that."

Xander shrugged. "Let me see for myself, and I will."

Logan listened, thankful again for his friend. Without him, this investigation would have taken much longer. Xander was a natural bullshitter and his connections had proven very useful.

The dungeon monitor scowled, then sighed. "See, they're here, mostly unharmed. Help me clear a space. Sire just left and said to make room for another last-minute delivery."

Logan's blood ran cold. Another delivery? And Sire had left? It had to be Sterling. God, this was going to destroy Tara. But now everything made sense. Kantor and Jordan had backed away from Tara so fast because Sterling had told them she was FBI and to keep their distance. If her stay ended without incident, then Darcy would be sold, Sterling would be richer, and it would take the Bureau more time to amass another investigation. By then, Tara's stepfather could have hidden his tracks—again.

Fuck! Logan clenched a fist. He had to get to Cherry before Adam did.

"Where is he getting the other girl?" Xander asked.

The other guy shrugged. "The usual, I guess. Some slut dumb enough to come here with an inattentive Dom, and no one back home to care what happens to her. Help me move this body."

Body? Fighting the fear that he was too late to save Darcy, Logan shoved down his anxiety as Xander, walking beside the guy, stuck out a leg. The other man stumbled, and Xander grabbed his hair, shoving his forehead against the wall. The dungeon monitor slithered to the ground.

That obstacle cleared, Logan ran into the little room, hurdling over the fallen man to the two shackled women. He couldn't stay long, but he had to make sure they were okay—and find out about that body.

Xander rescued Allison, swiping the keys from the unconscious man to unshackle her. As soon as he'd finished, he tossed the keys to Logan, who hustled to the other woman. The second he got a look at her, even beneath her dirty face and red nose, he recognized Darcy from her picture.

"Agent Miles?" he prompted softly.

Her head came up as he released her wrists. She wiped her tears away. "Who w-wants to know?"

"I'm Logan Edgington, a Navy SEAL, here to rescue you."

"Yes, I'm Miles. Help me. They k-killed Robert."

"Agent York?" Shock reverberated through him.

She pointed to a bundled blanket in the corner. Horror whitened her face, and she looked like she was torn between racing to the body and fearing to set her eyes on her dead coworker and boyfriend.

Darcy began sobbing. "He abandoned his assignment as Tara's

pretend Dom because he knew it would never work. He took a job as a waiter to save me, but they discovered him."

And killed him. That's who they'd been talking about when he and Cherry had broken into Kantor's office.

Logan made his way to the rumpled blanket and pulled it up, shielding Darcy's view with his own body. Sure enough, York had been double-tapped in the back of the head. Half his face was gone.

Grimacing, he covered the body again. Darcy began sobbing uncontrollably.

Logan went to her. "You're safe. More agents will be en route soon. I'm here with your friend, Agent Jacobs."

Darcy's blue eyes widened. "Oh God, Tara *is* here? Her stepfather is—"

"Sire. I know. I've got to go hunt him down."

"Quickly! I think he means to grab her and sell her with the rest of us—tonight!"

* * *

KANTOR stared at her through accusing eyes while Jordan fawned over her barely clad body. Tara held in her nausea and terror. The resort manager knew exactly who and what she was; Tara could see that all over his face. The dungeon master didn't have a clue.

Her heart broke into a gallop in her chest as she considered her possible methods of escape. They were absolutely limited, but she had to wait, give Logan and Xander as much time as possible to locate Darcy.

Surreptitiously, she stared at the clock on the wall. They'd been holed up in here for nearly thirty minutes. She and Logan had agreed to rendezvous back at their suite at eleven, twenty minutes from now. She racked her brain to come up with some other distraction to keep the two men busy, but she'd nearly overplayed her pitiful sub hand, dragged out her medical attention, and Kantor would never believe it if she came on to him. So now what?

The phone at the manager's belt rang. At the distinctive ring, a

smug grin uglied up his face, and he all but jumped to answer. "Yes."
He paused, listen. "Yes, right away."

As Kantor slipped the phone back into its carrier, he smiled.
"Jordan, take a spin around the Pit and check on things."

Oh, hell no. What had just happened? Had someone caught
Logan and Xander? Was that why he'd looked so self-satisfied? Just
in case, she couldn't let Jordan go down there and sound the alarm.
And God knew that she had to avoid being alone with Kantor at all
costs.

She clutched Jordan tighter and batted her lashes at him. "Don't
go! I'd love to play, Sir. I would be more than happy to continue my
submissive journey with someone as experienced as you."

Jordan's chest all but puffed up, and he turned Kantor. "I'll take
her with me."

"Get your brains out of your dick and get the hell out," Kantor
snarled.

Jordan released her and left with a scowl. Tara backed away from
the manager.

"Now, you'll come to my office with me," he demanded, gestur-
ing impatiently.

"No."

God, she wished she'd been able to hide a weapon anywhere on
her body. Now being in character was really going to come back to
haunt her.

"My dungeon master may be fooled by a pretty face and a submissive disposition, but I'm a businessman, not a Dom."

Then he pulled a Glock from the back of his waistband and
pointed it at her. "You and I both know that you're here to bring
me down. I won't let it happen. I didn't tell Jordan about you because
he's a terrible actor. He would have given us away. Come with me
now."

As he grabbed her wrist and pulled, Tara's mind raced. She had
no doubt that if he got her alone, he'd either kill her or sell her. No
way was she going down without a fight.

For a moment, she dropped her gaze and her shoulders in defeat, let Kantor get comfortable with the thought that the little woman wasn't going to struggle. As soon as she drew closer, she shocked him with a knee to the balls, then delivered a round kick to his face. He stood as much as his aching testicles allowed and threw her a mean right cross. Tara bobbed out of the way, sent her left fist screaming into his jaw, then her right into his nose in a nasty one-two. When the impact of the blow shoved his head back, she charged, grabbing his salt-and-pepper waves, then slammed his forehead onto the desk beside him once, twice.

With a grunt, he fell to the floor.

Panting, her fists hurting like hell, Tara took a moment to shove Kantor under the desk, throw the blanket on the cot over him in case someone peeked in, then looked around for some rope or cuffs to secure him with, but found none. With time of the essence, she could only pick up his gun that had skittered across the floor, then shove her way into her sheer dress, which Jordan had left behind.

Turning off the light to the little room, she locked the door behind her and rushed out onto the dungeon floor. She had to find Jordan and occupy him before he reached the Pit. But she also had to get that backup out here pronto. The second Kantor woke, he'd be screaming for her blood. Their cover would be blown, and they'd be unable to go back to their room and contact Bocelli and the team for help. Outnumbered and outgunned, they'd be toast.

And Logan had no idea what was coming for him. There wasn't a moment to lose. She had to hope that Kantor would be out for a while.

Clutching the gun in the folds of her dress, she scanned the dungeon for Jordan, but he was nowhere to be found. *Damn!*

Running all the way to her room, taking stairwells and lesser-traveled hallways in case Kantor came to, she finally reached her room. It was empty, and Logan's smell lingered here. Their intimacies hung in the air, and she prayed desperately that they both came out of this alive.

She dug out the sat phone and quickly placed her distress call. A male voice advised her that backup was en route and would be on the island within minutes.

Tara just prayed she could find Logan and that they lived that long.

She stared at the bedside clock, anxiety eating into her gut. Logan should be back by now. But eleven rolled around and he didn't return, she called Xander's cell. No answer.

Anxiety became panic as Tara threw on a pair of harem pants in an earthy bronze and a matching bandeau top that covered her breasts but didn't conceal the rosy pink of her areolas. Very submissive, and she wondered where—and when—Logan had bought this stuff for her. She hoped like hell she got the opportunity to ask. At the moment, she was more thankful that the sheer pants, while showcasing her bare pussy, had pockets at each thigh. She slipped the gun into one, a can of pepper spray into the other.

As much as she wanted the shoes for running, she didn't dare tip off any of the other resort employees that anything was amiss. Instead, she left her previous costume on the bed. If Logan returned, he'd know at a glance that she'd been here and hopefully wait for her.

Cracking the door open, Tara peeked down the hall both ways. She didn't see Kantor. Pressing her hand to her nervous stomach, she stepped into the hall and around the first corner, toward the dark hall that led to the Pit's elevator.

Her hallway joined with another in a T, and as she passed it, she turned to see a familiar, out-of-place figure in a dark suit bearing down on her.

"Tara!"

She blinked and tried to reconcile his appearance. "Adam . . . what are you doing here?"

"Thank God, I found you." He pressed a hand over his chest. "I've been worried sick."

"You're not supposed to be here!" She was on a mission, and he knew it. Why the hell would he turn up here and blow her cover?

"It's fine, Tara. It's over. Darcy has been recovered."

A warm rush of profound relief went through her. "Thank God! How did you find out?"

Adam sent her a sheepish smile. "I asked Bocelli to contact me once things were over. He knows how worried I've been, so he gave me the green light to find you and take you home."

She held in a groan. As a former agent, Adam had to know that showing up here at the conclusion of her mission was, in short, embarrassing. If her own stepfather didn't think she could take care of herself, then no one who worked with her would believe she could, either.

But she'd worry about that later. Darcy was okay, and that was more important than anything. Except . . . "Who found her? And how? Were there other active agents on the island?" And why hadn't she known about them?

"Bocelli didn't give me details. I was just so grateful that he let me come and assure myself that you're safe."

Tara frowned. That sounded unusual. Bocelli wasn't old enough to be soft or sentimental. He struck her as a straight-up agent with a will of steel, so the man telling her stepfather that he could take her home right away, before debriefing? *Really* unusual. And she'd just talked to someone from the ground team Bocelli had set up moments ago. None of them had said a word about the mission being over to her. How would Adam have been close enough to get the news and get here?

"I've been so worried, and I'm relieved that you're unharmed and well."

This felt like a bizarre dream, where things happened but none of the events were logical. She frowned.

"Princess?" He walked closer and held out an arm, as if he meant to embrace her. "Come with me, and I'll take you to Darcy."

Your stepfather killed my mother. Logan's words flashed through her head. Twenty minutes ago, she would have never believed it. She wasn't sure she believed it now. Her stepfather was former FBI—one of the good guys, right? He'd never exhibited a violent tendency. But his presence here didn't add up.

What reason would Adam have for lying to her?

Up the hallway, the sudden pounding of footsteps grabbed her attention. She turned to find Logan charging up the hallway, gun in hand, pointed at her stepfather.

Did Logan mean to subdue Adam or just shoot him?

"*Tara!*" Fury poured from his eyes as he stopped a few inches from her and jerked on her arm. "Get behind me."

She resisted. "What is going on?"

Logan didn't veer in the least, just lined Adam up in his pistol's sights. "Move out of the way. Not only did this fucker kill my mother, he runs this place and tried to sell your friend, Darcy, to a Saudi oil sheik. Xander is with her now. She's a mess. Adam's minions 'disciplined' her within an inch of her life. He had Robert York killed as she watched. Baby, your stepfather is Sire."

Everything was happening too fast. Tara blinked, rooted in place, staring at her stepfather. Logan's allegations sounded so far-fetched, so surreal. She waited for Adam to vociferously deny them.

Her stepfather glared at Logan. "That's a lot to hurl at my head. You can't back that up. You just hate me because I tried to separate Tara from your bad influence."

"You lying motherfucker."

Adam loosed a long-suffering sigh. "Are you trying to hurt her again? Wasn't once enough? You brutally broke her heart and left her, then you walk back into her life and expect her to trust you"—he snapped his fingers—"like that? She's wiser to you now. This attempt to come between us . . . are you hoping to win her over, separate her from my support, then crush her again? Is this some sick game to you?"

Tara sucked in a breath. She stung as if she'd been slapped all over. Adam repeated all the secret worries she'd harbored since

Logan walked back into her life. He gave voice to her fears that she was nothing more than a trophy to him.

A glance at Logan showed the stark angles of his face set with determination, his mouth a grim line, and his eyes the iciest blue she'd ever seen. He wouldn't look at her, didn't say a word against those accusations. Inside, her heart broke a little. She wanted to take her stepfather's arm, and sink into the familiar parental comfort he offered, ask him to take her to Darcy.

But a niggle of doubt tugged at her.

"Logan, just . . . put the gun away."

He clenched his jaw. "You're going to believe him?"

Honestly, she didn't know. Neither man's story made sense. "I'm trying to sort it out, but I can't think when you're pointing that in his direction."

"I'm not lowering the gun. Don't ask me to trust him. On surveillance monitors, I *saw* him in the Pit, watching some sadist take a crop to Darcy while she cried, and he just smiled, Tara. Smiled, like it was a sunny fucking day, then sliced her with the crop himself."

Tara flinched. Logan had *seen* that? Really?

"Are you sure?"

Because that didn't make sense. But then Adam's presence here didn't make sense, either. Why had her stepfather been lying to her?

"What's going on here?" She turned to her stepfather.

"Besides Logan losing his sanity? I told you, princess. The mission is complete. Darcy's been found. You can come home with me now."

"Don't listen to him, Tara," Logan roared. "You should know by now that I love you and I'd never hurt you again." He shifted his attention to Adam. "I left her once—because you threatened her life. I'd blow you away before I let you touch a hair on her head. I know who and what you are."

"Ah, yes. A would-be murderer and criminal mastermind capable of a worldwide sex ring. Tara, does that really sound like me?"

No, and that's what she struggled with. Though he had retired from the FBI, he seemed like a fairly easygoing guy. He went to church nearly every Sunday, was respectful to everyone he met. He'd never had so much as a parking ticket.

But he hadn't denied Logan's accusations, either.

"Cherry, he's trying to confuse you," Logan insisted. "Ask yourself how many identities he assumed as a field agent for cases over the years, sometimes for weeks or months. Maybe the good suburban dad was just another cover so that no one would suspect his real activities. Please, baby, believe me and step behind me."

Her big, bad Dom was begging her. An angry scowl slipped across her stepfather's face, but he just shook his head, as if befuddled.

Glancing between the two men, Tara realized that it didn't matter if Adam had bullied her boss into letting him on the island or if Logan was mistaken in thinking that he'd seen Adam on the video monitors. Whatever was happening here, she had to choose between them. Past or present? Head or heart? Her thoughts spun as she heard the mental clock ticking.

"Tara," Adam said with a sigh in his "be reasonable" tone.

Logan gripped his gun tighter with one hand and held out his other to her. "Please. Let me keep you safe."

Instinctively, the submissive in her didn't want to disappoint her Dom. The woman inside her responded, seeking the shelter of her man. The memories from earlier that day seared across her brain, the trust she had placed in Logan's hands and the gentle way he'd worshipped her body, revered her. He'd felt perfect entwined around her, packed tightly inside her. He'd felt like home and tomorrow and all the things she craved. If all Logan wanted was some twisted revenge, he'd given up the opportunity to avenge his mother's death with an easy kill. Instead, he'd started explaining to her. Even if he proved to be wrong about Adam, he was the right man for her. If she failed to put her faith in him now, they would have nothing.

Heart beating wildly, she reached out to him, their fingers brushing, his a warm flare of warmth and strength.

Before he could take her in his arms, an arm curled around her waist and dragged her backward against a hard chest. She felt cold metal jammed up against her temple. It took her a moment to realize that her stepfather now captured her in his forceful grip and held a gun to her head.

"Adam!"

"Shut up, you ungrateful bitch. I *raised* you, and you did what? Chose the guy who fucked you good over me."

Shock washed over her. Ice spread through her veins as she struggled against his hold. "What are you doing? Let go!"

"I don't think so, princess."

"Do it, you motherfucker! Let go now," Logan yelled. "Or I'll blow your head off."

Adam held firm, the gun biting into the soft skin of her temple. Tara realized that he was using her as a shield so that Logan couldn't take a clear shot. And Logan clearly knew it. Terror and frustration burned from his blue eyes. He stared down the gun at Adam like an avenger, his finger taut around the trigger, just waiting for any opportunity.

"Not before I blow hers off first." Adam's arm moved from her middle to loop around her throat—and squeezed her windpipe.

Tara choked. Before this, she would have never believed her own stepfather capable of hurting her. Now, she had no doubt he'd do exactly as threatened.

"Why?" she gasped out.

"Once my buddies in the Bureau told me that you'd broken into Kantor's office, I knew it was only a matter of time before you figured everything out. You always did well with puzzles."

"What are you saying?" But Tara had the sinking feeling that she knew.

Her stepfather was everything Logan had claimed. Inside, the fury and betrayal swirled, beating deep. She thrashed and elbowed Adam in the stomach. He grunted but held firm.

"Nice try, but I'm much better at this game than you, princess. I played it for twenty years for the Bureau. I got a lovely watch and a very modest pension as a 'fuck you very much' from Uncle Sam. That wasn't going to do. I had the contacts to go into a very lucrative business for myself, so I did."

"Selling women and little girls against their will as sex slaves?"

"Stop with the righteous indignation," he tsked. "You're young and you have twenty-plus productive, money-making years ahead of you. You couldn't possibly understand until you get older and your nest egg isn't enough to really live on. I wasn't about to suffer the rest of my days in the thoroughly middle class income bracket after risking my life over and over. These girls don't matter. Most come from poor families who can barely feed them. And the women . . . I'm just giving them a permanent outlet for their kink."

She gasped, shock like a sledgehammer in her chest, pounding all the air out of her lungs.

Damn it, why hadn't she believed Logan sooner?

Now, it might be too late. Because Tara knew for certain that Adam had no problem stepping over her dead body to get what he wanted.

Snaring Logan's gaze with hers, she let the thousand regrets pouring through her show on her face. She might not see him again or live long enough to say it, but she wanted Logan to know how sorry she was. She wished she could tell him one last time how much she loved him and to go on with life if something happened to her. No more hiding in clubs, denying himself the pleasure of laughter, passion, and love.

But she'd run out of time to say anything.

"Another two days—at most—and you both would have known the truth," Adam said. "Kantor has been sloppy, and left too much of a paper trail to me. But I'm not going down. I just need a little more money and the means to skip this country and live rich. I got both when I found a buyer for you, princess: a Russian businessman with my Swiss bank account numbers, a taste for sadism and redheads, and a private plane waiting to take me anywhere I want to go."

Terror staked its way through her heart. Adam meant every word of that.

"Over my dead body," Logan vowed.

"Oh, that's the best part. You're going to put your gun down and stand still like a good target, or I'm going to instruct my Russian friend to make the rest of Tara's life as painful as possible."

Adam had deceived her, and lately she'd dismissed his odd hours and phone calls as necessary for someone self-employed in the security business. But it was the activity necessary to make money from human trafficking. If he'd betrayed her about everything else, he'd do exactly as he threatened.

She had to keep him talking. The more time she could buy, the more likely she or Logan would think of some way out of this mess, or her FBI backup would find them.

"Why did you kill Logan's mother?" she blurted.

At the question, Logan jerked as if he'd been jolted with a live wire.

"You finally figured that out?" Adam addressed Logan.

"The necklace," he choked out.

Adam nodded. "That chain was in my way when I was trying to slash her throat, so I yanked it off. I thought it was a fun little joke that Tara wore it. I knew I absolutely had to separate you then, but even before I killed your mother, I was never going to let you have Tara. I'd already begun plotting ways to separate the two of you, you little prick. Your mother was just another nuisance to be dealt with."

"Was she your girlfriend?"

"No," Adam scoffed. "I wouldn't have minded that. She was one fine-looking piece of ass."

"I'm going to rip you apart, motherfucker," Logan vowed.

"No, you're not. You're going to shut up and die like Amanda did. She tried to do good when she found out about my business venture.

I was just getting off the ground, and discovered the sweetest little fifteen-year-old runaway—one of Amanda's students. For a few hundred thousand dollars, I found her a new master in Saudi. Your mother somehow caught on, and was about to blow the whistle. I couldn't let that happen."

So Adam had ended her life.

The truth crushed her, and she felt so terrible for Logan and all he'd endured.

Suddenly, Kantor limped down the hall behind Logan, who stiffened when he heard the threat at his back.

"You've finally arrived," Adam drawled.

"Your bitch of a stepdaughter took me by surprise and beat my face into a table." He rubbed at the goose egg on his forehead.

Adam laughed, then tightened his hand on her neck. "I'll let you repay her back in pain on the airplane."

"Damn straight, the little cunt. We just have to get rid of Romeo first."

The last puzzle piece snapped into place. That voice, the reason she'd recognized it when she and Logan had first reached the resort—he'd called Adam hundreds of times over the years.

She gasped. "Kantor is an assumed name. You used to be FBI!"

Kantor smiled, still massaging his forehead. "Agent Stoltz, at your service. Took you long enough. Too bad for you that it's too late. Did you know that, before I left the Bureau, I was known as the Interrogator. For the last few years, they sent me to Guantanamo to extract information from the detainees. You and I are going to have a lot of fun." The he pressed his gun to the back of Logan's head. "Weapon down, and I'll make this quick and painless."

Slowly, he lowered the gun to his side. Tara pressed her lips together as terror spiked through her blood and her heart raced. This couldn't be happening. But she and Logan were outnumbered and outgunned. And she had only herself to blame. If she'd listened to Logan sooner, if she'd trusted what he was trying to tell her . . . if she'd tried harder to retract the shield around her heart, this would have all turned out differently.

Now, Logan was going to die for her mistake.

Tara refused to let that happen without a fight.

"Now put it on the ground," Kantor instructed.

Locking gazes with Logan, she tried to communicate silently to be ready for anything. He tensed and lifted his chin like he understood.

Suddenly, she went completely limp in Adam's grasp. Unprepared to hold her dead weight, he stumbled forward and lost his grip on her. As she went down, Tara shoved her elbow in his balls. Predictably, he grunted and doubled over. Then she reached in her pocket, grabbing the gun she'd stashed there, and pointed it straight at Adam with one hand. With the other, she surprised him by misting the pepper spray in his eyes. As he coughed and struggled, she kicked his weapon out of his hand.

Behind her she heard the blast of a gun, and whirled with a shriek to find plaster flying from the wall beside Logan's head. Kantor had grabbed the barrel of Logan's gun and shoved up, forcing Logan's finger away from the trigger. With his other hand, Kantor was lining up his kill shot.

Tara didn't blink, didn't hesitate; she pulled the trigger. The bullet hit Kantor right between the eyes.

Logan turned back to her, and his eyes grew impossibly wide, fixed behind her. She whirled to see Adam with a wicked blade raised, coming straight for her.

She threw herself against the side wall, then gained her stance to fire. But there was no need. A heartbeat later, Logan squeezed off three rounds. The first two hit him right in the heart, the third dead between the eyes, each shot's retort deafening in the low-ceilinged hallway.

Adam slithered down, dead before he hit the ground.

Then she stood alone with Logan, their enemies vanquished. The enormity of the night hit her immediately. The adrenaline racing through her blood began to drain, making her cold and shaky. He stood, staring at her, not moving, not speaking. A look of such anguish crossed his face that Tara's heart wept for him.

She ran to him and threw herself in his arms, praying that he could still love her, even though she'd waited so long to trust and believe him. If Logan let her, she'd spend the rest of her days making it up to him.

He hesitated, breathing so hard, his entire body so tense. Tara stiffened. Did he resent her? Had she killed his affection?

"Logan?" she touched his arm, her eyes searching his wild blue stare.

Finally, he wrapped two steely arms around her, dragged her body against his, and buried his face in her neck, their hearts beating as one. "Thank God you're okay."

A long moment later, he pulled back enough to stare straight into her eyes, and she was shocked to find her tears mirrored in his.

As she opened her mouth to ask him why, Bocelli came running down the hall, gun drawn with a team of agents at his back. And Darcy, wrapped in a blanket, brought up the rear, hair matted, cheeks smudged, ankles and wrists bruised and screaming red.

"Oh my God! Are you all right?" Tara asked her friend.

Darcy nodded mutely, shivering.

There was no way Tara could not hug her. Darcy sobbed on her shoulder, and Tara let her cling. No doubt, her friend had been through a terrible ordeal, but she vowed to be with her during every step of her recovery, both mentally and physically.

Bocelli broke them apart, then gently cupped Darcy's shoulder. "Now that you've seen Tara is okay, cooperate with medical, Miles. That's an order."

She nodded and allowed an agent to take her away.

Her boss turned back to her. "Good work, Jacobs. We've already arrested Jordan, the little slime." Then he spotted Adam's body, and a scowl passed over his face. "Are you all right?"

Tara gave him a shaky nod. "I'll be fine, sir."

He took her by the elbow. "Let's go, so you can tell me what happened."

Bocelli nudged her forward, and she looked back to find Logan watching, staring. With all the evidence and the carnage, she knew it would be long hours, maybe even days, before she saw him again. She wished she knew what the hell he was thinking. Logan was glad she was still in one piece, but as long as it had taken her to really listen and trust him . . . could he still love her?

Chapter Twenty

LOGAN paced outside the quaint white gazebo at one of the parks in Tyler, Texas, as the small crowd chatted, awaiting his brother and sister-in-law's vow renewal. Hunter and Kata had been married one year today. The sun was shining and the birds were singing. He was damn happy for them both.

But misery tore at his insides. The ceremony started in ten minutes, and Tara hadn't yet appeared.

Kata's saucy blond friend, Hallie, winked at him. Whether flirting or trying to cheer him up, he didn't know and he didn't care. And yeah, he could probably be more gracious, but it was fucking hard when his heart was breaking. The rest of his life stretched out as bleakly as the twelve years before, with only one brief week of paradise between.

And now, paradise was gone.

He replayed those events on Fantasy Key in his head, over and over. Tara had eventually trusted him, come to see that he was right about her stepfather. Hell, they'd saved one another's lives that day. She'd trusted him with her safety, her body. Even her heart . . .

Or so he'd thought.

Was she angry that he'd killed her stepfather? Sterling had been a crappy excuse for a human being and deserved to be six feet under. The world was better off without him. With a few bullets, Logan had erased him. But Adam had been a father figure to her for many years—the only one she'd had. The fact that he was a class-A scumbag didn't mean Tara had been ready to see him dead. Or have her fiancé put him there.

Or did that last battle at Fantasy Key put him into the ex category again?

Logan clutched the box in his pocket, looking again and again toward the parking lot, willing her to show up.

"You're going to wear out the grass if you keep pacing over the same spot."

Logan turned. Hunter looked happy, far more relaxed than he'd ever been before marriage. He was happy for his brother—but he wanted that for himself.

"Is it time?"

"Almost. Don't worry; she'll show."

Logan had to face facts. "She won't. I've been calling and texting for two days. Not a single reply other than 'We'll talk soon.'"

"Tara will make good on that."

"Maybe too much has happened." Logan paced again.

"Maybe the only thing that's too much is your worrying."

Just then, Kata wandered over, looking absolutely gorgeous in a white sundress that was cleavage central. Her sable hair was piled in an upswept do with baby's breath. A simple veil hung halfway down her back. She glowed with happiness, all but floating into her husband's arms, who cuddled her close and pressed a tender kiss on her lips.

"Hi, honey. Did I tell you that you look absolutely stunning?"

"You did." She sent him a saucy grin. "But feel free to say it again."

"You look stunning. How soon can we ditch this party and, um . . ."

She slapped his shoulder. "It'll be later. If you're not good, *much* later. Caleb and my mom are calling this their first 'official' date. We have to stay and chaperon."

"No. C'mon, my dad will be on his best behavior."

She snorted. "I'm not sure my mom will. I think she has it bad for your dad."

"See, we should let the grown-ups have their fun so we can go off and have our own."

"I don't need to hear this." Logan was tempted to shove his fingers in his ears and tune out.

Kata laughed, then faced her husband. "Humor me, huh? This is the wedding we didn't have for our friends and family."

Hunter turned sober. "I was teasing you, honey. Of course. I know how important it is to you that your brother is here. And . . . when it's time for the honeymoon activities, I'll be really excited."

Logan winced. "Take your sucking face and whatever else privately, huh?"

With a laugh, Kata kissed his cheek and walked toward Hallie, acting as one of her bridesmaids. Kimber, their sister, had agreed to stand in as the other. In the background, Kimber's husband Deke juggled their son, little Caleb, currently trying to scramble from his dad's hold and test his newfound walking skills. Hunter followed the others, laughing at the baby's antics.

"You sound grouchy," a familiar voice said. He whirled to find Xander and scowled.

"I only invited you so you can help me get really drunk if Tara doesn't show. I don't need your shit."

Xander laughed. Yeah, he was always freaking amused when someone else's balls were on the chopping block.

"I heard you on the phone with Thorpe the other day. He wants your membership card?"

Another sore spot with Logan. Tara didn't yet wear his collar, and he couldn't prove that she'd agreed to be his wife. If she'd get her sweet ass over here, he'd take care of that. If she didn't . . . "I told him to shove his membership up his ass."

"Definitely grouchy. Really, Logan. Hunter is right; she'll come."

"Yeah, then where has she been for two fucking days?"

"I don't know, but trust me, she loved you then, and she loves you now. You just have to know that, no matter what happened in the past, she's opened her heart to you again."

God, how badly he wanted to believe that.

Fuck this. Even if Tara didn't show today, he would come after her on his next leave. And his next. And every single one after that, each and every day, until he wore her down. Because he wasn't living his life without the one woman who meant more to him than every sunrise, every moment of life, every single breath.

Logan let out a deep, shaky breath. "Thanks, man."

Xander slanted a teasing glance at him. "You think I'm full of shit?"

"Pretty much."

"How about a friendly bet? Fifty bucks."

He glanced at his watch. Two minutes before the ceremony. She wasn't coming. And she'd be facing a really pissed off SEAL at her door as soon as this shindig was over.

"Sure." Unfortunately, it would be the easiest money he'd ever made.

"Yeah?" Xander smiled broadly. "Pay up."

With a lift of his chin toward the parking lot, he clapped Logan on the back.

He whirled—and his heart jumped into his throat. *Fuck me, she's here.*

Blood rushed and roared through his body, most of it leaving his brain and settling into his cock when he saw her in a gorgeous dress in a shimmering gold, its thin spaghetti straps clinging to her pale, lightly freckled shoulders. He didn't think she was wearing a bra. She flashed him a shy smile, her eyes peeking out from behind her bangs.

Hell, if she was wearing a bra, he could get it off in a few seconds with a little privacy. Her panties, too.

Tara slowed as he jogged toward her. She stopped a good two feet away. "Hi."

That was it? Just 'hi'?

"Thank you for coming. Are you okay?" Damn, he didn't know what else to say.

She nodded. "You said that you wanted me here, so I wasn't going to miss it."

Hope wrenched at his heart, but there was still a long way between showing up to his brother's vow renewal and wearing his ring. For all he knew, she'd come out of pity—or guilt.

"I'm glad you're here." He took her hand, pulled her closer, gratified when she didn't pull away. "I've missed you. I'm sorry about . . ." God, he could be here all day apologizing for his multitude of sins—everything from shooting Adam to being a complete pervert. "Everything."

She closed her eyes as she drifted near, but her face tightened, her pouty lips trembling. Damn it, she was going to cry.

"Cherry . . ."

Covering her mouth with her hand, she tensed and sniffled. "I—I've missed you s-so much. I owe you my life. And I'm so sorry that it was almost too late before I believed y-you. I spent so many years trying to convince myself that I hated you." She drew in a shuddering breath.

She wasn't pissed at him?

"Get it all out," he encouraged. As long as she was talking, he was listening.

"I knew better. I never got over you. But when confronted with a choice, when I knew that you would never deceive me again, I didn't let go of what I thought was the truth and just believe you. I know trust in any relationship is really important, but in a BDSM rel—"

"Shh." He wanted to take her in his arms so badly, but feared she'd only back away until they'd hashed it all out. "Trust is important, but I shattered yours completely years ago. You had a long time to live with that betrayal. You had no way of knowing that I'd never stopped loving you. I'm willing to take whatever time we need to build the trust back up."

She sobbed again, and this time he did pull her close, right against his chest. Damn, it felt so good to have her against him, and he cradled her head against his shoulder.

"But you needed me to believe you, and I didn't."

"I *wanted* you to believe me," he corrected. "I needed you to come through, and you did. If you want to talk about it, I'm here for you."

"No." She shook her head. "I've spent the last few days getting myself in order. I've had my debriefing, and psych has checked me out. Darcy was released from the hospital this morning, and I got her settled back at her place. She misses Robert, but she's going to be okay. I finished making Adam's burial arrangements. I also quit the FBI. I'm not cut out for fieldwork, and my relationship with Adam hasn't helped my reputation at the bureau. I'll take my analysis experience elsewhere. And during all that, I've worried that I ruined everything between you and me."

Hope settled into his chest, making it light until he felt like he could soar.

"Don't worry about what you *think* I feel or could happen. Just answer me one question, Cherry: Do you trust me now?"

"Absolutely. I'll never doubt you again." She did her best not to sob.

He thumbed away her tears. "Good girl. He was your stepfather, so I know it must be hard. I wanted him to have to stand up for his crimes, face the families of his victims and pay. Shooting him wasn't my plan. But I couldn't let him hurt you."

"I'm sorry he hurt *you*." She caressed his cheek, thumbed his dark brow. "That he killed your mother."

"You had nothing to do with that," he assured. "Now tell me, what do you want next?"

"I want to spend my life with you. I love you."

Relief and delight poured through him, a warm fall of abiding devotion and a yearning to grow old with her.

"I'm sorry he took so many years away from us," she added.

"But we're together now."

She gave him a watery smile, shades of joy lighting up her face this time. "Yeah . . ."

Logan dragged her over to a nearby folding chair and fished in his pocket as he pulled Tara into his lap. "Cherry, baby, I loved you at sixteen. I love you now. I'll love you always. This was my mother's." He opened the box and showed her Amanda's engagement ring.

She gasped and started crying again.

"I'd be honored if you'd be my wife. Will you belong to me?"

"Yes." She nodded as fresh tears streamed down her cheeks. "Always."

Tara threw her arms around his neck, and he curled her into his embrace, burying his face in her neck. They'd overcome so much, grown back together, and were stronger for it. Now, they only had to pick a date and a time and state their vows before God and their loved ones, and he would hold her for the rest of their days.

Around them, people started clapping, and his brother rushed over to give him a hearty handshake. As he tried to get his shit together and not bawl like a baby, he slid the engagement ring on Tara's finger. She gave him the most beautiful smile. It lit up his heart.

"When can we get married?" The idea of waiting another six months for his next leave didn't thrill him, but he knew it took more than ten minutes to plan a wedding. Damn it, he didn't need all the pomp; he just needed Tara.

"The sooner the better." She put his hand on her flat belly, then bit her lip and smiled again. "Just in case."

Holy shit! He hoped that their love had taken root in her womb and would soon give them a child. If he had his way, the first of several.

"How does a quick trip to Vegas sound?" he asked, grinning. "Like tonight?"

In the background, his father groaned, and Hunter just laughed.

Tara kissed his lips soundly. "It sounds perfect."

KEEP READING FOR AN EXCERPT FROM
SHAYLA BLACK'S NEXT EROTIC NOVEL

Mine to Hold

COMING SOON FROM HEAT BOOKS

"TYLER, are you aware that all the girls at Sexy Sirens have nicknamed you Cockzilla?"

He laughed. That rich, deep sound Delaney Catalono hadn't heard for two long years sang in the humid August air, making her heart clench. After all the trials and miles—and lately, the bullets—she never believed she'd hear Tyler Murphy's voice again. Certainly, she'd never imagined to hear it in BFE, Louisiana, hiding in the shadows of his back patio like some sad stalker. She wasn't at all surprised to hear that some group of girls had given him a moniker about his sexual prowess. Delaney remembered exactly how good he'd been.

Her heart clenched again.

Peeking around the corner, she saw Tyler's broad shoulders and upper back encased in a charcoal gray T-shirt. His blonde hair had been cut brutally short, exposing his sun-kissed neck. He clutched the chair, his forearms looking bronzed, heavily veined, and vital under the patio lights. Around a table, he was surrounded by a virtual harem: two redheads, a platinum blonde, a Latina brunette, and an auburn-haired model-type—each totally gorgeous in her own way.

Some things never change. Tyler, with his sparkling green eyes and Hollywood smile, had probably had girls chasing him since puberty. Not that it mattered to her anymore.

Been there, done that. Burned the T-shirt.

"And that's a bad nickname, why?" Tyler returned to the stunning blonde beside him, picking up his bottle of beer and taking a long swallow.

As the other women laughed, Delaney glanced over her shoulder, hoping like hell that she hadn't been followed. She breathed a sigh of relief that she was alone. How nice would it be if her most pressing problem were others' opinions. How nice would it be if someone didn't want her dead.

"Ladies . . ." the blonde's voice warned. "This is not funny. Remember the plan?"

"Alyssa is right," said the brunette with the sinful curves. "We're worried about you."

"That's very sweet, Kata, but acting like you care isn't going to persuade me to watch another crappy *Twilight* movie with you."

"You liked it," Kata accused.

Tyler snorted. "You wish."

He had probably liked it more than he wanted to admit. Tyler liked high-testosterone thrillers, yes, but he'd admitted under the influence of Señor Cuervo that he kinda liked chick flicks, too. Once upon a time, he'd been her buddy of choice to curl up with on the couch and rent movies, Delaney remembered with a wistful smile. Then she frowned.

You burned the bridge. Move on.

"Focus here." Alyssa's voice brought the subject back around. "This is an intervention. Morgan, Kimber, Kata, Tara, and I are united about the fact that you need help."

"A what? C'mon. I'm not a drug addict or an alcoholic. I'm no danger to myself or others."

"That's debatable," the auburn-haired beauty cut in. "Can you make it a whole day without getting in some stripper's thong? Our guess is no."

Delaney winced. It was just as well that she was here to ask for his help, not his hand in marriage.

"Ouch, Kimber. You wound me." Tyler slapped a hand over his chest dramatically.

"Cut the crap," she demanded. "You *can't* make it a whole day, can you?"

"Sure, I could. But why torture myself?"

"It's bad for my business," Alyssa chimed in again. "I don't need any more catfights on stage about who's getting Cockzilla tonight."

"Hey, your patrons loved it. Better than Jell-O wrestling. Got a rise out of me."

Delaney heard the humor in his voice. The women in his life were staging an intervention, and he wasn't taking it seriously. No surprise there. What was a surprise, however, was that none of the women seemed to be fighting over him themselves. Not yet, anyway.

Another woman scoffed and waved her hand. "I haven't known you that long, but seriously, a stiff wind could get a rise out of you."

The lovely redhead with the sultry brown eyes wore a wedding ring. Then again, bands of gold had never stopped Tyler before. She ought to know.

"You noticed, Tara? I'm touched." Tyler slapped a hand over his heart.

"Don't give me that," Tara scolded. "Alyssa is being really serious. We all are."

With a sigh, Tyler turned back to the blonde. "Okay. What's up, boss lady?"

"I can't have girls fighting and quitting because you're too busy playing musical beds," Alyssa said. "Someone is going to lose every time, and it's creating a fucking mess that I don't have time to clean up. I hired Jessi to replace Krystal, who left because she didn't like being last on your booty call list. Tyler, Jessi has been there three days. Three! I found out this afternoon that you've already tapped that, more than once."

He shifted uncomfortably in his seat. "After her first shift, she asked for an escort to her car. The parking lot was dark and empty. I helped her out."

"By nailing her in the backseat?"

"There's more room in a Civic than you'd think."

"I don't care." Alyssa sounded pissed off. "Jessi came crying to me when she found you and Skyler in the dressing room last night after closing. Do I need to enact a strict 'no anal sex' policy at the club?"

"I've bounced at the club for almost two years. What I did with the girls has never bothered you before. What is this really about?"

There was a long pause, and Delaney watched a few of the women lift glasses of wine and sip nervously.

The other redhead, the one with the baby bump, clutched a water bottle and shifted in the seat. "We think it's time you settled down."

"Morgan . . ." he warned. "Don't try spreading your matrimonial joy on me. Just because you're all blissful with your monogamy doesn't mean I'm in any hurry to get there."

So the redhead's baby bump wasn't his doing? *Never mind. It's irrelevant. Focus on getting his help and staying alive.*

"You're going to have to grow up," Morgan pointed out.

Alyssa wagged a finger in his face. "Skyler just turned twenty-two. You're what, a decade older?"

Actually, Tyler was thirty-four. Delaney knew that well. She remembered his thirtieth birthday party, during happier times, back when she and Eric—

She shut down that thought and listened to the conversation.

"I didn't know she was that young. Sorry." Tyler shrugged. "We weren't exactly exchanging vital statistics."

"No," Alyssa jumped in. "Just bodily fluids."

"Hey, I wore a condom."

Tara grimaced as several others groaned. "Eww. I don't want details."

"I'm just saying . . . Let's not get technical," he defended. "So I'm older than her. I'm not the first guy to date a younger woman."

"Fucking in the back of the club isn't dating." Kimber sighed.

"We love you, but you've gotta clean up your man-whore act." Alyssa looked dead serious. "Or in ten years, you're going to be a walking stereotype, a middle aged Lothario hitting on young chicks with your snazzy sports car."

"I don't have a sports car, and even if I did, with a name like Cockzilla, everyone would know that I'm not overcompensating for anything I might be lacking."

Alyssa smacked her hand on the table. "Damn it, are you listening to us at all?"

Tyler sighed. "Okay, joking aside, I appreciate your concern, but seriously, I'm not looking for any kind of happily-ever-after."

"Too bad," Kata cut in. "We're going to give you one."

He stiffened. "Oh, I get it. You have someone in mind."

"Well, I thought it would be nice if you'd talk to my cousin, London," Alyssa suggested, as if walking on eggshells. "She just moved here. She's very sweet and could use a friend."

"Hell no."

Kata stood, putting her hands on her very curvaceous hips. "Are you refusing because she's not a size two?"

Tyler shook his head. "I've got nothing against girls with a little extra cushion. But that one has purity written all over her. No fucking way. Alyssa, you don't like the way I treat your dancers, but you want to unleash me on your little virgin relative?"

"So what if she's a virgin?" Alyssa argued. "You have a really kind, loyal side that would be good for her."

The gorgeous blonde had gotten that part right. He'd once proven that he'd do *anything* for a friend.

"He does," Kata agreed. "I might not be here if that weren't true."

"If you can just keep your pants zipped long enough, she'll see it. And you'll get to know her, too, and—"

"Nope." Tyler finished the last of his beer and slammed the bottle on the table. "I'm done here. If you ladies want to stay and finish off your wine, you're more than welcome, but there's no way you're pairing me up."

"Where are you going?" Tara, closest to the sliding glass doors, moved her chair to block his path.

He scooted her out of the way with a nudge of his thigh. "Any-where else. Bye."

When he disappeared inside the house, Delaney panicked. It had taken her forever to track him down. She was at the end of her cash reserves and the end of her rope. Time had run out. No way could she wait until he felt like coming home to confront him. There was too much at stake.

Dragging everything she loved and owned behind her, Delaney clung to the shadows, watching for anything suspicious, and ran for his front door.

* * *

THE doorbell rang before Tyler even got near the front door. Now what? If this was another meddling female trying to tell him how to run his life, he was going to shove a bottle of wine in her hands and send her out back with the rest of the interfering females. He had better things to do, like slap some sense into his buddies. What the hell had possessed all of them to marry such pains in his ass?

Clenching the knob almost as hard as he clenched his teeth, Tyler yanked the door open, a curse on the tip of his tongue. It died abruptly.

He stared at the familiar, petite brunette, unable to take a breath. "Delaney?"

The sight of her hit him like a fucking two-by-four in the solar plexus. Was it even possible she really stood at his door? Or was he hallucinating after two silent years of wondering what the fuck had happened to her?

"Hi, Tyler."

She shifted nervously, looking too damn tired, as if she'd been traveling for days. Her dark hair barely hung together in an unravel-ing braid, no makeup, dark circles under her deep blue eyes, wrin-kled T-shirt. By her side sat a black duffel bag on wheels. Something else squatted near her, around the corner. He couldn't see more of it than a tall plastic handle.

What the hell? She didn't speak to him for two years, then brought everything she owned to his door?

"You're a tough man to find," she murmured, then looked over her shoulder.

He crossed his arms over his chest. Yeah, he should invite her in, but last time he checked, she'd thrown him out of her life.

Of course, she wouldn't show up now with luggage unless she was desperate . . .

"I was under the impression you'd rather I get and stay lost."

She shook her head, her dark braid swaying in the valley between her soft breasts, the ones with the pretty, berry red nipples he'd never quite forgotten. He swallowed back the memory.

"It wasn't like that. I swear." She bit her lip. "Look, I know this is awkward—"

"As hell. Yeah. Where's Eric?" He glanced down at her left hand, clutching the rolling duffel bag. Her ring finger was bare.

"We're divorced."

Fuck. And there came the two-by-four to his gut again. Tyler didn't want to ask why; he was pretty sure he knew the answer.

"I'm sorry."

And he was. But there was a selfish side of him having a full-on, get-down party at the news. He shoved that greedy reaction aside.

Self-consciously, she rubbed her thumb along the back of her naked ring finger. "Thanks. It was final fourteen months ago. I haven't seen much of him since." She pursed her lips together, glanced behind her again. "He doesn't want to see me at all."

Why the hell was she so nervous?

"Delaney . . ." Tyler stopped. He didn't know what to say. It wasn't *all* his fault. But a good deal of the blame rested on his shoulders.

"It's okay. I know you have company, and that this is awkward. I know I handled everything between us badly. And I'm sorry."

Delaney's blue eyes filled up with tears. As she fought them back, Tyler resisted the urge to comfort her as he had in the past when they'd been friends . . . then more.

"Can I come in? There's something we really need to talk about."

Everything inside Tyler seized up. The last time she'd wanted to "talk," she'd thrown him out of her life. Whatever was on her mind, he could bet it would be heavy. She hadn't come all the way to Lafayette from Los Angeles to shoot the shit.

How the hell could he say no? He'd ruined her life, and had been pretty damn sure what would happen when he was doing it. Tyler knew that he owed her. Besides, he'd never been in love . . . but he'd come damn close with Delaney.

"Sure." He swallowed, grabbed her duffel, and stepped back. "Come in. How did you know I had company?"

Delaney glanced at the object with the tall plastic handle beside her, hidden by the exterior wall of the porch. She looked distinctly uncomfortable. "I rang the doorbell a bit ago, and no one answered. So I popped around to the side of the house and . . . saw that you weren't alone."

"They're my buddies' wives." He'd meant the words as an explanation, a defense. Then he winced. God, Delaney probably already imagined that he was fucking them.

"It's none of my business." She glanced at the hidden object beside her again, then the empty street behind her. "I came because I need your help. Really badly and right now."

He nodded. "You look tired, Del. And too thin. Come in and tell me what I can do."

She drew in a deep breath, then bent to the item with the tall plastic handle. A trunk? A dolly? Did she mean to move in?

A moment later, she straightened up, clutching a little boy. He was dead weight in her arms, half asleep, his face against her shoulder, thick blond hair askew. Tyler's heart skidded to a stop.

The kid's meaty hands and feet peeked out beyond the arms and legs of his Spider-Man pajamas that were just a bit too small. He hooked one arm around Delaney's neck, then began rubbing an eye with his little fist. Then the kid turned. That little face possessed the

Murphy nose. His own green eyes, uncertain and watchful, stared back at him.

Tyler's entire body went cold. His jaw dropped. His mind came to a screeching halt. *Oh god. Oh fucking god . . .*

"Tyler, meet your son, Seth."

Before she'd said a word, Tyler had known this kid was his son. A thousand emotions pelted him at once. Shock blazed through his system first. Wonder and anger crashed in together next.

He had a son. He and Delaney had created life together that beautiful May night when he'd finally stopped seeing her as a friend and had no choice but to touch her as a woman. Then the thunder of his fury caught up. Gritting his teeth, he tried to push it down for the boy's sake.

"Hi, Seth." He spoke in soft tones, then speared Delaney with a glare that dared her to defy him. "Can I hold him?"

Suddenly, Tyler ached to. This was his son. *His . . .* with her.

At her nod, she kissed the little boy's head, then whispered, "It's okay, little man."

Seth frowned and watched him suspiciously, but went without a fight. Then Tyler was holding his son for the first time, wrapping him as tightly in his arms as he dared.

He tried to swallow, but his throat felt too tight. His jaw ached. His heart beat fast, like a fucking racehorse at the Kentucky Derby. Something warm flooded his chest. Tyler had never fallen instantly in love with anything or anyone, but Seth seized his heart in a single moment. He kissed the little boy's forehead, and the feeling swelled ten-fold.

"Why am I just now finding out about him?" Tyler tried to keep his voice calm, even. But his eyes accused her. What he really wanted to know was how the fuck she could have robbed him of the first fifteen months of his own son's life.

She glanced around apprehensively and shimmied out of the porch's light. "You have every right to be angry. That things were complicated and you became impossible to find once you moved out of state are true facts—but poor excuses. At the end of the day, I didn't know what to tell you or if you'd even care. You can take it out of my hide later. I'm sure I deserve it. But right now, I need your help. I need you to protect Seth with your life. Someone is trying to kill me."

Shayla Black

The author of more than twenty-five sizzling contemporary, erotic, paranormal, and historical romances, national bestselling author Shayla Black (who also writes as Shelley Bradley) lives with her husband, her munchkin, and one very spoiled cat. In her "free" time, she enjoys reality TV, reading, and listening to an eclectic blend of music.

She has won or placed in more than a dozen writing contests, including Passionate Ink's Passionate Plume, the Colorado Romance Writers Award of Excellence, and the National Readers' Choice Awards. Romantic Times has awarded her Top Picks, a Historical K.I.S.S. Hero Award, and a nomination for Best Erotic Romance of the Year.

A writing risk-taker, she enjoys tackling writing challenges with every book.

Visit her website at www.shaylablack.com.